The Best Postboy In England

Stephen Frost

Burnt
Orchid
Press

BURNT ORCHID PRESS

THE BEST POSTBOY IN ENGLAND

A CIP catalogue record for this book is available from the British Library.

The Postboy's face courtesy of cottonbro studio at Pexels

www.stephenfrost.info

ISBN 978-1-7394309-0-0

To Tracy

Part One

Prologue

Exeter, 1940

3 Townley Street
Exeter
24th June 1940

Officer in Charge
Children's Overseas Reception Board
C/o Thomas Cook & Son
45 Berkeley Street
London

Dear Sir,

I am writing in reply to your advertisement in the June issue of Post Office Magazine for the position of Volunteer Escort for your Overseas Evacuation Scheme.

I have been a Post Office employee for twenty-four years, beginning as a clerk at Fore Street Post Office in Kingsbridge and rising to the position of Assistant Manager at the main GPO on the High Street in Exeter.

Since the outbreak of war in September I have also trained staff and been especially instrumental in mentoring our younger recruits, which I believe would be of great benefit to your scheme if I were chosen for it. I enclose a reference from my manager, Mr Jarvis, which I hope will aid you in considering my application. I have no family ties and would be able to travel at a moment's notice.

In respectful anticipation,
Yours faithfully,
Billie Bedden.

No family ties. That probably swung it. A reply to his job application had landed on his doormat a week ago and the position was his: Overseas Evacuation Escort. Poor little blighters, little parcels of fear and sorrow, shipped across the ocean, three thousand miles from their homes, schools, and parents. He felt sorry for them and genuinely wanted to help.

It was, however, the destination, Nova Scotia, that had really caught his eye in the advert, and was his true reason for travelling. After all these years, he was still stalked by duplicity. He sighed through his nose and cigarette smoke followed, rolling timelessly against the pane of his bedroom window. Somewhere out there, beyond the skyline, beyond the sky, was another version of himself, his ghostly twin, cruising the attics and cellars of the past. An echo of flesh and bone that travelled by another name entirely. Freddie Lovegrove.

No one had called him that for years.

He was Billie now, Billie Bedden, assistant manager, Exeter Post Office. Freddie had long since ceased to exist, though not so much as a death, more a letter lost in the post.

Despite the closed window, Billie could still detect the gluey stench coming from the collar factory opposite, strong enough to overwhelm the smell of his own cigarette. In the back yard below, a dozen men wearing threadbare suits smoked droopy roll-ups and drank beer through rotting teeth. Billie wondered why more of these fit young men hadn't been called up, they couldn't all, like him, be in a reserved occupation. He supposed their luck would run out soon enough, then he gave a dismal snort that the war to end all wars had been closely followed by another. Its predictability made it no less ludicrous.

Muffled echoes of chat and laughter were wafting up the stairs – the sound of family ties, the rumble of guilt. He had been in his bedroom for half-an-hour, long enough for the party below to begin to wonder where he was, but he couldn't face the idea of going back down. He had instead turned to memories of his mother, about whom he felt few regrets, worn down and erased by the passing years. Except one memory lingered – not that he had never told her he loved her, nobody did that, but that he had never shown it. Since he had first read the job application in *Post Office Magazine* his mother seemed to increasingly occupy his thoughts, which surprised him, unsettled his days, and sometimes his match-hand would shake when he tried to light up. Unsettled his nights too – one in particular, sweat-ridden, with an ending too dark and shadowy to confront until now: why not just say "dead" and be done with it? For all he knew, his mother was lying in Eagley graveyard along with the rest of them. So strong was the thought in fact, he wasn't sure if he'd said the word out loud.

"Talking to yourself again?"

He glanced round to see Ellen leaning against the door frame, arms folded. Her dress was old and over the years a few extra pounds had begun to push gently against the seams, revealing more of her shape, which Billie continued to desire. He, on the other hand, was so skinny he thought that when they made love their bodies were entirely incompatible, so he would sometimes avoid it, as if he was undeserving of her. But he loved Ellen in other ways and knew he would return to her. Once he had done what he needed to do.

Billie looked back out of his window and leant across the small dressing room table to stub out his roll-up in the ashtray there. Normally he would press it down three times, then extinguish what was left of it with a twist. But this time he didn't bother. He had something to say and he might as well get on with it.

"I have to go."

He waited for a reply, filling the gap by thoughtlessly putting his hand up against one of the window panes. Thoughtlessly, yes, but not without purpose. His palm and outstretched fingers prevented him from seeing her reflection.

"Go? What d'you mean?" she said.

He dropped his voice to a whisper. "I mean I have to go."

"What, now?"

There was a quake in her throat, a sudden nervous shiver that suggested she knew he meant more than a trip to Short's Stores for a pack of Golden Virginia. That going meant leaving.

"Not now Billie," she said. "Everyone's here for you. Wet the baby's head you know...?" Her words petered out, leaving only the rich aftertaste of her Exeter accent, something Billie always relished. The way she pronounced his name, how she poured it out like hot chocolate, each syllable carrying equal weight, equal love. But the name no longer sounded like his own, not today, not enough anyway to make him turn to face her.

"I'm leaving. For a couple of months. Give or take. There's fifty pounds in the Post Office account."

Then from downstairs came the sound of a crying baby – needy, heart-tugging, hungry – and Ellen turned her head towards it, distracted and split in two. "Two months? Now? What you talking about?

Where the hell are you going? Where d'you get that kind of money?"

"You'll be all right."

He'd heard that before. You'll be all right. The words stirred up another old memory and he could see the face as clearly as his own reflection in the window, smell the breath as pungent as smoke, as vile as glue...

The floorboards creaked under Ellen's tentative approach, and she repeated herself, more desperately. "Where the hell are you going, Billie?"

Someone downstairs had begun comforting baby Millicent, but as the little one's tears were soothed, Ellen's began. Billie could hear the salt in her words and in their mistimed delivery. There was nothing for it, he moved towards the wardrobe, opened its doors and waited for a moment before finally turning to look at her, finding her eyes with his.

"Do you have any regrets, Ellen?"

She pinched the waist of her dress, absent-mindedly tugging at it as she fixed Billie's stare. "Is it another woman?"

Billie reached inside the wardrobe and pulled out a suitcase. "It's not another woman. Not in the way you mean anyway."

"In what way is it not another woman?"

Billie felt a brief, wry smile pass across his face. It had always been an effort for Ellen to sound angry. Another breath, this time a sweet one, filled his nose, a shadow from his past flickered across his eyes, someone who could have been standing there now if only a black door had remained shut. Someone else who was incapable of anger. He drifted further, thought he could smell wet straw, remembered lying in it and wanted to do so again. But there was no going back to the barn. Instead he had to continue what he'd started, placing the suitcase on the bed, clicking open the latches and lifting the lid, allowing one rush of memories to be brushed aside by another. His clothes were folded neatly enough, but not how Ellen would have done it, lovingly organised with shirts here, socks there, suit on top, as she had when he'd gone away on a week's secondment to Bristol four years ago. Instead, a muddle. And then there were the letters, rubber-banded up. She would have put those down one side to keep them safe instead of having them lie on top where they might fall out, perhaps getting lost entirely in the confusion of his journey. This, Ellen would have done, not through matrimonial obligation but through a kindness she was unaware she possessed, and for which, therefore, she needed no repayment. Kindness was not kept in a ledger, not by Ellen.

He picked the letters up, removed the first one from the rubber band and handed it, uncertainly, as if it were an injured bird, to his wife. "You need to read this."

Ellen wiped her eyes with her sleeve so she could see more clearly the address on the envelope. She read it, glanced up at Billie, then back down to read it again. "Where the hell is Nova Scotia?"

Billie stood perfectly still, watching her, watching himself too as if surveying the scene from above, waiting for her next move as she examined the envelope more closely and rubbed her thumb over the postmark, her anger turning to incredulity.

"It says nineteen-sixteen."

"Yes it does," said Billie. "It's about time it was delivered."

Ellen sat down on the edge of the bed, next to the open suitcase. Billie looked at her beautiful face, beautiful even when she was sad and crying; perhaps, because of the tears, more so. Everyone said he punched above his weight. She looked a lot like Joan Fontaine, a resemblance he'd only just noticed the night before when they had been to the Mayfair to see "Rebecca" together, thanks to Ellen's mother offering to baby-sit. Their first night out since Millicent Rose had been born. She was plumper, yes, and because there was no money, less manicured, but Ellen still retained her Hollywood, black-and-white elegance in the way she held herself and tilted her head; every bit a leading lady, though she didn't know it, or didn't let on.

Watching her take the letter out of its envelope, Billie had the whimsical feeling it was he who was being decanted, and that if he thought hard enough, he could think himself right out through the window to disappear like cigarette smoke, somewhere far across the ocean.

"This is your handwriting," she said.

"Yes it is."

"Then who is Anne?"

1

Eagley Village, Summer 1916

It was early, half-past-six. Freddie had arrived for his first day at work half-an-hour earlier than the appointed time, finding himself already in the back room of the Post Office, eager to impress. With the help of George Franklin the Postmaster, Freddie was being fitted with his new postboy uniform. New for him, at least. It was a hand-me-down, one size too big, but he liked the dark blue cloth with red trimmings, relished the way it made him feel older than fourteen. Important, serious. Up until then he had never really been noticed – children should be seen and not heard, that was what the grown-ups said, though sometimes you were lucky even to be seen – but no one could ignore the postboy, especially in wartime. He was puffed up in another way too, entirely secret, one that he didn't fully understand but reminded him of Millie, who delivered the milk.

When George had leaned in close to straighten Freddie's collar he had offered some advice: *"Don't get involved. Don't get drawn into conversation and never say you're sorry."* A subtle urgency had engulfed the village on the outbreak of war, a faint nervousness possessing everyone, especially the women, and as the weeks and months wore on Freddie had become increasingly aware of it. So George's words resonated, making the job of postboy still more important. But he was not sure why he might have to say sorry, and would have asked George to explain except for the old man's rank breath of smoke, eggs, and beer. All he wanted to do was retch and escape.

Twenty minutes later the smell was still stuck in his nostrils, even though he was now in the open air and on his first round, so he dismounted his new postboy bicycle, took out his handkerchief, blew his nose and examined the contents to look for evidence. Disappointed that his snot was just transparent slime, apparently uncontaminated by George's breath, Freddie raised his eyes to look out across the arid fields surrounding Eagley.

Standing on the ridge of Bath Hill gave him a view for several miles in every direction, and he felt a flush of guilt that he was now being paid to stand still, less than half-an-hour into his new job. If George found out, Freddie would be in trouble, so he returned his handkerchief to his pocket and climbed back onto his bike. He was about to push off when something stopped him, made him look out across the fields again, his eyes following their contours as they sloped into a tranquil valley.

There, in the distance, partly hidden from Freddie's vantage point by a small area of woodland and the curve of a hillock, was a manor house. He had noticed it before on his many childhood excursions, though never seen it up close, and it had always been a place he used to dream of owning, presumably as some landlord who didn't need to work: an artist, or a minor dignitary, or a writer. He knew it was called Tendring, because he'd heard it being talked about in whispers loud enough to be overheard. The occupants went to church, Freddie had seen them there, but they kept their distance from everyone. Or everyone kept their distance from them; it was hard to tell.

Freddie pushed hard on his pedals and set off down the slope towards Tendring to follow George's next piece of advice: *"If you've more than one telegram, start with the rich and work your way down."*

George had instructed him to knock once, then for a second time if necessary. But it was not possible to raise his knuckles to the door at all, since it was already open. Propped up against the side of the portico was a ladder leading mischievously to nowhere, and Freddie wondered why anyone would put it there. The door's brass letterbox and knocker had been removed and placed on the threshold next to a pot of paint, and a shining wetness of black covered each rail and panel of what seemed to Freddie to be an unnecessarily large door. He felt slightly nauseous at the smell of the paint – his lungs reflexed, breathing the fumes in more deeply, the last thing he should have done because it caused a brief flash of light to rip behind his eyes. Certain smells would often trigger a headache.

Since he couldn't knock, Freddie felt unable to move either forward or back. He had received no advice for this situation. This was his first delivery, his first telegram, and he was already stuck. *"Sometimes you deliver the post,"* George had said, *"sometimes telegrams, and sometimes both. You're not supposed to, but you do. There's a war on."* It seemed to Freddie that people said "there's a war on" all the time and used it to justify almost anything. He wondered how he might use it in conversation with Millie, but he wouldn't have known what to do next, just as he didn't now.

Freddie put his hand into the leather pouch that hung from his right hip and pulled out a telegram. He examined the name and address, then looked behind and around to check he wasn't being watched, knowing he was about to do something he shouldn't. Convinced it was safe to go on, he negotiated his way around the paint pot, stepped into the hallway and so into a more adult way of doing things, breaking the rules because it seemed necessary to do so. His new uniform seemed to give him permission. Or was it the doorway itself, acting like some magician's portal? It certainly felt like it.

"Telegram for Mrs Harkness!"

To his surprise his words – the very first words in his capacity as postboy – were emphatic and bold, as if rehearsed. And in a way they were. He was used to his Ma calling him from downstairs and he was well-practised at raising his voice from his bedroom in reply. That would be it. As he waited for an answer he tried not to look further into the hallway, but couldn't resist, persuading himself you needed to see something first in order to avoid looking at it.

His pupils widened reflexively in the gloom of the hall. On the right side was a small table and chair, also a grandfather clock, and a glass-fronted gun cabinet fixed at eye-level on the wall. On the left side were stacked some metal frames. He wasn't sure what they were, but they clearly didn't belong there. In his days of growing up, he had trespassed across the fields and into the orchards, through the woods, and sometimes even into Bedden's empty barn, but this was a new experience of being both thrilled and frightened, crossing the threshold of another's private house. His temples pulsed against the sides of his shako hat and he felt a sudden urge to escape, but he forced himself to move further in, taking one more step into the hall. There was no messing this one up, his first delivery.

He called out again. "Telegram for Mrs Harkness!"

In the stillness, the hanging chimes of the grandfather clock resonated to his call like a humming choir of insects. The sound of heat.

"That would be me."

She had spoken, each syllable an exotic sound, strange glottal stops entirely new to Freddie's ears; feminine, deep and thrilling. He turned round to see a woman framed in the doorway, and although he had occasionally caught sight of her in the village and at church, her sudden appearance here was nevertheless a shock. With her long, loose black hair and paint-splattered white smock, she looked like an apparition, fictitious yet true. He recalled a story that had once done the rounds in the school playground – if you walked past a ghost you would never know, because they were just like real people. The idea sent a shiver down his back, and he felt the same thing now.

He remembered once standing behind her with his mother in the Post Office and noticing that when people met her they smiled, then said "good morning" and then stared, in that order. Her brown skin meant she was from India, he knew that, but it made no sense because she didn't look anything like the Indian on the cover of his Boy's Own Annual. If anything, she reminded him more of the suffragettes he'd seen pictures of in the newspaper. They looked exotic too, the shadows across their faces exaggerated by an excess of printer's ink.

It was an uncomfortable, unnatural reversal of positions, Freddie standing in the hallway of this woman's house and her outside looking in, as if she were the visitor and he the owner. Silhouetted as she was against the daylight, it was hard to discern her expression, so Freddie was relieved when she spoke again, his trespass apparently forgiven; possibly unnoticed.

"You're new," she said.

"Yes ma'am. Telegram for you." He held it out for her to take.

"Would you read it for me please?" She was trying to sound kind, Freddie thought, and may even have been smiling, but he detected a nervousness beneath her words that made him feel anxious too. No, he couldn't do that, couldn't read it for her. He scratched the side of his nose, until he recalled George's final piece of advice, which he duly paraphrased. "Can't ma'am. It's the rules. Unless you're blind of course, then we make an exception." George hadn't told him what to do if someone was illiterate, but Freddie calculated it was not a consideration here because Mrs Harkness sounded too intelligent and educated for that.

"What's your name?"

"Freddie, ma'am. Freddie Lovegrove."

"Well Freddie Lovegrove, sometimes we have to break the rules," and by way of explanation she took a step towards Freddie and into the hallway, out of the light, then held out her hands, palms up, to reveal more of the black paint. He looked at them, and then he looked into her eyes, which in the shade of the hallway had now become visible. Her irises were such a deep brown it was hard to see where they ended and the pupils began. There were bold black lines painted around her eyelids that reminded Freddie of the charcoal pencils he kept at home. He felt the urge to draw her eyes, a compulsion he frequently had when he saw something distinctive, and he wondered if he would attempt it later, when his bedside candle was supposed to be nipped out but which he usually left to burn down into the small hours. That time of night, the time of sleeping, when he would stroke thick edges of charcoal into life and hatch the shadows they cast across his paper. But then he'd tried to draw from memory before, and had failed miserably, so perhaps he'd just stick to copying from his Boy's Own Annual after all.

Freddie looked down again at Mrs Harkness's hands. The wet paint on them gave him no choice, so he opened the telegram and read the message out loud.

"Celandine Hall V.A.D. wish to... dispatch soonest. Can you be ready for... three men Tuesday early? Captain Hurley."

He looked up, seeking approval. Instead, hands on hips, she examined the door frame like a workman inspecting the paintwork, as indeed perhaps she was.

"Will you be replying ma'am?" asked Freddie.

She grimaced at the half-painted door. "I suppose I'd better."

Freddie delved into his leather pouch for his pencil and notepad and began, to his surprise, to feel substantial; growing into it, his uniform suddenly seemed to fit. When he got home, he would proudly tell his mother all about the important messages he had delivered. Though he wondered if, when it came to it, the words would stick in his throat.

"To... Captain Hurley... Stop..." She was measuring each syllable so that Freddie would not get behind. "Celandine Hall. Stop. Tendring... Ready... Tuesday." Then, with a change of pace: "How much is that?"

Freddie counted the words with the tip of his pencil and said, "Ninepence, ma'am."

"Very good," she replied, casually brushing Freddie's arm with her hand as she walked past him into the hallway. He barely noticed the touch, yet something deep had registered. His mother would not have done it.

She called over her shoulder and pointed into a room off to one side. "Wait for me there, Freddie."

He turned his head but not his body. It would not be the last time Freddie tried to face in two directions at once.

Freddie found himself alone in the library, having been left there by Mrs Harkness who had gone to wash the paint off her hands. Yet he did not feel alone, far from it, watched as he was by three young men in army uniform, balanced on an easel in an unfinished portrait. Unfinished, however, only by degrees – the soldier on the left was complete, the face in the middle still in need of finishing touches, whereas the figure on the right was no more than pencil strokes on canvas. This face in particular seemed to be watching Freddie. Even though it had no colour, no shape or depth, it seemed to exist by dint of its absence, like the pupils of Mrs

Harkness's eyes.

He turned away, only to discover that someone else – or some*thing* else – was also regarding him closely. Further along, near the back wall and on a wooden pedestal, was a statue: life-like, yet unlike any person Freddie had ever seen before. Sitting cross-legged, its face and arms were a vibrant, menacing blue, its right hand raised like an archbishop's blessing. Freddie felt unsettled by the statue, it didn't belong in an English country house, in the middle of rural Kent. But it was his very unease that drew him towards it, until suddenly their eyes were level and his arm started to move, to reach out to touch the cold, blue skin, to check that it was stone, not flesh. But he knew that he mustn't, having trespassed enough in the house already.

"Shiva," explained Mrs Harkness as she re-entered the library. Freddie dropped his arm back down by his side and wondered how long she had been watching him. She smiled and then walked towards Freddie with her hands held up to show her inky palms once more. "I've no idea where the turpentine is." Again, she had pretended not to notice his transgression. He was not used to that. Harsh words, or a clip round the ear, was how his life had been defined up until this point. But Mrs Harkness was different, in ways he understood, and in ways he didn't.

Halfway between the portrait and Shiva was a writing desk, and Mrs Harkness came to a stop in front of it, pointing to one of its drawers. "You'll find ninepence in there. And a penny for yourself."

Freddie innocently obeyed, went to the drawer, opened it, looked inside and took out nine pennies. Then he was torn, unsure whom to obey next, no idea who came highest in the unwieldy hierarchy of adults, George or Mrs Harkness. All he knew was that he, Freddie, languished at the bottom. In the end, his boss prevailed. "Thank you ma'am, but I'm not allowed to take your penny."

"Oh, the rules?" said Mrs Harkness. "Well you know what I think about the rules. Please, take the penny. When you are down to your last one you can think of me."

She had sounded harsh, but then she winked. It was like the throwing of a switch or the opening of a door, and with it her otherworldliness disappeared. She was definitely not a ghost. Emboldened by this informality and the unfamiliar equality that came with it, he took the penny, then tried to think of how to thank her, and it suddenly came to him: some printed text he had learnt off by heart.

"I can save up to a maximum of thirty pounds per year and interest is paid at two and a half per cent per annum on whole pounds." Then he added: "It's a Post Office savings account."

"I see. And for what are you saving?"

"America ma'am."

Her eyes widened. "America? Well, you are a penny closer." Then she looked at the palms of her hands. "I would shake your hand, Freddie, my apologies. It's been nice to meet you. If you like you can call me Suhani."

"I'm not permitted, ma'am."

She smiled, which Freddie took to be a concession. She was allowing that one through, and he was grateful, for he knew – and perhaps she did too – that to use an adult's first name would catch in his throat, as forbidden as swearing.

"Very well, Freddie," she said, and then appeared to have an idea. "Wait for me outside if you will. I have something else for you."

Freddie was left waiting for a second time, this time by the portico, astride his bike and ready to leave, feeling that he had already been taking too long. To run late on his first day would be a mistake. He looked up at the top of the ladder, wondering who the last person to climb it might have been, and why. This mysterious domain, its peculiar inhabitants. If he just set off he would leave Tendring behind and it would disappear, with everything in it, into the dark hollow of a memory. His job as postboy could then properly begin. He had the uncanny feeling that if he left now, his life would be much simpler. But the telegram was real, George Franklin had handed it to him, therefore all else must follow, and sure enough Suhani came out and stood on the front doorstep.

"Here. Hold out your hand." She placed a small object in his outstretched palm and he rolled it suspiciously around his fingers until he could fathom out what it was. Made of brass and not much larger than a thimble, it had a face he recognised.

"We have many Gods," she said. "But three main ones. Brahma, Vishnu, Shiva. Brahma is the creator of the universe, while Vishnu is the preserver of it. Shiva's role is to destroy the universe in order to re-create it." With a final flourish she winked again. "He's my favourite."

In all the dreams he had ever had, no one had done that, not even Millie the milkmaid. Mrs Harkness seemed to straddle two worlds, the present and the past, heaven and earth, distance and closeness. An angel that winked at him? He couldn't reconcile the two. But he was glad, after all, that the post would bring him back to this place. He put Shiva in the same pocket as his penny, certain it would give him no choice but to return.

"Thank you ma'am."

"I will see you again on your next round, Freddie."

"Yes ma'am."

But he was troubled by something, a question that had been nibbling away as he'd waited outside for her, and if he didn't raise it now he never would. "Ma'am? The painting. Why isn't it finished?"

She looked at the freshly painted door and put her hands on her hips again. "We are all trying to do three jobs at once Freddie. That's war for you."

Freddie realised she had misunderstood. “No, I mean the one in the library.”

“Oh.” She moved her hands from her hips and absent-mindedly clasped them to her stomach. Freddie felt she had retreated somewhere. India, perhaps.

“Well, because he is the artist. He had to leave rather suddenly. He is in the army.” Then she nodded over Freddie’s shoulder as if she knew in which direction France might be. “He’ll finish it when he returns.”

“Do you know them?”

“Of course I do,” she said, wiping her hands on her smock, in the measured way a mother might smooth her child’s hair. “They are my sons.”

Since the moment he had first seen Mrs Harkness standing in the open doorway he had watched her and listened intently, but her demeanour seemed to have changed now, some quality in her smile that made him feel like his presence had become an imposition. It was time to stop watching, stop attending to this extraordinary creature, and he should leave her be. So he nodded a wordless goodbye and pushed down hard on his pedals, aware that those deep brown irises were following him down the drive and out through the open gates, guarded by two stone eagles. He thought it odd he hadn’t noticed them on his way in. In the same way too, he now realised, that he had never noticed her sons in the village, or at church. Perhaps they had been packed off to boarding school from an early age. Or perhaps they had always been there and Mrs Harkness was beginning to teach him how to see.

2

"Swifter than the antelope!"

They were working quickly, Suhani folding a bed sheet that had been handed to her by Hannah, who was unpegging another sheet from the washing line in the garden at the back of the house. Hannah was a strong, wiry young woman whose red hair billowed out from beneath her bonnet. Her life had been forged in the hills and rivers of Ireland, had made her way to England in search of better pay, or any pay at all. Eagley village seemed prissy compared to the country of her birth and whenever she walked across the lawn of Tendring, even in bare feet as she sometimes did at night, she felt disconnected from the earth beneath it. It was this that made her think she would go back to Donegal one day, when the time was right.

Phoebe by contrast was so fragile a man might fear she would break in his arms. Despite this, or perhaps because of it, she had once folded sheets with a man – one folding more than she had expected by the age of seventeen. And so it was that Phoebe seemed distracted from the task at hand.

"...or the Tamarin," continued Suhani, smiling, as she pressed on with the business of the laundry, allowing sheets and pillow cases to fall into the basket by her feet. "We must open all the windows and clear the sills. And push the Chesterfield to one side for now. Hannah, did you place the extra order?"

"Four o'clock ma'am."

"And you'll have these ironed by tomorrow morning?"

"Yes ma'am."

"Good. We will move Shiva nearer to the door. We'll need all hands on deck for that. Are you feeling strong Phoebe?"

But Suhani could see that Phoebe was not feeling strong, in fact looked paler than the sheets she was folding. Not only that, she appeared not to have heard the question.

"Ma'am?"

Suhani said it again, more softly so that she might be listened to. "Are you feeling strong Phoebe?"

"Actually ma'am, I'm not feeling very well."

Suhani paused with the laundry, hugging a half-folded sheet up against her chest. "Then you must go and lie down. We can manage."

Phoebe curtsied, "Thank you ma'am." She began walking through the garden and towards the house, each step turning into a skip, though not a joyful one, and Suhani presumed Phoebe would soon be reaching for the nearest sink or toilet bowl.

Suhani finished folding her sheet and placed it in the basket, which made Hannah obediently do the same with her own. Service had long ago become second nature.

"Anyway, first things first," said Suhani, brushing aside Phoebe's exit. "Before we can make the beds, we have to make the beds."

They stood in the hallway, Suhani and Hannah, neither of them quite sure what to do with the metal frames propped up against the wall either side of the library door.

"I can't say they look very comfortable, ma'am," said Hannah, her broad Irish accent particularly suited to understatement.

Suhani grabbed hold of the topmost frame. "But more comfortable than the trenches. This looks like as good a piece to start with as any."

And so they began to build the beds that would line one wall of the library, transforming it into a makeshift hospital annexe ready for the delivery of three mud-caked souls from the battlefields of France. The Chesterfield was moved, Shiva pushed to one side, and the unfinished portrait taken upstairs into Tristan's bedroom, where Suhani realised it should always have been stored. Painting was Tristan's joy, but more than that it was, she understood, his sole purpose, motivated by something beyond art: it functioned as a record, an entry in the register of life, of himself and his two brothers. These were Suhani's three sons, which the war had turned into men before they were ready, and which might kill them all before they had truly lived.

A war, in fact, that had taken her firstborn the previous summer. Her grief had been endless and gripped her tightly, never letting go, in silences that were her only defence against it. That was when the front door first became black, and she had secretly resolved to paint it every summer in remembrance. Laying out the freshly washed sheets and blankets in the library brought back the memory of nursing her children, and this made her feel useful again.

"These are near to breaking," said Hannah, poking one of the frames with her foot. "They'll be lucky if they last the night. The beds, I mean."

"Well, at least there will be no gunfire," replied Suhani. Though she thought to herself that if her husband had the garden foxes in his sights, these beds would rattle to the discharging of a bullet, sure enough.

Phoebe lay on her bed, wondering what it was she had eaten, and what chance she had of keeping it down. In her hand, resting on her stomach, was a letter that she hoped would distract her, so she held it up above her face and not for the first time began to read the opening lines.

"My darling Phoebe, I can hear the whistle of the train..."

But it failed to stop her lurching stomach, so she leapt off the bed to get to the bowl by the window, and threw up.

Freddie cycled back into the village. He knew how many items he had left to post because George Franklin had counted them into his hand before he'd set off – twelve letters, three Field Service Postcards and two telegrams, the first of which had already been delivered, leaving fifteen to go. His round was not supposed to take more than two hours, but looking up at the church clock he saw he was already running late. The twenty minutes he had spent at Tendring should have taken no more than two. Still, he knew the village well, everyone in it and where they lived, so he thought he'd be able to catch up.

As he delivered each letter they were received with varying reactions, but rarely with what he felt was his due: gratitude. Often he was greeted with a blank stare until the letter was examined, sometimes opened up on the doorstep there and then before he was finally thanked – but falsely so, with what seemed more like relief than indebtedness. They smiled with their mouths, but never with their eyes. He wondered if he was doing something wrong but couldn't work out what. Talking to his ma about it would not be possible because he wanted her to be proud, and as the man of the house it was his duty to show strength, not weakness. He sensed his growing up necessarily involved increasing the distance between them, he and his mother, like fruit seeding the ground furthest from the tree. And there was no point speaking to George because he would only say *you'll be all right,* as he had done several times earlier that morning already. The despondency Freddie felt made the pedals harder to push, like riding through mud, because his job as postboy involved meeting almost everyone in the local area, every day, yet was already making him feel lonely. In some curious way he felt as if he was letting the whole village down.

Freddie was especially unnerved by Mrs Girling, whose eyes bulged so much it looked like they might pop out. He hoped he wouldn't have to deliver too many letters to her. Mrs Pratt had a nice round face, but her clothes smelt of fish; Mrs Gardiner had a large mole on her top lip and a young daughter called Leslie who clung to her mother's side and never seemed to go to school; meanwhile Mrs Chilvers had ankles like an elephant's. It was odd, none of these things had ever really caught his eye in all his years living in the village. Perhaps he had never looked at anyone properly before, not even, come to think of it, Millie Bedden, who he realised was prettier the more you thought of her and the less you looked.

He had now delivered fourteen of his items of post with impressive efficiency, and had caught up on his shift. Later he would tell his mother how he'd gone about it; that much at least he could tell her, perhaps even face to face, rather than in the way they usually spoke to each other through his closed bedroom door. That way he'd be able to tell if she was proud or not. She might even say he was becoming more like his father.

One more letter to go and his first shift would be done. He looked down at the name and address: *Mr & Mrs Mawby, 3 Broad Street, Eagley, Kent.* This delivery would be the simplest. Mrs Mawby had taught Freddie when he was at school, and although, like all teachers, she had kept her distance – except of course when executing some measure of discipline – she would often smile kindly at him, and so he knew that he was well liked by her. It was because of Mrs Mawby that Freddie could read and write with such ease and skill. Advanced for his age, she had once told his mother. So he thought he would knock, to say hello.

The Mawby's letter looked more formal, the name and address not handwritten but typed, the envelope an unusual hue of cream. Mrs Mawby would be pleased to receive such an important looking item of post, Freddie thought, so he confidently knocked on his former teacher's door and whilst he waited for her to open it he wiggled his shako hat into a straighter, if slightly less comfortable, position. The door could do with a lick of paint, he reckoned, and wondered if black would suit it.

He lingered for a while but after nearly a minute, and another knock, he began to doubt she was in. He was on the verge of giving up and just pushing the letter through her letterbox when the door scraped open, halfway, with Mrs Mawby's head tilted to one side. For a moment he didn't recognise her because he had expected her to smile in the way she used to do every morning in school. In fact she looked angry, with the beginnings of a snarl spreading across her mouth.

"Morning Mrs Mawby," said Freddie, unsure but undeterred, and handed her the letter. She took it and stared at the address for several seconds, far longer than seemed necessary or normal. Then Freddie became alarmed as Mrs Mawby's head started to shake as if she were freezing cold and he wondered if she was coming down with something. She pulled at the letter carelessly, too quickly, tearing the envelope right through the address as if she wanted to destroy it, make it undeliverable. He was surprised, however, to see the letter itself had survived the assault, and she shakily flicked it open, like the striking of a match, and began to read. But she only studied it for a few seconds before looking straight at Freddie and screamed with her mouth so wide open he could see the many gaps in her teeth, all the way to the back. The waft of her breath swept across his face with a smell that reminded him of a ploughed field, and when her lungs were empty she breathed in and screamed again, her face going red and the veins in her neck bulging so gruesomely that Freddie imagined they might burst and squirt blood over his new uniform. Then she screamed for a third time, scrunching up the letter to put it to her face where the noise she made changed to a wail, a fathomless moan which Freddie instinctively understood to be her calling out for help that would never come. She fell to her knees and leant forward until her forehead touched Freddie's shoes. Instinctively he retreated half a step as she rocked back and forth, her moaning muffled by the letter she had cupped around her mouth. Flustered and hesitant, Freddie looked from left to right, expecting to see Mrs Mawby's neighbours arriving with a helping hand, but none came, although he thought he caught the flicker of a net curtain being pulled at by a plump, grey hand. Then Mrs Mawby fell on her side. Except no, it was more than that, she had thrown herself there, deliberately, her head hitting the cobbles with a crack. The sickening noise of it summoned the trace of a memory, of when he was seven or eight years old and on his way back home from picking apples – or stealing them, if truth be told, though his mother had simply told him to *go and find some cookers* – Freddie had witnessed the shooting of a horse. Four people gathered around the poor animal, a man who held the bridle, a second man who held the gun, and a woman who was hugging her young daughter to her chest. The little girl was crying and looking up at her mother, who stroked her daughter's hair. Freddie was watching this sombre tableau from behind a hedgerow at the side of the field, and although he wasn't exactly hiding, neither did he wish to be seen for fear of disturbing them. He watched the man with the gun put a bullet in its chamber and then immediately place it against the horse's forehead. What seemed odd to Freddie was that the horse didn't flinch, even though of course he knew the creature was not capable of understanding what was about to happen. In the final second before the shooting, the horse was as it had always been and always would be, simply and permanently alive in a split-second of existence, an eternal present. It was this taking away of innocence that made the execution seem like such a terrible act of betrayal. As Freddie looked down at Mrs Mawby he thought of the horse collapsing to the crack of the gun, and the pointless thud as it hit the ground.

Surely the neighbours would come out soon? If they didn't, Mrs Mawby would continue to wail forever and Freddie would be late back for his shift. He looked from left to right again and to his relief heard the click of a door being opened. An older woman, who Freddie knew to be Mrs Hope, stepped out from her house next door and leant down to put one hand on Mrs Mawby's shoulder, the other to tend to her badly grazed cheekbone, then looked up at Freddie: "Why are you hanging about? You've done what you came to do."

Freddie blushed, suddenly feeling tears rush upon him, and realised he would have to walk away in order to hide them. But he found himself remaining for a moment longer, trying to recall a postscript that George had given him, a line he didn't understand at the time but which now seemed clear: *Sometimes they catch your eye and wish they were dead. Or wish you were. But you don't worry about that. You just do your job. You can't change the message.*

Mrs Hope looked up at Freddie again and said: "Well?"

"Ma'am," nodded Freddie, as he blinked away the wetness, climbed on his bike and pedalled off to the end of his very first morning's shift, complete, ahead of time, job done. Then a cloud passed across the face of the sun and Freddie was alone, without so much as his own shadow to accompany him home.

3

Freddie ought to have been tucked up in bed asleep, but as darkness fell on his first day's work he lay on top of his blankets, still wearing his uniform. The flickering from his candle mingled with the moonlight to cast strange shadows on the ceiling that sloped above his head as he focused on a crack in the lime mortar. He was trying to convince himself his day had been a success. After all, he had done his job, just as George had told him to, and everything had been delivered with efficiency and punctuality. He had not made any mistakes. Yet he couldn't dismiss the melancholy that enveloped him, the idea that his world had irrevocably changed for the worse, that there was no going back to scrumping for apples, climbing the bales of wet straw in Bedden's barn, or walking through a field because there was nothing better to do and discovering that there really was, as it turned out, nothing better. Even Millie had shifted in his mind. He didn't see her hands anymore but fingernails that were bitten and dirty, and the split skin in one corner of her mouth where before there had been only unblemished lips. Her milk was on the turn. The feeling of despondency was not dissimilar, he thought, to the dreary glow of needing to empty one's bowels, except there would never be any relief. He'd been a fool to think that the job of postboy was anything other than the bringer of bad news. This was war and people died in it. He was hardly likely to be welcomed with open arms.

As he looked up he imagined the lime mortar falling in on him and almost wished it would. He wondered if he might feel better if he removed his jacket and forgot about being the postboy for a while. There was a knock on his bedroom door and a muffled voice called from the other side: "You asleep Freddie?"

"Yes Ma."

"Candle out?"

Freddie twisted his neck to look up to his windowsill where his candle was defiantly burning. "Yes Ma."

"You sure? You know what happens when you don't get your sleep!"

"Yes Ma."

It was a lie of course, but an insignificant one. He had lied to her this way so many times that it had become a kind of truth, even to himself. It had crept up on both of them over the years, in the same way her blindness had. These days he could say the candle was out when it was lit, and she would never know. There was a pause after he had said so, as there always was, familiar and warm, that meant he could time his goodnight wishes to coincide exactly with his mother's. He didn't even have to think about it, and nor did she, but on this day of all days his timing was off, he uttered the word later than hers and he felt she had let him down, or worse, he had let her down. After his father had died Freddie and his ma had become very close; now they seemed to be more distant than ever. He waited a few more seconds listening to her footsteps disappearing across the landing into the other bedroom, and thought they might be slower than usual. Everything was on the crook tonight. He rolled off his bed to stand by the window.

He took out the small statuette of Shiva from his jacket hip pocket and placed it on the windowsill next to the candle. Its mottled bronze sheen reflected the candlelight, which for an uncanny moment made it appear to move. On one side was a thin smudge of black paint – it must have rubbed off Suhani's fingers. He thought if he kept repeating Shiva's mantra – *destroy the universe in order to recreate it* – it would eventually make sense, because right now the words sounded like double dutch to him. Then, from the same pocket, he removed the penny. It was an old one, almost black, with Queen Victoria on it, and he put it on the other side of the candle to the right. The placing of it felt like the ending of an old life and the beginning of a new; but as he took his hand away, he wasn't sure he wanted either.

He removed his jacket and hung it on one ear of his chair, where his shako hat hung on the other. Then he wound up his G.P.O. alarm clock and the turning of its gears made him feel better. He assumed this was his life now, that he would do the same thing every night and the routine would prevent any more changes. A simple world in which he would repeat himself over and over, until he was seventy years old, just as George Franklin had done. It would surely take forever to live that long but then he remembered Mrs Mawby and how her son – for he presumed it was her son – had not managed it. The calming effect of getting ready for bed hadn't lasted long, and his dismal mood returned.

However, there was one element of his routine he could reach for, the one thing that was guaranteed to lift his spirits. From underneath his bed Freddie pulled out a bible-sized book, his Boy's Own Annual; and in a way, it was his bible. He lay back on his bed, propped the book on his knees and opened the stiff cardboard cover, then flicked through the pages, skimming past the factual stories – *The Channel Swimmer, The Race to the South Pole, Rustic Woodwork for Boys* – to pause and marvel at the many intricate illustrations that accompanied the fictional tales of exploration and derring-do from the British Empire. The smell of the paper and the ink thrilled Freddie as much as if he was at Jephson's Public School or in the Syrian Desert himself.

He stopped turning the pages to allow a loose sheet of paper to fall out onto his lap, his own drawing, half-finished, a copy of the front cover of the Annual. An American Indian was looking up into the sky. His long black hair was tied back by a red bandana and a belt of bullets hung diagonally across his red top-shirt that billowed in the North American wind. Legs apart, he held aloft his rifle, the proud and imperious custodian of the land he stood upon.

Freddie had been working on transferring this picture every night for over a week and it was now nearing completion. Sometimes he was so lost in the process it felt as if someone else was moving his pencil for him, and was thinking so deeply as to be unaware of his own thoughts, oblivious of how extraordinarily accurate the end result would be until it was actually finished. Someone, perhaps Mrs Mawby, had once said he had a gift, that he was born with a pencil in his hand. But Freddie just drew. It gave him genuine peace, and in this moment it took him back to the Freddie he felt he was already beginning to lose, and wanted to become again.

The Indian would be his best drawing yet. There was a chance he could finish it tonight before the candle burnt itself out – although another part of him wished for the act of drawing to continue until the morning. Or better still, for the process to last forever.

A fox walked across the lawn of Tendring, pausing nonchalantly to sniff the ground. Suhani wondered why it moved in a zigzag, perhaps it was following the shadows cast by the branches of the copper beech so that it would not be seen by predators or prey in the moonlight. She watched it pause again, nearer, a matter of five yards away, and this time it looked straight into her eyes. It was not so much a challenge as simply an acknowledgement of each other's presence that passed between them.

But then Suhani was suddenly startled as the fox let out a scream, a noise that, were it not for the evidence of her eyes, could be mistaken for the cry of a woman in pain. Her stomach clenched as it took her back to the unearthly sound she had once emitted at the birth of her first son, and again at his death. The fox yawned and walked off into the trees as if they had done nothing more than pass each other in the High Street.

By day, Suhani wore the clothes of an English lady, but at night she took to her sari. Sometimes she told herself this was an act of defiance, but in reality it was more one of practicality and comfort. She was simply able to breathe and to move through the air uninhibited. As she stood underneath the copper beech at the bottom of the garden, she was glad to be alone without the weight of Englishness on her shoulders.

Under the branches and next to where she stood was a marble pedestal on which sat a small glass cabinet. At its base were strewn delphinium petals and inside it was an unlit candle, a matchbox and a miniature framed photograph of her lost son. She opened the brass-hinged door and put her hand inside to remove the picture, accidentally disturbing some of the delphinium petals so that they floated to the ground like feathers. Why did nobody smile in photographs, she thought? He was a young soldier who looked both confident and fearful at the same time. Suhani felt that if only he'd smiled, the fear would have disappeared. But it was not to be, and she returned the frame to its place on the pedestal, next to the cabinet.

She was removing a match from its box when she became aware of the sound of soft footfall on the grass behind her. She did not turn round.

"Suhani. I've decided. I'd like more light in the house." It was a man's voice with a dismal cadence to it, which, like the footsteps, she had become so familiar with she rarely noticed anymore. She struck the match and leant across to light the candle.

"Stephen, you're very late again."

"The Cawley's have a generator in their dairy. It's about time we had electricity installed. What do you think?"

Suhani blew out the match and spoke as softly as she could. Any difference of opinion needed to be handled carefully. "The days are long enough already, don't you think?"

She turned to face her husband, a man twenty years older, bolt upright yet somehow rather trivial, with a Kitchener moustache that gave him the air of a drowned man. He looked tired and sounded irritated.

"Why is the front door open? We'll have foxes in the house."

"The paint is still wet." She tried to smile. Stephen used his top lip to push the hairs of his moustache up into his nostrils. Suhani knew that he was counting to ten in order to calm his nerves, an exercise he did so often she wondered how there was ever time for him to do anything else.

"And I thought we agreed. Not the library. Upstairs for those men. Where am I supposed to retire for the evening?"

"Stephen, you're hardly ever here in the evenings. It won't be easy to get them upstairs. And then down again for air. The library is so much more practical. Doctor Herring said we must give them – "

"Perhaps Doctor Herring would like to have them in his house then," Stephen interrupted. Suhani was so used to it she barely noticed.

"Move them please," he continued. "You can open the upstairs windows."

"Stephen, they're coming tomorrow. First light. There isn't time – "

"Then you will have to move them in their beds. We agreed. What's the point of having the discussion? Suhani?"

Suhani stared at Stephen for a moment and thought he seemed in physical pain, his anger pushing at the inside of his chest. He was right, there was no point in having the discussion. Calmly she turned her back to him, choosing a different tack. She picked up the photograph again.

"Do you think any of them will come home?"

"What?" Stephen breathed out heavily, impatiently. "Well, they have God on their side."

"It hasn't helped so far," she replied, returning the photograph once more inside the glass cabinet, then realised she had unintentionally used a sarcastic tone and quickly spoke again to rectify the impression. "I worry about Tristan in particular. You know how much he hates thunder storms. He jumps at the sound of the dinner gong." There was a silence, which she felt compelled to fill. "And he's left-handed."

"Whose fault is that?" he snapped. Her attempt at levity had backfired, Suhani felt hurt by the edge in his voice, and she knew the immediate calmness that followed was just an act; a welcome one, in a way, but an act all the same. "I apologise," he said. "It's been a difficult day. What is your opinion then? Of electricity?"

Suhani picked up the candle and turned back to face Stephen, though she kept her focus on the naked flame rather than on him. "Do you think, one day, in the future, there will be no more candlelight?" Only then did she look up fully into Stephen's eyes, who seemed thrown by her question, so she answered him directly. "But yes. I agree. Our house could do with more light."

He nodded, appearing to accept her answer as a declaration of peace. She replaced the candle and looked at the photograph of her dead son, Arthur Lancelot Harkness, a name she had not chosen, or liked. The sound of it tolled in her head like a funeral-bell.

"I'm going to water the roses, then reset the snare," said Stephen. "That damned fox makes a mockery of our lawn."

"Must you?"

"Well, you won't let me poison it. What would you have me do?"

She wanted to ask him to let the fox live, but he would never understand, not now, not since the change in him. "I think you should shave off your moustache," said Suhani as she walked past Stephen. "It would be nice to see your face again."

He seemed utterly thrown by her request. As she padded softly across the grass towards the front door and away from Stephen, she reflected that there had once been a time, long ago, in another time and another garden, surrounded by roses, when her words would not have been a mystery to him, when their conversations would have sounded like prayers, or singing, instead of what they had become, a noise like the clatter of a typewriter and the scything of dead wood.

4

The alarm clock by Freddie's bed rattled its bells in a wild fury that could have woken the whole street. But he was already awake and getting dressed. He leant down to switch off the alarm and then straightened up again to fasten the final button of his jacket. Next, he wiggled his hat into place. He had no mirror to check what he was doing, but George would give him the once-over before he set off on his deliveries. Finally, he threaded his leather pouch onto his belt and tightened it. For the time being, this was as close to being a soldier as his fourteen years allowed. He knew his mother would like to see him in his uniform, and in a way he would have liked to show it off, but of course her eyes didn't work and she would have said how natty he looked based purely on the sound of his voice, not the smartness of his uniform. There would have been a time when she would have used her hands to see, to feel the thickness of the cloth, the sharp edges of his collar, even the shining smoothness of his shoes. But that was for small children, not boys becoming men, and by remaining aloof he was able to push her away. Best to leave it for another day. Though he wondered if such a day would ever come.

In the final minute left to him before setting off for work, Freddie pulled out the Boy's Own Annual from underneath his bed, along with his drawing. He looked from one to the other. The likeness was remarkable, even Freddie thought so himself; all the same, he felt there was some deficiency there. He saw a shine on the face of the original that was missing from his copy. In his own drawing the white war-paint under the eyes was simply the absence of cross-hatching, whereas on the cover of the Annual it seemed to be the actual presence of a white glow, an effect he had not been able to re-create the night before, leaving him feeling dissatisfied then, and even more so this morning. But he would have to solve it later, he had work to do. He replaced the book and his drawing under the bed and stood up as straight as he could, the top of his hat only an inch from the low ceiling. In all respects, he would do better today.

When Freddie arrived for work there was a despatch rider waiting for him outside. She had left her motorbike running and was lifting out a small canvas bag of post from the sidecar. She handed it to Freddie as she nodded at the front door of the post office and shouted over the noise of her engine: "Can't bloody wake him – as usual!"

Freddie didn't know what to say, instead he just took the bag from her. He wondered whether, underneath her flying goggles and riding hat, she was pretty or not. He thought the wisps of hair sticking out from beneath her hat meant that she must be. Her fingernails were tidier and cleaner than Millie's, and her teeth were straighter too. Freddie wanted to speak to her but the ten years between them might as well have been ten trips to the moon and back and he couldn't even muster a thank you. She climbed back on her motorbike and called out over the spluttering engine "See you later!" then revved and disappeared in a cloud of purple petrol fumes. Millie had competition.

George was asleep in his chair, just as the despatch rider had predicted, and Freddie rushed to switch off the Primus stove that he spotted was boiling a small kettle of water on the counter for tea. George had allowed it to nearly boil dry and the whiff of alcohol in the room explained why. He was not merely asleep, but unconscious. Freddie wondered if George had even gone home yesterday or had slept in the office all night. At least this state of affairs meant Freddie could get on with his job, uninhibited by George's endless instructions.

There was, however, one instruction he couldn't ignore. On the counter was a parcel with a note attached to it, on which George had written: *Recieved in Error. Return to Sender.* Freddie noted – thanks to Mrs Mawby's teaching – the incorrect spelling, then lifted the note to see the address where the parcel was supposed to be going: *GHQ Stationery Office, Montreuil-Sur-Mer, France.* He turned the parcel over to check the sender's address and saw that it had come from the War Office in London. He saw, too, a brief description of the contents printed on the back, along with their quantity: *Field Service Postcards, 500.* But George had yet to instruct Freddie about how to return-to-sender, it was bound to be unnecessarily complicated, so he put the parcel in the drawer which George used for everything that didn't have its own designated place, and was therefore already overflowing. Freddie decided he would sort it out later, when he had a moment. Right now he had more urgent things to do.

It took him less than a minute to sort out the twenty letters he'd poured out of the despatch rider's canvas bag. There were only three pigeonholes that covered Freddie's rounds – Eagley North, Eagley South, and Eagley village itself. In reality, North also covered West, and South covered East. The system seemed random and pointless to Freddie. Surely he could just take all the letters and deliver them in one go, organising the different areas as he went, and he wondered what would happen if he did. In one of George's lectures yesterday he had proudly told Freddie that the Post Office employed over two hundred and fifty thousand people and that's why they needed rules. Staring at the pigeonholes, Freddie realised that it was immaterial whether those rules made any sense or not, they were simply there to keep the machine turning. Perhaps the system had made sense once, long ago, but now it was just there, like an old tree the farmer had to plough around. In the end, Freddie decided that things are done a certain way simply because they are. But it irked him.

Freddie gathered up the Eagley North pile and put it in his leather pouch. He looked around the room, a cluttered, chaotic space, not remotely conducive to doing the job efficiently. Obviously George hadn't heard the rule about tidiness. There were two recruitment posters on the wall behind the counter. The first had John Bull pointing directly at him saying *Who's absent? Is it you?* and the second showed soldiers in desert uniform with the slogan *See the world... and get paid for doing it.* Freddie had taken over the job of postboy from Jimmy Gardiner who had run away to volunteer for the army a month before, and Freddie thought it was just a matter of time before he too could go off to fight in France. He wanted to go, not least because his Boy's Own Annual told him to. Anything less and he'd be the recipient of a white feather. He'd heard a whisper, though, that Jimmy had lied about his age and had consequently ended up in Lincoln. Freddie would have to bide his time.

He continued to look around the room and at last saw what he was looking for. In the past Freddie had stolen apples, with his mother's blessing, so a small piece of chalk seemed nothing in comparison. It would not be missed. He took the piece of chalk and put it in the hip pocket of his jacket.

Freddie stood astride his bike, as bold as the American Indian, looking down the gentle slope which promised much more than he could actually see. In truth, the view to be had across the fields from anywhere other than the very top of Bath Hill was mostly blocked by tall hedgerows either side of the lane. So he chose instead to look straight up into the sky, a clear blue lustre that baked his face in the early sunlight, causing his cheeks to tingle. He scrunched his eyes and then closed them altogether, holding this position for a full minute, until an unexpected noise made him open them again. The sound reached his gut before his ears, then he worked out what it was, the approaching roar of an internal combustion engine. At first he thought it might be the despatch rider on another run, but then he caught sight of an aeroplane, its stacked wings rocking as it made slow progress over Freddie's head. He smiled, raised his arm to wave, and laughed out loud when the pilot waved back. He felt a heady pleasure in being spotted by a character straight out of his Boy's Own; then he felt the strangest notion that this event was already a memory, that he would become someone who would look back and remember it, this day in the sun, with the aeroplane overhead. But having the feeling was not the same as understanding it, and it disappeared as surely as the plane itself, over the hedgerows and beyond the horizon.

He wiggled his shako hat to make sure it was secure and pushed off down the track. The ridges and potholes caused his bell to ring of its own accord, and as he picked up speed the boy who wanted to be a man became a boy again, stuck out his legs and laughed at the wind.

As his bike bounced and skipped musically down the lane, Freddie heard, for the third time that morning, the sound of an engine. This time it was more familiar to him as he had often heard trucks passing through the village carrying soldiers to the coast, and the noise he heard now seemed to be the same. But he realised he was no longer quite in control of his bike, and had an eerie premonition that the two things, truck and bike, were about to be combined. His whole body contracted, his backside squeezed his bicycle seat and his fingers tightened on his brakes, which stopped the wheels from turning but not the forward motion of the bike itself as it began to skid, throwing up dust and small stones into the air. A makeshift ambulance was making its way along the road at the bottom of Freddie's track, and they were seconds from an unplanned rendezvous. Freddie rapidly twisted the handlebar of his bike back and forth, with nothing but instinct keeping him upright, until he tumbled past the front of the ambulance, missing it by inches and ending up in the ditch. The driver of the ambulance, a young woman, had slammed on her brakes but didn't stop, instead accelerating off and yelling curses out of her open window, "You bleedin' idiot! What the bloody hell do you think you're doin'? Stupid bugger!"

Freddie crawled out of the ditch, stood up and watched the ambulance take a bend in the road until he could no longer see it. He looked at his bike and at his hat lying nearby. Both seemed undamaged, but he himself felt queasy. A sticky substance was dribbling into his eye which he investigated with the tip of his forefinger. Blood. His eyelids flickered and he fell and rolled over, in a faint, back into the ditch he had just climbed out of.

Although it was still early, Tendring house was fully awake and Hannah was hard at work in the kitchen. The act of preparing food reminded her of home, which sometimes filled her with such wistful joy she would sing out loud, and today was no exception, rolling out the pastry to the rhythm of *Jolly good luck to the girl who loves a soldier*. Hannah and Phoebe had been to see Vesta Tilley the previous Saturday at the Theatre Royal in Margate, and the song had stuck in Hannah's head. But what had also stuck, and was even harder to shake out, was the sight of men queuing up on stage to volunteer. Vesta Tilley had become *Britain's Best Recruiting Sergeant,* as the posters outside the theatre proclaimed, but Hannah thought the men were having their arms twisted, as did the wives and girlfriends who looked up at them from the auditorium, though none would admit it. There was something sinister about the carnival atmosphere, and Hannah for one was not falling for it. It was not volunteering, she thought, if you had no choice, it was just another form of conscription, and they were being herded like young bulls to the slaughter house. She had heard the stories. Jolly good luck, indeed, to the girl who loves a soldier.

In her reverie Hannah had rolled out her pastry too thinly. She sighed and was about to start again when Phoebe walked in, carrying a wicker basket of vegetables.

"They'll be here any minute," said Phoebe, as she dumped the basket onto the table, next to Hannah, who thought Phoebe looked miserable.

"We've no time for all this extra work," said Hannah dismissively, pummelling the pastry back into a ball in her hands.

"We must do our bit," said Phoebe.

"That's what they say, isn't it. Well you need to be careful. That's a heavy delivery and make no mistake." Hannah, who had become vigilant in recent weeks, noticed Phoebe looking at the basket of vegetables as if her own heart had fallen into it, and saw the corner of her mouth begin to tremble. So Hannah dropped the ball of pastry back into its bowl, brushed the flour from her hands and turned to face Phoebe with open arms. "Come here you silly goose," she said, and gave Phoebe a hug. "Go and put water on the tables. I'll be with you in a minute."

Hannah ended the embrace in a matter-of-fact way, and despite there being little difference in their ages she smiled at Phoebe like a mother to a daughter, which made her think all the more of Vesta Tilley and her invisible, treacherous fishing net.

Being hugged by Hannah raised Phoebe's spirits. She went over to the sink and filled a large porcelain jug with water, which she then carried out of the kitchen through the narrow corridor under the stairs and into the hallway. She caught sight of Suhani standing in the open front door, silhouetted by the early morning sunlight, where she was busy with her screwdriver reattaching the letter box. Although Phoebe didn't stop, because there was no time, she felt a familiar comfort being merely in Suhani's presence. She could never possibly be her friend – they lived on different levels in more ways than one – but she felt Mrs Harkness would be there for her, always listen, never judge. When Phoebe accompanied her into the village, as she had often done in the three years since she had first started service, there were stares and whispers that made Phoebe feel protective, though it would often manifest itself the other way round with Mrs Harkness shielding Phoebe from the sly put-downs. Phoebe saw it from time to time, Mrs Harkness coming to the aid of scapegoats and outsiders, and because of it she was drawn to her as someone with whom she could share secrets. Except the one secret Phoebe owned was not yet ready to be shared. In any case the idea was so fleeting she was already in the library focused on distributing glasses of water, and Suhani had probably not even seen her.

It was strange to see three empty beds in the library, two on one side, the other opposite them creating a triangle, and Phoebe was unsettled by the change. It was like a different room. She looked at the nearest bed and the clean white sheets made her consider how many people besides Hannah had physically touched her in her life and decided it was not many. She compiled a list in her head. Her father, a lot, her mother, not so much, her two sisters and one brother; and then the touching of hands as she passed money or bread in Mrs Jenner's shop, though she wasn't sure if that really counted; or the man she had sat next to in the Theatre Royal, who seemed to lean in and point his pipe more towards her than to his wife; or Mrs Harkness informally touching her arm as they spoke, a social transgression that made Phoebe feel strangely elated; and then, finally, one other, the secret one, sometimes kept secret even from herself.

"Daydreams are all very well, Phoebe." Stephen stood in the doorway, checking his pocket watch.

Phoebe turned round and curtsied briskly, as if she had been caught stealing the silver. "Sorry sir."

He smiled at Phoebe, but she could tell it was the smile of someone who no longer quite understood its purpose.

Other than continuing to turn the screw, Suhani didn't move when Stephen squeezed between her and the door frame. She noticed that, as usual, he made sure not to brush her dress as he passed. Without stopping he said: "That is man's work, my dear."

Suhani had timed the rhythm of her reply...*there...are...no...men...*to synchronise with each tightening of her screwdriver, but it seemed Stephen had already stopped listening; instead he had stepped out of the portico and was making his way down the main drive of Tendring, negotiating the rows of delphiniums that grew on either side, striding formally down the middle, as obediently as a train riding its tracks. But there was an odd cadence to his gait, the suggestion of a limp.

He called out to Suhani over his shoulder: "I will probably be late again. Depending on the whale oil..." Suhani did not reply. In more ways than one, he was too far away. She felt the edges of the letterbox to check they were true before looking up to watch her husband as he headed towards the open gates. He hadn't mentioned the requisition of his library, almost as if he had forgotten about it. But that was often his way, to keep quiet for a day, and then explode when she least expected it. How small he seemed, how hurt, and she felt an unexpected ache of protectiveness, not for the Stephen as he was now, nor even as he used to be, but for some small child that was imprisoned inside him. An orphan, abandoned by the loveless man he had become.

The pang was short lived. An ambulance was turning the corner into the drive and Stephen had to quickly step aside. At this distance Suhani could not make out the expression on his face, but she was familiar enough with his body language to know that he was annoyed. She watched him pause for a moment to glare at the ambulance as it drove towards the house, then he turned with an irritated snap, almost losing balance on his shorter right leg, before leaving the stone eagles behind.

The ambulance pulled up in front of the portico and the driver, a young woman in nurse's uniform, switched off the engine. Suhani stood and waited, wondering if she should speak to the driver, but before she could decide another figure climbed out of the passenger seat. It was a second nurse, but Suhani was in no doubt that in every other sense she was the first – her Matron's uniform was more formal and starched, like the woman herself. She walked up to Suhani, clutching some papers under one arm.

"You must be Mrs Harkness."

"Please, call me Suhani," she said, then held out her hand, registering for the thousandth time the slight pause between the offer and the acceptance, insignificant but acutely painful, like a paper cut. It was no longer a surprise after so many years, yet she had never got used to it.

"Nurse Collins is easiest, if you don't mind." The handshake was brief, with the apparent excuse that she needed to hand over her paperwork to Suhani. Then Nurse Collins spoke without any intention of being interrupted.

"There is one wheelchair, which will have to be shared as required. We will leave you with enough carbolic lotion, gauze, and bandages to keep you going until I return on Friday. There is also laudanum with instructions that must be strictly followed. Use it last thing at night if you can, for your benefit as much as theirs. I will try to send a nurse every second day but that may not be possible and if any of their conditions deteriorate quickly, telegram Celandine Hall for advice, or if necessary I will come back myself. They are all walking-wounded and two of them are on the road to recovery already. I suggest you don't fall for this shell shock nonsense. They will know the ropes better than you I suspect. The third patient is more difficult. Doctor Herring was not... well...do you have a strong stomach Mrs Harkness?"

At first Suhani didn't hear the question. She had been watching a farcical dance going on over Nurse Collins' shoulder and had become distracted. The driver had removed a wheelchair from the back of the ambulance and by then Hannah and Phoebe had come out of the house to help, the three of them guiding the first wounded soldier out of the ambulance and into the wheelchair, then pushing it up to the portico where the steps meant they could go no further. So they lifted the soldier out again, his arms around the shoulders of Hannah and Phoebe, who walked either side of him into the house, past Suhani and Nurse Collins. The driver tried to push the empty wheelchair up the steps but lost balance and had to let it tip over in order to save herself from falling.

Nurse Collins turned her head to see what was happening and her nostrils flared as if she had been offered a rotten egg. "You will need some kind of ramp."

Phoebe was with Hannah, taking the soldier into the library and helping him down onto the edge of the first bed. Hannah placed the soldier's canvas bag down by his side.

"Thank gawd for that," he said. "Jack. Jack Lloyd if you like, pleased to meet yer. Go and 'elp the others, ladies, I can manage from 'ere. And what moniker do you go by, if you don't mind me askin'?"

"Phoebe will make sure you're comfortable, Mr Lloyd," said Hannah, pulling herself up to her full height. "And my name is Hannah. If you like."

Phoebe looked at Hannah – she could deal with the likes of Jack, all right – then watched her leave the library to go back outside. Hannah was strong, clear-sighted, and Phoebe was envious.

Jack looked down at his heavily bandaged foot and grimaced up at Phoebe, who didn't know what to do next. Jack seemed to sense her awkwardness, so she was relieved when he spoke. "I can manage, don't you worry. I wish they'd cut the damn thing off though. More trouble than it's worth sweetheart. They should just cut the damn thing off, don't you think? When the left ain't right, better to be left with the right. Surgeon in France told me that one. Too clever by 'alf."

Phoebe had no idea what he was talking about or whether she was supposed to say yes or no, so instead changed the subject entirely. "Mrs Harkness says you can read any book you like."

Jack was lifting himself onto the bed to lie down, but he paused to look around the walls that were covered in books. "Well sweetheart, you'll 'ave to learn me to read first." He gestured to the door. "Go on. I'm safe enough 'ere in me crump-hole."

Phoebe looked at Jack's hands. He smelt strongly of soap and yet his fingers looked dirty; grey, yellow, puffy things that appeared older than

Jack himself. Phoebe thought the dirt was not on his skin, but somehow beneath it. She wondered why most men she had ever met seemed to be scuzzy, inside and out. All except one, that is.

Hannah had stepped back outside and was helping the second soldier out of the ambulance. He had no obvious injury, but he seemed wary and skittish, on the lookout for the next threat, mumbling words that presumably would have made sense at some time in his past, though now meant nothing: "Pineapple, chocolate, cigarettes." Then for the first time he looked directly at Hannah and said, as if it was a question she would be able to answer, "See you in Southend?"

Nurse Collins called over to offer Hannah some advice, "Take him by the arm...no, other side," and then handed over more paperwork to Suhani. "That is Gabriel. He has a shrapnel wound to the side of his chest. It's not healing. He is also showing signs of nerves. What he needs is laudanum and kindness, in that order."

Suhani looked through the sheets of paper in an attempt to reconcile the names with the numbers. "But I thought there were three."

Nurse Collins turned to walk towards the ambulance. "Indeed. Come and meet Christopher."

She had said it like the closing of a story, though Suhani sensed it would be the opening of one.

5

In the short space of five minutes there had been several comings and goings. No sooner had he settled himself in his bed, Jack then asked if he could go back outside. So Suhani placed a small breakfast table by the portico where he sat down to play chess against himself. He'd exited the house much more easily than he had entered it – Tendring seemed to have worked a medical wonder. She watched him for a few moments before returning to the library to join Nurse Collins, as well as Hannah and Phoebe, who had by now gathered round Christopher's bed. He was lying flat on his back, propped up by three pillows. Hannah and Nurse Collins stood attending on either side of him, with Phoebe standing a step back, ready to help if need be, although she appeared reticent, at one point swallowing hard, followed by a nervous cough. Suhani positioned herself next to Hannah and although it felt wrong to stare at Christopher, his condition – along with the lecture from Nurse Collins she knew was about to come – compelled her to do so. A bandage was wrapped around Christopher's head at an angle so that only one eye was exposed. On the other side of his face was some cotton padding that had become engorged with blood and his wounds were accompanied by a sickly smell causing Suhani's stomach to lurch. She noticed the elegant symmetry of Christopher's nose, the steel blue of his iris, an eyebrow that was neat and black, and thin, strong lips that suggested he was not just handsome, but beautiful. All of this, along with his grey skin that was drained of blood, reminded her of those twelve-foot high, monochrome, American faces she had seen at the Gaumont. The right side of his face, at least, was extraordinarily striking. For a split second he glanced at her, so she looked away, found guilty of staring. He must be used to it by now, she thought. In that, at least, they had already become kindred spirits.

She was also struck by how still he was, as though he couldn't move, though she knew this was not the case because she had helped him walk from the ambulance to the library. He had possessed a quiet serenity then, which persisted now. So quiet, in fact, he had not yet spoken. Or perhaps, because of his injuries, he was unable to.

In any case Suhani understood he would have no wish to draw attention to himself. Along with the damage to his face, Christopher had no hands. His forearms were bandaged stumps that lay by his sides, and pus was already seeping out of the dressings onto the sheets, spreading out into pale patches of yellow.

Nurse Collins pointed at Christopher's eye and face as if he were a zoological specimen. "You will need to change all bandages at least twice a day. Clean the wounds with saline and then carbolic lotion. Be careful here on the face, parts of the flesh are still loose. More surgery is required but I'm afraid there is a list. The stumps are infected. Give him laudanum in order to sleep or otherwise when required. Obviously he will need help with feeding, and also toilet. One of your girls can do that. They'll get used to it."

Suhani smiled first at Nurse Collins, and then at Christopher, to show him he was in safe hands. "I am a mother, Nurse Collins."

"That's as may be. I assure you it's not the same. If he gets too much for you, I can try to arrange a swap."

Suhani leant forward to make eye contact with Christopher and touched her hand on his shoulder. He blinked with his one eye, some unknown thought passing across it. She said, "I assure you that won't be necessary, Nurse Collins."

"Well, let's see."

"Yes. Let's see."

"That is all, I think. I will see myself out."

"Let me show you."

They walked together in silence towards the library door and then through it, but in the hallway Nurse Collins turned to have the last word. "It's your house, Mrs Harkness, do what you wish. I can see you know your own mind. But you'll find after a while there is a natural order to these things. There is in England, anyway. There's really no need to show me out. Good day." Suhani followed her through the open front door anyway, just to make sure, out onto the portico and past Jack's solitary game of chess.

The driver turned the crank at the front of the ambulance to start the engine, which coughed into life, and Nurse Collins climbed in. As she made herself comfortable in her seat, she turned to stare at Suhani in a way that looked like an expression of regret. The subtle dismissal of Suhani's brown skin, followed by the imperceptible, unspoken confession, was a reaction Suhani had been familiar with since she was a child; familiar, but never easy. She nodded at Nurse Collins in order to accept the implicit apology. The driver climbed in and drove the ambulance down the drive, catching some of the delphiniums under its front wheel.

Suhani watched the ambulance disappear through the stone gates before turning to Jack and his chessboard. "I can play," she said, offering herself as an opponent. "Well, I know the moves at least."

He drew on his roll-up as he smiled at Suhani. "The bloke who learnt me got 'imself blowed up. Just like to play against meself now. Can't lose can I?"

"I suppose not."

He chuckled. "Though I can't win neither."

"Well, I'm sorry that you lost your friend."

Jack flicked his thumb over his shoulder in the direction of the library. "I ain't lost 'im. He's in there."

Jack blew out a huge lungful of smoke whilst Suhani made some quick calculations, but she couldn't decide whether he meant Gabriel or Christopher. "Oh. Well you were lucky not to be separated," she said.

"Not luck Miss. Got meself injured the same day and then yer just speak to the right people. Pouch o' Golden goes a long way. He always used to watch my back. My turn now. Just need to get 'im home somehow." Jack looked out across the lawn. "Peaceful here, innit."

Suhani nodded in agreement. "I'll bring you some tea." She would have left there and then, except she saw that Jack wanted to say something more. He was staring at her differently and after another drag on his cigarette, spoke differently too.

"I knew an Indian fella in the trenches. Had some funny ways but he was all right. *Awal* something or other. Kept wondering why he was there though."

"Didn't you ask him?"

"I was a bit scared of 'im to be honest. He didn't really belong, did he, should've been with 'is own, if you know what I mean. Then one day he wasn't there, just disappeared. Awal went awol. That kept us goin' for a week."

"In a strong wind, the leaves fall outside the forest."

Jack stubbed out his cigarette and looked out across the lawn again, but this time beyond it, beyond even the horizon.

"If you say so."

Hannah and Phoebe were in the kitchen, facing each other straight on, like boxers before the bell, each waiting for the other to make the first move. Eggs and bacon were sizzling in the background, unattended and already overcooked. Hannah, being the older and senior of the two, tossed a coin and Phoebe called, without enthusiasm, "Heads." Hannah revealed the result to Phoebe, which only worsened her early-morning nausea, her tightened lips saying everything. It was always the wrong face of the coin these days.

"Best of three?"

Hannah sighed and dropped the penny in the front pocket of her apron, then reached up to tidy a curl of Phoebe's hair that had fallen loose from underneath her bonnet. "I'll do it."

Phoebe tried hard not to look relieved. "We can't have the cook wiping arses."

"I wipe me own, don't I? I'll do it. I did it for my da and his da before him. I'll do it all right."

Breakfast was finished and Tendring began to embrace the early signs of a new routine, planting its seeds in the first of what would become identical days. Jack remained outside playing chess; Gabriel was walking around the outside of the house, having made the trip five times so far, talking to himself, or to an invisible collaborator who walked beside him; Hannah and Phoebe were back in the kitchen, clearing, washing up, knowing their place and the security it granted them.

This left Suhani and Christopher alone in the library. The silence was consummate; even the sound of the grandfather clock's ticking, despite it resonating through the floorboards of the hall, went unnoticed, like all clocks, because of its constancy.

Suhani was feeding Christopher honey on a teaspoon.

"I'm not hungry, thank you ma'am." These were his first words at Tendring, and the sound of them was a surprise to Suhani, the soft lilting inflections from a continent as far away as India, yet infinitely different, separated from it by oceans of salt and time. North America. His accent had a rhythmic and melodic beauty she was not familiar with, and she was all the more moved by his efforts because the bandages and injuries made speaking difficult.

Suhani persevered with the honey. It reminded her of feeding her sons when they were very small children. "It is not food, it is medicine. It will ease the infection."

"It's difficult to eat ma'am. The infection'll run its course soon enough."

"One spoonful, that's all..." and she thought of Tristan in particular, who had always been a fussy eater as a baby and would regularly and furiously throw his food on the floor.

"I'd like to write a letter ma'am."

Suhani withdrew the teaspoon. It was an odd, untimely request. She thought at first the sudden change of subject was more about rejecting the honey than writing a letter, but that gentle flow of words, that musical line again, suggested it was important to him.

"Now?"

"I'd like to write a letter to my wife if I may. It's been two weeks and she doesn't know where I am. I'd like her to know." He raised his arms a few inches off the bed. His hands would have expressed something meaningful, the subtle movement of a dancer, or a musician, but with mere stumps it was an ugly, futile gesture, though Suhani found herself moved by the desperate beauty in it. He quickly dropped his arms back onto the sheets then closed his one exposed eye.

Suhani placed the spoonful of honey on its saucer. It looked sickly now, too sweet – too similar to putrefying flesh. It was time to stop treating Christopher like a child.

"Very well, I'll get a pen and paper," she said as she stood up and turned with the intention of walking over to the writing desk at the far end of the library, next to Shiva, but Christopher interrupted her before she had taken a step.

"Ma'am…There are some things I need to say that I don't want you hearing, you being a woman and all. Personal things, if I can put it that way."

Being a woman… personal things… Suhani looked at Christopher and wondered which was worse, to lose your face or your hands. "Christopher, I'm an army wife. There is nothing I haven't heard before."

"That's as may be, ma'am. You might be able to hear it, but I won't be able to say it. I can't explain it better than that."

Suhani sensed there might be some unspoken scheme behind his request, but conceded the point. "Very well, Christopher. Your friend. He's outside. I'll get him."

Again he pulled her back by declaring, "Jack's a smart man in many ways, ma'am, but he can't read or write."

Suhani cocked her head to one side, trying not to appear discouraged. "Gabriel then?"

"Hmm." Christopher emitted a brief, chesty laugh. "He's a cat stuck up a tree." But the joke immediately seemed to cause him pain, and he grimaced. "Someone else," he said. "I don't know. Someone. Someone else."

"Christopher. You are making this a little difficult. There are no other men in this house at present and I can't just wave a magic wand."

But there was suddenly a loud knock at the front door, as if she had. Christopher jumped at the thudding sound that resonated through the entire house, and immediately Suhani stretched over to place her hand on his shoulder again. "It's just the door, Christopher."

"I realise that, my apologies," said Christopher, in his foreign metre, trying to regain his breath before emitting another feeble chuckle. "I've heard too many coffin lids being nailed down recently."

Suhani welcomed the knock at the door, the distraction would give her time to think. "Excuse me for a moment," she said, as she walked out of the library and into the hallway.

Outside, under the portico, Freddie stood at the shining black door, brushing some grit off his trouser-knees. Then he removed his shako hat and touched the graze on his forehead, which immediately he realised was a foolish thing to do. "Ow."

Jack looked up from his game of chess. "What 'appened to you?"

Freddie turned towards Jack. Obviously the soldiers promised by Captain Hurley must have arrived. Of course, it all made sense now, they had been in the ambulance that nearly ran him over. But Freddie didn't want to go into those details because he was running late again, so decided he would simplify the story. "Fell off my bike. No harm done."

"Well you've come to the right place," said Jack, "welcome to our little toy hospital." But before Freddie could answer, the door was opened by Suhani.

"Oh, Freddie, hello."

"Morning ma'am," he said, in an attempt to sound cheerful and professional, but it rang hollow in his aching head as he handed over a handful of letters to her, all addressed to Major Harkness.

"What happened to you?" she said.

He looked across at Jack. Here we go again. "Fell off my bike. No harm done."

She put her hand to Freddie's temple in order to turn his head towards the light. "I'll be the judge of that."

"How's your spelling Freddie?"

They were in the kitchen, Freddie sitting on a stool with Suhani standing over him tending to his wound. It was a nasty graze, just below his hairline, worse than he had realised.

"I can spell well enough, ma'am – *ouch.*"

"Hold still – and your handwriting?"

"I can write well enough too. Mrs Mawby taught me extra after school. My letters lined up like soldiers, so she said."

Suhani finished cleaning Freddie's graze, dabbing and patting at it with a damp swab, followed by a final inspection. "You'll be all right. It'll be gone in a week." Freddie found her attention contrasted with the increasing distance between himself and his own mother, whom he no longer allowed to touch his face. There was a different air about Mrs Harkness, disconcerting but irresistible, that was drawing him in.

"It sounds like your handwriting is second to none," she continued. "Those are special gifts Freddie. I think we should use them." Then, somewhat unnecessarily, she dabbed again.

Freddie looked at her through wincing eyes. "Use them for – *ouch* – what?"

Despite the addition of its three hospital beds and a superficial air of practicality, the library still held an atmosphere of mystery for Freddie. Perhaps it was because of the bizarre, almost humorous juxtaposition of beds and books, of injury and learning, of being too ill or exhausted to read the books that filled the walls, that perplexed him. And even though Shiva had been relegated, tucked as he was into the corner at an asymmetrical angle, he seemed just as enigmatic, possibly more so. He still had secrets to give up, thought Freddie.

Christopher's bed was alone on one side, opposite the two others. Freddie sat by it with his feet on the lower rung of his chair so that he could balance a silver serving tray on his knees. On this he held down a sheet of writing paper, which he stroked between the tips of his forefinger and thumb, finding the surface unlike anything he'd known before; smoother, like skin, with a soft down that reminded him of his top lip. This paper was expensive. Even the warm sound it made as he rubbed it was different to the thin crackle he was used to. Freddie had the urge to draw on it, to sweep his charcoal pencils across the page. But never mind, filling it with words would give him almost as much pleasure.

Looking at the piece of paper was also a way of not looking at Christopher. Freddie had seen wounded soldiers on the truck that came through the village on its way back from the coast, but only from a distance. Being this close, he found Christopher's freakish, unnatural stumps wretched, then felt ashamed and guilty that they repelled him, but he couldn't help it. Examining the piece of writing paper meant he could hide behind its tactile essence and ignore Christopher's gaze.

"What happened to you?" said Christopher.

Freddie continued to avoid Christopher's eye. How many more times would he have to explain? But it made him realise they were both specimens, in their own ways. "Fell off my bike. No harm done."

"We've been in the wars, haven't we, you and I?" Though speaking was clearly painful, there was a kindness in Christopher's baritone that put Freddie at ease and he saw he was not in the presence of a monster after all, but a man like any other. He wanted to say he was sorry about Christopher's condition, but George's advice came back to him – *never say you're sorry* – and in any case it seemed a pointless thing to mention.

He thought it safer to bat back Christopher's original question.

"What happened to you?" As soon as he said it, he wondered if he should have done. It was one thing to ask about a graze, quite another to ask about missing limbs.

Christopher lifted up his left stump a few inches. "This one blown off at Sanctuary Wood." Then he lifted up the right. "I held on to this one for a while but it turned gangrenous. It's in a military hospital near Dover. Well, ashes now I presume. All of which means I need an amanuensis."

Freddie was confused. What was that word? Was it Greek? Or Latin? Or some consequence of delirium? He must have looked baffled, because Christopher raised his head an inch off the pillow to explain.

"It means you're going to write a letter on my behalf. That makes you an amanuensis. Mrs Harkness said you were just the man."

Freddie glanced back down at his piece of paper, this time through embarrassment. He couldn't think of what to say in reply, but then snatched at some fragments of his conversation with Mrs Harkness so it would feel like it was her, not him, blowing his trumpet.

"Well...I have a special gift sir. My spelling is very good and my handwriting second to none."

"I'm very glad to hear it. And what do you intend to do with this gift?"

Freddie saw a hint of a smile across one half of Christopher's lips. Any more than that would probably have been too painful. "I like drawing," said Freddie. "Copying actually. Copying's what I do most of the time."

"I see. Well copying is an excellent way to learn. I learnt the piano that way." Christopher absent-mindedly lifted up the stumps of his arms, as if hovering over a ghostly keyboard. Freddie glanced down, but pressed on.

"Paper's hard to come by but...Mr Franklin has extra. Ma says I was born with a pencil in my hand."

"I'm sure she's very proud of your drawings."

"Yeah, I suppose, she would be, but she doesn't see them."

"Ah, well, you'll show her when you're ready."

Freddie didn't feel like explaining that it was not him but his mother who needed to be ready, yet never would be. His mother had learnt to see with her hands, had done so for as long as Freddie could remember, but Christopher would never feel anything with his one remaining eye. Nothing except distance and loss, anyway. No point rubbing salt in Christopher's wounds, thought Freddie, then grimaced at the grizzly vision he had of doing so.

In the silence that followed, Christopher tried to shift his weight, leant back into his pillow and looked up at an elaborate plaster ceiling-rose above his head. The mood had changed. "You must promise me you will send this letter Freddie. Every word of it. Can I trust you to do that?"

Christopher's voice had softened, his energy seemed to be draining, and a bubble of red spittle was caught in the corner of his mouth. Freddie didn't see why he might not deliver the letter, what possible reason he might have not to do the one job he was assigned to do, deliver letters, but he gave the answer he felt was needed. In any case he wanted Christopher to trust him. "Yes sir."

Christopher continued to look up to the ceiling, his one eye staring, unmoving. "So, Freddie, how should we spell Anne?"

Freddie took up his pencil and pulled the serving tray on his lap an inch nearer. "With an E?"

Christopher nodded. "That's right. Anne with an E."

His words had become slow and methodical through the sheer effort of speaking but this at least allowed Freddie the time to write them down. Perhaps that was also Christopher's intention. Matter-of-fact and unemotional, he began to recite:

"Anne Ellis, Memory Cove, Nova Scotia, Canada. My dearest Anne, forgive my haste, I've just a few minutes to write. I'm sorry it has been such a long time since my last letter, the war makes it hard sometimes. I don't want you to worry but I have injuries that make it difficult to write."

Difficult, thought Freddie. That's an understatement.

"Today I have an amanuensis called Freddie."

Freddie stopped to look up at Christopher. "I don't know how to spell that."

"My apologies Freddie," and he slowly spelt it out, letter by letter. "Got it?"

"Yes sir."

Christopher then tried to wet his lips with his tongue, but the effort seemed to cause him discomfort and was not successful, so he returned, dry-mouthed, to his dictation.

"I'll be here for some while. I hope you are looking after our house, and I hope it is looking after you. If I don't get back in time, remember to paint the windows before the storms come, they won't last the winter. Don't forget Joseph said he will help, if you need him to. I think about you often. In actuality I think of nothing else. Time drags without you and sometimes I don't see an end to it. I can't say for sure when we will see each other again. My leave has been cancelled and as soon as they have put me back together they will return me to the front."

Freddie put down his pencil again, not this time because of a word he couldn't spell, but because it was beginning to dawn on him he might be the unwitting participant in a conspiracy. *Put me back together... return me to the front.* He looked at Christopher, and Christopher looked at him.

"Please."

Christopher blinked two, three times, imploring Freddie not to break the fragile contract that hung like a cobweb between them. Please. The word had been no more than a whisper, for Freddie's ears only.

It gave him responsibility beyond his years, and he did not need it, or want it. So he handed it back, told himself that he was in Christopher's hands – he *was* Christopher's hands – and that the deception belonged to this foreign soldier, not to him. His role, like all young boys of the age, was simply to do as he was told. *Don't get involved.* He picked up his pencil to continue with Christopher's letter, wrote down the lie that would heal the soldier's wounds, put him back together, return him to the front, and keep their thread intact.

"I'm ready," he said, and Christopher continued.

"France is beautiful, and England looks after me like a favourite aunt, but it is not home. My goodness, Anne, I even miss the north-easterly blowing across the water and rattling our windows. Well, I must finish now, Freddie has work to do. He's the postboy here, my Hermes, excellent in all the tricks. Don't worry if you don't hear from me for a while. Get the piano tuned every six months won't you. God bless you Anne. Your loving husband, Christopher."

Christopher had spoken each word with patience and precision, and had helped Freddie to spell Hermes. In the end Freddie chose to be more connected to his own neatness, the shape and beauty of the letters, than the meaning of the words. They were both selecting their own pathway of deception, to look but not to see. He didn't know what some of it meant anyway. He wrote down the last word, Christopher's name, and was about to fold the sheet of paper in three when Christopher interrupted him.

"Actually Freddie, I have a postscript."

Oh, he thought. So Freddie settled back to begin writing again. In fact he was pleased that a few more words would fill in the blank white space at the bottom of the letter that currently made it look unbalanced.

"P.S. My darling Angel..." Christopher quickly interrupted himself to say to Freddie, "with a capital A please," before returning to his letter, *"Don't forget what I once said to you on the steps of our home. Let my*

hands be the wind. It was something of a joke then, of course. Less so now."

It didn't seem to mean anything to Freddie. He suspected there might be some coded message in this postscript, but it was not for him to decipher. Instead he continued to focus on the page as a whole, rather than the details, with a sense of satisfaction at the proportions and spacing of the text. The lines were level and true, and there was a regular frame of white space around the edges. It gave him the same pleasure as a drawing. And in a way it was just a drawing, the meaning of the words reserved for Anne alone.

"Is that it, sir?" Freddie asked.

Christopher closed his one exposed eye.

"It will have to do," he said.

6

Is that you, Christopher, my restless wanderer?

At the end of my path I stand and face the sea before sprinkling the ashes, gathered from our fire grate, onto the flower beds that grow along the garden fence. The waves beyond the harbor always catch my eye, as they have done every day since I was a child, and before that as a babe in arms, rocked by my mother's singing. Each seascape is different I think, each roll and swell unique in its combination of time and place. Sometimes, when I stare for long enough, the pinpricks of sunlight reflecting on the waves remind me of the stars, so I feel surrounded by them day and night. I want the moment to last forever. But of course it will never do – I must get the washing in before the rain comes.

I run my hands across the bottom of the bed sheet as it hangs on the line. Its cool dryness tells me the wind has done its work, but the air is freezing as it blows around my dress and raises goosebumps on my arms. You wouldn't think it was summer here. Best to move quickly. I should have put my coat on, but when I do I feel like I'm leaving. I unpeg the sheet, and the pillow cases too, and the table runner I use to protect the top of the piano.

Once inside, I make the bed. I have become skilfully adept at catching the air under the sheet as I unfurl it, and it covers the mattress with little need for adjustment, except for tucking in the corners. I do it every day because he may come home at any moment and also because it helps me sleep. When I go to bed at night I want to think about him of course, but I have to get my rest, and clean sheets help me, I don't know why.

When the post comes, which is not often in Memory Cove, I feel both joy and fear – not one after the other but at the same time. The war touches us lightly on this distant coastline, but I've still heard of local hearts being broken, now and then. His last letter, weeks ago, was vague, saying nothing about where he was, or when he would come home. The Postmaster blames the censor, and perhaps there is something in that. His letter says he is happy, not in danger, as fit as a fiddle. Well, that will do for me. But I worry I haven't heard from him for a while.

The piano hasn't been played since he left. I can play Camptown Races slowly with one finger and sometimes without a mistake – he taught me with such patience! – but I would rather wait for Schubert, and for the man who plays it. I set down the table runner along the top of the piano, smoothing it with my hand, and then replace the silver teapot, a wedding gift handed down from my grandparents, on top of that. It seems out of place on the piano, but we have no space for it elsewhere. Then I dust the keys, because I like to keep the lid open. Sometimes I strike a note accidentally, and I have the idea that he can hear it...though of course that's a foolish thought.

Although it is only ten o'clock in the morning, I go lie on the bed. It's something I've taken to doing every day and is the moment I think about him most. It's the moment, after all, when I least need sleep. Ironically there are no photographers in this place called Memory Cove, which means I have no picture of him. We would have to drive into Halifax for that. I try to conjure up an image of his face but as each day passes it becomes more difficult, his features harder to imagine. I know his eyelashes are dark and long, but I don't quite see them...not quite. What has happened to him in the four months since he left for Europe? This is the man I have always loved, yet even in such a short space of time he is becoming a shadow and my memory of him increasingly unreliable. Of course I know what he looks like, I'm being silly, I can piece together the shapes of his eyes, his nose, his lips, but it is a caricature that seems to miss everything else that's important; everything that connects. I can see the parts, but can't make out the whole of him anymore.

And so it is, at ten o'clock every morning, as I lie on our bed, that I think of other things too. We are not naïve here in isolation on the coast, we know more than the people in the cities. We are closer to the earth and to the meaning of it. I have watched the horses on Rainbow Hill climb clumsily on top of one another, I have heard the pigs squeal and watched the dogs hunch their backs in a fleeting, furious embrace. When the foals are born, there is no mystery to this piece of magic, so there was no embarrassment when my mother explained how to avoid a child, and why. On this bed, on the evening of our marriage, there were no surprises. Indeed, I was the teacher, and the calmer of his nerves.

Christopher works at the Cunard Steamship Company, based in Halifax, and they've given him something called a retainer whilst he is in Europe. The company looks after me while he is gone, so there is enough food, and I have a roof over my head. I still help out at my mother's shop in the afternoons and I enjoy the routine of my life. I am very lucky, I know it, but I wish with all my heart to be with Christopher again. And I wish more than that, I admit, to be the bearer of his child, despite mother's dry counsel.

But I have a child already, after a fashion, which is our house. It is rust-red with white trimmings and was built of corrugated iron by my grandfather, not as a dwelling but for storage of grain and tools. When our wedding was announced he installed some windows on both floors and made safe the door, and we have lived in it for three years since. It is modest and functional, but I'm content with that. Modest, too, is my life with Christopher, but all I ever wanted. The waiting now for its return is interminable, like an Arctic winter's night. Or like Eddie Hunter's silence – but I'll tell you more about him later.

The windows could do with a lick of paint, truth be told. I might ask Joe for help, or perhaps, since I have the time, I will do it myself. In the meantime I must go. Today is the day my mother and I drive into Halifax to get provisions.

The waiting will have to wait.

7

Freddie stepped out onto the portico of Tendring House. Jack was still pondering his chessboard and Gabriel was sitting opposite him, though unaware of the game. Then, suddenly, Gabriel caught sight of Freddie and scuttled under the table, shaking like a cornered fox.

"It's the uniform probably," said Jack, moving a pawn forward one square on his chessboard. "Shell-shock. He'll be all right."

Freddie was holding Christopher's envelope, looking down at the address he'd transferred from the letter in bold capitals. He'd not yet sealed it because he was thinking about showing it to Mrs Harkness. He felt there was some unfinished business within it and needed her opinion.

He looked out across the lawn. It seemed to have no purpose, it propagated nothing except an emptiness of grass, a monotony of colour, unlike anything he saw in the fields and woods of his childhood. But then he realised that was the point, its sterile perfection a statement of wealth and privilege. His heart sank. He would never be able to afford to cross the Atlantic. At school, geography had been of little interest, and Mrs Mawby had tried to kindle it by lending him an atlas to take home, but he'd put the book on a shelf and forgotten about it. He had a rough sense of where Canada might be, but no idea where Nova Scotia was until he wrote down Anne's address and put the two together. Now having heard Christopher's accent he knew what the people who lived there sounded like. He feared this was as close as he would ever get.

"Hey, Billie," said Jack, throwing a penny towards Freddie, who caught it before he had time to think about it. "Penny for yer thoughts."

Freddie turned the penny over in his fingers... another Queen Vic... the veil flowing down to her shoulders. The urge to draw her, capture the sideways glare, the double chin. "It's Freddie, sir."

"Well, heads or tails, makes no difference to me. I'm Jack." He gestured to the shaking figure under the table. "This is Gabriel. We're pleased to meet yer, Freddie."

"And you sir." Though he wasn't. He didn't want to speak to anyone.

Jack turned the chess board round and pushed another pawn forward one square to counteract his previous move. "Well Freddie, those letters aren't goin' to post themselves."

"No sir." But instead of getting on his bike, he went back into the house.

"Did you forget something?" asked Suhani who stood by a table in the middle of the drawing room. She had been pulling petals off some cut delphiniums and placing them in a wicker basket, but stopped when Freddie walked in.

"Ma'am...sorry but there's no stamp for this." He made a faint gesture with the letter he was holding and then removed his hat, tucking it under his arm.

"Oh dear. Where's it going?" She held out her hand, an instruction for Freddie to walk across the room to give her the letter. She took it from him and examined the envelope. "Of course. How much for a letter to Nova Scotia?"

He didn't know, he should have checked before entering the drawing room. His rate card had its own pocket in his leather pouch, difficult to reach quickly, so he had to fiddle for several seconds until eventually pulling it out. Then he scanned down the list until he reached Canada, near the bottom. Whatever order there was to it, it was not alphabetical.

"Tuppence ha'penny, ma'am."

"Well if I give you tuppence ha'penny will you stamp it for me at the Post Office?"

"Yes ma'am."

"The drawer in the library. You know the one. You can take the money from there." Suhani handed the letter back to Freddie.

"Thank you ma'am. Good day."

"Yes Freddie. I believe it will be. Make sure to wash that graze again when you get home," and she returned to picking off her delphinium petals.

Freddie wanted to leave. In a strange contradictory way he wanted to leave because he had more to say, something difficult, and the conflict meant he was stuck, a feeling he was becoming familiar with in Tendring. He watched her as she continued to place more petals into her basket.

"Was there anything else, Freddie?" she said.

"Not really, ma'am."

"Not really? I see."

Freddie could see she was amused by the game they were playing, but he was not. He looked down at his shoes. The library was opposite the drawing room and both doors were open, so there was a chance they could be overheard. Although he knew he was taking a liberty in closing the door without permission, he walked over to it and did so, then returned to his spot in the middle of the drawing room and lowered his voice.

"He's not telling the truth."

Suhani put one more petal in her basket before turning her attention to Freddie.

"Christopher?"

Freddie was now holding the letter with both hands as if there was a danger he would drop it. Suhani walked over to him, took the letter and casually scanned the address again, though Freddie knew she would find no evidence of truth or lies on the outside of the envelope.

"What about?"

"He says...well, he says he's going back to the front. He won't be will he. He can't, can he."

Suhani kept her gaze on Freddie but he saw her thoughts drift elsewhere. She was thinking many things, a calculation in progress. Then she pursed her lips briefly in final judgement.

"No, he can't."

"What should I do?"

She handed the letter back to Freddie with a finality that suggested she did not want to see it again. "Seal it up and post it. It's none of our business."

He looked at the envelope again. This was not the result he had wanted, and he felt the need to challenge her further. "Very well ma'am. But what if...?" he trailed off, unable to finish his sentence. He needed more help from her and she must have known it because she added, in a gentler tone, "Sometimes people want to be lied to Freddie. Or need to be. But we have a saying back home. The truth rises with the sun."

Freddie thought about Suhani's words but wasn't sure what they meant, which made them unchallengeable, so he could do nothing else but replace his hat on his head. "All right, ma'am," he said, though he was not convinced it was. "I'll be back at two, if there's more post."

"There's always more post Freddie." She smiled at him and then returned to plucking delphinium petals in a way that indicated nothing more needed to be said. So he left the room.

He closed the drawing room door behind him and stood in the hallway. It was true, there was always more post, so far most of it addressed to Major Stephen Harkness and in official-looking envelopes. The address was usually typed. He must be important, thought Freddie, and he wondered what he looked like, close up. Or rather what would it feel like to stand next to him? He'd seen him at church but only from a distance, and hardly ever in the village, as if the man did not wish to be seen. A faceless, unsketchable figure, an unfinished portrait in human form, warning you to keep your distance.

The library door was open and it was possible to see from where Freddie stood in the hallway that Christopher was asleep. He put the letter in his pouch, and took the few steps required to enter the library to retrieve his tuppence ha'penny. This was the third time he had been there but the first time he had felt like an intruder. Perhaps it was the exotic, unfamiliar Indian furniture that made him feel like he didn't belong, that he was merely an observer, not a participant, as if in a museum. He closed the library door behind him and walked further inside, hoping the act of shutting out the rest of the world would make it feel less like trespass.

It was possible, if he stood in exactly the right place, to make eye contact with the statue of Shiva, and Freddie took several seconds positioning his head and eyes to do just that, trying to work out how this entity, with its eerie, quiet stillness, its expressionless face hiding much and revealing nothing, could destroy anything, much less the universe. He didn't understand its unfathomable story. He recalled a section in his Boy's Own Annual about *Island Universes,* and wondered if Shiva would have to destroy all of them, or just one. He could no longer find actual words to manage the ideas in his head.

And then he became aware of the sound of bubbling in Christopher's breath, which aroused the queasy recollection of porridge coming to the boil only that morning. The speed of Christopher's breathing was increasing and making him agitated. It had never occurred to Freddie until now that Christopher might be dying.

Freddie reached the writing desk and opened the drawer to take out the three coins needed to purchase Christopher's stamp. As Freddie pushed at the drawer to close it, Christopher called out. It was not a word that Freddie recognised, probably it wasn't a word at all, more like the tremor of a bleating sheep, the serrated edge of a dog's bark. Whatever it was, Christopher had woken himself up with it and made Freddie jump to such an extent he inadvertently slammed the drawer shut. The library resonated with an embarrassing echo.

Freddie expected Suhani to come out of the drawing room in response to the commotion, but she didn't, and now he regretted closing the library door. There was no one else to tend to Christopher, who seemed disorientated, so Freddie reluctantly went over to stand at the foot of his bed.

"You all right sir?"

Christopher's breathing was still fast, and he was looking around the room with his one eye and lifting his head, trying to work out where he was. It was only when he saw Freddie and blinked his muddled thoughts into some kind of focus that his breathing became more regular.

"Freddie?"

"I came to get money for your stamps. I'm sorry if I woke you."

"You didn't, Freddie. It was...someone else."

"Well, I'll be off then." He felt guilty that he was not able to help, and regretted that what he said next had a sense of finality he did not intend.

"Goodbye."

"Goodbye, Freddie."

Freddie walked to the door and opened it, then he had an idea. "I'll come and write your next letter whenever you want me to."

"Thank you, but that won't be necessary."

Although the dismissal was spoken kindly, Freddie felt deflated by it, as if he had signed a contract without knowing what was in it, leaving him with no option but to exit the room. Christopher raised the corner of his mouth again, Freddie's signal to leave. On doing so he left the door open so that, although there was no one else in the library, Christopher would not be alone.

When he stepped outside onto the steps of the portico, the sunlight made Freddie squint. Jack was leaning back in his chair, contemplating his chessboard, whilst Gabriel was nowhere to be seen.

"See yer later, Freddie," said Jack, who saluted, which, along with the sunlight and fresh air, cheered Freddie up, made him feel important again and much better about Christopher's letter. The problem was not his, surely, but belonged to the General Post Office. It would just be sent, and that would be that. What else could he do?

"Sir," answered Freddie as he climbed on his bike and pedalled off down the drive, wondering if Christopher would ever see Nova Scotia, or his wife, again. By tomorrow he might be dead, his already diminished body shovelled into a box and dropped into a hole in the ground.

8

Suhani stood in the drawing room and trailed her fingers through the loose delphinium petals in her basket, a small act of intimacy with nature which she carried out most days. A variation of delphinium flowers grew in Maharashtra, and the English buds were similar enough to make her think of home and family. These days, they were one of the few things that did. To abandon something she could never let go of was Suhani's endless struggle. Sometimes she would wake thinking she was back in India, other times it was hard to remember where she came from – though the village of Eagley would remind her soon enough.

The difference in social status between her servants and herself was undeniable and palpable, almost as immutable as the caste system Suhani had grown up with. She had tried over the years to subvert it, coming down to their level and bringing them up to hers, ignoring the narrow lanes around Eagley that led to narrow minds. She knew her attitude annoyed Stephen, and that he dealt with it by sometimes treating Suhani as a servant herself, increasingly so as the years went by, bringing her life full circle back to Maharashtra. It was difficult to remember her parents who, although still alive at the time, had orphaned her into servitude, and secret meetings with her mother became less and less frequent until they faded away to nothingness. It was the English lady in the big Indian house where she worked who showed her, if not love, then affection. Suhani's first job, aged six, was to sweep the verandas of the Imperial bungalow, owned by the East India Company and occupied by a British Army family. Thus began her slow journey to England, at first by heart and then, years later, by boat.

Suhani watched how Hannah and Phoebe dealt with the hierarchy of Service. Hannah seemed to find it easier than Phoebe and somehow rose above it, perhaps because she wasn't English and therefore had not been bred to follow English rules. Phoebe, on the other hand, continued to play the role of servant, but knew what she was doing, an actor inhabiting a part. There was a kinship between them, Phoebe and Suhani, and Suhani recognised this was because she was the only one of the upper classes Phoebe was not intimidated by. For her own part, Suhani had come to dislike the idea of servants, having once been one herself. This was why, when the need arose, Suhani was willing to do what Hannah had been designated to, and become the wiper of arses.

She came out of the drawing room to see Christopher standing in the open doorway of the library.

"I'm looking for Hannah," he said. "I need some help." His bloodied words dribbled out of his mouth, his jaw movements inhibited by bandages. The sleeves of his pyjama top hung down loose and empty by his sides, and he looked ashamed. Suhani spoke as if she had done what she was about to do a thousand times before, which, when her sons had been babies, she had.

"This way."

She was to be mother and servant to him at the same time. Empire and India.

Christopher leant forward on the toilet seat, his arms resting on his knees and his stumps sticking out like two fat coat hooks. The bandages around his head and face were discoloured with blood and pus, their changing overdue. As Suhani cleaned the crack of his anus with a damp cloth, he thought of the last time he'd made love to Anne. It was hurried and gave neither of them much pleasure. They were doing it simply because it might be the last time. He had, therefore, expected it to have extra frisson, but the opposite was the case and he would have preferred after all to have stood with her at the end of their garden to watch the sea. He suggested they do so, but too quickly after he had rolled off her, and regretted that the ending had been as unsatisfactory as the beginning. His dictated letter to her had been an attempt to rewrite the ending, but now he felt guilty about the deception. Foolish, too. His injuries brought humiliation in many forms.

Christopher watched Suhani rinse the cloth in a bucket of water, wring it out and then wipe again. She glanced at it to see if it was clean and he saw what she saw, a streak of blood. But they both knew there was nothing to be done so she turned it round and wiped for a third time. Her free hand was resting on Christopher's back and she pushed gently.

"Can you lean forward a little?"

He moved his elbows forward a few inches and looked at his stumps. They were not even equal in length, their lack of symmetry adding to their ugliness. He wondered if they would support his own weight with Anne underneath him. Would she want to be touched by them? Would he be able to reach up and stroke her hair, and would there be any point? Would their cauterised nerve endings send any messages back to his brain and his loins? Or to hers?

In the end they had chosen to stand on the step of their front door to watch the sea. This was their last moment and made up for their forced, cack-handed attempts to say goodbye half an hour before. This would be what they both remembered, standing next to each other, holding hands, like novices. Gently he had pulled her close and whispered in her ear, a postscript, which made her laugh, and then the wind obliged as if commanded by his whisper, and caused her dress to billow around her body. She kissed the side of his face, the side that was now, six months later, mostly gone. As Suhani wiped and rinsed one final time, Christopher thought it would not be love-making he would miss the most, but one hand inside another.

"All done," said Suhani. She was trying to sound matter-of-fact and professional, but Christopher felt it reduced him to a small child being potty-trained, and when she lifted him to his feet so that she could pull up his pyjama bottoms his humiliation was complete.

The clock in the hallway chimed the quarter-hour.

Then, to his surprise, and out of the depths of his shame, Christopher felt an overwhelming sense of peace beginning to rise up through his whole body, a glow, almost an ecstasy, as he realised he was content with the decision he had made in his final letter to Anne. The shame was gone.

Or was it merely laudanum that had transported him to Paradise?

Freddie was sitting next to his discarded bike under an apple tree on the road between Tendring and Eagley. In the wheatfield behind the tree was a scarecrow, and if Freddie squinted he could make it look like a real person. He spent several minutes pinching his eyelids together until his eyes wandered up to the tree itself, to the branches hanging overhead. There was an orchard opposite, but this tree was not part of it, and he wondered if it had been seeded by a discarded apple core several years before he was born. He thought about how such an insignificant act could magically produce such a large and consequential result. How a pip could become a tree. Finally he went back to the reason he had sat under the tree in the first place: reading Christopher's letter.

He was feeling frustrated he had written the letter in pencil. Everything else about it was perfect. Its lines and proportions had a mathematical beauty that he had instinctively crafted as he wrote, and he was beginning to understand why Mrs Harkness had not been the first to say he had a special gift. But the pencilled words felt temporary, as so often they were at school, constantly threatened by Mrs Mawby's eraser, and he wondered if it would matter if he inked them in. He could take it home tonight where he had pen and ink, or if George was asleep he could do it at the Post Office, and then post it in the morning. What difference would a day make? Ink was immutable, permanent, and that seemed important to Freddie as he read the message over. But he was stopped by Christopher's sentence about returning to the front. The Front sounded like a wall, and he could not get past it. Because Mrs Harkness hadn't read the letter there was no way for her to understand the depth of the deception, so Freddie wasn't sure that her advice was sound. Now he wasn't at all sure about inking it in either, which would feel like collusion, an accessory to the crime. Sending the letter gave him a deep sense of foreboding, sucking him into an adult world before his time, a world where lies spread like the common cold on the sighs of men and women who for some reason no longer had a choice. But neither did he. Folding up the letter he returned it to its envelope, then slipped it back into his leather pouch. He stood up and put on his hat, gathered up his bike and cycled off towards Eagley. The road was little more than a dirt track, bumpy and sometimes dangerous in places. His journey was an uncertain one.

Suhani was improvising a screen around Christopher. He watched her as she placed two wooden room dividers along the sides of the bed, then a third at the end, before hanging several sheets over them to create a private space.

"That's not necessary, ma'am," he said, but only once she had finished.

"There's no reason not too, either," said Suhani. "I'll open them up when we're done."

He knew she was trying to be kind, and in some ways he was grateful for the privacy, but it left him feeling isolated too, the freak hidden away. He resigned himself to the fact that, in the grand scheme of things, his feelings about it didn't matter, the screens were unimportant. For whatever reason he wanted to not rock the boat, to please her in some way, because he felt he was in the presence of someone who was primordially sad, a quality he recognised in himself. It made him want to play music to her, to speak without words. It was as if he had forgotten, and then remembered, that he could play the piano. Some Schubert perhaps, or Chopin.

Suhani began removing the bandages from his severed arms, first the left, then the right, before washing the wounds and replacing the dressings with fresh strips of linen. He observed that she was slow, confident and gentle, and realised this was now the limit to which he would experience the affections of a woman. Why else, except to disinfect his wounds and wipe away his shit, would a woman lay her hands on him?

Christopher had managed to avoid mirrors, except for one occasion in the hospital in Calais. Jack was in the bed next to him – somehow he always arranged to be with his friend – and was shaving. Jack had turned the mirror in order to see better and Christopher caught sight of his own face. He was several feet away and it was only for a second, but he saw enough to understand that no amount of surgery would be able to save him from a lifetime of disfigurement. From now on, the small children in Memory Cove would freeze on the spot and stare in horror, before running away.

He watched Suhani intently as she removed the bandages from his face. If she remained impassive, there was still hope, and she almost did, except her nostrils flared momentarily and she blinked twice in quick succession. She tried to cover up her reaction with one of her soft, peaceful smiles, but he was not fooled by it. The mirror in Calais had told him that the skin around his left eyebrow was missing and the white bone of his skull was visible there. His left cheek, without the support of bandages, hung loosely down to just below his jawline, exposing his two rows of teeth. The flap of flesh looked dead, bereft of blood flow, waiting to fall to the floor and be swept up by one of the nurses, were it not for one small piece of skin that connected it to his face. He had not, however, lost his sense of smell, and now that Suhani had removed his bandages the air was pungent and rancid and her eyes began to glisten.

She cleansed the wound with one hand whilst supporting the loose flap with the other. The stinging was almost unbearable, but then he became distracted from it: he began to hear a melody. Suhani was singing to herself, humming a gentle tune he did not recognise, as if she were doing something ordinary: sewing, or rolling out pastry. He was unsure whether the tune was for herself, or for him, to calm her own nerves or to smooth his pain.

"What is that tune, ma'am?" he said, as she began to tie his bandages under his chin.

She stopped. "I'm sorry, I forgot myself."

"Please, what's the tune?"

"It's a lullaby."

"Does it have words?"

She returned to the bandaging as she spoke. "It's called The Moon Thief. If the baby won't go to sleep, the full moon will come down from the sky and steal them away. My mother sang it to me and I sang it to each of my sons." Suhani continued the process of wrapping Christopher's face with clean dressings, and she seemed lost in it, no longer affected by his appalling injuries.

"It's a frightening story for children," said Christopher.

"It would be if they could understand it. The tune is for the baby, the words are for the singer."

"I'd like to write it down. If I could. The tune, I mean."

"Are you a singer, Christopher?"

"No ma'am. I play the piano. It's only a hobby. But I would have liked to be able to write it down."

Suhani tied the final bandage under Christopher's chin, but she did it slowly, seemed to be stalling, giving herself time to think, before finally resting her hand on his arm.

"If you write it down, it won't be able to change and eventually it will die. Then it will be like a dead butterfly pinned inside a display case on the wall. The colours will fade in the sunlight, and the wings will turn to dust. All you'll have left is your memories, which is what you had in the first place. So there's no need to write it down."

Suhani smiled and stood up to go, but stopped when Christopher lifted up his arms, as if to invite an embrace. Instinctively she reached out to take his hands but immediately he saw regret in her eyes, the wrong decision made. But it was too late to withdraw so without pausing she folded her fingers around one of Christopher's severed forearms. And then because his other arm was in the air, waiting to be held, she reached out and wrapped her hand around that one too.

They both wanted to speak, and yet both waited for the other, until finally Christopher said, "I'm sorry you are so very sad, ma'am."

He watched her intently, saw that she was considering a thousand different answers and doing what he thought only men did, had seen it constantly in the trenches, choosing some stoical answer that meant they would not cry.

"There must never be another war like this one."

He understood. Then she let go of his arms and a defiant tear petered down her cheek anyway. She stepped silently, past Shiva, out of the library, shutting the door behind her. If all went to plan, thought Christopher, he would never see her again. He had always assumed Anne would be the last woman to lay eyes on him, but now, he was reasonably content with Suhani as a substitute. In truth, given the state of his arms and face, he was grateful for it.

9

For once George was sober, or appeared to be. In fact Freddie thought his boss had perhaps drunk something with exactly the opposite effect of alcohol, but he couldn't imagine what that might be. The mystery chemical, whatever it was, made George excessively talkative and uncharacteristically fidgety, so much so that he had tidied his desk several times over, and continued to do so. This was going to make Freddie late if he didn't extricate himself somehow. The conversation, if you could call it that, seemed rehearsed, more like a well-honed lecture from his boss that pinned Freddie to the counter, about how things used to be and how they were now. How before the war there had not been much post in Eagley, how most talk was done in the street, in the living room, or over the garden fence, how unless you could afford a telephone the post was the only way of communicating over greater distances. Letters were generally to and from people of substance only, said George, pumping out his chest with self-importance. The doctor, the vicar, the policeman, the school teacher sometimes, the Postmaster himself, but for the rest, they all lived and died within the boundaries of Eagley, their entire world. To some, George laughed, the post was a complete mystery. "But the war's changed that," he finished, in a melancholic afterthought. "Letters are as common as table salt." His tidying finally complete, he returned a bottle of rat poison back under the counter by Freddie's feet.

Eventually Freddie was able to pull himself away from George and cycled off on his next round. It consisted of two other villages, some distance apart, and he had twelve letters on an eight mile circuit that would keep him occupied until early afternoon. Though he was still troubled by Christopher's letter, he found that by focusing on his current deliveries he was able to push it to the back of his mind. It was only his second day but he was beginning to feel things were falling into place, and that he was a loyal servant of the system. On his round he proudly and regularly straightened his hat. The more often he felt like an adult, the sooner he would become one.

Sometimes his bike enabled him to make good progress and he could get ahead of his schedule. At other times, on bumpy cobbles or prehistoric tracks, it was more of a liability so it was quicker to get off and push, which was what he was doing as he approached a house in Denton village, his furthest port of call, with his twelfth and final letter. His back wheel was making a funny noise, the rim was rubbing on one of the brake pads, but he chose to ignore it. After all, there was nothing he could do about it.

Freddie leant his bike against the outside wall of the house and checked the address on the letter: *William Roper, Worshipful Master, Denton Lodge, 3 Trinity Street, Denton.*

The name rang a bell, but he couldn't place it. Worshipful Master? Whoever this man might be, he was clearly important. A dog barked from behind the door as Freddie pushed the letter through the letterbox. He heard it hit the hallway floor, landing and then sliding on wood, bouncing on expensive floorboards. Done. Freddie's first round was finished and he could cycle back to Eagley, arriving by three o'clock when he would run the shorter afternoon delivery that would take him until five to finish. He was beginning to understand the ironic effect of routine: keeping boredom and madness at bay.

His bike, however, was going nowhere. As Freddie was about to re-mount, he saw that the back tyre was flat and airless. Not only that, it had slipped off the rim of the wheel.

"Shit," said Freddie under his breath. The swearing was supposed to have the effect of making him feel grown-up, but on the contrary he felt faintly ridiculous, as if he was yet to learn how to do it properly, and was glad no one had heard him. The bad language, however, had still been necessary – Freddie would have to walk for two hours to get back to Eagley. He kicked the back wheel so hard the whole contraption flew into the air.

Freddie propped up his crippled bike against the counter and found himself standing alone in the sorting room at the back of the Post Office. He was looking at the envelope of Christopher's letter and thought it was time to seal it up. No doubt it was a sackable offence to read any letters from the public, and he wondered if the same regulations applied to writing one, but no one had mentioned it and he thought there probably wasn't any rule one way or the other. If he'd written it, there was surely no harm in reading it again. He was so intrigued by the word amanuensis that he said it out loud, twice, rolling his lips around it as if to exercise them.

"What's that?" said George from the shop on the other side of the door. Freddie had to act quickly before George came in, he couldn't be caught reading a private letter. He wanted to reach up to put it in the Overseas pigeonhole and be done with it but because it wasn't sealed, and there was no time to do so, posting it would be risky. It might even be returned to sender. So instinctively he slid the letter underneath the large leather blotter that was on the counter, to be dealt with later.

"I haven't got time for this," said George. From the crook of his elbow hung a rubber inner tube, which he transferred to the handlebar of Freddie's bike. Then he removed his pocket watch from his waistcoat to look at the time. "Cribbage tonight. We'll fix it in the morning. Half five. You can open up. I'll show you." Then he brazenly knocked back half a bottle of gin, as if Freddie wasn't there and couldn't see him do it. It was a small bottle, but half of it still seemed like a lot to Freddie.

"There's a knack," said George, wiping the damp corners of his mouth with his sleeve. They were standing outside and George was showing Freddie how to lock the door, twisting and pulling at the octagonal iron door handle. "Like... this. Otherwise-it-comes-off. Pull-the-door-t'wards-you-when-you-turn-the-key." His words were running into each other as if his sentence was just one long meandering syllable, and Freddie kept his distance in order to avoid George's appalling halitosis. "Come on," said George. "Haven't-got-all-day."

"Yes sir," said Freddie, who took the large iron key from George's outstretched hand, but before he could attempt to lock up, both he and George were disturbed by the sound of an engine. They looked down the High Street towards it until a motorbike came into view.

It was the despatch rider. What was she doing here so late? The bike pulled up and the rider lifted her flying goggles onto her forehead so she could see more clearly into her satchel. For a fragment of Freddie's time, like the moment when the second hand of a clock appears not to be moving, she looked at him and smiled. He envisaged a future where he was a young, fully-grown man who had married her and where she did nothing but look at him in the way she did now. But then the second hand started moving again, she was no longer smiling at him, and his future with this girl was over before it had begun.

As usual she had to shout over the noise of her engine as she handed a telegram to George. "Telegraph caught bloody fire! We're behind! Sorry!"

George took the telegram and examined it as if some crime had been committed, seemed irritated, and snapped at her. "We just locked up."

"Well it's the law, ain't it," she said, shrugging her shoulders as she did up the belt of her satchel. Then she replaced her goggles, revved her engine and pulled away, leaving George and Freddie to stand and watch in a cloud of exhaust fumes. As the motorbike disappeared around the corner of the High Street, Freddie was already looking forward to seeing her again.

George was reading the address on the telegram and seemed to take longer than necessary over it. When he finally spoke it seemed more to himself than to Freddie, and didn't look up. "Lock the door like I showed you." So Freddie followed George's instructions – twist, pull, lock – and then dropped the key in his jacket pocket.

He studied George for a moment. The rounded shoulders seemed more upright than usual and the muscles in his face had tightened around his skull. Freddie wondered how long George had been a drunk, or whatever he was, because in that brief moment he saw him as the man he must have been before the booze had wrecked his body and mind. Freddie thought the gin swallowed the man, not the other way round, and couldn't understand why anyone drank it. Gin had seduced George in the way an apple, made suspiciously sweet by the maggot inside it, forced you to take another bite.

When George spoke again it was as if he had miraculously sobered up. "Take it in the morning," he said, handing the telegram to Freddie. "That's soon enough."

Freddie took it from George. He wanted to please him, cheer him up somehow. "I can take it now."

But it seemed to have the opposite effect. George sounded tetchy. "In the morning I say. It's another noddy. It won't make any difference. She might as well have one more decent night's sleep."

Freddie looked down to read the address on the telegram. He felt a dullness in his stomach. Something was wrong, or missing. He thought of the unfinished painting, had a vague sense of what was coming, without fully understanding it, and wanted to put the telegram in George's overflowing, sort-it-out-later drawer. When he looked back up he saw that George had already begun to walk away and was calling over his shoulder: "Night Freddie."

Freddie called after him. "Night Mr Franklin." Then, to catch George before he slipped out of earshot: "What's a noddy?"

George stopped and turned to answer with a grim smile, then a chuckle. "Keep up lad. That little black cross in the top left-hand corner? Notification Of Death. N.O.D. Sometimes it's there and sometimes it isn't. And sometimes on the front, sometimes on the back. You'll get a feel for it. This one's clear enough." He saluted Freddie and walked off, with a final apologetic flourish. "No need to ask for a reply. You'll be all right."

He'd be all right, always all right. Noddy had sounded like the name of a pet dog, or a children's toy, or the thirteenth bun from the baker; an off-cut, or a song you sang as you brought in the harvest, or a gift of some kind, a corn dolly perhaps. The word protected itself from what it really was, shielding itself from its own message – your son is dead, and there is nothing to be done. Freddie's breathing quickened as he remembered that Mrs Harkness had asked him to read yesterday's telegram out loud, and he prayed she wouldn't ask him to do so again.

He feared she might scream in the same way Mrs Mawby had done. He looked down at the address again: *Major and Mrs Harkness, Tendring House, Eagley, Kent.*

The graze on his forehead began to throb, and the ache in his stomach turned to a pinching feeling he more normally associated with off milk. It seemed to regularly happen in the summer, creamy spots floating on the top and at some point later in the night a tightening inside his gut, then the milk would be thrown up, followed by watery acid, until he could slip back under the sheets for some fitful sleep. But there was no way to purge himself of the telegram or the message it contained. His only option was to deliver it and that would have to wait until tomorrow. He resigned himself to feeling nauseous all night, with no medicine to relieve it.

Freddie stood outside the Post Office and leant against the pillar box to watch the butcher's opposite shut up shop for the day. They were lucky, he thought, because their tomorrow would be no different from today. He put the telegram into his pocket and started what little was left of his daily routine – the fifteen minute walk home.

He had tried to go to sleep, but neither thoughts of Millie Bedden nor even the despatch rider could help. So Freddie lay on his bed, flicking through The Boy's Own Annual. He was familiar with every single page, having studied them many times in the last six months, but for the first time they seemed dull and uninteresting. Each turning of a page was an act of disappointment, every picture tired and unoriginal, each tale – the swimmer, the explorer, the home-made wooden bench – a dismal recycling. He dismissed them all. Or worse, his eyes ended up following not so much the words but the white spaces between the lines, moving side to side and up and down like a marble in a maze, because that had come to be more engaging than following the story. The scrape on his forehead continued to throb, so he closed the book quickly, the thud of which at least was satisfying, and got up to look out of his window.

There was not much to see above the tiny back yard and the flint wall at the end of it. The sky was a sheet of dark purple behind the silhouetted roofs of the cottages opposite, with one star shining next to a chimney stack. Freddie had never noticed this drop of light before. Was it new? Its bright whiteness was infinitely more interesting than anything in his Boy's Own. Suddenly, it reminded him of what he needed to do.

First, out of the hip pocket of his jacket he removed the large iron Post Office door-key, then placed it beside his alarm clock. Next he removed the penny that Jack had thrown him, putting it on top of yesterday's haul on the window ledge, making a grand pile of two. And finally he groped around inside the same pocket for the borrowed piece of chalk, the thing he was actually looking for.

Freddie stretched down to pick up his picture of the American Indian that was lying on the floor by his feet, and he used the palms of his hands to flatten it out on his table. He had begun vaguely to realise why it didn't look finished, even though he could think of nothing more to add; a conviction, in fact, that what was missing was not the mark of a pencil but the absence of one. So he took the chalk and, without pausing to think, made a small but bold stroke on the face of the warrior. It was simple but, he thought, brilliantly executed. Freddie felt he was no longer someone who drew pictures, but had become an artistic genius. The Indian had come alive with one effortless mark of white chalk that made a drop of light reflect off the war paint on his face, and at last he understood what everyone else had said: he had a gift.

"Freddie! What time is it?!"

It was his mother from the other side of his bedroom door, as usual. Earlier they had sat in silence over dinner except for one question from her about how his day had been. He'd said it had gone well, and she sighed as if she knew that was not the case. But then he couldn't say what he was really thinking, that his day had ended badly and would be even worse tomorrow, thanks to the Noddy. Better keep his thoughts to himself. It seemed they communicated best through closed doors.

"Nine!" he called, glancing at his alarm clock.

"Go to sleep Freddie!"

"Yes Ma."

It was true, he did feel tired. Without thinking, he undid the belt of his trousers. The throbbing graze on his head had turned into a proper headache and he wasn't sure he was thinking straight. He had delved into his jacket pocket three times, for the key, the penny, and the chalk, and on each of those occasions he had brushed his hand past the telegram, pretending it didn't exist. Indeed the wish had been so strong he now felt the need to make sure it had not come true, so he put his hand in for a fourth time to check. Of course it was there, the telegram, between his fingers. The paper was hard and cold, and when he gripped it more tightly it made a sound like toilet paper. He pulled it out and read the address again, but he found it difficult to focus. His head hurt so much he curled up on his bed, though he knew that this telegram, and its unwanted message, would never allow him to sleep tonight.

10

Jack was sitting by Christopher's bedside, setting up a chess board on the top of a small round pedestal table, lit by candlelight, when Hannah peered through the gap between the two dividers at the foot of the bed. She pinched her lips together, which Jack took to be the holding in of some kind of reprimand.

"Won't be long," he said, putting the final few pieces in place.

"You'll get me into trouble," said Hannah.

"Chance'd be a fine thing," said Jack, who turned to wink at her, though he knew he had no chance whatsoever, a position confirmed by Hannah's dismissive smile and by her calmly drawing the sheets across the gap.

"Ten minutes," she said, as she walked away.

Jack returned to the chessboard, neatening up the ranks, ready to begin. "Worth a try," he said, winking again, this time to his friend.

"Your turn to be black," said Christopher. He sounded unenthusiastic about the prospect, and looked exhausted. Despite being dosed up on laudanum, he was still in considerable pain.

Jack emitted a chuckle. "Memory failing yer is it? No mate. I'm white this time."

"Please, I'd like to be white," said Christopher. Some red spittle was caught between his lips. He tried to lick it away but he grimaced at the effort and gave up.

"Come on," said Jack, "Give us a chance. I never won you when I'm black."

"I want to be white."

"Well you can't." Jack chuckled again.

Christopher lifted his head from his pillow and looked at Jack for the first time, probing him with his one vigilant eye. "Please. I need to be white."

Jack sensed a cooling in Christopher's words, a whisper now, a sort of muffled anger, a determination that meant there would be no more discussion. It had the odd effect of making Jack blush.

"All right stumpy, keep yer hair on, what's left of it." He turned the board around and mumbled in good humour: "Fuckin' hell." And then another of his chuckles. "Might as well throw in the towel now."

Christopher rested his head back on his pillow and closed his eye. Jack watched and waited for his friend to speak, but Christopher remained silent.

"Come on," said Jack, "We ain't got all night. We ain't got ten minutes even."

"Well, that should be enough." Christopher grimaced with pain.

"Don't rub it in, mate."

There was another pause, long enough to become aware of the ticking of the clock in the hallway. Then Christopher dictated his move.

"Pawn to F-Three."

Jack leant across the board to move Christopher's pawn. It was an unusual opening move and at first Jack seemed suspicious, pulling the corners of his mouth southwards, but then he sat back in his chair to contemplate the board.

"All right then," said Jack as he moved his own first piece. "Pawn to E-Five." He leant forward again, resting his elbows on his knees and his chin in his hands. Christopher opened his mouth to speak, but then seemed to decide against it. Jack started to whistle, then broke off to say, "Ready when you are."

Christopher tried again. "Pawn...to G-Four."

Again Jack stretched across to make Christopher's move but as soon as he did so he realised he'd been set a trap, though not the kind he had been taught. He kept his hand on the pawn, allowing for Christopher to change his mind.

"Oi, don't be daft."

"Pawn to G-Four," insisted Christopher.

Jack looked at Christopher, confused and suspicious.

"But that's Fool's Mate, mate. First fing yer taught me. What's the point of that?"

Christopher sighed and then took a deep breath in. "Please. Pawn to G-Four."

Jack slowly removed his fingers from the pawn to leave it on the G-Four square. He realised this was no longer a game of chess, never had been. And then fragments of a conversation they had shared in the trenches weeks ago came back to him. Some euphemistic flannel, with a nod and a wink, about helping each other, pulling the trigger if the need arose. They hadn't spelled it out then, and did not need to do so now.

"It's time, Jack."

"Time for what?"

"Time to move your Queen, my friend."

Suhani stood, as she did every night, at the marble pedestal under the copper beech. The sky blossomed with stars. There was no breeze, it was still warm despite the late hour, and the heavy heat reminded her of home. As she tended her shrine, she wondered if she would ever go back to her place of birth, and what, if anything, would be there to go back to. No, her memories were best left where they were, swept under the carpet of an East India Company veranda. She had uprooted, and replanted, and her children were all here, one way or another. She looked at the photograph of her son and realised that, after a year, she could never recover from his death, didn't want to, but had come to some arrangement, some contract signed, that by allowing a part of herself to die with him, the rest of her could live.

For the second night in a row, the fox came to see her. She paused from gathering up yesterday's delphinium petals in order to watch him walk through the space between the beech tree and the shrubs that lined the end of the garden. He stopped to look at Suhani and she rather welcomed the idea that she might now have to add this visitation to her nightly ritual. She noticed a quality in his coat she had not registered the previous evening, that he was different from all the other foxes she'd seen padding across the lawn. His legs, tail and throat were darker, almost black. This fellow was new to the area. What had pushed him into this unfamiliar territory? There was a boldness and nonchalance to the fox's attitude, as if he owned Tendring, but he must have enemies from which he needed to keep his distance. Like Stephen, she thought. He was also one who hid behind a mask and was very rarely seen by day.

As happened most evenings she heard his footsteps, her husband approaching, a soft brushing of leather on grass, the sound of which made the fox turn and scuttle off into the trees. Stephen was late home from work again. This, too, had become part of her ritual, its predictability a source of comfort to her, even if the man himself was not. And as usual she felt no need to turn in order to speak to him.

"Hello Stephen. I suppose whale oil has to be delivered when it can."

She wasn't particularly surprised when he didn't reply. This usually meant he was building up to some reprimand, or some criticism, some release of the day's pent up anger. In any case, she was absorbed in the process of placing fresh delphinium petals around the photograph of her dead son and didn't want a conversation, so she made sure that what she said next was a question requiring no answer.

"I wonder how many whales have died for King and Country."

The silence continued and part of her welcomed it, but another was starting to feel vaguely uncomfortable. The longer the wait, the fiercer the admonition would be. She wished he would just go to bed and save his rebuke for the morning, when it would probably be forgotten anyway, so she tried once again to finish the conversation by making her words rise and fall like the end of a bedtime story.

"We have had a successful day. There are three sleeping soldiers in the library. I am grateful to you Stephen."

If it had worked, he would at least have acknowledged her gratitude and said goodnight, but he uttered no words. Suhani suddenly felt cold, goosebumps on her arms, as if some wind had picked up, blowing through her skin and into her bones. But there was no wind that hot summer evening. Once more she tried to speak.

"One of them is quite badly injured." There was a faint tremor in her voice. And then she knew. From somewhere in the trees, the fox screeched as if to tell her that it was not Stephen who stood behind her, but the angel of death.

"What are you doing here so late, Freddie?" she said, still with her back to him, wanting his answer to sound as cheerful as her question. What would it be? Had he forgotten his hat? Lost his way? But there was no hope of such a thing, she understood that perfectly well. Having tried everything else, Suhani at last turned around, her strained face imploring him not to speak. Although she knew full well he would.

"Telegram for Major and Mrs Harkness."

The telegram was already in his hand and he was holding it out to her. She looked at it, then at Freddie, then back down at the telegram again. Her eyes flicked quickly up and down and from side to side, her lips tightened up and began to quiver, and she breathed in with an audible gasp.

"Why now?" she said.

Jack quietly gathered up the chess pieces, not wishing to wake his friend who had finally been dragged into sleep by the laudanum even as Jack had been moving his Queen into her final position. What was the difference between sleep and death? Standing up to look down at his friend, Jack thought the answer was that sleep couldn't be chosen. He folded up the chessboard and tucked it under his arm before walking round to the foot of Christopher's bed.

"Sleep tight, mate. Make 'em sweet, if yer can..."

Freddie had not expected Suhani's question and he realised he didn't have an answer. To visit her so late had been the selfish passing on of pain, an unburdening, a ruse to stop the throbbing in his head, to allow the incubus to jump from his chest onto hers so that he would sleep through the night, whilst she would not. He had refused to be the custodian of her grief for one second longer than necessary but realised now he had been thinking of no one but himself, that he could have waited until the morning, and he felt ashamed. Perhaps George had been right after all; allow her one more night's decent sleep. Too late now.

Then he remembered. "Late delivery ma'am. Telegraph caught fire."

He felt relieved that what he said was true, making it easier to say. She looked unconvinced, but took the telegram from him anyway and began to open it too quickly, tearing at it so she could get to the message it contained. What was the black mark in the corner of the envelope for, Freddie wondered? To ensure it was prioritised? Surely that was the point of a telegram in the first place. And how would it break such bad news with so few words allowed? *Regret to inform?* He watched her scan the words and was at first relieved to see that Suhani's reaction was different to Mrs Mawby's. No anger, instead a kind of begging. But the sound she made was the same, like physical pain, a retching up and emptying out of the soul, an inhuman sound from thousands of years ago, deeply pitched, as deep as a man's. He wondered if all mothers who lost their children made the same noise, and how many more times he would have to hear it on his rounds. If it were a hundred, or a thousand, he would surely never get used to it. He wanted the war to end there and then, right now. He wanted to no longer be the postboy, he wanted his mother to be able to see with her cloudy, milk-grey eyes and he wanted his father to be there when he got home. With this litany of impossible desires his eyes suddenly welled up in communion with Suhani. It was not that he was crying, at least not in a way he ever had before, there was no shaking of his head or trembling of his lip, it was just as if someone had turned on a tap. He had started to sweat, that was it, and the salt water was irritating his eyes. So they both looked at each other, both shimmering through each other's tears, both willing the moment to end, or to never have started. Freddie noticed a sudden pungent smell of freshly trampled grass in his nostrils, and looked down at his shoes, allowing a tear to drip on them.

Suhani put her hands to her face in order to stifle the noise she was making, using the telegram almost like a handkerchief. Her wet face glistened in the moonlight and Freddie slowly became aware of the absolute silence that now followed after Suhani's scream. No birds sang, the sheep were sleeping in the fields, and there was no wind in the branches above them. But then he swore he could hear the grandfather clock ticking in the hallway fifty yards away. So much so, he wanted to look to see if Suhani had left the front door open, but there was some kind of spell between them that was impossible to break. They were both becalmed in the eye of the storm, and he couldn't look away. Then, just as he thought the moment would never pass, Suhani gasped through her hands that were still clenching the telegram in front of her mouth.

"Thank you, Freddie. I...appreciate you coming out so late."

It was an utterance so completely at odds with the situation, her words seemed to come from a different place than her weeping, as if she was able to stand outside of herself. Her sari glistened in the moonlight, he was in the presence of someone remarkable, unlike anyone else he had ever met, or could ever imagine. Yet the sense of it passed as quickly as it came, with one tick of the clock as he, too, found he was looking at himself from above, with horror at his own unbidden words: "Will you be replying ma'am?"

It was an entirely stupid thing to say. He blamed George who, by telling Freddie not to ask for a reply, had put the very idea in his head. It would not otherwise have occurred to him. He felt as witless as she was extraordinary, they couldn't be further apart, all his efforts and desires to become an adult wasted by this senseless utterance. Yet in her moment of profoundest grief, through her tears and her crumpled telegram, Suhani was able to be kind, amazing Freddie once more with her ability to forgive.

"No, no thank you, Freddie. That won't be necessary." He looked up at her and saw that she was smiling. He wiped his face with the back of his sleeve and smiled back. Her words were a gift, he decided, a gift that he would keep safe, a simple act of kindness to be repaid at some point in the future, and he would not forget it.

Suhani closed her eyes. The mood changed as quickly as the blowing out of a candle – except no, it was simpler than that, the actual candle on the pedestal by the photograph had blown itself out, even though there was no wind. Freddie knew it was time to go. "Well…Good night ma'am," he said, too cheerfully.

"Good night, Freddie." Her eyes remained closed as she said it, her hands still up to her face, the telegram damp from the moisture in her breath and the tears that continued to fall from her eyes.

There was nothing for it but for Freddie to turn away, to abandon her, and to take the first few steps of his long walk home. What was this job, who was this blue be-hatted postboy, except the breaker of hearts? These bereavements were not his fault, why was it left to him to be death's emissary? As he walked across the grass towards the driveway and wiped his eyes with his sleeve again he was expecting at any moment for the sound of Suhani's weeping to return, but it did not. Perhaps she was waiting for him to pass through the open gates and out of sight. He was tempted to look, to see if she was still standing there, frozen under the branches of the beech tree, in the territory of the fox, but he chose not to and walked on, further, away from her, towards his own mother.

If he had looked, he would have seen Suhani lying on the ground on her front, her arms stretched out above her head with her fingers digging into the ground. Her saliva had moistened the earth and some soil had stuck to the side of her face. Her gaping mouth made her look as if she was screaming, although she made no sound at all. Freddie had heard nothing because her chest was empty and she was struggling for air, some hidden force of grief compelling her to wring it out again, to empty out even more of it from lungs that were already empty. She pulled at the earth in order to drag her body closer to the marble pedestal, her sari gathering grass and dirt as she did so. When she got there, face down in the soil, she continued to dig, clawing into it with her fingernails, removing handfuls of earth and dropping them again. And then, finally, she wailed, but into the ground so that she would not wake the soldiers or the servants in the house.

11

Stephen allowed his torch-beam to light the road home. Although there was enough moonlight to see without it, the torch had been supplied to him as manager of the munitions factory and it made him feel vaguely important. At this late hour he would rarely meet anybody on his journey, and it was the one part of his day when he felt some level of contentment, without anger or the need to lash out. Sometimes he was even happy enough to start whistling, and the uneven swing of his limp would settle into a more comfortable rhythm. So it was more resentment than surprise when he saw a figure approaching in the opposite direction. Once they were within ten yards of each other they both stopped, and Stephen abruptly ceased his whistling.

"What on earth are you doing here?"

Stephen saw that Freddie was nervous of him. It was what he did, and enjoyed the effect, making the enemy hesitate to give one an advantage in battle. Yet he hated himself for it too.

"I was...I had a puncture..." said Freddie. "There was a telegram."

Stephen pressed home his advantage. "I see. But it must be ten o'clock."

"I thought it might be important."

"Was it?"

"I think so."

Stephen didn't like the answers he was being given. "Has Mrs Harkness replied?"

"No sir."

"I see."

He took a few steps nearer in order to examine Freddie's face more closely and his eyes flicked rapidly, trying to assess what the boy was hiding. But he left it. He would find out soon enough when he got back to Tendring.

"Well. Good night. You're lucky there's a full moon."

"Yes sir. Good night sir."

Stephen stepped aside and pointed his torch along the road behind him, indicating to Freddie that he was allowed to leave. Freddie took a few nervous steps to get past whilst Stephen stood and watched the boy until he had turned the corner and was out of sight.

It was another ten minutes before Stephen arrived home. Sometimes whistling and sometimes not, his irregular steps alternated between good news and bad. Telegrams were not uncommon at Tendring what with Stephen's work, his Masonic links, and now, he presumed, Suhani's connection to Celandine Hall. It was odd to have deliveries so late, but on the other hand war did stranger things than puncture a postboy's tyre.

Normally he would walk straight past the two stone eagles at the open gate of Tendring, but on this late evening he paused to examine them with his torch. The first signs of this year's lichen were beginning to appear on their cracked surfaces and he wondered if he might start to remove the yellow-green layer now, at ten o'clock, in the darkness. He would not be needed in the house, or missed, nor was he tired. That way, by staying out, he would not hear about the telegram until the morning. But then the fox screeched, as if calling him, so he thought he should investigate the snare.

It was untouched; no sign of the fox. No sign of Suhani either. She was not at her shrine, which was unusual. He realised he might have come home even later that evening than he normally did. That would probably explain it. The candles around the photograph were out, Suhani must have gone to bed. He leant down to pick up a stray delphinium petal at the base of the shrine, but in doing so noticed the earth had been churned up by something. He looked towards the woods and muttered "Damned foxes." Kicking at the broken earth he then padded it down with his shoe, but some of the soil stuck to his sole. The ground was moist. There had not been rain for several days but still he looked up to the sky just to make sure, an illogical gesture. It might be the fox marking its territory, though he couldn't smell it. There seemed no explanation for the dampness of the earth.

Stephen stood at the closed door of his wife's bedroom. He was listening without any particular expectation of hearing anything from the other side, but was aware his listening was an intrusion, that somehow he was invading her privacy. Normally he would have simply assumed she was sleeping, thought nothing of it and gone straight to his own bed across the landing, or more likely down to the library to read, but the conversation with Freddie had stirred up some unspecified doubt that prevented him from letting it go. He lifted up his hand and tapped once with his knuckle on her door. It was so timid that if she had heard it at all she would probably have dismissed it as the creak of an old house cooling down after the day's summer heat. So he tapped again, twice, more resolutely.

"My dear? Suhani?"

He wasn't sure how she would react. She had closed her bedroom door many years ago, because he had stopped entering it, and the domain was hers alone. If she came to the door, he would have to take a step back. But she did not.

He put his fingers on the door handle. In doing so he revisited an ancient memory, before his own war, a time when to touch the handle, and her, did not require permission because it was not only taken for granted, but desired. In fact the two things were indistinguishable – to allow was to ask, to open was to enter. But the door handle was cold and so was the recollection, gone before it had chance to take hold, and he stood amongst the pile of lifeless years that lay emptied out like dirty linen on the landing outside her bedroom.

He pushed down on the door handle and opened the door, just enough to be able to see inside. The curtains, still open, allowed the moon onto her bed. Suhani was not there and the bed remained unslept in, untouched since Phoebe had made it up that morning. Stephen breathed in slowly and thought the whole room felt musty and lifeless, like a museum. He walked in and past the bed to stand by the window to look out across the lawn, as if she might after all be under the copper beech, but he didn't expect her to be there, any more than he had actually expected her to be in her bed.

Back out on the landing he quietly closed his wife's bedroom door behind him. Perhaps Hannah would know where Suhani was. He had noticed that they'd become close since Hannah had joined the household, and he was both envious and disapproving of their relationship – though it might have its advantages now. Stephen descended the stairs and entered the library, standing in the doorway. Hannah looked up at him from her chair, quickly put her book down, stood up and curtsied.

"Sir."

"Have you seen Mrs Harkness?"

"Is she not outside sir?"

"It seems not. When did she go out?"

"Usual time sir."

Stephen looked around the library to buy time to think, barely noticing Jack and Gabriel in their beds, and a third bed opposite them, shrouded in hanging sheets. "Go to bed Hannah. It's past ten."

"With respect sir, I shouldn't leave them alone."

"You can't stay up all night. I'll watch them. Go to bed."

Hannah picked up her book and pulled her shawl more tightly round her shoulders. They both knew she was in no position to argue. "Very well sir."

Stephen watched her leave, waited for the sound of her footsteps climbing the stairs to fade to nothing, and then sat down in the chair she had vacated. For years sleep had eluded him, and so he would either walk into the small hours, or, if his wound was troubling him excessively he would sit reading. On many mornings he would wake up not in his bed but in his chair in the library with a book pressing on his chest. Occasionally he wouldn't sleep at all, having read an entire novel. Now these soldiers had invaded his space he resented it, and wanted to take it back. He resented too Suhani's undeniable logic that the library was the best place for them, fuelling his frustration and irritation still further. Yet something made him want to stay, to guard them in their sleeping, to secure the consolation of their dreams, since he knew, for some of them at least, dreams were all they had left.

Only then did he notice one of them was awake and had propped himself up on his pillow, one arm behind his head, the other resting by his side, perhaps having been disturbed by the conversation Stephen had just had with Hannah. He saw in the soldier's hand a small object that he rolled around his fingers: a chess piece. Without concern for the other two patients, Stephen called over to him.

"Can't sleep?"

"Nah. Waste of time sir, don't yer fink?"

"Yes. Now you say it, I'm inclined to agree. Why don't you go for a walk? You can borrow my coat."

"I might. Why don't you?"

"I'm keeping watch, aren't I."

"No need for that. We won't come to no harm. Been in worse situations, that's for sure."

Stephen glanced across at Christopher's veiled bed. "Who's in there?"

"Him? That's Christopher. Christopher Ellis. Captain, Second Canadian Division."

"Why is he hidden? I think his sheets should be drawn back so he can see out."

"He ain't very pretty, that's why."

"Well, that's why we're all here, isn't it? Nothing to be ashamed of. And nothing I haven't seen before."

Jack looked sceptical. "Where?"

"South Africa. Death is death, you know."

"Some deaths are better than others, I reckon."

"That's as may be. Let's draw back his sheets." Stephen slid his arms back in order to push himself out of the chair but Jack raised his voice to stop him.

"He's fine," said Jack. "Leave him be."

Jack seemed to hold some advantage over Stephen, which irked him because in every way – class, rank, education – Stephen was the superior of the two. There was a tussle going on between them and there hung in the air an infinity of possibilities that seemed to be summed up by one trifling, meaningless choice: which one of them would leave the library to go for a walk? To do so would feel like a surrender, but to what? The question seemed petty and inconsequential, but then he knew from experience that most battles began with the flick of a kid glove. The triviality of the moment served only to make it more intractable.

Stephen made one more effort. "Perhaps I should talk to him."

"He's asleep."

And that was that. They spoke no more to each other. The silence seemed to disturb Gabriel, who turned in his bed, but didn't wake. Jack put the Black Queen up to his lips and kissed it, an incongruously fey thing to do, though his eyes remained resolutely fixed on Stephen.

They didn't know it, but they had both had the same thought, Stephen and Jack, that the future might split and send them off in two directions, where one went for a walk, or the other. And they wished all games and battles could end this way, not with a draw, but with both sides winning in two different worlds.

They also didn't know that Christopher, inside his shroud, had not been sleeping but listening, like a fox in the woods, and was about to ask one of them to stay, and the other to leave; as if he could read their indecisive minds, and decide on their behalf.

Having earlier slipped secretly out of his house, and somehow managing to avoid his mother's bat-like hearing, Freddie couldn't face creeping back in, so he sat in the darkness under the apple tree on the Eagley Road. He took his leather pouch and threw it as hard as he could into the ditch opposite. He had wanted this job more than anything, but now he wished desperately to go back in time, retrace his steps, take a different path, one that would lead not down the lanes of Eagley but along the trenches of France – to the job he really wanted, where he might do his bit to change the war for the better, instead of the war changing him for the worse.

He wiped his wet face with his sleeve and then cradled his head on his folded forearms to weep in a way he had never done in his life before, not even, because he had been so young, when his father had died. At four years old, all he could remember was that his father was there one day, and gone the next. His mother never talked about it, and Freddie never asked. Once, he had sought him out in the graveyard and found a headstone but no story engraved upon it, except the dates of his beginning and his end, and the unnerving epitaph that Charles Lovegrove was not dead but sleeping. He found the metaphor disturbing enough to keep him away, and he never went back to that corner of the graveyard.

Freddie decided to retrieve his pouch from the ditch to tuck it under his head as a makeshift pillow, though he suspected it was really no more comfortable than the ground itself. If he remained under the apple tree and kept perfectly still, the day might drift away from him, its anguish replaced by dreams, diminishing and fading to nothing. It had not been his intention to go to sleep, he didn't think he was tired, but despite everything he would be out like a boxer as soon as his head hit the stiff leather hide of his pouch. The sheep in the fields behind Freddie started bleating as if they were concerned for his well-being and wished to help. But they were just sheep, stupid sheep – he had once seen them willingly queue up for slaughter – and he knew, as he fell asleep, that help would not come tonight.

The sheep had gone silent and he had been out for the count for two hours when he woke suddenly, disturbed by a noise. A distant rumble, a throbbing that was more a feeling in his chest than a sound in his ears; a mere rumour of sound. He panicked for a moment, wondering where his bike was, and then remembered it was still awaiting repair in the Post Office. Only half awake, he tried to focus on the noise and listed the obvious culprits in his mind – the ambulance, the despatch rider, the aeroplane – but once he shook the sleep out of his head, none of them seemed to match this strange new sound.

He looked up through the branches of the apple tree and saw that there were fewer stars in the sky, and the moonlight was muffled by a thick covering of cloud that had drifted across from the east. The rumble was clearer now and could no longer be dismissed as the fag-end of a dream. Like the throbbing pain in his head the noise seemed to come from everywhere, directionless, enveloping Freddie's entire body. He looked in both directions along Eagley Road but without moonlight he could see nothing.

He stood up and stepped into the middle of the road, thinking he might be able to see more clearly there. The noise was getting louder, and it was no longer possible for it to be mistaken for anything earthbound; it was now so loud that the ground was vibrating under Freddie's feet, like thunder. Once more he looked up and watched as the last remaining stars switched themselves off, one by one, and then the clouds disappeared, taking with them the remnants of moonlight. The rumble changed to a whine, like a cry for help, as perhaps it was. Only then did Freddie finally realise he was witnessing an alien craft struggling to stay airborne. He felt not fear but awe, in the presence of a superior being, as if Shiva had taken to the air, and he watched, open-mouthed, as it slipped across the sky.

Zeppelin.

The airship was approaching Tendring, and the dim noise of it woke

Hannah. She was in the bedroom which she shared at the top of the house with Phoebe, who continued to sleep undisturbed. Hannah climbed out of bed as quietly as she could and walked over to the window, although the table made it difficult to get close enough, meaning she had to crook her neck in order to look up into the sky. But it turned out there was no need, instead the sound came from straight ahead and immediately she saw an unfathomable shape, a monstrous black shadow drifting slowly across her field of view, beneath the clouds, not one hundred yards away from the house. Then she realised what it was. There had been a newspaper story less than a month ago of a Zeppelin that had crashed in Oakston Marsh, a village on the other side of the estuary in Essex, and Hannah feared the story was about to repeat itself, but much closer to home. The article included a photograph of the mangled skeleton of the craft in a field, and stories of bodies so badly burnt they could not be identified.

The Zeppelin's engines throttled and wheezed, then cut out, and then just as quickly restarted. Hannah watched it losing its battle with gravity, and she became fearful not just for the Zeppelin but for the house, Tendring, to which it was flying parallel. She prayed the ghostly machine would not change direction.

She stretched across to open the window and peer out. Being able to see the whole of the lawn, she sensed an urge to protect it, to prevent the Zeppelin from getting any closer, as if she could push it away by simply willing it. She had another feeling too, and at first couldn't work out what, until it surfaced of its own accord, a sense of shame that she was intruding on the final, private throes of death. Yet she was obliged to watch, her helplessness making the spectacle all the more compelling. The engines had cut out again and she wasn't sure if in the silence she could hear the occupants in the airship's gondola yelling and screaming at each other, the sound of terror, more frightened than she was. She blasphemed, Holy Mother of God, though in a whisper so as not to wake Phoebe, as the craft came dangerously close to clipping the tops of the trees at the far end of the lawn.

Just as it seemed an accident was inevitable, that she would be the witness to a firestorm and the unimaginable bonfire of a score of German crewmen, the engines cut back in and sounded suddenly healthier, stronger, their pulse more regular and their pitch rising harmoniously. Either the crew had solved the problem, or it had solved itself, and the airship immediately gained some height, slowly but consistently changing direction away from the house. Only then did Hannah realise she had been holding her breath. She let out a sigh and then for several minutes watched the Zeppelin manoeuvring itself up into the sky and across the fields, back towards the English Channel.

Hannah turned her head to look at Phoebe in disbelief that her room mate had slept through the commotion. As she often did these days, Hannah felt the desire to stroke Phoebe's hair, like a mother would do, because they would have to contend with a commotion of Phoebe's own making not so long from now.

Hannah turned back to the window. As she watched the airship completely disappear from sight, she felt it was odd that no one had come out on to the lawn to watch. Surely she was not the only one to have been woken? As mistress of the house Mrs Harkness would most certainly have investigated. Or no, perhaps she had watched from her own bedroom window, just as Hannah herself had done, for fear of missing any part of the spectacle by going downstairs. Her bedroom was on the same side of the house after all and that was what one would do. But why wasn't there now the sound of doors opening and closing? Perhaps no one wanted to make any noise, for fear of waking those that had remained asleep. She could find logical answers to all her own questions, but none of them seemed to ring true. The Zeppelin had not been as eerie as the silence it left behind.

She stretched her arm back up to the window and was about to close it when a movement caught her eye. A shadow on the lawn, a figure walking across from the trees towards the front door. The sky was completely cloudy now and there was no light at all from the house, so it was impossible to see any detail: no face, no attire, just a spectre on the inky grass.

Except she knew it was a man, and he had a limp.

Jack stretched out his leg to alleviate the pins and needles in his injured foot. He was sitting on the floor of the library by Gabriel's bed, hugging Gabriel tightly, trying to reassure him by gently rocking. Gabriel was whimpering and mumbling the only words he seemed to know: "Pineapple... chocolate... cigarettes." It was the sound of the trenches, Jack thought, more jumpy than gunfire, more throat-constricting than Lyddite smoke.

"It's all right mate," said Jack. "All over now. All done."

There was a lit candle behind the shroud that hung around Christopher's bed and Jack watched the shadows it cast on the sheets, but it seemed it had burnt through to the wick's end and finally extinguished itself. Jack wanted to know what the time was and turned his head to look at the grandfather clock in the hallway, but then he remembered he had closed the library door.

Stephen sat on the edge of his bed, rubbing his sore leg with one hand and holding one of his shoes with the other. There was mud on the sole and part of the leather upper, so he took his handkerchief and began to wipe it off. Then he noticed a flash of blue, and delicately removed a fragment of delphinium petal. He held it up to examine it closely and it added profoundly to his sadness, grief upon grief. He dropped the shoe onto the floor and buried his head in his hands to try to stifle the noise as he became the second person, after Gabriel, to weep into the night.

The third had been Freddie. He'd finally made his way home and was now in his own bed, having cried himself to sleep. Still in his uniform and lying on top of his blanket, he drifted in and out of a dream: Millie, Suhani, and the despatch rider appeared to know each other, like sisters-in-arms, and all three seemed to be angry with him. They either shouted at Freddie, or ignored him, or, as was the way with dreams, were able to do both simultaneously. Whatever he tried to say or do to make them appreciate his point of view – though he didn't himself know what it was he was trying to convince them of – they would look down at him like giants, impatient because they couldn't understand what he was saying, and stepping around him as if he was broken glass. At one point, Millie was waving to someone in the gondola of the airship. It was the American Indian, except it wasn't a man but a young woman, smiling and waving back with a letter in her hand. Was this Anne, setting sail from Nova Scotia? Meanwhile Suhani tended to the graze on Freddie's forehead, even though she had no hands, dabbing at the wound with her stumps. She seemed cross, or disappointed, or dismissive, that she was unable to tie the bandages so she walked away as if Freddie's injury no longer mattered. Except no, she didn't walk off, she was already there to rejoin her friends, along with Anne who was now magically back on terra firma, in a discussion that was no doubt about the useless postboy, or worse, about another boy, one they actually appreciated and fussed over. Yet these different women pulled relentlessly at him: he wanted Millie to kiss him, the despatch rider to marry him, Anne to forgive him and Suhani to be his mother. But they always seemed to be walking away. Where was his own mother when he needed her?

And then, the last thing he would remember from his dream before waking, was that the four of them had turned some corner or other and were not coming back. And Stephen – or was it Jack, or some human portmanteau of the two? – appeared from the library and took him across the lawn and into the woods.

The fourth person to weep into the night was Suhani, who had run two miles from Tendring to the church, a medieval sanctuary so familiar to her, yet so foreign, so unlike the India that carried the oxygen in her blood, that she felt she belonged nowhere, the reason why she had sought it out. A place where the stone floor she lay on numbed her body with the cold, the smell of polished pews stung her eyes, and the air cooled her lungs and eased the pain that was burning into her heart, turning it to ash.

The only time she closed her eyes all night was when an inquisitive rat scuttled by, pausing momentarily to sniff her face. She felt no disgust, barely flinching. Then it was gone, and she was completely alone.

12

In my mother's shop we sell what people need, most things anyway, groceries, bread, soap, coffee, newspapers, and so on. Everything, I suppose, except meat – go round the corner to Castle's Butchers for that – and fish, you can get that fresh off the boats. It was quiet today. Every day is quiet, truth be told, but it was odd, because Tuesday is often a busy one due to early closing on a Wednesday. Perhaps they are steering clear of my brooding countenance. They still have to eat though, don't they?

Since Christopher left, there has really been no one to converse with apart from Mother. I can talk to her about almost anything, so I was glad the shop had been empty most of the time. I said I was worried I'd not heard from Christopher in a while. I said I felt he had left the house for good, and I was terrified he was dead. I burst into tears and she held me in her arms, hugging me tight. She said it was natural to feel these things but they were only feelings, not facts; facts could not be changed but feelings could be, and you could choose different ones. The papers were full of stories of U-boats sinking allied ships in the Atlantic, she said. Christopher's letter was probably on the seabed somewhere between here and Europe. He would write again, and the letter would come. For a while I believed her, and felt a little better. But it didn't last.

I can't help the sense of emptiness that washes over me as I approach our house, although I haven't felt well all day and wonder if it is the beginnings of a cold. I open the front door, which sticks at the bottom and so needs a good shove with my foot. It's the change in temperature as the summer comes on, Christopher had said, altering the shape of the door frame. At least it isn't draughty, he would joke. I hang my bag on the back of the door and then close it with another push of my foot. My grandfather had taught me to be practical and independent, and I have inherited his carpenter's tools, so I know I could mend the door myself, but I need a reason for Christopher to come home. So the door sticks, for now.

I kick off my shoes without undoing them. It's lazy, then I feel guilty about my laziness, so I pick them up and untie the laces, noticing the sole of one of my shoes is coming away. We sell shoes at my mother's shop too, just a few pairs, practical, ugly things that came as part of a food consignment by mistake. Practical and ugly – sometimes I feel that would be a good description of myself, so I go into my bedroom and look in the mirror to check.

It's too small to see the whole of me, but I can piece myself together by tilting the mirror back and forth, up and down. Today I'm wearing trousers, once forbidden, but now given tacit permission by the war as so many things have been. They are dull and masculine – six months ago I would have hated them. Today they feel as essential as a uniform. We are all soldiers now. My blouse is a hand-me-down, once frilly and puffed up, now hanging miserably in all the wrong places, and my hair is tied back, as tight as an anchor's rope.

Then I do something I often do on returning from work and quickly change into a dress. Plain, but pretty enough, it was the one I had worn when Christopher first took me dancing. I pull it over my head and let it fall over my trousers before I remove them. My modesty is unnecessary of course, there is no one here to see, but I have accumulated odd habits that come from pretending not to be alone. Sometimes I am coy, sometimes I'm free with my nakedness, either way it is because I imagine I am sharing the house. In particular, I undo my hair as if Christopher is watching; or not necessarily watching, but simply in the same room. I run my fingers through it and I'm not sure if it's an attempt to tidy it up, or to make it look used and bed bound – or windswept, because Christopher would often talk about the wind, and how beautiful it made me. My mother had warned against men like that – they flatter you into bed, she said, and that's where the flattering stops – but she was wrong about Christopher. I understood him completely, I knew he meant every word and needed nothing in return, which seemed to me to be the very definition of love.

I twist the mirror so that I can see my face again and, without warning, for the second time that day I begin to weep. I don't know why, but I no longer need to pretend to be alone, as if others have joined me, a whole boatful of wet and dripping ghosts. It's a very different kind of crying from earlier, there is more grief to it, because I don't believe my mother's story. There is no letter on the sea bed, and if a message is ever to be delivered it will not be from Christopher, but *about* him, and the words of his demise will be as black as tar. That is what I believe, in my darkest hours. I think I'm in mourning not for one death but for a family of lost souls: his, and mine, and the sailors that would have gone down with his letter, because to keep Christopher alive would be to drown a hundred innocent men. Would I take that bargain, if I could? Mother was wrong, no one chooses their feelings.

But this will never do. In any case, there is a knock at the door. I brush down my dress with one hand and wipe away my tears with the other.

It's Joe, with a tin of paint.

13

As the sun rose, Tendring seemed to rise with it, the house stirring itself awake. The bricks and mortar expanded and the old wooden window frames creaked in the early morning summer heat, the sunlight baking their south-facing paintwork, peeling the edges away like dead skin. Sometimes Stephen thought Tendring woke him in the mornings as it sighed itself into life. Though there was no need to be woken this morning since he wasn't sure he had slept at all that night.

There was an inch of water in his bowl. Stephen dipped a cloth into the surface of it and used it to shine the toecap of his shoe with small circular movements. He examined the end result in the sunlight streaming through the bedroom window and was satisfied with the reflections. Then he took the opportunity to trim his moustache. You can leave the army, they said, but the army never leaves you. He had hoped his early morning schedule would in some way be restorative, a process military life had taught him, but then he looked more closely at his face in the mirror and saw it was riven with the salty remnants of tears. This startled him, shocking him into topping up the bowl with freezing water from the ewer and washing his face for a second time, more thoroughly, rubbing in haste, as if he were still shining his shoes. Then he grabbed a hand towel to pat his cheeks and unexpectedly thought he might start weeping again. But he was able to fight it back by straightening his shoulders and looking at himself in the mirror as a sergeant would to a foot-soldier. There did indeed seem to be two of him, and he knew which one must prevail. So, with meticulous attention, and yet without thinking, he finished getting dressed.

There was a connecting door between his bedroom and Suhani's, but it was locked and the key long since lost. In any case, Suhani had put her dressing table against her side of it and the lock had been painted over on both sides, many years ago. He remembered the day when he had originally locked it. It was a Sunday, Suhani had gone to church with their three small sons and the staff, but Stephen had stayed at home with a bad cold, or possibly the 'flu. He had not planned in advance to lock the door, or intended it to be permanent, it was more that he simply didn't want to be disturbed that day. It was hard to believe he and Suhani had once, long ago, lived so passionately, that despite the difference in age they loved each other equally as they danced through those early years together. The wagging tongues had rejected the idea it was Suhani who had been the first to unlock their affection and allay his doubts, and yet that was how it had been. The gap between them existed only in the minds of others. But that was then, and this was now, so when Stephen had turned the key to the door between their bedrooms it felt final, in some way sealing his heart to protect it from more pain. When she had come back from church that day, she didn't mention the locked door.

He stepped out of his bedroom and onto the landing, listening out for signs of life. He heard a door close downstairs, probably the kitchen. It was a comforting noise, the house waking up as usual with its predictable familiarity, nothing untoward, and he had the urge to do what he always did, slip away unnoticed and go to work. But he knew this was not a normal day and that he would have to knock on Suhani's bedroom door once again.

When there was no reply he opened the door and stepped fully inside. For the second time in a matter of hours he stood in a room he had not previously entered for many years. The bed was as made up as it had been the night before, so he walked over to the window and looked across the lawn to see if she had returned to her shrine under the copper beech. It would have been a strange thing for her to do so early in the morning, it wasn't part of her routine, although today might be different, everything else seemed to be. But she wasn't there.

Stephen went back out onto the landing and decided to investigate the other bedrooms. She might be in one of those. He suspected it would not be the first time she had slept in Arthur's room, her first-born, lost to the war, so he checked there first.

The door creaked, due to lack of use. The servants weren't allowed in to clean, though Suhani would wipe its contours from time to time, at least that was what she said she was doing. There was no sign of her. Sunlight exposed a week's dust on the surface of the bedside table and Arthur's uniform lay neatly on the bed, so Suhani could not have slept there. He picked up Arthur's peaked cap off the pillow and rubbed his fingers over the sewn-up bullet hole. There was also a parcel on the bed, a soft package of brown paper and string, containing all of Arthur's belongings from the front, still unopened, and lying there in lieu of a body. Stephen placed the cap back on the pillow; he had been in this room long enough.

Edward's room was on the opposite side of the landing, away from the sunlight, and had the opposite feeling too. It was not so much a bedroom filled with hundreds of books as a small library with a bed thrown in for good measure. Edward would spend every waking hour with his head in a book and, given the early hour of the day, was probably doing so now in the trenches. But Edward's intelligence was the right kind, Stephen thought, for army life. He was brave on the cricket field, and a leader, and would thrive in the trenches. Again, the bed was made up, undisturbed.

Stephen moved back across the landing this time to Tristan's bedroom, though by now he was not expecting to find any evidence of Suhani's presence, he was merely checking due to a compulsive need to complete the process. The triple portrait on its easel took up most of the space between the foot of the bed and the far wall, and Tristan's unfinished face sent a shiver through Stephen's body, even though he didn't believe in ghosts.

The four walls were covered with paintings, some rather childlike, others expertly executed, and some between the two extremes. A story of artistic improvement from gifted child to young artist, from the literal to the metaphorical, a journey that Stephen neither approved of nor understood. He felt alienated by Tristan's choice of weapon, the paintbrush, and the distance between father and son had grown with each stroke of it.

There was one painting in particular, done when Tristan was about six or seven, that caught Stephen's eye because he remembered the day it was painted. It was a view from his mother's bedroom window of the lawn and the copper beech. Tristan had proudly presented it to his father but Stephen had been in considerable pain and had dismissed the effort. Later on in the day, when the pain had eased, Stephen had felt guilty, but he had not been brought up to apologise to children, especially one's own, so the deadly cycle persisted and Tristan continued to cry for the rest of the day. From then on, Stephen noted, Tristan only ever showed his pictures to his mother.

As Stephen walked the Eagley Road, his hip was causing him discomfort and making it more difficult than normal to hide his limp. He was always brusque and grumpy when the pain was this bad, and combined with a sleepless night it meant he was unable to think clearly. His decisions, such as they were, were instinctive and he felt vaguely annoyed to be at their mercy. And so it was that he turned left down a bridle path that was a cut through to the church; quicker, but more difficult to walk, which only made his hip burn more fiercely. He couldn't be sure he would find Suhani at the church, but she often visited it and it was the nearest location to check. In any case, it was where he'd found her the last time she'd gone missing after bad news from the front.

The two-mile trek was rugged in several places, so it was at least half an hour before Stephen walked through the lychgate and along the path that led through the graveyard. Before he got to the south door of the church, he stopped to turn right, another detour that seemed instinctive rather than planned. He picked his way through the uncut grass towards a marble monument that stood out as both newer and more ostentatious than the mossy gravestones surrounding it. Stephen had devised the shape and style of this six-foot high construction, a design which Suhani didn't like, and she had chosen the inscription, which he didn't like. He would have preferred a simpler, more straightforward text, less poetic, more befitting of a soldier and a man, and he would usually avert his gaze from it. Today, however, he found himself reading the words that still looked freshly carved, still unbleached by the sun:

"To the beloved memory of Arthur Lancelot Harkness, Captain Rifle Brigade, who fell in the attack on Fromelles near the Aubers Ridge, May 9 1915, aged 22. First son of Stephen and Suhani Harkness of Tendring in this parish. My days are gone like a shadow and I am withered like grass."

He walked all the way round the monument and then tapped the base with the tip of his shoe, as if checking the structure's integrity. It was the least emotional thing he could think to do.

When he reached the church door, Stephen twisted the handle and a heavy iron clunk echoed inside the building. Once inside, he saw the sun passing through the stained glass windows, casting red spots of light onto the floor. Stephen instinctively stepped round them, avoiding them as a child might, then made his way into the church towards the choir vestry that was under the tower. He could see the bell rope hanging straight down – someone had forgotten to tie it up – and it even seemed to be very slightly swinging. He concluded there must be a draught caused by the church rapidly warming up in the sunshine. Or perhaps it had just been his opening of the door. Either way, he didn't like the swinging rope, it made him feel slightly nauseous, so he went over and tied it up.

He looked up the aisle towards the altar at the far end of the church and there she was, lying on the stone floor, parallel to the altar rail. She had her back to him, so he couldn't tell whether she was asleep or awake. He walked towards her, over the shining tomb lids that led up the floor of the aisle like brass stepping stones, trying to make his footsteps as regular as his crumbling hip would allow, so that, if she was awake, she might not know it was him.

He stopped as soon as he could see her face. It was clear she had not slept all night, her eyes bloodshot and staring unblinkingly straight ahead in the direction of the altar, though he doubted she was looking at it, or at anything. Her hands were under her chin, clutching a telegram. Stephen knew he had to speak and wanted to be kind, but what actually came out was harsher than he intended, as it so often was.

"Why are you wearing your sari? People will see."

Suhani didn't appear to react, she lay there unmoving, as if she hadn't heard him. Perhaps she hadn't. Stephen was about to repeat the question when suddenly she spoke.

"I'm sorry. I haven't slept."

Stephen leant down slowly to extract the telegram from Suhani's grip. He was careful to avoid touching her hands or face, and when he took hold of the envelope she did not resist. He stood back up, removed a pair of spectacles from his inside jacket pocket and with one hand tried to put them on his face. To his shame he seemed to be shaking, and he had to try more than once to hook them over his ears.

"Which one this time?" he asked quietly as he began to open the telegram.

He breathed in deeply and got a strong whiff of the mould and dampness that always filled the air in the church, of every English church, whatever the weather or time of year. It reminded him of being a very small boy, of a school dormitory that was a hundred miles away from his home and from his mother, and of the sickening feeling when there was no one to turn to. The corner of his eye began to twitch, and although he knew it felt more substantial than it really was, he clenched his jaw to try to stop it. Reading the opening lines, he broke off when he got to the name.

"Ah. The lion."

He removed his glasses and put them back inside his jacket, then folded up the telegram and slipped it into his hip pocket. He had spent years and years blocking his emotions in the presence of another human being, denying the existence of his feelings and their consequences, building a dam that would never be breached. So it was not difficult to suppress them here in front of his wife. In any case, he had wept the night before, in private, for reasons he had not fully accepted at the time, but understood them now. From this moment on then, his grieving would stop and would not be allowed to run its natural course. At least, that was his intention.

"You must come back to the house now."

For the first time Suhani moved but with only the merest twist in order to ease the pressure that the hard stone floor put on her hip bone.

"Would you like to say a prayer first?" she said.

"There'll be plenty of time for that sort of thing. I'll walk with you. Come with me please."

Suhani blinked for the first time. Stephen saw how red her eyelids were, and then caught sight of some snot falling from the end of her nose. She sniffed it up, then wiped away the residue with her sleeve before making a pillow with her hands. "Well, I suppose I have prayed enough for both of us. Not that it ever does any good." It was almost a whisper that Stephen could barely hear, Suhani talking to herself as much as to him. "How do you think I should break the news to Tristan?" she continued. "They were...three peas in a pod. It will break his heart to be the only one left. Can you say that? Three peas in a pod?"

Stephen felt irritated by her frivolous question, but decided for once to hide it. "I've never heard of it." Then he changed tack. "The soldiers need you."

He knew what he was doing, manipulating her kindness, a skill honed over many years, and it seemed to do the trick. She closed her eyes for a few seconds, then shifted her weight in order to stand up and Stephen made a tentative move to help, but thought better of it, quickly withdrawing to watch her rise to her feet on her own.

"They don't need me," she said. "They need their mothers."

They stood together, but apart, both looking straight ahead at the cross on the altar as if they were about to get married. She brushed away the wetness from her face with the palm of her hand, and then wiped her hand on her sari. It was a matter-of-fact gesture, signalling a change of mood.

"There is to be no more post. Tell Mr Franklin to burn it. Burn it all."

He looked at her. She had always been strong willed, and there was a time, long ago, when he could match her, ride the same rearing horse together, which was one of the things that had given them their immutable bond. But all he could do now was parry with weak excuses that sounded pitiful as soon as he uttered them.

"I can't do that. You're being ridiculous. How are we supposed to..." but she had already turned to walk away down the aisle, further diminishing him.

She called over her shoulder, "Burn it."

"But what about my work? The house? It would be quite impossible...Letters from Celandine...Letters from...Life must go on."

He knew it was those last four words that made Suhani stop and turn back to face him in an irrational rage he had never in his life seen from her before. Her face turned purple and her veins bulged inside her neck like worms trapped under her skin, and she screamed so loudly there was no room in the church for its own echo.

"Burn it! Burn it! Burn it!"

In the silence that followed he finally understood her madness. If there was no post, Tristan would be trapped between two worlds, between the living and the dying, forever returning from the front. Death's emissary could be held at bay, and there would always be hope.

14

Hannah stretched up to the gun cabinet, not for the guns but for bottles of saline and morphine. She grimaced – guns and medicines, side by side, they seemed to sum up the whole of the war. Mrs Harkness had suggested the cabinet in the hallway of Tendring as the most convenient place to store the medicines, the guns themselves taking up little space. Hannah imagined Major Harkness would disapprove of the appropriation, and she hoped he hadn't noticed on his way out to work. She examined one of the bottles of morphine and saw it was already almost empty, but she wasn't the only one administering medicine so thought nothing more of it, except that perhaps the gun cabinet ought really to be locked.

As she placed the medical provisions on a metal tray that was balanced precariously on the small rosewood table beneath the cabinet, she said, "It's a fortnight mechanism, so we only need to wind it up once every two weeks. We switch off the chimes just after six o'clock every evening."

Gabriel was standing in front of the grandfather clock, turning its key.

"And on again just after quarter past six in the morning. Otherwise they go awry. Would you like to do that for me?"

Gabriel looked sceptical, but nodded. Hannah took a sideways step to be beside him and pointed to the chiming pin that was on the right side of the clock face, embedded within the Roman numeral number three.

"Well, it's quarter past six. Go on."

He reached to push up the chiming pin and the clock duly struck the quarter hour. He briefly smiled at Hannah, who saw the glimmer of an uncomplicated human being behind his troubled façade, though it only lasted a second before he turned to walk off towards the open front door, as if their conversation had never happened. Hannah followed, sensing she might be the person best able to help him re-enter the world, and went to stand next to him in the open doorway to look out across the lawn.

Jack was there at his table as usual, a blanket round his shoulders to protect him from the nip in the early morning air, hunched over his chessboard. He'd got there unaided, and Hannah's suspicions were once again raised about the way Jack always seemed to be more mobile when no one was looking, his injury varying according to circumstances. He lifted his head to wink at her, which initially she took to be his way of saying good morning, but he lingered too long and without the smile that usually accompanied his wink, as if he was afraid she could read his mind. Finally he looked back down to scrutinise his chess pieces.

Hannah put her arm through Gabriel's. She sensed him recoiling, and he looked at her as if she was the one who was mad, but she held on until she could feel the muscles in his arm relax. It was like training an abused dog – in fact, she thought, with a pang of sadness, that was exactly what she was doing.

The silence between the three of them, on the lawns of Tendring, seemed important somehow, the war a million miles away. Sometimes, with the wind in the right direction, it was possible to hear the shelling from France, the bass drum of death, soft blows of carnage echoing across the channel. But today the air was still, and Hannah wondered if right now it was as peaceful over there in the trenches as it was here on an English lawn. She wanted to ask Jack about it, how much time was spent fighting and how much waiting, but now was not the right moment. The point of the silence was not the questions it raised, but the answers it gave.

Just as Hannah was beginning to wonder how to break the spell, what excuse she might find to start speaking – a call to breakfast, perhaps – she saw two figures turn the corner at the bottom of the drive. Hannah should have instantly recognised them but she was blinded by their unexpected arrival, it being in the wrong place at the wrong time. Major Harkness should have been walking away from the house at this hour of the morning, not towards it, and Mrs Harkness should have been at her desk in the drawing room, or, as she more often chose to do these days, in the kitchen helping out. So although it was obvious who they were, Hannah took several seconds to decide she wasn't dreaming them. Their pace was measured, Stephen a yard ahead of Suhani. He was slowed by his limp, which seemed more pronounced than usual, whereas the force that pulled from behind Suhani was invisible, as if she were walking uphill on the perfectly flat lawn. It felt suddenly wrong for Hannah and her two patients to be there, an unwelcome welcoming party, so she tugged gently at Gabriel's arm. "Come on," she said. "Breakfast." But before she turned, and even at this distance, Hannah caught Suhani's eye and felt pushed away by it. There was more glancing from one to the other – Stephen stared at Hannah across the outstretched lawn, Suhani glanced up at her husband, even Jack had looked up from his chessboard to see what was going on, and Hannah felt they were all sharing an unspoken secret. She thought of hers, the crippled Zeppelin, and the figure on the lawn in the dark. What made her eventually able to turn was seeing Stephen stop momentarily to rub his hip, and she pulled once more at Gabriel's arm to take him back into the house.

"Well, my dear. I have to go to work. In fact I am late now."

Stephen was standing by Suhani's bedroom window, looking out through the open curtains that allowed sunlight to fill the room like fog. She lay on her bed, curled up on her side with her knees almost touching her chin, the same pose in which he had found her earlier at the foot of the altar. Her stillness made her seem untouchable, which came as something of a relief to him. When she finally replied, her voice sounded flat and hoarse, sore from screaming.

"Of course."

"Will you be all right?"

"There is plenty to occupy me," she said, though Stephen wasn't sure she meant it. If anything, it sounded like she would never move again.

"Are you sure?"

"Thank you for your concern, Stephen."

He took a step towards the door, which meant he could no longer see Suhani's face. He dug deep into his army training. They had taught him that being practical and matter-of-fact would help to ease your comrade's anxiety. In any case, he had no other way of dealing with it, incapable of showing any sympathy. "I will speak to Mr. Franklin on the way."

But there was no reply, no stirring of her muscles. For a moment he wasn't even sure if she was breathing and he had to squint to see across the room in order to check. There was no option for him but to continue, though with each hesitation he wished he could stop.

"About the post that is...and I thought I would drop in on the Randolph's...on the way home. To get things...going...organised, I mean. I know it's very soon but...we must...the village will..."

She filled in the final gap: "...expect it."

He waited for his untimely suggestion to dissipate into the air, even raised his head to make way for it, but then stupidly tried to justify all that had gone before, which only made things worse. "No point hanging about."

"No. You must go to work, Stephen."

He wanted to wish her a good day, to sign the moment off neatly with a full stop, a clean cut, but all the words he could think of struck him as hopelessly inept. So he simply slipped out of the room. It seemed he couldn't even reach out to her with his usual form of connecting, that of anger, his heart being too cold for that now. All he could do was close the door behind him as quietly as possible. Standing outside her bedroom door he imagined for a moment he was dead, pictured his own funeral, and wondered who might turn up.

Hannah took her second tray of medicines and bandages through to the library. She walked past the unoccupied berths of Jack and Gabriel and headed towards Christopher's shrouded bed. She balanced the tray on one hand and pulled back one of the hanging sheets with the other.

"Oh."

Her first thought was that he had taken himself off to the toilet, but surely she would have seen him pass her in the hallway. Besides, he would have needed to ask for help. She put the tray down and walked across to the nearest window to see if he was in the garden. She knew Gabriel had gone back outside to sit with Jack, so perhaps Christopher had joined them. But there was no sign of him.

Then for the second time she jumped, this time to the sound of a voice.

"What time is the first post?"

Stephen was standing in the doorway of the library. Hannah felt as if she had been caught unawares and made to feel guilty about it, an effect he often had on her. It made her independent Irish blood boil – only an Englishman could create such a malignant feeling inside her without even trying.

"About seven, sir."

He pulled out his pocket-watch to check the time, then walked over to stand next to her, unnaturally close. His half-whispered words made her feel like a co-conspirator, though in what plots and schemes she didn't yet know.

"At a quarter-to-seven I would like you to go and intercept the postboy on the Eagley Road. Tell him that today and at all times in the future he must deliver to the back door, via the rose garden, approaching the house through Sandy Woods. Do you know the path?"

"Yes sir."

"Then this morning you can show him. Tell him to enter the kitchen without knocking and to give the post to you or Phoebe. Put everything in my office. Mrs Harkness is not to be troubled. Can I trust you to do that please?"

"Yes sir."

He slipped his pocket watch back into his waistcoat pocket. "Thank you." Then he walked off and was in the doorway of the library before he stopped again to face her. "By the way, I suppose you should know that we have had some bad news. I'd be grateful if you could keep an eye on Mrs Harkness. She's not taken it well." He turned again to leave but Hannah interrupted his departure with a simple word, though it contained within it a much more searching question.

"Sir?"

She was a servant but no fool, she knew he would have to answer. But she jumped for the third time when he snapped the conversation shut.

"Edward."

Freddie was pumping up his back tyre. George stood over him, hovering, hands on hips like a school teacher, waiting for Freddie to finish.

"Bloody Zeppelin. Get what they deserve, droppin' their bombs on women and children. Have you got that telegram?"

For a split second Freddie had to think what he meant before realising George was referring to the telegram he had already delivered the night before. He stopped pumping but kept his eyes fixed on the tyre. He would have to lie.

"Yes sir."

He feared his hesitation would be enough to expose him, but George appeared to put it down to Freddie's reticence. It was, after all, bad news that would be difficult to deliver.

"You'll get used to it lad."

Freddie went back to pumping the tyre and felt he had learnt something new: it was easy to lie if you said what people expected to hear.

This time, the downhill seemed less inviting as Freddie stroked the graze on his head. The wound was healing with a dry, rough surface that felt like an old brick, and he no longer had a headache, but he had other reasons to feel dizzy, having managed perhaps two hours of erratic sleep, and no breakfast. When he had said to his mother he didn't want any, she had told him not to be silly, but didn't pursue it further. He was glad she couldn't see his graze or his exhausted eyes, though he could never tell for sure that she didn't know what she couldn't see. Sometimes he felt she knew everything, other times he wanted to tell her, but always the consequence of his needs was silence. These days they barely breathed the same air. He wished it was otherwise and wondered if she did too.

Most of all, however, his stomach churned at the prospect of returning to Tendring so soon after his visit the night before. When George had handed him more letters addressed to Mr Harkness his heart had sunk. Perhaps he would be able to hand them over to one of the servants and make a quick escape. What would the place be like? Would everyone be weeping, prowling the grounds like miserable ghosts? Would Mr Harkness be full of rage that he had not been told the whole truth when he encountered Freddie on the road last night? Would Freddie hear Mrs Harkness wailing inside the house? When he started to free-wheel his way down the incline between the hedgerows, he did so with heavily applied brakes, not only to make it safer than the day before but also to extend the journey time and delay his arrival.

At the bottom of the incline the road levelled out and Freddie began to pedal, passing the orchard on his left and the rogue apple tree on his right. He thought about stopping but in the end decided there was no point making himself late for the rest of his round, it would only make things worse. He continued cycling along the Eagley Road whilst going back and forth in his head, stopping and starting, his mind unable to persuade his legs to stop, when he saw a figure standing at the crossroads fifty yards ahead. It was an odd place for someone to stand.

As Freddie approached, he thought the girl must have heard the soft gravelly noise that his tyres made on the road because she looked up and turned towards him, then took a step into the road as if she wanted to block his way. He was a few yards nearer when he realised that was what she was doing, raising her hand in order to bring him to a stop.

He recognised her face, he must have seen her in the village, although initially he couldn't place her more precisely than that. But she was obviously a servant and he quickly put two and two together. Tendring. She was from the house. Then he became gloomily suspicious that this rendezvous was to do with the night before, and cautiously he pulled up, still several yards away.

"Are you on your way to Tendring?" she said.

At first, Freddie was so intrigued by her lilting Irish accent that he didn't properly hear what she had said. Suhani, Christopher, and now this one, they all talked funny at Tendring.

"Beg your pardon?"

"Are you on your way to Tendring?"

"Yes miss."

She smiled at him. "Follow me."

"Where to?" he said, perhaps too abruptly, but her bossiness was beginning to aggravate him.

"A different route. Same destination. I'll explain on the way. What's your name now?"

She had already set off, so Freddie had no choice but to follow. It was more awkward to push his bike than to ride it, which added to his irritation.

"Freddie Lovegrove. Where are we going?"

"Tendring, I told you, but a different way. Through Sandy Woods. Mrs Harkness is not to be disturbed today or for the foreseeable future. You will do this every day, for every delivery, whenever it is necessary."

"But..." He stopped pushing his bike. "I haven't got time for that, miss."

"Oh," she said, her Irish accent swinging happily in the air, "you've no choice and make no mistake. You'll make time. You'll hand over each and every delivery to me or Phoebe, or Mr Harkness if he's there."

And so it continued, off and on, for twenty minutes, Freddie asking questions or raising objections, and Hannah batting them all away. For a while she talked about Ireland but Freddie didn't really take it in, more concerned about this annoying delay and the effect it might have on his job.

"Telegrams have to be handed to the addressee, it's the law," pleaded Freddie.

"Mr Harkness is the law as far as you're concerned. Leave your bike here. It gets narrow through the woods."

They had reached the edge of Sandy Woods and Freddie was grateful to be able to park his bike, which he leant against a sign that said *Private*. Hannah opened a small rusty iron gate and led the way along a path that was clear to begin with but became increasingly choked with nettles and brambles.

Ever since his mother had first let him out alone at the age of five, Freddie had explored every coppice and woodland in Eagley, but because it was private property he had only been to Sandy Woods once. Until two days ago, it was the closest he'd been to the hidden curiosity of Tendring. He had only vague memories of the woods, but he thought the path was surely more overgrown now. Pushing the brambles aside, he pretended he was hacking his way through the rainforests of Ceylon in his Boy's Own. The adventure was getting the better of him.

"What's Ireland like?"

"Well, it's true, it does rain a lot. But I miss my family. Still, you go where the work is, don't you now."

The path itself was becoming easier as it headed up towards a small ridge, though there was less light as the canopy of branches thickened overhead.

"I'm sorry you miss your family."

"Well, half of them have gone to America now to be sure. So it doesn't matter where I post myself to."

"America?" Freddie's ears pricked up. "How much does it cost to go to America?"

"Oh, I don't know. Depends how you go and who you know. I fancy it's not expensive if you rough it."

They were nearly at the edge of the ridge and Hannah turned to offer Freddie a hand.

"I'm fine, miss, thank you," but as soon as he had said it he tripped over an exposed root and had to put his hands out to soften his fall. Hannah leant down to help him up, but again he rejected her advances. "I'm all right." Boys needed no help from girls in the jungle.

Freddie stood up straight and was about to set off again when something caught his eye, a shimmer that initially made no sense, a stroke of colour, a flash of pale blue in the trees that didn't belong there. The ridge fell away into a dip, a bowl-shaped hollow, and a childhood memory suddenly returned to him, a rope tied to the highest tree from which you could swing for an entire summer. Then he worked out what the pale blue was: pyjamas, worn by a body hanging by its neck from an outstretched branch.

Hannah saw Freddie's reaction and immediately turned to see what it was that had drained the blood from his face.

"Holy Mother of God."

They both looked at the body for several seconds. The branch it was hanging from creaked, and the corpse was turning slowly a few degrees back and forth, though with its back to them it was impossible to see the face. Freddie felt as though he was watching a magic trick at the Margate Theatre Royal, that the figure would swing round and take a bow and the audience would break into laughter and applause. But it just hung there like a pheasant in the larder. It was then that he noticed the man, for it was a man, had soiled himself. It was a blessing not to be able to see his face, and nor was it necessary: his identity was clear, the standard issue pyjamas, the bare feet, and most conspicuously of all the empty sleeves that hung loosely down by the sides of him where his hands should have been. Freddie prayed without words for it to be otherwise and he stared at Hannah for some solution, but she was elsewhere, thinking fast, a step ahead, working out what to do next.

"Go and get the police. I'll go back to the house."

15

The windows look much better for a lick of Joe's paint.

Now he tends the garden for me, says I don't have the time, some of the work is heavy, and I suppose he is right. I'm grateful to him, the garden is neater than it's ever been. And yet I feel a kind of resentment, as though the house is moving on, as if wood and nails and paint could be unfaithful! As if removing weeds could erase the past.

Of course, Christopher always said a garden should be left to follow its own course, that it should be part of nature, not separated from it, and I would laugh back saying that was just the excuse of an unenthusiastic gardener. He would concede with one of his disarming smiles – a smile which I attempt, and fail, to re-imagine now as I look up at the gleaming white window frames and the weedless garden. My house – my life – slowly contaminated by purity, destroyed by perfection. You see, it's the flaws that I remember, the fleck of green in the brown iris of his left eye, the loose joints in his hands and subtly squashed fingertips from the constant playing of the piano, the crooked tooth that he would allow no one else to see; the tiny birthmark on the top of his right hand, about which he had a sweet, childlike self-consciousness.

When we grow old, it will be only the imperfections that are left, and that's why, I suppose, I have begun to catalogue them now.

So I wonder how long it will be before I step outside with my paint-scraper and start scratching the fresh paint off the window frames. Will I ever have the courage? But then, there's nothing to be gained from hurting Joe, is there. Above all else, Christopher taught me kindness. But it is not easy, and sometimes I'm angry at him for leaving me here alone, to watch the never-ending tides come and go, and the cliffs fall into the sea.

16

Three days had passed since Hannah had knocked on Suhani's door with the news about Christopher. Suhani had been unable to respond. It should have been a shock, but her own grief did not allow room for any more of it and the circumstances of Christopher's death left her unmoved, though guiltily so. It was true she had bonded with him over the one day of his stay at Tendring, one cleansing of his wounds, but she didn't know him, having merely chanced upon the soldier from Nova Scotia. Hospitals were for dying as much as anything; best not to get attached. Mourning him was for others. She thought of his wife, therefore, and continued to do so for three days and nights until finally she sat down, still in her room, still in her sari, and wrote a letter to Mrs Ellis. She was sorry she didn't know her first name.

"Dear Mrs Ellis, it is with much regret that I write to inform you of the passing of your husband in the early hours of Wednesday the 5th of July."

Suhani paused. That was the easy part. Immediately she wished she hadn't started it, and the more she thought about what to write the more difficult it became. But she had to find a way to put a human voice behind the official army report, the kind of voice Suhani herself had desperately missed not only three days earlier but also a year before that. In any case, there had been no contact from the Canadian Army, as if they'd forgotten about him, or lost him in a bureaucratic fog where wounded Canadian soldiers had been spread too thinly across the whole of Kent, so it was her duty to write. Returning her pen to the paper she decided to allow the words to appear of their own volition.

"Christopher was a kind and generous man who, in his brief time here, made a lasting impression on all of us at Tendring House. He spoke very affectionately of you, Mrs Ellis. Indeed, I can say that he loved you very much. It is a rare gift and although I am deeply sorry you had so little time to share it, please be comforted to know that you will surely be loved from heaven."

Suhani closed her eyes for a moment, hoping that what she was about to write next would not, on this occasion, rise with the sun.

"Christopher was brought here for injuries sustained in France, but he died peacefully in his sleep and was in no pain. If you can find any comfort from it, please know that Christopher did not die alone and that I held his hand as he passed away. I will write again to let you know where Christopher's body will be buried. Your husband's personal belongings will be forwarded to you at the earliest opportunity.

With deepest sympathy, Suhani Harkness, Tendring, Eagley, Kent."

She read the letter through. Mrs Ellis did not need the truth. Christopher had made that decision himself. He had died, and that was truth enough.

Suhani had not eaten for three days and had actually drunk water from the jug that was meant for washing. The thin layer of scum that had accumulated on the water's surface wouldn't have put her off even if she'd noticed it. There had been several knocks on her door from Stephen, from Hannah, and once even from Phoebe, but she had either ignored them or made it clear she was content to be incarcerated in her bedroom. On the first day Inspector Roper had also come knocking, but Suhani didn't answer and to her relief he did not persist.

She would listen out for the house to become silent before escaping across the hallway to go to the bathroom. No one saw her and she found some comfort in her primitive existence. For the most part she was looking out of her window, or sitting on her bed, or sleeping. At one point she had picked up a book, but to read it felt pointless and she didn't even open the cover. Half the time she wept as if she would never stop, for the rest of it she was empty of tears, and almost dead.

However, she had no address for her letter to Christopher's wife, which meant at some point she would have to leave her room properly. And so for the first time in three days she walked down the stairs towards the library.

Hannah and Phoebe were both there. Suhani had no idea of the time, but it looked like lunch had been served and empty plates were being collected from Jack and Gabriel who were sitting upright in their beds.

"Hannah, where is Christopher's paperwork?"

Her first proper words for three days brought everyone to a standstill. She dragged her fingers through her tangled hair in an attempt to tidy it, and looked down at her bare feet, almost as if she were not interested in an answer to her question.

"They took it away with the body, ma'am," said Hannah.

"Oh yes. I suppose they would." She held out the letter for Anne. "I saw the address but I didn't take it in."

Everyone was looking at her, Hannah, Phoebe, Jack, even Gabriel, but no one wanted to move or speak, so in the end Suhani broke the silence. "Did Mr Harkness stop the post?"

Hannah hesitated. "Yes ma'am."

"Perhaps I was a little hasty." She became resigned to not posting her letter. Nothing mattered to her, nothing would relieve her desolation. What difference would this letter actually make? How would it help with the pain? She stared into space, almost trance-like, exhausted. But then she had an idea and addressed Hannah with it.

"Does Freddie deliver to Celandine Hall do you think?"

"That'd be too far I expect, ma'am."

It was another knock back, though without any other direction to go she decided to persevere.

"Perhaps he could make an exception. They will have the address there don't you think?"

"I imagine so ma'am."

"Could you catch Freddie somewhere on the Eagley Road?"

"He doesn't come this way, does he ma'am. What with the post stopped and everything."

Suhani sensed Hannah was lying, wasn't sure why, but had no desire to investigate further. "No. Of course." She opened the sheet of writing paper and then folded it again as she considered one final option. She held it out for Hannah to take.

"Please, take this to the Post Office with a blank envelope. Tell Freddie to go to Celandine Hall, tell him to ask for Christopher's address and then post this letter as soon as possible to Mrs Ellis." Then she pointed to the writing desk. "And take tuppence ha'penny for the stamp."

Hannah handed the dinner plates she had been holding to Phoebe and took the letter from Suhani's outstretched hand. "Very well ma'am."

In those same three days Freddie had buried himself in his work. The police had insisted he should go back to his job and not mention the body to anyone until there was time for them to question him. So, in a daze, he carried on delivering the post and didn't even mention the gruesome discovery to his mother, though in any case he wasn't sure he wanted to. It would have invoked a long conversation, which he wasn't ready to have. He felt a dull but constant sickness from what he had seen in the woods, wasn't able to concentrate, and on several occasions couldn't remember posting any letters at all, even though he knew he had done because his bag had got lighter, and then it was empty. He went from house to house without thinking or reacting. At least none of the news he delivered was bad, as far as he could tell.

So he did as he was told and kept quiet about his discovery. At first it weighed heavily on him, but keeping quiet about Christopher became easier as time wore on and he began to feel like a cog in a celestial mechanism, turning because everyone else did, the gears of silence running smoothly, and never needing winding up. He was, at least, no longer an outsider.

But there was one delivery that he dreaded, a run-of-the-mill letter addressed to Mr Harkness, which meant he would have to go through Sandy Woods again. The last three days had got progressively worse, the horror increasing with each visit. He toyed with the idea of saving this latest delivery until tomorrow in order to postpone at least one trip today, but if the letter was important he might get caught out, even lose his job.

He leant his bike against the gate of Sandy Woods and began to pick his way through the overgrown path. He had already trampled it down twice with his two deliveries yesterday but it seemed to have sprung up again, renewed, wilder, more prickly, annoying. As he walked up the slight incline to the ridge he once again had the grim, recurring fantasy that another body would be hanging from the tree. Of course there was nothing. Indeed, by now there was no evidence at all of Christopher's final moments, except perhaps a slash of exposed white wood on the branch where a saw had been used to cut through the rope. There were birds singing and a benign breeze ruffled the leaves above his head. To his surprise, he suddenly felt peaceful. The dread had diminished, was almost gone. Whatever Christopher had done, whatever his reasons, Freddie felt that some of the words and phrases in Christopher's letter to Anne had taken on a new, if mysterious, meaning. *Get the piano tuned every six months won't you...*

As he was looking up at the branch he thought he heard the crack of a twig. Someone was approaching. The noise made him shiver and triggered a startled flock of wood pigeons. Two unrelated thoughts occurred to him almost simultaneously, notions he should have had three days earlier but had been suppressed by the foggy gloom of his depression. First, his face filled with hot blood when he suddenly remembered he hadn't posted Christopher's original letter; it was still under the blotter, waiting. Second, it had not occurred to him until now that it was impossible for a man with no hands to hang himself.

It had, however, occurred instantly to Inspector Roper. He had spent three days thinking about it, off and on, but mostly off as he and his men had been distracted by the Zeppelin crash in Little Risborough, six miles west of Eagley. Eighteen charred bodies had been found, but there were rumours of an escapee, someone jumping clear before the airship hit the ground. Whether that was true or not, the site needed securing and sightseers kept away. The reasons behind the hanging in Sandy Woods receded in his mind as the mangled flying machine took up both his mental and staffing resources. And it was the bigger story.

On the day they'd discovered the body, there had been no one much to question. He had been forewarned by one of the servants that Suhani was grieving and not to be disturbed, though he did try knocking on her bedroom door simply to see how she was. She was the wife of his Masonic friend and despite their age difference and her Indian aloofness he had grown quite fond of her, so it seemed only right to check on her. But there was no reply. He would speak to her later, and to her husband too, though Stephen would certainly know nothing.

On the way out of Tendring he had stopped to ask Jack if he had seen anything untoward, but he had shrugged, "No sir, nothin'." He had asked Gabriel the same question, but Roper couldn't understand his reply. He thought he heard the word pineapple, though obviously it couldn't have been. He'd left in a hurry with Constable Waveney, as they were already running late to get to Little Risborough. The whole episode had been a distraction, less serious in his mind than it ought to have been.

Nevertheless, a man with no hands cannot hang himself. It niggled him at the time and it niggled him now.

For three days Hannah found herself running the household, with Suhani having locked herself away. The two remaining soldiers needed meals prepared for them but they chose to wash themselves and Jack even changed his own bandages. With Christopher gone, it became more of a hotel than a hospital.

But she was distressed by Suhani's behaviour. Hannah was leaving trays of food outside her room three times a day but they were never taken in. She would tap on the door and sometimes get a muffled reply of gratitude, but more often silence, which Hannah presumed was Suhani sleeping.

From the very beginning their bond had been strong. They were in many ways similar personalities with a certain disdain for rules and authority and their respect for each other was not so much as mistress and servant but more as allies, so Hannah was concerned that Suhani was not able to talk to her now. All the same she did not press her. There was a time for talking and a time for distance.

Food and other provisions needed to be ordered, so she had to write notes to the shops in town who would deliver the same day. Freddie had collected twice yesterday, coming to the back door and into the kitchen. She handed him her notes, he handed her his post and that was that. Apart from saying good morning, how are you today, they didn't speak.

But something troubled Hannah during those three hot, becalming days at Tendring. The police had asked her nothing about Christopher, indeed their only question on the first day was to ask her for Suhani's whereabouts. They seemed to be in a hurry and she felt invisible. The Inspector's pompous and superior attitude rubbed her up the wrong way, but that was the English for you. For each of the three days she expected the police to return to ask questions, but they never did.

And then she heard a noise from upstairs. Hannah had lived at Tendring long enough to know the sound of each individual door and their place in the house so even though she was in the library where she and Phoebe were collecting the detritus from lunch, she was almost certain that Suhani had opened her bedroom door. Initially Hannah wanted to step into the hallway to greet her, but it would have been wrong to address her with a handful of dirty plates, so she waited in the hope that Suhani would come down into the library.

When she did, what Hannah saw was a shock. Suhani's long hair would always be tied back during the day, but now it hung down, unbrushed, wild and slept-in. The kohl around her eyes had run and greyed her cheeks. She also had nothing on her feet, which made her look like a child disorientated from a night's sleep, still only half awake. Suhani put her hand up to her hair and stroked it, before asking incongruous questions about Christopher's paperwork, which Hannah answered as best she could. When Suhani then asked about the post, about whether Stephen had stopped it, Hannah felt that neither the lie nor the truth would suffice, but, after a moment's hesitation, she took the easier path and said that he had.

There was an aura around Suhani that made her look completely alone and Hannah wanted to take her hand to comfort her, but in present company that was impossible. In any case she was still holding the plates. So all she could do was to continue to answer Suhani's questions, which revolved around trying to obtain Christopher's address in Nova Scotia. Finally, with all other options exhausted, Suhani had come up with a convoluted plan for Hannah to take the letter to the Post Office with a blank envelope, ask Freddie to go to Celandine Hall to obtain the address, and then for him to post it. Hannah handed the dinner plates she had been holding to Phoebe and took the letter from Suhani's outstretched hand.

"Very well ma'am."

In agreeing to it, Hannah had needed to lie, knowing that in fact she would instead be intercepting Freddie on his latest back-door delivery, which was due in less than half-an-hour. She regretted the deceit, but the truth was too complicated. Suhani went back upstairs to her room and Hannah gave instructions to Phoebe to finish tidying up.

Despite the heat, Hannah wore her shawl to step out of the house, anything less would have not been respectable. Holding the letter and a blank envelope, and with three coins jangling in her front pocket, she went out of the front door, heading in what was the wrong direction for Sandy Woods, down the drive, in case she was seen. Suhani might be looking from her bedroom window. Only after she had passed the stone eagles did she take a sharp turn left that would take her back round the rear of the house and then through the meadows to rejoin Freddie's new route, though in the opposite direction. A path of trampled grass had been created by Freddie's previous visits and Hannah followed it as quickly as she could, almost running. It was none of her business what was in the letter, and there had been enough deception between her and Suhani for one day; but for a second she was tempted to look.

She was glad, then, that she was in too much of a hurry to stop and read it, instead climbing over the stile that took her into the trees and down into the shadows.

There seemed to be more birdsong than usual, a sound she would more normally associate with daybreak or dusk. It was as though they were watching her, as if the birds were discussing her movements. She knew, however, that what she was really feeling was a foreboding as she approached the hollow – the tree, the branch, the rope, the body, all lining up in her imagination – and coming from the other direction she would now see Christopher's swollen, open-mouthed face. But she was being silly, there would be no body – she had stood as part of a small guard of honour when Christopher's shrouded corpse had been placed in the back of the ambulance and driven away. Nature would already be claiming back its land and space, she thought, and there was nothing to fear. Perhaps this was why the birds were so full-throated. She heard a breeze blow through the upper branches as she picked her way further into the woods.

She was perhaps a minute away from the hollow when she stepped on a dead branch on the ground, dry and brittle, with a crack that reverberated through the trees. A distressed flock of wood pigeons flapped their way through the branches, slapping their wings against the leaves.

The snap of the branch beneath her foot had caused some pain and she limped for a few steps to walk it off. Once again the limping figure slipping across the lawn three nights ago stirred her mind's eye. He had come from the direction of the copse, not Sandy Woods. She tried to make connections and disentangled them again. When the police came back, if they ever did, she would tell them. But what? It was not so much a thought as a feeling, unarticulated, residing deep in her gut, and it disappeared before it had a chance to fully form further up in her consciousness. In any case, something had distracted her.

Freddie was standing in the hollow, looking up at the branch from which Christopher had twisted and swayed, when he saw Hannah at the very same moment she spotted him. He watched her warily as she approached and came to a stop by his side.

"Mrs Harkness would like you to go to Celandine Hall." She held out the letter and the envelope for Freddie to take, but he didn't move.

"That's miles. I don't even know the way."

"Mrs Harkness would like you to do it."

"I haven't got time, miss."

"It's important."

"Every letter is important, miss." He thought he'd made a good point, like a devastating chess move, but Hannah countered with a change of tone, one he would have to take more seriously.

"Please, Freddie."

And so he knew at some point he would have to give in, though he battled on for a moment longer to save face.

"I don't know where it is. I don't know how to get there." It wasn't true, he had a good idea where Celandine Hall was.

"Eagley Road, then Storrington Road. It's signposted for goodness sake."

"Why doesn't she just post it?"

"She doesn't have the address. That's the whole point. When you get there ask for Christopher's address. Mrs Harkness thinks they will have it there." She pointed at the envelope. "Write Mrs Ellis followed by the address you've obtained. Then make sure to seal it up and post it."

Freddie had run out of excuses and became resigned to visiting Celandine Hall; then he began to look forward to it. It was true the journey would make him very late on his rounds, but he decided it was an interesting adventure, which he felt would perk him up. Then something else occurred to him, a new twist, a plot so obvious he had only just seen it. He took the letter and envelope from her, keeping the plan to himself.

"All right."

"Oh." She seemed surprised by his sudden capitulation. "Thank you."

"What about the stamp?"

Hannah put her hands in her front pocket, removed three coins and handed them to Freddie. "Here."

Freddie put the coins in his pouch along with the letter. He kept his hand inside it in order to remove another letter, the one for Stephen Harkness.

"You might as well take this, miss, save me a bit of time."

She took it from him. "I hope this doesn't make you late."

"I'll be all right."

He would be. What Hannah didn't know was that Freddie had worked out why he wouldn't need to go to Celandine Hall at all.

On the first of the three days, Stephen Harkness had managed to hide his grief, not least from himself, by diving into the practicalities of life and work. He had, as promised, called in on Randolph's Undertakers to give them the details of Edward's death. There would be no corpse, but there would still need to be a funeral service. And at some point the monument would need updating. He had not, however, fulfilled his other promise to go and see Mr Franklin at the Post Office. As the manager of the Milbridge Munitions Factory and as a Mason – Worshipful Master elect – he needed deliveries of post to continue. Letters for him were almost always important. It was unfortunate having to send

Freddie through Sandy Woods, the long detour must be objectionable, but it was the only solution for now.

When he had returned home late that evening, he had gone straight into the library, dismissed Hannah as he had done the night before and again ended up talking with Jack in the semi-darkness, surrounded by beds and books.

"Everything all right?"

Jack was sitting up in bed, tapping the bedstead above his head with his fingernail, as if he hadn't moved from the previous night.

"I'm all right. Others not so much." Jack nodded across the way. "Empty bed now."

They stared at each other. Stephen was unsure what to say next, but knew it needed to be words that sounded kind.

"I heard. That's why I asked. I'm sorry." It was too sympathetic. He pulled back. "But I can't say I'm surprised."

"How did yer hear?"

"The police telephoned me at work."

"He hung hisself, poor bugger."

Stephen remained impassive, trying to judge Jack's mood and giving himself time to formulate his next question. "How did he manage that?"

"Good question. The police'll work it out. Once they've talked to everyone."

"Let's hope so. I'm sorry, bad luck, I know he was your friend."

"Yeah I suppose he was." Jack's voice cracked and he swallowed hard. "Didn't have a single thing in common 'cept an enemy, but we just got on somehow. Understood each other without using any fancy words, if you know what I mean."

"Well I'm very sorry." The repetition sounded vacuous to both of them.

"It's for the best, don't yer think?" Jack turned his head to look across at the sleeping Gabriel. "Anyways, I got other friends." It was a cruel, dispassionate postscript, but Stephen knew that was what soldiers did, shrouding their grief in black humour and moving their affection on to the next convenient recipient, like an abandoned dog looking for a new family.

It seemed like each was waiting for the other to say something more, even if it was only goodnight, but in the end the silence won out, broken only by the creak of a bed as Gabriel turned over in his sleep at the far end of the library. Instead, the two men nodded at each other, neither knowing quite what they meant by it, except an indication they were sharing an unspoken covenant, an agreement to remain silent, a secret they both had knowledge of and yet were keeping from one another.

There was nothing left for Stephen to do but leave the library and go upstairs. There was candlelight coming from under Suhani's bedroom door, but he ignored it and went to bed. He felt he was neither welcome nor needed in his own house.

On the following day Stephen left for work so early and came home so late he wondered why he didn't just sleep at the munitions factory and be done with it. So on the third day, that was what he did.

It was five o'clock and Freddie had finished his rounds early. He leant his bike against the outside wall of the Post Office next to the pillar box and went inside, where he found George asleep. It seemed he slept increasingly often as Freddie learnt more of the job, which made him wonder what George did all day. He considered the possibility that he, Freddie, was not so much an assistant as a replacement. Everything George had taught him had been a shortcut, a bending of the rules if not a downright breaking of them, despite the fact he was always stressing their importance. There's a war on. That familiar excuse for sloppiness.

How George dealt with people coming into the shop was a mystery. Presumably he had developed the technique of both waking and going back to sleep at the drop of a hat, or the ring of a bell. So Freddie crept in, making sure not to wake his boss so he could just get on with his job.

Standing at the sorting counter, Freddie took out the letter Hannah had given him and the envelope that came with it. Then he lifted the blotter to remove the other letter he had hidden there four days before. Had he really forgotten it? Certainly, he had not remembered it, but that didn't quite feel like the same thing. It had been more of a problem to be solved tomorrow, and tomorrow never came. The chances of it being discovered by George were high and yet Freddie had not considered the possibility. To be under the blotter was to be stored in a part of Freddie's memory that he could cover up, choose to forget.

Freddie took Christopher's letter out of its envelope and re-read it. He felt again a surge of pride at the neatness and overall architecture he had instinctively constructed. How clever he was with the pen! But a replacement letter was now at hand, a gift, which presumably contained the truth. Christopher's own letter of deceit was no longer required. There wasn't even any need to write the address on the new envelope because he already had one. The fact that the original had lain there hidden for four days felt, after all, like it had done so for a reason, taking the decision out of his hands.

But he began to feel uncertain, unwilling to cooperate with fate. Even though the promise was with a dead man, the contract was still alive. He was about to put the new letter in the old envelope, and so let the problem solve itself, when he caught sight of the opening salutation, *Dear Mrs Ellis,* followed by the first few words. He looked across at George who slept heavily, so there was no chance of being caught. It wasn't exactly that he intended to read it, but having started it the stone just kept on rolling down the hill. He read the next line. The subjects and objects were kind and comforting, not only their meaning but their rhythm, and he imagined Anne sitting in Nova Scotia, scanning them with a sad smile on her face. There was a neat and conclusive quality about Suhani's text that would enable Anne to grieve comfortably, he thought.

But then he stopped. What was this about Christopher dying peacefully in his sleep and without pain? Freddie saw Christopher hanging in denial by his rope and he gasped out loud at the image, sharper than a dream, as real as the oak counter in front of him, then had to shut his eyes to make the vision go away, for a moment not daring to open them again. His own pulse filled his ears, so loud it felt it might wake George.

Sure enough, George stirred with a snuffle. Perhaps Freddie's gasp had disturbed him and he might have to move more quickly now. He opened his eyes to read the rest of the letter, practicalities about possessions and places of burial, until he had to stop once more. It was a final flourish of deception, a lie that Freddie could not at first understand, and when he did he could not sanction. *If you can find any comfort from it, please know that Christopher did not die alone and that I held his hand as he passed away.* He tried to understand why Mrs Harkness would not tell Anne the truth, and in a way it was obvious. She was being kind. What difference would it make? Sometimes people want to be lied to, she had said that, hadn't she?

Two letters, two different lies. Perhaps he didn't have to decide. But there was no point sending both. They were unlikely to arrive at the same time and he couldn't make up his mind which was the crueller – to deliver despair followed by hope, or the other way round. Then the hollow in the woods came back to him again, a watery apparition where this time the body swung, then started to turn, and Christopher's distorted face mouthed a single word. Please.

George called out in his sleep, some muffled syllable of distress... Ah, perhaps in reality that was what Freddie had heard, not any noise from Christopher. He didn't know which path to choose, which letter to send, so he stalled by deciding, after all, to relinquish responsibility and just follow orders. He copied the address onto the blank envelope and then licked a stamp, which reminded him of the two pennies and the halfpenny in his pouch. Dropping them into the petty cash drawer, each coin made a distinctive metallic clink. He had the odd feeling he was being watched, not by Christopher anymore but by himself, or rather some other Freddie Lovegrove, or some other postboy who was Freddie but went by a different name altogether. And he suspected too that by throwing the coins into the drawer, he was trying to wake George up so that he might be caught.

17

I told my mother it was a bad cold, and I suppose it feels like one, but in truth I know my three days in bed to be a malaise of the heart. Despite the loneliness, I don't want to see anyone. I did rise once, and found myself sitting at the piano, but it is so horribly out of tune that I stopped after a single chord. The thing couldn't have sounded more dismal if I had rung a funeral bell. A cold air blows in through my open bedroom window and the herring gulls squawk their wicked laughter. How I wish I could sleep as soundly as a drunkard. Why won't it come to me? The clock in the living room is ticking so loudly I can hear it as I lie awake in the room next door, and it makes time pass more slowly than ever. I turn to be held in Christopher's arms, to be piano keys under his fingers. Poor, foolish, out-of-tune melody that I am.

Part Two

18

Autumn

Freddie was lying in his bed wondering who on earth could be ringing the bell. It was early but he had already been awake for an hour or more. His curtains were feeble at the best of times, but in autumn the sun's angle warmed his face and roused him more reliably than his alarm clock, which he often left unwound because he preferred to be woken that way. His routine had become second nature, to the extent that on a Sunday George no longer troubled himself to turn up for work at all, knowing Freddie could do everything perfectly well on his own.

And the fact was, with the shop shut on Sundays, the job was not difficult. You collected, and you delivered, and by now he knew where everyone lived, the numbers of houses that had no numbers, the gates that had to be lifted and pushed to be opened, the barking dogs behind letterboxes that demanded a cautious delivery, the people who lived alone and wanted to talk, and how best to avoid them, and those who wanted to avoid Freddie and twitched their curtains as he approached. The post he had delivered over the last two months or so had either been good news or inconsequential, and although he was now enjoying his job, it was also beginning to feel mundane. At least that might mean there would be no more letters with black marks. It was only a village, after all. He wondered if he would reach George Franklin's age and still be delivering the post. It seemed to him that was what everyone else did, the same thing, over and over again, until they stopped at the far end of their lives.

The most challenging thing for Freddie was trying to juggle what was in reality two jobs – the ordinary post, and the telegrams. The station Fly brought the post, usually one bag, first thing in the morning, and the despatch rider would bring telegrams, if there were any, at some point later. Or they would swap times, and sometimes even roles, for no apparent reason, which made things even harder to predict. In any event it made sense to wait so that both could be delivered at the same time, but on the other hand he couldn't wait forever. The despatch rider's arrival times were always different and sometimes she didn't come at all. The Post Office may have been highly efficient on a national level, but Freddie was sometimes amazed it worked locally, or that more post didn't get delayed or lost altogether. His judgement today was that he shouldn't bother to delay. In his experience a delivery of telegrams was less likely on a Sunday, because they were more expensive.

Freddie was feeling unusually sleepy as he lay on his bed looking around his bedroom through half-opened eyes. He glanced up first at his collection of coins: seven piles of twelve pennies each, and one pile of ten halfpennies. Then he scanned his walls and ceiling as he did every morning. It was not pride – that came before a fall, his mother said – but a feeling more akin to saying good morning to old friends. Since borrowing a box of drawing pins from the Post Office he had been able to cover his walls with characters and landscapes copied from his Boy's Own. More recently, having reproduced every picture in the annual, he had taken to replicating pages from the old atlas Mrs Mawby had given him and in which he had not until now taken much interest. Having run out of wall space he'd pinned a copy of every continent into the lime mortar above his head as well as several individual countries. It was only when he'd sketched the North American continent that he had properly found out where Nova Scotia was. He'd drawn in the shipping lanes too, and noticed with some unspecified excitement that Nova Scotia was a stopping-off point to New York. In the atlas it had been coloured a pale pink, but Freddie had left it as white, a reflection of the music of its name, *Nova Scotia,* which sounded cold and desolate. As he saw it in his mind's eye, he couldn't imagine anyone actually living there, though he knew that at least one person did, since he had sent a letter to them.

A letter. One of two. Had he sent the right one? The question had nagged at him for weeks. No one mentioned Christopher anymore. The haunting circumstances of his death continuing to torment Freddie whilst everyone else seemed to have forgotten about it, including the police. The job of postboy may have become mundane, but the responsibility of it made the pedals of his bike increasingly hard to turn.

As he traced the coastline of Nova Scotia with his eyes, he carried on listening to the church bell. Why was it being rung so very early in the morning? Who goes to church at half-past five? Surely someone had made a mistake. It was only when he closed his eyes again and felt the creeping weight of sleep return that something forced him out of bed with a jump, his actions preceding his thoughts – he was the one who had made the mistake. For the first time ever, Freddie Lovegrove, postboy, had overslept.

Nurse Collins walked slowly down the narrow gangway between two rows of five beds each, squeezed neatly but uncomfortably into Tendring library. Shiva had been moved ever more tightly into the corner at an angle and was no longer in a position of power. That, unequivocally, belonged to the equally androgynous Nurse Collins.

Five of the beds were occupied with wounded, bedridden soldiers. Next to each of the other five bunks were soldiers either seated or standing, dressed or dressing, two of them assisted by young nurses. Jack had been moved to the far end, where he stood in a dog-eared suit next to his own bed, lighting a cigarette. When Nurse Collins reached him, she stopped.

"Why are you still here?"

"I'm ill ain't I."

"Remind me what is wrong with you?"

"Infected foot."

"You had an infected foot two months ago. You should either be better, or dead. Who tends to your wound?"

Nurse Collins picked up Jack's clipboard and read it. She watched him put his cigarette to his mouth for another drag.

"Hannah."

"And who fills in your report?"

"Hannah."

"Always?"

"Always."

She replaced the clipboard and looked at Jack with disdain. "Commonplace accident, isn't it, shooting yourself in the foot. You know that men have been executed for less. We are desperate for beds. I want you out of yours by tomorrow. You are not wanted. Here or anywhere else."

As she walked away, Jack called after her, "Where the 'ell am I supposed to go?"

She stopped and turned to face him, speaking impassively to make her words sound all the more cruel. "As far as I'm concerned you can go to hell, Private Lloyd."

Only once she had said it was she shocked by her own contempt for him, not sure where it had come from, except she had not slept for over twenty-four hours. Or was it that men were sleeping on the floor in the corridors of Celandine Hall and were more deserving of Jack's bed? She was sure Jack was not deserving of her pity, and made sure he didn't see it, but all the same she was sorry she had given him directions to hell.

He took another long drag on his cigarette. "I just come from there ain't I."

They looked at each other and an understanding passed between them, recognising in each other's eyes their mutual hatred of the war. She straightened her back. "Then I suggest you go to church and pray for guidance. I will arrange for a train ticket for tomorrow morning with leave of absence. Go home, where you will no longer be any of my concern."

And then she had an afterthought, lowered her voice in such a way that Jack was only just able to hear.

"I hope I never see you again."

The meaning was ambiguous, which was the limit of her compassion. In the silence that followed, it was just possible to hear the church bell from four miles away, its sound caught in the breeze.

Hannah and Phoebe had been up since five to make breakfast. It always seemed that on a Sunday there was more time, the proceedings less frantic, and the air fresher. There was no logic to it, as there was as much to do on a Sunday as any other day and in addition they had to get ready for church. But still, there seemed to be time for quietness and contemplation. God brought order to the chaos, they presumed.

Occasionally Suhani would come down for breakfast but more often than not Hannah would leave a tray for her outside her room. She had noticed, as the days and weeks wore on, that Mrs Harkness gradually took more trouble in her appearance until she seemed to be back to her usual self, her English boundaries returned, with the exception that she now wore her sari all day rather than just in the evenings. But this was merely an outward expression of normality. Her smiles were joyless and her words ephemeral to the point of being difficult to hear. Hannah no longer had meaningful conversations with her and the melancholy sometimes became infectious.

The only other change in Suhani that Hannah had noticed was in and around her eyes. Tiny furrows of skin at the outer corners, a slight swelling and darker colour under them, and between the lower lids and the whites of her eyes a gap, so subtle as to be almost undetectable, that collected salty water there. At best, Hannah thought, Mrs Harkness could only ever be cat-napping through the night. When Hannah had left the breakfast tray outside the door of Suhani's bedroom that morning, her gentle knock was answered with a faint, delicate clearing of the throat, the waking up of a voice that was now rarely used, followed by a thank-you that cracked either because Suhani was crying, or simply because she was exhausted. There was no point in enquiring further.

Suhani usually had breakfast in her own room and so Stephen preferred to do the same, although increasingly he was not there at all, instead choosing to stay overnight at his munitions factory. If his bowler hat was hanging in the hallway, Hannah knew to leave a tray outside his room. When the hat was not there, she felt relieved, and noticed that Suhani was more likely to come down for breakfast on those days. Presumably she must be awake enough every night to hear whether Stephen's bedroom door had opened and closed or not. This morning, however, the bowler hat hung on its stand, discharging its silent orders.

Hannah was beginning to feel unhappy working at Tendring, and if it weren't for her attachment to Suhani she might have considered leaving. As she stood by her bed and got out of her work clothes and into her Sunday best, she wondered if even that close bond would be enough to keep her here. But her job for now was to look after her mistress, especially on this day of all days when painful memories were bound to be reawakened. She walked across the room to Phoebe who was already dressed for church and helped her put on her coat.

"You won't get away with this much longer."

"He's mine and I'm going to keep him."

They both looked down at the now rather visible swelling of Phoebe's belly that separated them. It could pass as lamb's fat for now, thought Hannah, who was doing up the buttons of Phoebe's coat like a mother helping a small child, but another month would not even fool a fool.

"You know that's madness. You'll be in the workhouse before your baby hits the floor. I can help. I can tell you what to do. But you must do it soon."

Hannah thought her words had sounded harsher than she intended, so she put both her hands up to Phoebe's face to cradle it. Phoebe looked like she was about to cry and her voice was shaky. "He wants to be born."

"Into this world? Not if he knew. And how do you know it's a boy?"

"They are always boys."

Hannah dropped her hands from Phoebe's face to do up the last remaining button, then she tugged gently at the lapels so that the coat would hang more naturally, hiding Phoebe's bump.

"Let's go and say a few prayers for him then. That's the next best thing we can do."

Stephen looked in the mirror that hung between his wardrobe and the window. He was trying to do up the button of his shirt collar, a white starched linen band, stiff as cardboard, that went right round his throat and was designed to push his head back so far that a feeling of superiority was inevitable. His fingers became increasingly exasperated with the button because the collar was too tight. It took him several goes, but once it was done the stiffness in his neck drained down into his entire body and the cravat, waistcoat, and frock coat all added to the impression he might be a mannequin in a shop window. He turned his head to look out of his own window to assess the temperature. He thought he would be too hot in this attire but of course he had no choice, Sunday being Sunday – especially this one.

As he waxed his moustache and leant forward into the mirror to see more clearly, he found himself looking into his own eyes, unable to remember the last time he had done so. The irises were dark grey, the colour of rain clouds, and merged into the black pupils that widened as he leant in. He combed for over a minute, far longer than was necessary, trying to remember where he had seen eyes like these before. Then it came to him: from his time on the battlefields of South Africa, he remembered that most of the dead bodies had their eyes open.

He picked up his Homburg, stepped out of his room and across the corridor to Suhani's door. Her breakfast tray was at the foot of it, untouched, so he put his hat down on the floor, picked up the tray to balance it on one hand and knocked on the door with the other. He waited, but there was no reply. He was about to try again when he decided instead to dispense with formalities and pushed open the door with an abrupt turn of the handle. He had no idea where this new boldness had come from. Perhaps he was still annoyed by his stubborn collar button.

Suhani was sitting on the end of her bed, still in her night clothes, looking in the direction of the window. Her sari was laid out neatly beside her, and the sunlight fell on it. When Stephen went to place the tray on her bedside table and walked round to stand in front of her she ignored him as if he were invisible, so he straightened his shoulders and spoke quietly, as he always did when he felt confrontation coming on.

"Suhani. My dear. Enough is enough."

An ancient thought entered his head for the first time in years: that she was still very beautiful, that she hadn't really changed, could still be sixteen, except for her exhausted eyes. And he wanted to feel what he would have felt then, or even a small fraction of it. But all he had now was an emptiness that he could fill only with anger, and because Suhani was ignoring him, this began to rise from his chest and squeeze his neck ever more tightly inside his collar.

Her response to his entreaty was to lie down on the bed and curl up onto her side, next to her sari, an act of clear defiance that increased his irritation further. The more he tried to suppress it the more it boiled up inside him. When he spoke it was almost a whisper, like the hissing of a snake, and his sentences began to run into each other.

"It's been two months, you were not as bad as this last time. You have to be there, with me, otherwise I will look ridiculous. You have an hour to get ready."

She sighed heavily, but otherwise didn't react. He knew that by ignoring him she held all the power and he would be unable to negotiate anything, so he resorted to what was the natural way of things: order and obedience, a crushing and an acquiescence, one life at the expense of another. A man telling a woman what to do. He walked over to the wardrobe, pulled out a black dress and threw it onto the bed above Suhani's head.

"Get up. The whole village will be there."

She did not move or speak.

He started counting to ten but got no further than three. "The epitaph is as you asked. Against my better judgment but there you are. Isn't that enough for you?"

At this, she stirred. Stephen was unsure why. Perhaps mention of the monument made her realise she had to go, because it had in fact been her idea. She sat up, slowly, and brushed the sari that was by her side with the palm of her hand, following her fingers with her eyes as she traced the lotus leaves printed on it. Then she spoke as if she were in the middle of a conversation and had been talking with Stephen all day.

"It is not two months. It is one day less than two months. But very well, I will go." She continued to stroke the silken fabric of her sari and seemed mesmerised by it. "On condition that I go as me."

Stephen glanced down at the sari. "You know that's inappropriate. It is not for you to set conditions. Absolutely not. You will wear black."

"If you had wanted an English wife you should have married one."

Stephen's jaw muscles twitched. "We had no choice."

Suhani turned her head up towards Stephen and looked directly at him for the first time. He sensed that she had become emboldened and he straightened himself up defensively. She rose to her feet, and although she was several inches shorter than him she was able to put her head near enough for him to feel her breath on his face. They were dangerously close to touching.

"We had every choice Stephen. We chose this life. I wanted you. We wanted each other. We knew what we were doing." Then she paused. He felt her glare penetrate him more deeply still, as if her eyes were being worked by an animal on the kill. "You can always choose who you fuck."

She spat the last word out, literally, a fleck of spittle landing on Stephen's cheek. He began to shake with fury. The sound of it, as much as the meaning, had shocked him into a state of disbelief. He had never heard her, nor any woman, use it before and was not only outraged that she knew such a word but that she understood what it meant.

He slapped her across the face. He had swung his arm back as far as it would go and brought the palm of his hand down onto her cheek and temple with such force that it knocked her to the floor. The strike had sounded like a horsewhip, Suhani crying out a split second later, yelping like a dog, and Stephen watched as she cowered and attempted to crawl part way under the bed. The force of his swing meant that his arm was still across his chest, frozen there, and his hand remained hovering just over his opposite shoulder. He looked down at what he had done, and couldn't bear the noise that Suhani was making, a whining that sounded like she was pleading for her life. At first it made him even angrier, his whole body trembling, but then his rage became shock and possibly a whole minute passed before he dropped his arm to his side while the rest of his frame remained resolutely still.

When he finally spoke, he snapped out, "I'm sorry." But his words sounded unapologetic and Suhani's whimpering continued. Being partly under the bed, perhaps she had not heard him. "I'm sorry," he repeated, louder, irritated that he'd had to say it again. His pulse was so fast and strong it was breaking up the rhythm of his words and he seemed unable to empty his lungs of air.

"Suhani? I didn't mean...I wasn't...I'm very tired." It was regret, but he knew it was the regret of a bully. Her crying was slowly abating but, apart from breathing heavily, she wasn't moving. Stephen stepped back and took several more seconds to gather himself, as if the whole village was observing – it was often the imagined sense of being watched that motivated him. Eventually he pulled at the lapels of his frock coat to straighten them up and then, in an attempt to control his breathing, went over to her wardrobe. Do something, he thought, anything, to restore some calm. He had been an invisible, distant husband, sometimes cruel, he knew that, but he had never hit her before. Words could be undone, or forgotten, this could not. You can't unscramble an egg, Suhani would say.

He quickly found what he was looking for in the wardrobe and placed it on the bed next to the black dress. Even now he was still shaking, but was nevertheless able to feign some level of composure, a skill he had acquired over many years, recovering more quickly than was appropriate. And suddenly it was as if it had never happened, his voice smooth and varnished, the cracks filled in.

"A veil might be in keeping today."

Not only would it be in keeping, he thought, but also necessary. He had probably left a bruise on her face.

19

Although Suhani's ear still rang in her head like a perpetual train whistle, its sustained note had become masked by the crunch of gravel under ten pairs of feet on the Eagley Road, bringing her some distraction. The marching created a rhythm that they had all fallen into naturally. The only one who couldn't slot in, even though he was leading the pack, was Stephen, whose limp didn't quite allow for an even stride.

Suhani noticed this as she walked beside him. Despite her stinging face, and in some ways because of it, she felt sorry for him that his steps did not synchronise, sorry for the man who could never fit in, and she became confused about who, or what, she was supposed to be grieving. Rejecting her sari that morning and putting on the black dress was not so much an act of compliance as one of necessity. She needed to wear the veil, and a veil without a dress would have looked preposterous. She knew everyone would assume that it was there to indicate her mourning but she had a more pressing reason, purple and swollen. Stephen had not needed to force the veil on her.

As she became increasingly absorbed in the sound of everyone marching, she tried to work out whose footsteps belonged to whom.

Behind her were Hannah and Phoebe, probably holding hands as usual, their footsteps a mirror image of each other and in perfect harmony. Jack would be following, his limp much improved – if indeed he now had one at all – and then there were two more soldiers, walking wounded, one with a bandage around his crown, the other with his arm in a sling. Next in line were the two nurses and finally, bringing up the rear, several yards behind, was Gabriel, who in the last couple of months had physically improved, but mentally withdrawn ever further into himself. She tried to picture them all. As she glanced down at the bouquet of white roses she was holding, she realised this was all merely a game of distraction, a way of filling her head to prevent her from collapsing in tears, or worse, turning round and running back in flight to Tendring.

Just as the rhythm of the marching had become relentless, almost self-conscious, Stephen turned left down the bridle path towards the church and everyone followed. Its narrowness meant the troops had to turn themselves into a single file and the marching fizzled out, replaced by disconnected footsteps and hitched up skirts, except for Suhani who didn't notice any of it and allowed the hem of her dress to catch the sharp flutes of straw that lined the edges of the path.

Although it was not yet nine o'clock the day was heating up, and picking their way across the field between stacks of hay was hot work for everyone, made worse by their layers of Sunday-best. Jack wiped his brow with the back of his sleeve and Stephen was singled out by a wasp that seemed attracted to the wax of his moustache. He flapped at it impatiently, without success. A bead of sweat had fallen into Suhani's bruised eye and the stinging sparked what was at first an unspecified memory. Although these were the early days of autumn it seemed the last days of summer were not yet ready to let go, and she realised it was home, India, with its heat-drenched summers, that she was thinking of. Yet was it home, really? Did she not belong here now? Or did she not belong anywhere at all? Dead or alive, all three of her sons were in

France, so perhaps, even though she'd never been there, France was her home now.

The path eventually widened out into a track again so the party resumed walking in twos, side by side, until they reached the lychgate of the church. They headed, not as they would normally do towards the south door, but off to the right and into the graveyard, where a crowd had gathered around the Harkness monument. Almost the entire village had turned up to watch.

Canon Lummis greeted them cheerily. "Hello Stephen. Mrs Harkness." He shook their hands and smiled broadly, but kept his voice down since official proceedings had not yet begun. For Suhani there was another quality about her veil that, as she looked through it, she found she was thankful for: it made the world remote from her own body. She was able to watch the proceedings without participating, not quite present. It felt, therefore, that it was not her but someone else who shook hands with Canon Lummis and smiled generously back at him.

"I thought if you two stood here and the rest of you gathered round behind?" He pointed to a spot on the ground a few feet in front of the monument and they did as instructed. Then Canon Lummis stood to one side, felt for the bookmark in a book that was too small to be a bible and opened it up. This was the cue for the village men to remove their hats and for everyone to bow their heads. Though there were two that did not bow: Suhani, and Jack.

She was aware of Canon Lummis's words as he began to read – the usual biblical aphorisms about a virtuous man, dying before his time, some fragment about the true measure of life, about understanding being more important than ripe old age. But she wasn't really listening and drifted instead into reading the newly carved inscription on the monument:

"Edward Reginald Harkness, Captain Irish Guards who fell in the attack on High Wood, July 1st 1916 Aged 20. Second Son of Stephen and

Suhani Harkness."

Suhani stepped forward, found herself doing so even though the vicar was still reading. Without understanding her own motives, she knew it was a grievous faux pas. Realising it would embarrass Stephen too, she even entertained the thought that perhaps this was why she'd done it. If it hadn't been for her veil offering some protection, she would probably not have had the courage to move. To her surprise, the veil was empowering her.

Out of the corner of her eye she could see Canon Lummis had stopped mid-sentence which left him slightly open-mouthed, though he quickly shut it. There were other looks too from the great and good of the village, silent criticism, small black marks in their books of judgement, accumulated over time. Stephen in contrast remained entirely passive, apparently unmoved by what she was doing, though Suhani knew that was not the case. On the contrary he was repressing his anger again, unable to react in front of the village. So she took another step forward, unbidden yet defiant, and knelt down to place her bouquet of roses at the base of the monument. She dragged her finger tips across the final five words she had been allowed to choose: *"Thy will, not mine, Lord."* Five Wesleyan words she had sung in church many times, Suhani was struck by how the congregation took one meaning from them whilst she understood them to have another. She envied their innocence.

When she stepped back and nodded her permission for Canon Lummis to continue, she then made a gesture that shocked even herself: she held out her hand for Stephen to take. The empowerment now seemed almost beyond her own control and she felt intoxicated by it. With Stephen's solitary act of violence one hour earlier, the strong had become weak and the weak had become strong, the sun had burnt away the clouds, and there was no returning to the old world they had left behind. Was she forgiving him, or making him look a fool? Well, she thought, that was not her choice, but his. Stephen looked at her hand, then at her face, and then finally at the ground in front of him. The village watched, the crows cawed. His rejection of her, years in the making, was complete.

Suhani dropped her hand and looked straight ahead beyond the graveyard. Her veil reduced the glare of the sun and she thought she saw some movement in the fields as Canon Lummis picked up where he'd left off, in the middle of a sentence: " – as he lived among sinners, he has been taken up. He has been carried off so that evil may not warp his understanding or treachery seduce his – "

"Stop."

Her disrespect, she realised, was deliberate, the need to fit in finally spurned, throwing off the ill-fitting coat of Englishness she had spent years trying to wear. Disrespect, or contempt? Whichever, they deserved it all. She wanted to walk away and the figure moving in the fields gave her reason to do so. This second, more abrupt interruption caused Canon Lummis to smile at Suhani, the sickly, superior smile of a disgruntled vicar, and the group of villagers became unsettled, some of them shifting weight from one foot to the other. All of them stared straight at Suhani, embarrassed, or appalled, and in some cases both. But the glaring spurred her on, she would slap them all across the face, and she turned to walk in the direction of the lychgate, meaning Hannah and Phoebe along with several villagers behind them had to step aside to make way. Stephen, red-faced now, looked like he was about to call out to Suhani, his mouth held open for a second, but he thought better of it, instead turning to the vicar.

"Please, carry on."

Canon Lummis had lost his place, having thoughtlessly closed his book in panic when Suhani had asked him to stop, so he flicked through the pages in the hope that the book itself would somehow fall open where he had left it. Stephen held out his arm to take the book from him and impatiently found the relevant verses.

"The Song of Solomon," he said.

Meanwhile Suhani had taken the fifty paces to reach the lychgate and arrived at the same time as Freddie. For it was Freddie she had seen in the fields.

The wood of the lychgate was beginning to rot and its thatched roof was in need of repair with green shoots covering much of it. It was probably the cobwebs and ivy that held it together, thought Freddie. Suhani sat down on the bench that ran along the inside of the lychgate, making the whole fragile structure creak, and Freddie stood a yard in front of her, breathless, watching, waiting for his orders.

"I haven't seen you in a while, Freddie," she said.

"No ma'am."

"That's my fault I think. I believe you deliver by the back door now."

"And at church on Sundays. Mr Franklin says we're not supposed to but it saves time. Kill two birds with one stone he says. There's a war on Mrs Harkness."

"Yes indeed." She stared straight ahead, yet to make proper eye contact with him. Then she seemed to have an afterthought. "There's a war on, certainly. Sometimes it's hard to believe." She placed her hand by her side to indicate where Freddie should sit. "Sometimes not."

He hesitated. "Mr Harkness says I'm not to bother you ma'am."

She turned to look at him properly for the first time. "You won't be bothering me Freddie. Please."

That word again, the one he'd heard before, in the library, alone with Christopher, and which still pulled with the same heavy undertow, meaning as usual he had no choice. After two months of being an ordinary workaday postboy, he felt he was once more standing at the boundary of a dangerous domain, about to re-enter it. Drawn in by a gravity he couldn't resist, didn't want to, he sat next to her with a gap between them, neither too near nor too far apart, like the Earth and the Moon.

Suhani leant back, once more looking straight ahead, and Freddie felt she was talking to herself as much as to him. "The seasons creep up on you don't you think? Like an assassin. We bring the harvest in and celebrate. But I think we also mourn. Summer feels like it will last forever. And then, suddenly, it is gone. Like the blowing out of a candle. Don't you think?" Suhani lifted her veil and turned to Freddie so that he could see her badly bruised face. "It's hard not to do what Mr Harkness says, isn't it."

The side of it was red, there was a swelling under her eye, and the eyeball itself was bloodshot. Freddie stared at it for too long until finally dropping his head to look down at his shoes. Eventually Suhani broke the silence.

"Do you remember Shiva's role?"

Freddie did. In an effort to understand it he had often repeated the words to himself, and although he would not have been able to say why, they were gradually emerging out of some opaque cloud of meaning. "To destroy the universe in order to recreate it."

Suhani pulled her veil back down over her face. "Then you may hand the post to me now."

Freddie looked at her. He loved his mother, of course he did, but Mrs Harkness too? He would think of Millie last thing at night and the despatch rider first thing in the morning. But Suhani filled an entirely different role, hovering over everything, as mysterious as Shiva, her auburn skin and cryptic eyes from an unfamiliar world as far away as his Boy's Own Annual had ever taken him, the glottal breaks in her accent from a foreign land, hiding in the furthest pages of his atlas. Yet somehow the two of them shared a common purpose, a secret that they kept from each other and even from themselves, and so he could not resist her entreaty. He put his hand into his pouch and pulled out the one letter he had brought for her. Handing it over, he noticed it had a muddy thumbprint on the back.

"Well, it is addressed to you ma'am."

She took the letter from him. "Ah yes. The rules."

"And courtesy."

Suhani examined the envelope and, to Freddie's surprise, opened the letter. He felt she had undergone a transformation, from previous circumspection to now needing the post, willing it into her own hands. He couldn't think what had caused the change but he wondered if the bruise on the side of her face had something to do with it. Tearing carefully through the top of the envelope with her finger, Suhani then pulled out the one hand-written sheet. She unfolded it but didn't look at the words, instead she slowly put the letter up to her face to breathe in its odour, holding it there for several seconds. Only then did she rest it on her lap to begin to read.

But she did not take long. It seemed she only needed to glance at the first sentence to understand the whole of it, after which she placed the letter down by her side in the gap between herself and Freddie, and looked over towards the monument. Freddie glanced down at the letter but straight away wished he hadn't, feeling he had intruded in some way into Suhani's private world. The first two words meant he should read no further: *"Dearest Maji"*. They may as well have said "No trespassing". What did they mean? He guessed it was an Indian word, probably meant Mother. Yes, that must be it, all the more reason to avert his gaze and change the subject.

"Do you have letters for posting, ma'am?"

Suhani continued to watch the memorial service running its course. Canon Lummis was still droning on, pouring out his meandering biblical contents, though he was too far away for it to be possible to determine any actual words. She picked up the letter, folded it and returned it to its envelope. Freddie could not make out what her reaction to it was, and at this angle it was almost impossible to see her face through her veil to perceive any expression at all. But he thought she was, at least, not upset. Possibly she was distracted by the contents of the letter because she didn't answer his question, instead asking one of her own.

"Will I see you in church?"

Freddie thought about it. He had once heard his Ma use the word atheist and at school the following day Freddie had asked Mrs Mawby what it meant, but this just sent her into a verbal spin about the Devil, which he stopped listening to after one lungful of censure. It was odd that his mother always insisted that he go to church and yet she did not do so herself. She took sightless steps into the village for shopping, so why not church? Her excuse was that it took her longer than most to prepare Sunday lunch. In any event, the result was that he always went to church on Sunday, and despite the fact that he was running late, today would have to be no exception, meaning there was only one possible answer to Suhani's question.

Freddie had spent the five minutes before the service walking the aisles and pews delivering several letters to various members of the congregation, and had thought if he could do this every day his job would be ten times quicker. Now he sat at the end of a pew next to Hannah and behind Stephen and Suhani. He was pondering the idea that sitting in church was an activity he liked, not so much for the service itself, which was always dull, but for the waiting beforehand when he could look around and read the epitaphs on the walls, of people who had died long before he was born. Husbands, wives and children, letters embossed in black or gold, brass plaques in loving memory of, parted by death and reunited in heaven, resting in peace, to the glory of God – and one in particular that always caught his eye, *"Here lyeth nearby the body of Mifs Sarh Jenner, you will knw the truth, and the truth will fet you free."* Why did they sometimes miss out letters? And why did the "s" look like an "f"? And why not always, why only here and there? It was messy and it vexed him. Every Sunday he had the same irksome thought. If he was ever to carve an epitaph he would space it out in advance in his head, like writing a letter, make the "s" look like an "s" and the congregation would nod and smile in admiration. Then, just as he visualised an actual hammer and chisel in his hands, he heard Stephen whisper angrily to Suhani.

"How dare you do that?"

Freddie saw Suhani try to hand the letter to Stephen in lieu of a spoken reply, but her husband refused to take it and remained rigidly facing forwards, saying, "I haven't got my glasses." The illicit sound of loud whispering was causing heads to turn in the congregation. Freddie was desperate not to eavesdrop, or at least not to be seen to be, so he looked over to one side in the pretence that he was not listening, though in fact it had the opposite effect, making it slightly easier to hear. Suhani turned to Stephen and finally spoke as she held the letter out in front of him.

"It's from Tristan. He is on leave from today. Home on Wednesday."

Freddie watched and waited. He noticed a mark on the back of Stephen's neck, a scar, a small injury that had long ago healed. The more he stared at it the more he could see it was pulsating with a vein that presumably was now closer to the surface of the skin than it should otherwise have been. Freddie knew from the addresses on the many letters he had delivered that the man who sat in front of him was a Major and therefore the injury might have come from a knife or bullet. What was the scar a vestige of, and how close had he come to death? How close, in fact, to becoming an epitaph on the church wall? *Here lies Major Stephen Harkness, you will know the truth, and the truth will set you free,* with each "s" as it should be, carved by Freddie Lovegrove, postboy, writer, and artist.

Freddie saw Stephen look up at the empty pulpit, which seemed to be a way of closing the subject, the last word on the matter of Tristan's arrival.

" It looks like the helenium will be in full bloom by then. It's late this year."

A moment later Canon Lummis walked up the aisle towards the altar and on a wave of obedience the entire village stood up.

The service had been dreary in the extreme. There had been some attempt at a harvest hymn but the error-strewn melody emanating from the harmonium had been almost impossible to follow. If the fields were to be ploughed and the good seed scattered, it would not be as a result of their singing. The congregation left the church in the order they had entered, wished well for a good day by Canon Lummis at the south door, with everyone squinting in the bright sunlight as they headed towards the lychgate. Freddie had slotted in between Hannah and Phoebe who walked in front of him as a pair, and Jack behind. He needed to get moving, he was later than ever, but the pace of the queue was painfully slow.

Looking down at his shoes again he nearly bumped into the back of Phoebe. The line had come to a stop. At first he couldn't see why, until he took half a step to the side to see through the gap between the two young women in front of him. Standing just beyond the lychgate were two figures, men, one of them in a suit, the other in a policeman's uniform, and there was a car parked a few yards away, a shining contraption with a black leather canopy stretched high over the seats like bat's wings.

The suited one stepped forward and stopped in front of Stephen. Freddie forgot all thoughts of being late as he looked at the man, then at the back of Stephen's head, at Suhani's black dress that had become creased on the pew, at Phoebe's shoes and her ankles that looked swollen. He turned round briefly to catch Jack's eye in case he had some explanation, but Jack simply dropped the corners of his mouth. He knew no more than Freddie. The man who had brought the village to a standstill put his hands in his coat pockets defensively.

"Hello Stephen."

Stephen flicked his eyes to scan his surroundings, then straightened his back and pulled back his shoulders. "What's all this about?"

"Instructions from Canterbury."

"Canterbury?"

"I'm sorry Stephen, to have to do this on a Sunday."

"Do what?"

"They're an officious lot."

"Who? Do what?"

"A witness has come forward."

Stephen narrowed his eyelids. "A witness to what?"

The man removed his hands from his pockets and put them out in front, palms up, a futile gesture of apology. "Look, it's...a...a formality I'm sure."

"It doesn't feel like it."

"Stephen. Please, get into the car."

Stephen turned to look behind. Everyone was staring at him. "I will not."

"Stephen, you do not have to say anything unless you wish to do so, but what you say may be given in evidence."

"Are you charging me with something?"

"I'm sorry..."

"Spit it out man."

"Come with us and we'll sort it out. We don't need to bother with handcuffs."

Stephen was beginning to shake with anger. "Indeed not. This is ridiculous. Step aside and let me go home."

"You must come with us Stephen. Your resistance now will not look good later."

"Later? There is no later. Let me pass."

Inspector Roper looked towards the uniformed policeman and nodded permission. The constable stepped forward, pulled out a pair of handcuffs and undid them. Within seconds they were on Stephen's wrists, which made him writhe with fury as the constable puffed up with sudden self-importance. "Stephen Harkness, you are charged with the murder of Christopher Ellis. You do not have to say anything – "

"That's enough," interrupted Roper. "We've done that."

The small crowd stood watching, pretending to be uninvolved, their faces emotionless masks that hid the thrill of the chase, the capture, and the kill. Stephen glared at Roper and held up his handcuffed wrists. "This is preposterous! Who is your witness?"

"I'm not at liberty to say, Stephen."

"For God's sake. I was at home that night. All of it. The night of the Zeppelin. Your so-called witness is lying."

Then it dawned on him that if there was a witness they would almost certainly be standing right behind him, so he turned to glare, at each in turn, lining them up like a firing squad and challenging them to look away if they dared. Then he pointed his stare directly at Suhani.

"Suhani! Tell them!" He was now shouting with frustration and switching backwards and forwards between Suhani and Roper. "William – Take these absurd handcuffs off me – Suhani, tell them I was at home all night – Damn your witness – Damn them – Who is it?" He was exasperated at not being listened to, not having his questions answered, not even with denials. Suhani's veil meant that he couldn't tell what her expression was, but he knew that silence, her chosen weapon, had condemned him.

"We have no choice Stephen," said Roper and he nodded again to the policeman who took Stephen by the arm to lead him away. The three of them headed under the lychgate and towards the car, with Stephen stumbling in the grip of the policeman and glancing back at the crowd of people watching. He called out one final time, though everyone could hear the pitiful futility in his voice.

"Suhani! Tell them I was with you all night. Why won't you tell them?" On the last beat of his sentence, an interrupted cadence, some spit flew out of his mouth, returning Suhani's earlier volley, caught like a pinprick in the sunlight. Moments later he was in the car and the policeman was cranking the engine to get it started. Stephen looked across at everyone, his face red and bloated, his lips tightly shut and his eyes choked with frustration.

The congregation watched the car pull away. Standing amongst them, somewhere, was the witness, and this made it impossible for any of them to move, except for the searching gestures of their eyes. Freddie looked at Jack; Jack looked at Hannah; and Hannah looked at Suhani, who sealed the covenant by directing her gaze towards Freddie. Only then did she lift up her head to speak to everyone gathered there in the graveyard.

"I'm sorry. It will burn itself out. All fires do. Let's not forget why we are here. Thank you for coming today, and thank you for remembering Edward. He would have appreciated your thoughts and prayers. He died so that you can bring the harvest in. Now, let us return home."

But just as she turned to go she caught sight of Gabriel, who was only then coming out of the church. Gabriel, the outsider, the wordless one who could not see but watched, who could not hear but listened; Shiva made flesh. And the stone eagles guarding the open gates of Tendring took flight.

20

Stephen's incarceration was, in fact, anything but. Inspector Roper had taken him to the police station, which in itself was little more than a modified house – so much so that the villagers called it The Police House. The room that Stephen found himself in had a desk with a leather backed chair and shelves on the walls that groaned under the weight of files of paperwork, most of which looked like they had not been touched for decades. The only thing that suggested a prison cell rather than an office was a timid, makeshift bed opposite the desk, though it looked comfortable enough with a thick mattress and two pillows. It would make no difference to Stephen, he doubted he was any more likely to fall asleep here than at home.

"You'll be taken to Ramsgate." Roper was removing Stephen's handcuffs as he spoke. "I'm not sure when. We have a cell here but I thought this office would be more comfortable."

Stephen looked at his friend to suggest comfort was of no interest to him.

"Look," said Roper, putting the handcuffs in his pocket, "I'll do what I can." With that he held out his hand for Stephen to shake. At first Stephen rejected it, so Roper tried again, gesturing more forcefully with his outstretched arm. "Stephen, if it were up to me..."

Stephen thought quickly, considered his options, finally deciding that if there was ever a point to being a Freemason it was now, so he accepted the offer and shook Roper's hand, signing off with a pinch of his knuckle. Over and above the Mason's symbol of secret mutual recognition, this was a sign that he needed help.

"I'll organise some tea," said Roper as he let go of Stephen's hand. He was leaving the room when he stopped in the doorway. "And I'll leave your door open, Stephen. The privy's at the end of the hall. But otherwise best to play it by the book."

Stephen wanted to be left alone, so went to sit at the desk, with his back to Roper.

"Thank you William."

He stared at the wall opposite where there were several recruitment posters and he waited to hear Roper's retreating footsteps, but instead his friend spoke again, still standing in the open doorway.

"You all right?"

One of the posters depicted a soldier, a private, holding a rifle in one hand and his other arm stretched out in front, rather like Roper had done a moment ago, with the text made to look like handwriting: *An appeal to You! Give us a hand old man!* In the car journey back from the church Stephen had become subdued, almost trance-like about this new state of affairs. In any case the engine had been so noisy that it made communication impossible so, only now, in the peace and quiet of the police house, had it properly begun.

"You all right, Stephen?" repeated Roper.

Stephen didn't move. Even his jaw seemed locked as he spoke. "Yes. Yes thank you."

Roper stepped back into the room. "Stephen. Why doesn't your wife speak up?"

Stephen looked down at the large leather-bound blotter on the desk and rested his arms on it, folding his hands together. He spoke slowly, to himself. "I think perhaps she despises me." Then he sighed, the sound of it acutely audible to them both as his breath passed through his nose and moustache. "Actually I don't blame her."

Stephen wondered how his friend would react to this candid response. Probably with embarrassment, and the silence that followed seemed to confirm it, until eventually Roper piped up with, "Milk and sugar?"

Good man, thought Stephen. "Thank you."

But then Roper added something that Stephen didn't understand. "Don't forget. I owe you."

Twelve hours later, Stephen was still sitting at the desk. What did Roper owe him? There was a clock on the mantelpiece that seemed to tick increasingly loudly as the evening wore on. An oil lamp cast a feeble light that barely reached the walls, and there was no window in the room to allow the moonlight in. His collar felt tighter than ever but to loosen it would be to suggest he would be staying, an admission of guilt, a confession imminent. He could feel the old injury on the back of his neck throbbing. Years of experience told him that to rub it would only make it worse, so he couldn't even use that as an excuse to move. He could, of course, go over to the bed and lie down, but that too would represent defeat. He had begrudgingly eaten, twice, and gone to the toilet once, but that had been the extent of his activities all day. The food had given him indigestion and passing water was always painful. Constable Waveney had brought and collected his tray, but they had exchanged no words. The less he moved, the less he was able to. With each tick of the clock he was gradually ceasing to be, a feeling that actually gave him some comfort, and although his descent was not deliberate, it was unavoidable, mercifully so. He was even pleasantly curious about how it might end.

Since the moment he had been dragged into the Police House he had thought more about Suhani, more consciously so, than he ever had since his return from South Africa. When he had struck her, the final misty traces of his own spirit had disappeared. What little purpose he had in life had been lost, any story he had left to tell had been crossed from the page with one single stroke of his own hand. There was no coming back from it, no apology that would ever suffice. His love for her, and hers for him, had proved immutable against the crude prejudices and expectations of the day, yet had now been consumed in a fire of his own making, and it was too late to salvage any embers from the ashes. He had tried to erase the last fifteen years of their marriage with his fist, but had succeeded in doing the opposite, rendering its desolate spaces as indelible as a freshly carved epitaph, and there was nothing to be done.

All day and all evening he had stared at the wall in front of him. He couldn't think what it was that Roper owed him, and he must have read the recruitment posters a thousand times whilst trying to work it out. These days the posters were now so familiar that it was hard to read them with a fresh eye, they seemed to state the obvious with a logic that could not be challenged, but his twelve hours of gazing at them had gradually revealed their persuasive qualities for what they were: deceit, their real message finally seeping through and exposed. Two were aimed at women, one an appeal to join the women's land army with *God speed the plough and the woman who drives it,* and another, showing a young woman, no older than twenty, donning an overall and getting ready for work with the message *These women are doing their bit, learn to make munitions.* He wondered how many shells she would help to make, and how many soldiers they would kill. The answer, of course, was that she was likely to have the blood of scores of men on her hands, perhaps hundreds. And where did that leave him? His factory had made over a million shells since he had become the manager. By now he could be held personally responsible for over one-hundred-thousand deaths. But he was insignificant, one small part of the process, in an industry that would carry on without him, meaning guilt was spread so thinly that in the end you didn't feel any.

And so those thousands of war dead meant nothing to him. Instead he remembered just one, from an earlier battle on the ridge at Vaal Krantz. This was the reason why he always resisted sleep because if he did the dream of his comrade being hit by a shell as he stood right next to him would return. The worst of the damage to his own body had been caused not by the shell but by pieces of shattered fibula from his friend's right leg cutting through his own flesh and arteries like glass. He would have bled to death were it not for the company surgeon being just yards behind. At the moment of explosion he happened to have been looking down and away to his left, otherwise he most certainly would have died himself from injuries to his head. Later, the surgeon had pulled out a tooth from the back of his neck. He had been lucky, though that had been the doctor's word, not his own. In reality, that was the day his luck had run out.

Finally, Stephen moved. He sat back in his chair, the end of his reverie. At last, it came to him, the word he had been looking for and which now seemed obvious. What he thought had been years of anger were in fact nothing of the sort. Instead they had been filled by something altogether more destructive and to which he could finally attach its correct name: shame. Infinite, eternal shame. It had directed his every thought and action, it fed on him every day, getting hungrier even as it took bites out of him, until there was nothing left of Stephen Harkness, like a snake eating its own tail. For years he had been desperate for Suhani to save him, yet he had always prevented her from doing so, devoted all his energies to it, and that was why he had hit the only person he had ever loved.

He glanced again at the wall in front of him and felt his body stir. The poster of the munitions girl had given him an idea, how he might make things right, and to his horror he began to cry.

At the edge of Tendring's domain, beyond the copper beech, far from the driveway and under the black sky of night, where the lawn met the trees and the grass gave way to bare soil, the fox, the special one with the black tail, was caught in a snare. The ground around it had been churned up by its unsuccessful attempts to free itself and there was blood coming from its mouth where it had tried to gnaw through the wire. In agitating the snare it had not only become tighter but had slipped down from its neck to its lower abdomen, and the more the animal had struggled the more the wire had cut through its fur to expose white bone and entrails, some of which were falling loose from the wound onto the ground. The fox had given up trying to escape and instead lay there panting, waiting to die.

Suhani pointed her pistol between the fox's eyes and pulled the trigger.

The sound of the gunshot made Jack jump. He had been stuffing his few possessions and spare clothes into his canvas bag but now stopped to look round in the direction of the piercing crack. Some of the patients in the library stirred in their sleep, others were already awake, and Gabriel began to whimper in his bed. Jack went over to him, sat by his bedside and placed his hand on Gabriel's arm. It appeared that Gabriel had not been woken up by the gunshot. Instead, Jack thought, the sound had probably become incorporated into another of his nightmares. Jack took several minutes to stroke and pat Gabriel's arm until he calmed down.

"Thanks for everything, my friend," said Jack. "I'll come and look yer up, one day, don't you worry." With that, Jack stood up. Gabriel had fallen back into a deep sleep and Jack thought that he looked, in that moment, like a small child, and was envious.

There was a creak from the hallway, but Jack thought it was nothing more than the house contracting in the coolness of the night, as it so often did. He headed back to his bed, did up the top button of his jacket, picked up his canvas bag and walked briskly towards the library door. But for the second time in as many minutes he jumped, this time startled by the unexpected sight of Suhani wielding a pistol in the hallway. They stared at each other, neither being dressed the way the other expected: Jack fully suited up and ready to leave, Suhani still in her black mourning dress. Both took a moment to regroup. Her veil had been pulled back behind her head, giving them permission to talk.

"We get a lot of foxes," said Suhani by way of explanation. "Stephen lays traps for them. Where on earth are you going?"

Jack avoided the question, instead nodding at the pistol. "That's an original Webley, ain't it?" He held out his hand so that he might be allowed to examine the gun, and after a moment's hesitation, Suhani lent it to him. He handled it like an expert, slowly turning the barrel and even going so far as to check the serial number. "I've shot a few in my time. They know what you're thinking, just before yer pull the trigger. That's what I reckon."

"It was suffering terribly."

"You did the right thing then dint yer. I look 'em in the eye and I reckon some of 'em are begging you to do it. That's what I reckon. They look you in the eye and beg yer." He handed the pistol back to Suhani and pulled the collar of his jacket up around his neck. “But then, yer know, one day I couldn’t do it no more. Lost me nerve you might say, ma’am. Had enough. And that’s that. Just want to go home now. Got a girl in Rye.” He gave a little snort to suggest he wasn’t hopeful. “Last time I looked, anyways.”

“Who discharged you? Your foot...”

“Ah, the miraculous touch o’ Nurse Collins.”

“It is indeed a miracle if you think you can walk fifty miles to Rye in the middle of the night.”

“Can’t sleep can I. And I don’t want no fuss. I’ll wait at the station and catch the first train in the mornin’.”

“You have leave?”

“I’ll take me chances. Always worked up till now.”

Suhani eyed him up. “I think you are running away.”

They stared at each other, Suhani’s challenge hanging in the air. Jack eventually looked away towards the front door at the end of the hallway. He didn’t want to look at her, but then felt compelled to. “Christopher was my only friend round ’ere, Mrs ’arkness. No reason to stay now.” He nodded at Suhani with a silent goodbye and turned to go but before he had taken his first step she stopped him.

“Are you the witness?”

Jack puckered his lips dismissively. “I dunno about that. Your husband’s a good man, Mrs Harkness. That’s all I saw.” He wasn’t sure if she believed him, but he didn’t really care and shrugged his shoulders.

“Do you have a forwarding address? The police will want to – ”

“Goodbye Mrs Harkness.” He smiled at her, a wide gap-toothed smile that indicated he wished to talk no more, then glanced at her bruised eye. “You need to watch yourself, walkin’ into doors like that.” He offered her his hand, which she took and held onto while she spoke.

“Goodbye Jack.”

“Goodbye Mrs ’arkness.” Then he felt emboldened by his leaving.

Nothing to lose. "Suhani. Does it have a meanin'?"

"My name? Beauty. Or pleasant. It doesn't translate very well."

They stood there, together, as motionless as spooked deer, looking into each other's eyes and with her right hand gripped tightly inside his, long after they had stopped shaking them.

"It's funny innit? We become what we're called somehow. Started off as Jack-the-lad, finished up as Jack-it-in. That's the trenches for yer." Jack dropped his smile, dropped Suhani's hand too, and disappeared out through the front door as quickly as a magician from the stage, knowing he would never be seen again. The grandfather clock made a resonant clunk as the mechanism bypassed the chimes to hit the eleventh hour.

Suhani contemplated the empty hallway and the space where Jack had been standing. Then she looked down at the pistol she was holding and slowly turned the barrel in the same way he had done. The gun felt uncomfortable in her hands, still warm from the shot, so she was glad to be rid of it. She opened the gun cabinet to put it back in its place, next to an identical weapon, their muzzles almost touching. But as she closed the cabinet door she caught sight of her own face reflected in the glass, and thought that in the semi-darkness she looked like a ghost. If anything the gloom made the bruise on the side of her face look darker than ever, and she put her palm up to it, an inch away, to feel the heat coming off it, warmer than the pistol. She held her hand there for a full minute, remembering, as clear as day, the last time Stephen had kissed her there, sixteen years ago. On the station platform, on the side of her face, the merest touch of his lips was as much as public etiquette would allow – though much less, of course, than either of them wanted. When the train had pulled away and Stephen smiled and waved from the carriage window, it would be the last time she ever saw him. Another man, another Stephen, would return, unrecognisable with his limp and his silence, having beaten the Boers but lost his own battle, a conflict he had never revealed to her nor, she suspected, ever resolved in his own heart. Courage and kindness, both gone. All she had left now of that final kiss on her cheek was the bruise on the side of her face.

Finally she dropped her arm down by her side and went into the library to check on her remaining patients. Most were sleeping, a few turning in their beds, but no one seemed in distress. In fact the place had acquired a calm functionality since Christopher's departure. No one talked about it, but everyone knew something was not right. Why had she not spoken up earlier today? Did she believe Stephen was guilty? At first she thought it was inconceivable, but then it depended, she supposed, on which Stephen it was. Perhaps, having been on the receiving end of his silence for so long, she was using hers to extract revenge. He had hit her, after all, and the desire to strike back was irresistible. His rejection of the offer of her hand, so permanent and irreversible just hours earlier, had left her no choice but to reject his change of heart, his need to take her hand now. But she knew revenge didn't flow through her veins, Shiva saw to that. Something was off, needed time to play out, and keeping her counsel had felt like her only option. She decided to take her thoughts with her to bed. Perhaps things would become clearer in the morning.

Suhani had only taken a few steps up the stairs when she stopped. Putting her hand up to her neck she tucked her fingers inside her collar and then pushed down until her whole hand was against her breast, turning her head to one side to make it easier. She pulled out the letter, the one she had kept close to her heart all day, then opened it to read the first line. Immediately something came to her, an idea, and she reached up to remove her veil as quickly as she could, then walked back down, taking a sharp right around the bottom of the bannister to get to the cupboard under the stairs, returning the letter to her breast as she went.

She knew where the trunk was, next to the croquet set. Even after so many years had passed, she fancied that both cases smelt of the scent of flowers and spices that had permeated the Indian house from where they had been shipped decades ago. The house where she had been bred like a hybrid rose, trained to be both English and Indian, becoming absorbed by the first as sure as she was slowly rejected by the second, at a time in her life when she felt the most happy, optimistic and alive, when love had been requited and uncomplicated. She was certain she could smell Frau Karl Druschki roses, Stephen's favourite, as she opened the trunk to pull out twenty yards of bunting.

Though there was the dull glow of moonlight, she still needed an oil lamp in the garden to help her see clearly enough to hang up the bunting. Otherwise it was straightforward. To begin with, the ladder was already there, and when she climbed up she discovered that, as expected, nails for tying the bunting around the portico had been left in place from last year's fête, held in April to raise money for the Prisoners Of War Fund. As she attached the last of the bunting to the furthest nail, she thought the fête had probably been the last time her three sons had seen each other; her three boys, so similar, so different, and so happy in each other's company.

Once her work was done she ought to have been satisfied, but instead felt uneasy, and wasn't sure why. Back in the hallway she reached inside her bodice one more time to take out the letter from her last remaining son, to double-check. *"Dearest Maji, We are out of the woods! Our boat departs from Calais on Sunday or Monday..."* Of course she hadn't misread it, of course he was coming home, Tristan's letter couldn't be clearer, but that didn't explain why she had run up the flags so many days in advance, and in the middle of the night. For a moment she thought she had tempted fate and should take them down again. But the feeling was as irrational as putting the flags up in the first place, so she ignored it.

Finally she went to bed and dreamed of ploughed fields, vast and silent, plains of sterile soil where no poppies grew, a land strewn with bodies that were not bodies but lifeless foxes. She woke with a jolt, remembering she still had to dispose of the carcass of her own dead fox.

21

There is no wind tonight. The moon reflects on the sea like spilled paint and a lone herring gull glides across the sky, beyond the cliffs, disappearing into the silence. Cold, watery fingers grasp my ankles, then withdraw. Holding on, letting go, each wave of the retreating tide stroking my bare feet a little less than the one before. Perhaps the wet sand will swallow me up, suck me down into the Earth, taking with me the unopened letter in my hand.

There is no wind, it's true, but a storm rages in my heart.

Joe had delivered the letter, two months ago, a favour to Mrs Callow in the Post Office and moreover, I presume, an excuse to see me. It looked innocuous enough, nothing official in its appearance. If anything the address of innocent hand-written capital letters could have been copied by a child. But nobody ever wrote to me except Christopher. I felt threatened by the letter's unfamiliarity and its taunting presence, daring me to unseal it. Joe waited on the threshold expecting me to open the letter right there in front of him and share its contents, as if his attendance might help. Perhaps I should have done, it would have saved me two months of self-imposed torment. Instead I thanked

Joe and said I looked forward to seeing him tomorrow, as usual.

I stepped back inside and nearly threw the letter on the fire. It took all my strength not to do so. Unlike Joe, Christopher would never mistake my courage for indecisiveness. He would say the beauty of a single note depended not on how you played it, but when. So instead I tucked the letter under the table runner on top of the piano, and made a secret pact with myself that when the time was right, when I was ready, I'd take the letter down to the beach to read it, alone, by moonlight, with no wind to ruffle the pages or blow away the words.

Perhaps it was the pointed glances from my mother, the fact that she had stopped asking me if I'd heard from Christopher, had remained silent until this morning when she'd said, "Dear, you can't carry on like this." Or perhaps the moment had simply arrived, the pact unsealing itself along with the envelope.

So this is why I'm here, on the beach, minding the receding tide, with the letter in my frozen hand. My grieving well-begun, my pillow fully soaked with two month's worth of tears, it's time to read the words I already know are there, already carved into my heart.

22

In the days and years before Freddie had first pulled on his postboy uniform, nothing ever seemed to happen in Eagley. Up until that point he had even been largely oblivious to the war. Yes, he had watched the trucks of soldiers passing through the village on their way to Dover, and could even hear the distant rumble of guns from France when the cloud cover was low and the wind blew in the right direction. There were the fund-raising fetes too, and the giving up of pots and pans to be melted down into guns. But these things didn't happen to Freddie, he seemed instead to watch them all from afar as a mere spectator. Then the blue uniform with red trimmings and the shako hat changed all that. Mrs Mawby, Mrs Harkness, Anne Ellis – Freddie had been the deliverer of their devastating news and in so doing he felt personally responsible for their grief. It was not, however, those tales that exercised the village jaw muscles, but that of Stephen and his scandalous arrest. With his story the gossip on people's tongues took on a different tone, the ends of their sentences raised along with their eyebrows. If Kaiser Wilhelm had walked down Eagley High Street it would not have been more shocking. Or more thrilling. No one seemed to care about the victim, the anonymous Canadian soldier, but Stephen Harkness was the subject of endless kangaroo courts held over the garden wall. Only Freddie seemed to care about Christopher, he thought. And about Anne.

Then there was Tendring. It was true his visits were not always pleasant, sometimes far from it, and a pall of sadness still hovered over the place, but Freddie was beguiled by it. There was a glow emanating from the walls when the sun shone, as well as a magnetism he did not understand yet found irresistible. So Freddie was disappointed there had been no post for Tendring on the Monday. More than that he resented his journey to Tendring being denied him, and briefly entertained the absurd idea that if he missed a day then the house might not be there on the following one. He realised he no longer thought of Millie; Tendring was his new infatuation. He wanted to be missed, to have his absence noted, questions asked. Absurd indeed. In reality he would turn up this morning, Tuesday, and the house would still be there, with the same people in it, he would hand over the post and be unlikely to say anything other than good morning.

As he opened up the front door of the Post Office – twist, pull, turn – his musings about Tendring quickly evaporated, replaced by the sound of an approaching motorbike and thoughts of the despatch rider. She was early.

Freddie tipped out the bag of post onto the counter. There seemed to be more than usual, almost double the amount, probably forty letters. Perhaps a bag had temporarily gone missing yesterday. It would not be the first time. That would explain why there had been no Monday post for Tendring. He glanced at some of the dates of the post marks and a few were a day older than they should have been, which confirmed his suspicions. It meant, of course, that it would take twice as long to sort and he wanted to get it done before George arrived otherwise it would look like he was slacking.

But in fact it made no real difference, taking him four minutes instead of two, filling up the Eagley North, Eagley South, and Eagley Village pigeonholes with the forty letters. Then he took the Eagley North pile, which included Tendring, and reordered them to follow his route. On his first few days on the job he had sorted them as he went on his rounds, because George had told him to, but he had found that doing it beforehand was more efficient. It seemed obvious to him. George didn't seem to notice, and often wasn't there to see it anyway.

The ordering meant that on top of the pile was a letter for Major and Mrs Harkness. By now he had learnt immediately to recognise a letter that had come from the front. There was the stamp of course, but also the censor's mark, the thin translucent paper, often some dirty fingerprints and even, he was sure, the smell of damp earth. He must have handled scores of them by now, but they were still as exotic as if they had come from Mars. He glanced at the address for a moment longer and checked, almost without realising he was doing it, for a little black cross in the top corner. There was none, nor did he expect there to be. He hadn't seen one for two months and was merely looking subconsciously, out of habit.

He heard the front door being opened. George was early. Everyone was early this morning – or was Freddie late again? Had his alarm clock lost time? He panicked, threw the pile of letters on the counter by his waist, stretched up to a small drawer where the rubber bands were kept and took out a handful, but the letters began to slip off the counter and he instinctively grabbed at them. The rubber bands went flying as he just managed to scoop up the letters in his cupped hands – all except one, which landed by his shoe. He bent forward to pick up the errant envelope that had come to rest face down on the floor.

Freddie could see George's grim smile in his mind's eye. *Sometimes on the front... sometimes on the back.* He felt sick. There it was, smaller even than usual, an apologetic black cross lilting slightly to one side, as if scribbled in haste. It would be missed by those who didn't understand. But for Freddie there was no mistaking the sign as it stabbed at him like a knife to his heart. No mother's sigh could ever erase the small black mark, put there by some army Captain in the trenches for reasons of mere bureaucratic efficiency, inked in so that the news might be expedited. Or might not. The officer was unlikely to have the time or energy to care. The cross seemed to be there solely for Freddie, to give the knife an extra twist. The angel of death was exercising its wings and taking flight again. He turned the letter over to read the address. Tendring was a graveyard and here was another cross to plant in it.

The letter shook in Freddie's hand. He thought of the portrait, the three sons, imagining the shrine under the copper beech where two pewter-framed faces were about to be joined by a third. Then he remembered the story in his Boy's Own Annual of how American Indians thought photographs were the thief of the soul – but he jumped when George clattered into the room, removing his jacket as he walked over to his armchair. Freddie felt flustered, jumpy, almost guilty, even though he had done nothing wrong.

"You all right?" asked Franklin as he sat down in his chair and flicked open his newspaper, not needing or expecting a reply.

"I'm fine," said Freddie. He was becoming an expert liar.

Suhani was applying make-up to her bruised eye with a small handkerchief. Having moved the mirror nearer to the window she could see that the paste she had mixed up using turmeric and helenium petals was turning out to be more effective than she expected, and the bruise began to disappear with each daub of silk. The story of her swollen eye was not one she wanted Tristan to hear. She wanted tomorrow, the day of his arrival, to go perfectly. Yesterday had been spent filling every room with flowers, washing the bedding and preparing special meals. On top of looking after ten wounded soldiers, this had turned Tendring into a place more resembling the Savoy, with everyone swarming around the house like a colony of ants. As she applied a final lick of makeup, Suhani made what felt like a heartless calculation: would the joy of Tristan's arrival trump her mourning for Arthur and Edward?

Covering up her eye, however, would do nothing to explain his father's absence. She would have to tell Tristan something, except she wasn't sure herself what the truth of the matter was. She thought of Stephen in the Police House. It was where she wanted him, away from her, beyond the reach of his grasp, his scowl, his fist. Yet she did not feel free. Moreover she wanted him to be guilty, but wasn't sure he was. He had become capable of cruelty, certainly, but not such an act of brutal, premeditated violence as this. If anything the hanging had been an act of kindness by whoever had helped; but then, as she leant forward to examine her face more closely in the mirror, she wasn't sure Stephen was capable of that either. Not anymore. A solution started to crystallise in her mind, some idea not yet fully formed. She knew, however, that it began by finding her way to the Police House.

The makeup was covering up another unpalatable fact, too. She was looking forward to tomorrow, longing to have Tristan home again, but she was also dreading it. In her weekly, sometimes daily, letters to Tristan she had shared everything except the one reason she would pick up her pen. Staring at the writing paper for several minutes, perhaps hours, she had been unable to find any words to tell Tristan that Edward had been lost to German bullets, not least because she hadn't, in truth, come to terms with it herself. Each time she tried, the task became ever harder, and in the end she thought it best to break the news when he came home. But that was cowardly, she knew it. In her grief she had not been thinking clearly, now she felt ashamed of the deceit. Suhani picked up her silk handkerchief and wiped away all the makeup she had just applied. The truth would have to be told; all of it.

Hannah stood with Gabriel in the hallway facing the grandfather clock. "There's a clock at Celandine Hall," she said. "Grander than this one. They'll be grateful for your help."

He looked at the face of the clock, then at her, then back again. She felt she wasn't getting through to him so she tried a different tack, lowering her voice and placing her hand on his arm. "I'll miss you Gabriel."

Gabriel's eyes flicked into life, as if she had switched the points on a railway track, and he replied in a whisper with such an extraordinary statement that Hannah's eyes widened in disbelief, as much at the quantity of words as to their content.

"Get out of this house. As soon as you can. There's demons lurking in every corner, I've seen 'em with my own eyes. Sooner or later they'll kill you. Escape the shadows and step into the light, while you still can."

Hannah was at a loss how to respond. She had never previously heard him utter more than five consecutive words, and usually those made no sense. This new speech, too, sounded in some ways like nonsense, yet was constructed in a way that was educated and intelligent – a lightning brain misfiring, Hannah presumed, thoughts and memories trying to make sense of their own faulty connections. Jack had called it shell-shock so, in the end, that was what she put this current outburst down to. These were the sounds of insanity, simple as that. She dismissed Gabriel's warning from her mind, though her heart, she suspected, might not let go of it so easily.

"Let's get you outside," said Hannah, taking his arm in hers as if they had just got married, and she walked him down the hallway, through the open front door and into the garden where the ambulance was waiting for them, and where Nurse Collins was talking to Suhani.

Nurse Collins handed Suhani some papers, which Suhani took but did not look at.

"Five removals, seven deliveries," said Nurse Collins. "I'm sorry, you'll have to find space somehow. The beds won't come until tomorrow. If any of you can speak a bit of German..."

Suhani interrupted as if she had not been listening. "We'll manage thank you. If necessary I will sleep with the maids."

"Will you indeed?"

"Well, I used to be one."

"I see. I'm sure you'll be very comfortable then. Now, where is Jack? Those are his leaving papers."

Suhani folded her arms, scrunching the paperwork in the process, to the obvious annoyance of Nurse Collins. "Jack has already left," said Suhani. "Under his own steam you might say."

"You just let him walk out?"

"He was quite determined."

"Well, they'll catch the silly fool soon enough. Then hopefully they'll shoot him."

Suhani couldn't decide if Nurse Collins was being sincere, or if it was an attempt at levity. She hoped for the latter, though Nurse Collins' face gave nothing away, and Suhani wondered if anyone had ever had the privilege of truly knowing this impenetrable woman.

"We can't dilly-dally any longer," she continued. "Where's Gabriel? Oh, there you are. Hop in."

She flapped some vague indication to Hannah for her to help Gabriel into the ambulance. They were passed by four injured soldiers who were making their way in the opposite direction into the house, new inmates to Tendring, helped by Phoebe and two nurses. Three of the soldiers all had their right arms in slings, like wounded triplets, and the fourth was more heavily bandaged, his eyes and face completely covered, clinging to Phoebe like a lost child, barely able to walk.

Hannah appeared to be saying goodbye to Gabriel, which provoked Nurse Collins even further and she called over, "Quickly please!" before turning to Suhani to hiss, "What a waste of time. He'll forget her by lunchtime."

"On the contrary," said Suhani. "That which is not written down is remembered."

"Oh really," she replied. "What exactly does that mean?"

Suhani shrugged. "It's an expression. From India."

Nurse Collins eyed her up. "India is an odd place I would imagine."

"India is many places, Nurse Collins."

They looked at each other for a moment and then to Suhani's surprise Nurse Collins took a step forward. She sensed Nurse Collins was looking at her bruised eye and thought some barb or cut was coming, but, in a moment of unexpected compassion, the opposite happened.

"I'm sorry about your sons Mrs Harkness. And your husband. All that business. If there's anything I can do to help."

Suhani wondered what sadnesses inhabited this woman's own life, whether she saw them reflected in Suhani's own eyes, but she knew whatever they were she would take them with her to the grave. She reminded her of Stephen, of most English people in fact, who kept their broken crockery at the back of the cupboard and never laid their table out. Suhani had to take a second to readjust to this unforeseen kindness before nodding her silent gratitude. But she was also buying time to think through the possibilities of a new opportunity that had just opened up. "Are you going to Eagley Village?"

"After Celandine, yes."

"Then I will come with you if I may."

"Oh," said Nurse Collins, clearly making some adjustments of her own. "What for?"

But Suhani was already taking the first few steps towards the front of the ambulance and calling over her shoulder: "Hannah, I'm going to the Police House. You're in charge. I don't know what time I'll be back."

Hannah and Nurse Collins looked at each other, equally perplexed, as they watched Suhani climb into the front passenger seat. Nurse Collins called out, "I don't know that there's room!" but Suhani was already nestling herself into the seat next to the startled driver.

"There's room," she smiled.

The ambulance bounced like a puppy dog along the Eagley Road with Gabriel and three other soldiers sitting in the back holding on to each other for stability. In some places the track was so uneven there was a danger the vehicle's hard tyres and lack of suspension would add to the occupants' injuries, entirely defeating the object of their journey to the rehabilitation ward at Celandine.

On the front seat Suhani was squeezed between the driver and Nurse Collins, which to some extent kept her steady, but it was by no means a comfortable ride and she kept looking straight ahead to avoid feeling queasy. She had tried shutting her eyes but that made it worse, and found instead it was best to fix her gaze on the road ahead.

The orchard was coming up on the right and the wheatfield fell away to the left where the errant apple tree was bearing rich, red fruit glistening in the sun. But then another flash of light caught her eye, out of place at the foot of the tree, a tangle of brambles inexplicably shimmering in the sunshine. It was only when the ambulance was upon it she realised that behind the brambles was a bicycle, lying in the grass, barely visible but reflecting sunlight off its frame, and dumped on the ground as if the rider had fallen off. Then she realised it was not just any bike, but Freddie's, so she thought about asking the driver to stop but by then they had already passed the spot and were beginning to round the next bend. She remembered the accident Freddie had suffered two months ago, but decided that not everything in this war was a catastrophe. Perhaps he was simply excusing himself behind the hedgerow. He must have been desperate, discarding his bike like a fledgling fallen out of the apple tree. Suhani turned round to look, forcing an unaccommodating Nurse Collins to lean over, but she felt foolish as there was no rear window to see through. All she was left to stare at was the wax in Nurse Collins' ear, which made her feel queasy again.

In fact Freddie had not fallen off his bike, but had tried to hide it amongst the brambles so that it would not be seen from the road. He had then walked into the wheatfield, although it had felt as if some exterior force had taken him by the hand and led him there. Fifty yards into its interior, he reached a spot where he thought there was no chance he could be discovered. What he did next he had not done for many years, but today it made him feel safe, untouchable to the world outside. Freddie laid down amongst the wheat and stretched himself out with his arms by his sides, listening to the birdsong, looking up at the sky, wishing the songs would last forever and the clouds would clear to reveal some trace of heaven.

He held the letter up at arms length for the blue light of the sky to pass through it. The paper was thin enough to see that there was writing but not enough to make sense of the sentences, the words themselves a blur. It didn't matter, he was sure he knew what they said. Although it was not a telegram and therefore the law had nothing to say about it, there was courtesy to consider. Courtesy. Freddie sighed heavily. There was nothing courteous about breaking such devastating news to someone who was already heart-broken. He slowly raised the letter until it obscured the sun, and although the writing did not become any clearer, his duty did, and it was finally Shiva who told him what to do. Destroy the universe in order to recreate it. They had been Suhani's own words, and they gave him permission. Death was to be delivered, on time, without fuss.

A flock of birds rippled across the sky above Freddie's head, disturbed by a noise, a sound that nature abhorred but one that Freddie was always excited by, another internal combustion engine. And not just any engine but a specific one he was familiar with, that of the ambulance – it had, after all, not so long ago brushed its fender past his nose. It was coming from the direction of Tendring, Freddie surmised, and was heading for Eagley. He imagined it driving past, wondered what its purpose was, who was being collected, who delivered, what selection of injuries they had, how much it would hurt to lose an arm or an eye. Or your mind. He waited a full minute for the sound to disappear before standing up, then put the letter back in his pouch and headed off towards his discarded bike. As he walked through the wheat, being careful to retrace the trampled path he had made on his way in, he wiped his eyes, only then realising he had been crying, having begun to mourn, in advance, the death of Suhani's third son. There was no escaping it, for her, or for him.

His approach to Tendring began to fill Freddie with dread, each turn of his pedals like the churning of spoiled milk. He wanted to change his mind. If only George had not explained what a Noddy was he could deliver this one in all innocence. Mrs Harkness had told him he no longer needed to go through Sandy Woods, but he wished with all his heart that he still did – any excuse to delay this delivery – or wished it with half his heart at least. The peculiar feeling began of splitting into two people, one who delivered, and one who did not. Finish the job, or abandon it. With each yard travelled, uncertainty flooded Freddie's road ahead.

He had not long dismounted by the stone eagles of Tendring and begun pushing his bike up the driveway when he noticed the portico was covered in bunting. His heart sank even further, thinking of the letter he had delivered on Sunday, such rare good news, and how the letter he had with him now would outdo it, the Ace of Hearts trumping the King of Diamonds, the bunting torn down by the storm he was about to unleash.

He lifted the lion's-head knocker. This was his last chance. He could go back, lose the letter in the hedgerows, have it taken up by the wind and left to rot with the autumn leaves – he could actually do that, and felt within him the power to alter the direction of Suhani's life. For a moment the idea surged through his veins, even lifted his spirits. But it was a ludicrous notion, it was not for him to change the message. Rules, courtesy, call it what you like, the letter had to be delivered.

He was about to bring the lion's head down when he heard footsteps approaching from behind the front door, saving him the trouble. It seemed Suhani could read his mind and once again Tendring was working its dark magic.

Except it was not Suhani, but Hannah.

"Oh. What are you doing here?" she said, whilst propping the door open with an iron boot scraper. "Round the back why don't you?"

There was the tapping of cutlery coming from the library and he could smell fried bacon. "Mrs Harkness changed her mind."

"Did she now? Well she's not here. You can give the post to me." She held out her hand.

Freddie's first thought was to do just that, to hand the burden over, walk away and leave the responsibility to others. He even got as far as opening his leather pouch, but then startled himself with a fabrication so unexpected it registered later in his own ears than in Hannah's.

"It's a telegram."

With that, there was no way back. In stalling the delivery, he'd made it inevitable. He had forced his own hand, and he wasn't sure where the lie had come from, except he could feel Suhani at his shoulder as if she were actually standing there.

"Well I don't know when she'll be back," said Hannah. "She might be all day."

"Oh. Right." He had no idea what to do next, and might have stood there until sunset except Hannah, after a moment's consideration, came up with a suggestion.

"Well she's gone to the Police House. To speak to Mr Harkness I fancy. But they're taking her via Celandine Hall, so if you go straight to the village now you'll probably catch her."

He did up the strap on his pouch. The village was next on his route. "The Police House?"

"Yes. Or you could give the blessed thing to me and be done with it. No one would be any the wiser. Still, if it's that important to you..."

"Thank you miss," said Freddie. It was very much important to him, he realised, this was what being a postboy was all about. And the Police House might be a better place to deliver bad news because Stephen would be there to comfort Mrs Harkness. Yes, that sounded right. In any case the letter was addressed to both of them. His impeccable logic made him feel better about it all. He wondered too, if he was curious about looking into the eyes of a murderer. So he nodded to Hannah, and was off.

The delphiniums that lined the drive had been cut back, or had simply died. As Freddie pushed his bicycle past the headless stalks and away from Tendring he imagined this would be the end of it, that by this time tomorrow Mrs Harkness would have no more sons to lose, no more twists and turns for her to face, death being the one certainty in life and that she could at last step forward into it. Destroy, recreate, that was what he thought as he mounted his bike and headed off in the direction of Eagley village, with the letter and its black cross in his pouch, pushed by the hand of Shiva, by rules, courtesy, and by truth itself. Momentarily he – or half of him – felt content. Destroy the boy, create the man.

23

Suhani sat on the floor cross-legged, one hand inside the other on her lap, palms up. She was facing the door with her back to Stephen, who in turn sat at the desk with his back to her. Suhani felt as if they had taken two steps in a duel before changing their minds and deciding to sit. A plate of food and a glass of wine was on the table in front of him, though so far he had touched neither. Roper had left the door of Stephen's room open to the corridor, as promised, but still Suhani found the air stale, smelling of cold food and sleep.

There was the sound of another door opening and closing at the far end of the corridor outside. Suhani looked up to see PC Waveney walk past their open doorway and assumed he was going to the privy.

"What happens next, Stephen?"

When he answered, after several seconds of thinking about it, there was a strange music in his voice, a gentle lilt that Suhani had not heard in years but brought back the same smell of roses she'd breathed in from the bunting.

"I believe they take me to Ramsgate to be formally interviewed. It was supposed to be today, but William got called away to Canterbury.

Looks like tomorrow now. Unless of course someone can disabuse them all of their misinterpretation of the facts."

"Why doesn't William interview you?"

"He is prohibited from doing so because we are friends. At least, he thinks so."

"Aren't you? Friends?"

"Well. I am his."

They both heard the toilet flush, then the footsteps of PC Waveney returning along the corridor and opening and closing the far door.

She rocked slightly in her seated position on the hard wooden floor. "Are you comfortable here?"

"What difference does it make to you?"

They were angry words, but his delivery was anything but. He was trying to sound kind and it unnerved Suhani. Was it kindness, though, or the dispassionate utterance of a murderer? Suhani was afraid of knowing, which was why she had her back to him, so she just said, "I'm not sure that it does."

"Then why did you ask?"

"I don't know Stephen. Force of habit?"

"In fact why are you here?"

Suhani looked down at her hands and turned the top one over to examine the veins on the back of it. One of them, near the middle knuckle, was visibly pulsing. "I think it was Jack. I believe he was the witness. But he's gone now."

"Jack? Where?"

"To Rye, so he said."

"You just let him leave?"

"Yes I did."

"Why?"

"It's not for me to tell a man what to do, is it?"

Suhani heard the clink of glass against ceramic. Stephen must have reached for his wine glass and caught the edge of his plate. There was a moment, perhaps taken up with the sipping of his wine, before he spoke.

"Why would he lie?" he said.

"Is he lying?"

"I imagine he is protecting himself." There was a sadness in his voice. "We could be over all this if you just told them I was at home that night."

Not just sadness though, thought Suhani, but more than that, an acceptance, a going-through-the-motions that sounded unlike any previous version of himself, either from before or after South Africa. He seemed relieved, despite his denials, to have been caught. This made it seem to Suhani both more likely, and less likely, that he had tied the hangman's noose. She couldn't fathom him, had no idea who he was. With each passing day they had moved further apart and now he might as well have been on the other side of the world. Back in India perhaps, having never met her, and having lived a life without her. The choice, all those years ago, which seemed so right then, had ended up like this, an unimaginable distance between them.

"Tell them I was at home all night," he reiterated.

"But I don't know that do I. I wasn't there myself."

"Tell them anyway," he said. "Nobody knows where you were. A wife has duties and this is yours. Go and tell them I was at home all night." His muted timbre had fallen further, almost to a whisper. "If you *are* my wife, that is."

For the first time since she had sat down on the floor, Suhani raised up her head to look at the bare wall two feet in front of her face.

"When was the last time you actually told the truth, Stephen?"

She was building up to something, the reason she had come, knowing she was going to hurt him, didn't want to but had to, and could already hear in his reply the pain she was about to inflict.

"When was the last time I lied to you? I've never lied to you. Tell me when have I ever lied to you?"

The door out in the hallway opened and closed again, but this time she didn't look up to see who it was. Instead she shifted her weight again, and sighed heavily. At first she didn't know where to begin, how to answer him, Stephen Harkness, the long-ago love they had once shared, when truth came easily and lies were unthinkable, and the only pain was the sweet kind, from the thorn of a rose he handed her at midnight. When had they swapped places, these two boatmen, truth and untruth, crossing time's river in the middle of the night?

There was a creak of floorboard which sounded like it came from out in the hallway, but Suhani had shifted her weight again, so she put it down to that.

Freddie had made his way to the village, to the Police House, and then to the desk where PC Waveney sat. At first it had been unattended so Freddie had waited until PC Waveney came back from the privy. Freddie had handed over the post for Inspector Roper, as he did everyday, but then explained he had a letter for Mr & Mrs Harkness, that he thought it was important and asked if he could deliver it here. PC Waveney might have considered it an odd request, but was busy with recording in his ledger the seven cases of poaching over the last fortnight, so absent-mindedly waved him through.

When Freddie had entered the corridor outside Stephen's room, he already had the letter in his hand, ready to deliver. He was nervous, but at the same time was empowered by the idea he was doing the right thing, his adolescent authority oozing out of the seams of his uniform. Immediately he could hear Suhani's voice and initially it was just a polite reticence that stopped him from interrupting; but as he got closer and could hear more clearly what she was saying, picking up a few key words that indicated an intensely private conversation, he became fixed to the spot. The longer he left it the more difficult it became to disturb her, and the guiltier he felt. He stood just outside the doorway where he could not be seen, but where he could hear, perfectly, every word, whether he wanted to or not, and the more she spoke, the more her words began to cut through him. Rising and falling, catching in her throat, her lament made little sense in Freddie's head, but in his heart rang as true as the church bell.

"You lie to me all the time."

Each word that Suhani uttered fell upon Stephen's shoulders like clods of earth on a coffin lid.

"You lie to me when you hold up your newspaper so we can't see each other across the dinner table and you lie to me by talking about the price of coal and you lie to me by coming home late at night in the hope that I've already gone to bed. That was never a duty Stephen, although I wouldn't mind even if it was, that would be something, except you are a ghost now. I don't know who you are anymore, and now, I don't care. Someone came back, but it wasn't you. You know, I often think about that, when you returned, walked up the drive at four o'clock in the afternoon. I remember it was so cold for the time of year and the ravens were circling. I should have taken that as an omen, shouldn't I. You walked towards me and the first thing I did was tell you that I loved you, but you looked at me as if you simply didn't know me, didn't want to, you said nothing. And that was when the silences began, with each passing day becoming longer and crueller until they were indistinguishable from hatred. Do you remember it, that day?"

At first Stephen thought it was a rhetorical question but she was waiting too long and he was horrified to realise she wanted an actual answer. The truth was, he remembered it like it was happening now, as many of his memories did. Sometimes it woke him from a dream, only to discover that in his wakefulness the nightmare continued, that whenever the words began to swell in his gullet his throat would tighten and close. He couldn't tell her about his love for her any more than he could tell her about the body parts he had been required to step over on the battlefield, or the pink mist of his friend, or the tooth in his neck, or the pools of his own blood he left glistening in the sand. She was right, he had his own way of lying, he was doing it now, leaving an emptiness that meant her question would remain forever unanswered, and she would have to fill the silence herself. As he listened, he gripped his glass of wine more tightly in his hand, wondering if it would break, until he knew she had given up on his replying.

"I'd waited three years but, my goodness Stephen, how the world can change in a single moment. I tried to talk to you but even Shiva can't unscramble an egg so in the end I stopped trying. You lied to me with your silences and you still do. Or when you do speak it is of nothing. Your words are like dust. I'm tired of hearing about deliveries of whale oil and burned seaweed and those poor women who look like canaries. I'm tired of it all. I used to try to tell you how I felt, properly, you know, and tried to understand you, but, worse than striking me with your fist, you would just squash me like a scorpion with one of your sneering English platitudes."

Stephen noticed a twitching nerve in his hand as he held the glass. It was only a few days ago when he would have exploded into a rage at Suhani's speech – indeed he would never have allowed her to get this far. Or more likely she would never have attempted it in the first place. But he felt no rage now. He had the peculiar thought, a kind of revelation, that he was glad he had hit her, because it allowed her to talk, and for him, finally, to listen.

"I caught my reflection last night. Do you know what I saw? My bruised eye for what it really was. It was the first time you had touched me since 1902. That is literally true Stephen. Have we even brushed past each other in the hallway? I really don't think we ever have. Why did you take fourteen years to slowly kill me when you could have just put a pistol to my heart? You taught me not to let a fox choke to death on the snare, so why do it to me? We sit next to each other at church and you place your prayer book between us. Every Sunday you do it. You were always shy and that was because you were kind but, still, we have three sons. They all wanted to be born, didn't they? Their need was ours too, wasn't it? How could you send them all to fight? In this ridiculous war? Where did your love for them go? You put guns in their hands and tried to put hate in their hearts, parcelling it up as duty. One of them was even too young to be sent to France. But you sent them anyway. Why? What was the point? I think you sent them because you didn't have the courage to finish yourself off. I think you are a coward. You have no medals from South Africa, do you, and now I know why."

Stephen opened his mouth to protest, but it was half-hearted and he shut it again. It was not his time to speak.

"Now I have one son left. Well, I will not lose him. When he comes home, he will stay, whatever the cost to you. You will make it so, you will pull your army strings Stephen, and I will tell them you were home all night. That's my bargain with you. You'll not send Tristan to his death and I'll not send you to yours."

Freddie stood in the shadows and stroked the black cross on the back of the envelope with his thumb. It was impossible to deliver it, not now, not after this. In those last few minutes when Suhani had been talking to Stephen, Freddie had the sensation that she had also been speaking directly to him, begging him to somehow commute the sentence of death. He considered for a split-second there might be a danger in not delivering this letter, but he couldn't think about the consequences because the alternative – breaking her heart again – seemed immeasurably worse. Suddenly he found himself crying, silently, walking away from the open door, away from Suhani's words, down the corridor and into PC Waveney's office, with the letter still in his hand.

But as he slipped away, wiping his face with his sleeve, he had the uncanny feeling that someone, or something, was going to help him out.

Once more, Suhani heard the click of the door in the corridor outside their room and thought perhaps PC Waveney was bringing them some tea, or coming to tell her the station Fly was waiting. She leant forward onto her knees, rose gracefully to a standing position and then looked across at Stephen as he sat at the desk.

"I'll tell them. I'll tell them I was angry with you about something that I have now forgiven you for. Perhaps something about grief clouding my judgement. And about my position in life. You know, my duty as a wife. Especially a native. It has its advantages. I expect they will rather enjoy accepting that." Suhani watched him. He was sitting perfectly still with his back to her. Then, having finally understood the power of silence, she simply walked towards the door to leave the room and Stephen in it.

She was surprised to find the corridor empty. PC Waveney was not bringing any tea. But there was a noise from behind her, barely audible, the rustle of clothes and the creak of a chair. Looking back through the open door she saw her husband had turned to look at her with hunched shoulders and empty eyes, and she noticed he was trembling slightly, as if he were cold. For a moment she felt sorry for him, knew he was desperate for her to reach out, offer a word of rapprochement, or even just a goodbye, a softening of the air like a sprinkling of rose water, but she knew she had none left in her. She had to finish what she had started, pull the trigger on the fox, so she plumbed the depths of her pity only to find contempt there. "I don't think you helped Christopher. You're too much of a coward for that."

Freddie rubbed his face with his hands as if it might erase what had just happened. He was desperate to escape from the Police House but PC Waveney was waving some post at him.

"Here. Don't go without this lot."

If Suhani saw Freddie it would be obvious to PC Waveney that Freddie's letter had not been delivered and his story would fall apart, so he had to get out, quick. He took the letters from PC Waveney and began to open his pouch, hoping that if he didn't speak then no conversation would ensue. But PC Waveney carried on.

"You took your time didn't you?"

Freddie had to think quickly. "They were talking. I had to wait."

"I hope it was worth it."

"It wasn't as important as I thought. Something about whale oil."

Whale oil. Construct the lie with fragments of truth, it was a good trick. By now he had stuffed the letters in his pouch but didn't bother to do it up, enabling him to leave more quickly. He walked out of the room calling over his shoulder, "I'm late, sorry!" and was gone.

As one door closed another opened. Freddie had just managed to miss Suhani, who came into the room moments later and PC Waveney politely stood up.

"Strange boy, that one," he said.

"Who?"

"The postboy. In another world half the time."

Suhani thought about saying she was sorry she'd missed him, but she felt protective of Freddie, wanted to defend him, and so took the conversation in a different direction. "Like Shiva, I suppose."

"Beg your pardon, ma'am?"

"Never mind. I have something important to tell you." It was a story she had fabricated as she'd sat in the ambulance on the way from Tendring, why she had kept quiet until now. And it seemed to do the job.

Freddie had spent the whole while until the end of his shift terrified that there might be more post for Tendring, devising all sorts of scenarios in his head in order to avoid delivering it. Even though in the end no more letters had materialised the mere possibility of a knock on the Post Office door or the revving of a motorbike engine had caused him distress for the rest of the day.

Freddie was about to lock up. George had left earlier, unusually sober and therefore in an irritable state, so Freddie was happy to be left alone. He needed more writing provisions to take home, more paper, ink, possibly a new nib for his pen. George had let him take them before, in fact he had originally suggested it, but Freddie still felt a pang of guilt because his boss wasn't there right now to grant permission. As he stuffed the supplies into his pouch he thought about the next part of his plan. There it was, sitting on the counter, hiding in plain sight, George's Primus and kettle, property of G.P.O. This was how he was going to steam open the envelope.

In the last few hours of the day, the air cooled, the autumn came and the villagers swept up its leaves. With the sun setting a few minutes earlier than the evening before, sleep came to many. Those that were married or shared a bed with their brothers or sisters held on to each other for warmth, whilst those who were alone slept under an extra coat or blanket.

Hannah and Phoebe slept back to back because it was more comfortable for Phoebe's unborn baby. Their door was open so that Hannah could hear the bell from the library, but mostly the soldiers slept and dreamed of fields of poppies, of the poppies that gave them laudanum, of the laudanum that gave them sleep, and the sleep that returned them to their dreams.

But there were three others, elsewhere in the house and the village, who did not, or could not, sleep. Three who in different ways needed one another, three who needed to speak the truth and have the truth spoken to them. They were waiting but could wait no longer, and each was sitting perfectly still in the light of a candle at their desks. An English woman who used to be an Indian maid, a man who had once been a soldier, and a boy who was becoming a man. All three yearned for the person they used to be; but there would never be any going back.

24

Stephen was the first of the three to move, and only then because he was told to. Inspector Roper had returned late from Canterbury, PC Waveney had relayed Suhani's story to him and so Roper had decided to take it upon himself to release Stephen. He went in to tell his friend he was free to go and five minutes later they were both outside, Roper leaning against the car and smoking, with Stephen standing in the doorway, looking up at the night sky.

"Want one?" asked Roper, holding up his lit cigarette. "Got a drawer full inside."

"No. No thank you. It's good of you to let me go. I presume it won't cause you any trouble?"

"I'll ring 'em in the morning. To be honest they didn't seem too interested."

"Even so. It's a risk, isn't it?"

"Well, I owe you, don't I."

That word again. Stephen looked at Inspector Roper, his Masonic friend, who was staring straight ahead and seemed to be studiously avoiding eye contact.

Stephen said, "Do you?"

"Well, let's stick together, eh? Enough said."

"Enough said about what?"

Roper threw down his cigarette and stubbed it into the ground with his shoe. He looked at Stephen and then turned his head away to speak in muted tones. "I know what Margaret told you."

"What did she tell me?" Stephen couldn't recall any conversation with Roper's wife of any substance. She was a woman who could effortlessly merge into the wallpaper.

Roper stroked his chin and Stephen thought he was back-tracking, trying to cover up a mistake, making a false effort to sound chirpy. "Well, water under the bridge now isn't it? So..." He held out his hand for his friend to shake but Stephen looked down at it suspiciously.

"I didn't realise you owed me anything."

Stephen could see Roper begin to quietly panic. "Well, doesn't matter, evens now aren't we, let's just stick together, eh?" The repetition sounded a false note as he moved his outstretched hand a little closer towards Stephen. They held each other's stare for several seconds before Stephen finally decided to shake it. Roper squeezed Stephen's top knuckle, but this time Stephen did not return the Masonic gesture and was the first to let go.

"I'll take you home," said Roper, nodding at the car and trying to waft away the smell of their previous conversation along with his cigarette fumes, even though the smoke no longer hung in the air. "Daft walking, it's miles."

"Thank you but actually I could do with the air. I have all night."

The moon came out from behind a cloud and Stephen walked away without another word, aware of a nervous Roper watching him. What did Roper think his wife Margaret had said? There were rumours, accompanied by a nod and a wink, it was true, and it was those that made Stephen decide to take the long way home, to see if there was anything in them.

Removing his pocket watch Stephen saw that he had been walking for two hours and notwithstanding the burning sensation in his hip he had been going like a train, so must have covered at least eight miles. He felt better for it, the walk had cleared his head. His thoughts made more sense, and the idea of walking forever, away from Tendring, appealed to him. He wasn't needed there, or wanted, he could not love or be loved, so what was the point? If he carried on walking, would he be missed? Only in the sense that his roses would die. But he had experienced that before, in India, and knew that they could always be replanted by someone else. In fact he felt more than contentment; he was actually at peace.

Until someone whistled. It was only then he realised he was no longer in the countryside and had reached the outskirts of a town, possibly Ramsgate, with houses either side of the road. He turned to look and saw someone standing in a doorway. She called over to him.

"Two bob, or three, dependin'." And he understood why he was there.

A minute later, at the most, he was in her bedroom. He had never visited a whore before, not even when the opportunities were legion and at their easiest during a war. It was not so much the dishonesty, the lack of faithfulness, although that would have certainly troubled him, it was just that he found the idea unattractive, not remotely erotic. Whores had rotten teeth and this one was no exception, so he was not sure why he was sat on the edge of her bed. Perhaps, he thought, it was in some pathetic way his last chance to be a man. But he didn't want to be there.

During his incarceration he had spent nearly three days essentially staring at a wall and now he was doing it again, examining the intricate patterns of mould on the girl's cracked plaster. The room stank of hawthorn and mistletoe, which was one thing in the open air, quite another in the confined space of a knocking lair.

She sat on the other side of the bed and was already removing her top layer of clothes. Stephen stood up to remove his coat, still with his back to her, and then spoke.

"I have an injury."

"Don't worry sir, soldiers my speciality these days, miracle worker I am."

There was another smell, a mixture of gin and morphine, both of which he was familiar with, and Stephen assumed that was the reason why the girl's speech was somewhat slurred and her eyes watery. He sat back down on the edge of the bed and began unenthusiastically slipping off his braces from his shoulders.

"I don't wish to be unfaithful to my wife."

She removed her shoe and put it to her nose to sniff it. "Really? Well that would be a bleedin' miracle."

The situation had suddenly become ridiculous and Stephen wanted to get out. He pulled his braces back over his shoulders and rubbed his forehead with his fingers. "Never mind."

She half-turned towards him. "Hang on sir. You a talker?"

She was right. "Yes. I suppose so. Would that be...acceptable?"

"Makes no odds to me. Cost you the same, mind. I mean, I can talk the hind legs off a donkey, I can. Or listen. Up to you."

She laid back on the bed, crossed her legs at the ankles and started rolling a cigarette. He looked at her properly for the first time, trying to judge if he recognised her, but after so many years, and so many men, it was impossible to say.

Suhani was the second of the three to move. She was sitting at her dressing table in her bedroom in almost complete darkness except for the light of the candle on her desk. She was exhausted but wide awake, unable to sleep, as was so often the case these days. Some household chore would usually serve as a distraction, and she could sometimes be found doing the laundry at two in the morning. But on this night she was in her room working on a task of her own, cutting out a picture of Edward from a larger photograph of the whole family. After two months she finally felt ready to place his image next to Arthur's in her shrine under the copper beech. It was unfortunate to be spoiling the photograph in such a way, but having searched every drawer in the house and every box in the attic, she could find no other suitable picture of Edward and therefore had no choice. It was a typical photographer's vignette, Suhani and Stephen standing with their three sons seated in front of them. In order to remove Edward, Suhani had to dissect Stephen's body. She paused before the final snip of her scissors, then cut through. It was only paper, but she couldn't shake off the feelings she experienced as she severed the bond: release, and betrayal.

In the cupboard under the stairs Suhani had found a second pewter frame for Edward's picture that exactly complimented the one she had for Arthur, and although she didn't believe fate could be tempted, she was secretly relieved she had not found a third. The photograph was now framed and ready to be placed under the copper beech.

Suhani put on a utility garment over her sari, an androgynous outdoor gown with metal buckles that would protect her from the cold air of the night. At the foot of the bedroom door was a pair of sandals from India she had owned since she was sixteen that would probably last as long again. She slipped them on as she left her bedroom to go downstairs, holding the framed photograph up to her chest so that it could not be stolen from her.

Descending the stairs she heard the quiet sound of sleep. It occurred to her she had not set foot inside the library since Sunday and had not remotely engaged with the influx of new arrivals. Stephen and Tristan had in their different ways taken up all of her thoughts and the ward system worked well without her, two day-nurses from Celandine taking the brunt of the labour and Hannah listening out for patients at night. But now, in the midnight stillness, she was at last drawn into the library, seduced by the disjointed purring of broken men and the creaking of their beds as they moved in their dreams. She found herself walking slowly between the two rows with their neatly hanging clipboards at the foot of each one. Watching and listening, she looked from side to side, her soft sandals making the wooden floor feel like grass. It was hard to believe the room was full of unimaginable pain. The miracle of laudanum.

Having reached the end of the library, Suhani turned around and walked slowly back again, towards the open door, her survey complete. Out of one dark corner, Shiva stared. Every time Suhani looked, Shiva had a different expression depending on the amount of light that fell across its face. Now he possessed a sullen countenance, brooding over the assembled beds as if about to pass judgement, a verdict and sentence she was not ready to hear. So she picked up her pace, trying to keep her sandled footsteps silent.

But she must have disturbed someone, because when she walked past the last bed she heard a voice, a single word, a fragile trace of another world.

"Bitte."

Suhani came to a stop and turned to look back along the rows of beds. There was no sign of movement.

"Bitte."

This time the word had required more effort, prised out with an ominous rattle from lungs that struggled to find air. Suhani walked towards the place where she thought the sound was coming from, a bed shrouded in shadow where she could just make out a face, except there was no face, instead a featureless bundle of bandages, as if the man had been mummified in advance of what was about to come. She realised he must be badly burnt. When the new arrivals had turned up she had not been paying attention and now felt ashamed that in not welcoming them she had let them down. Although she wasn't sure of the meaning of the word he was repeating, she felt the pull of what lay behind it and had no doubt he was asking for help.

Suhani picked up his clipboard and read the man's name: *Manfred Schreiber*. At first it made no sense, a German soldier recuperating in an English village, but then she remembered the circulating rumours about the crashed Zeppelin, about how one of the crew had escaped. That must be it. Hannah and Phoebe had been gossiping about it on several occasions. The police must have caught him, or perhaps he had handed himself in, or more likely, given his injuries, he had been found in a hedgerow by a bloodhound. Suhani wondered whether he had been sent here from Celandine in order to get better, or to die, and was struck again by the absurd madness of war. Putting bullet holes in a man and then sewing them up so he could return to the battlefields to be shot at again. The fact that he was German made it seem ten times worse. She read further down the page to see that he was a *Kapitänleutnant* and he was on large doses of laudanum, enough to put a horse to sleep at fifty paces.

"Bitte."

Softer now, the voice sounded reconciled to remaining unheard, which had the effect of drawing Suhani closer to it. Replacing the clipboard, Suhani went over to sit by the side of his bed. He tilted his head, he had heard her, and he tried a different word.

"Wasser."

There was no doubt this time what he meant, so Suhani poured a glass of water and put it to his lips through a thin gap in his bandages. He found it difficult to tip forward so she put her hand behind his head to offer support as he attempted to sip from the glass. She detected no resistance, except for the natural weight of a human head, which reminded her of a healthy newborn baby. He must be extremely weak, she thought. Suhani was not sure that he had actually swallowed any water, but wetting the bandages around his lips was presumably better than nothing.

"Sag meiner Mutter, dass ich sie liebe."

The words flowed quietly, as if he was praying to himself. Suhani put her hand on his bandaged forehead.

"I'm sorry Manfred, I don't understand."

"Sag meiner Mutter..." His voice died halfway through, turning into a whisper. "Dass ich sie liebe."

Suhani was desperate to understand and had at least picked up one word on second hearing and guessed what it might mean. The best she could do was repeat it back to him.

"Mother? Do you mean your Mother?"

"Ya. Sag ihr, dass ich sie liebe."

Suhani had no idea how to answer, so she stroked his forehead, smiled and nodded, a technique that had worked on all three of her newborns and seemed to work now, even though she knew he couldn't see the kindness on her face.

"Sag ihr, dass ich sie liebe," he repeated, several times.

"Yes," she said, hoping it was the right thing to say.

Suhani continued to stroke his head until Manfred eventually went back to sleep. Of that, at least, Suhani was envious.

Under the copper beech at the bottom of the garden, next to her shrine, Suhani saw another fox, though this one was without the distinctive black markings of its predecessor. It went to sniff where the snare had been and lingered inquisitively for several seconds before deciding to lie down there to guard the spot where his brother had died. He watched Suhani with a cat-like disdain.

She placed the picture of Edward next to Arthur. How much longer before she would have to take the shrine indoors, away from the cold winds that the autumn would bring to blow out her candles? She looked up at the sky, at the clouds across the moon, and decided it would be soon. For now, however, she lit the two candles inside their protective glass shrouds, and thought about her sons, though not with words. She simply wanted to feel that they were standing nearby, just out of sight, watching her as if they were about to speak. After the moment came and went, she felt certain they had visited, their arrival and departure one and the same, and she walked back towards the house, offering some kind of wordless prayer to Shiva that at least she still had Tristan, he was alive, and he was coming home.

Suhani had to do one more thing before going to bed. Back in the library, where the snoring had become as loud as the sleep was deep, she went to the shelf where the dictionaries were kept and which happened to be above Manfred's bed. There it was, high up, stuck between French and Italian, the largest book of the three. She stretched up and carefully took it down. Besides the word Mother, there was another that had caught her ear, of which she suspected its meaning but wanted to check. Liebe. She flicked through the pages until she discovered she was right.

The third of the three to move was Freddie. An hour before, his mother had, as usual, knocked on his bedroom door to check his light was out and to say goodnight. And, as usual, he had lied about his candle and said goodnight back. That morning he had seen his mother only hurriedly, and again even more briefly last thing before going to bed, but seeing was not the same thing as looking. In his own way, he was as blind to her as she was to him. He felt an overwhelming sadness, not because they had grown so far apart but because they had never intended it. What had caused their rending? And who was to blame? Love can flush into life like an unattended fire, he thought, but just as easily burn itself out.

Lit by one candle from the windowsill, Freddie was now sitting at his small table by his bedside, turning the pages of his Boy's Own Annual and reading an article he had previously dismissed each time he came across it, one that had only one picture and therefore too many words for his liking. But on this night, for the first time, Freddie's eye was caught by the title: *The Man Who Swam To His Death.*

So Freddie read about Matthew Webb, the first person to swim the English Channel. A man who had then become a celebrity by pursuing ever more dangerous stunts until he died trying to swim the Whirlpool Rapids below Niagara Falls, a feat that the article declared impossible, as indeed it turned out to be. Freddie wondered whether Matthew Webb had simply become over-confident, or whether it was in fact his fame that had killed him because it gave him no other option. He blinked thoughtfully at the idea of the man's inevitable path of self-destruction, and of him having no choice in the matter.

Something had been brewing all day. Not so much a thought in his head, nothing that could be put into words, but a dark shadow filling his body, the source of which eluded him. Or had it been for longer than a day? Perhaps it had been several, since the time of his conversation with Mrs Harkness under the lychgate. Or even for all the two months since his first morning of work, his first trip to Tendring when she had appeared in her paint-splattered smock and the door had already been open, drawing him in across the threshold. With hindsight, everything seemed connected. He looked at his alarm clock which said midnight and he felt more tired than he could ever remember being. But he knew the swirling feeling would never allow him to sleep, that he had a job to do. The right thing was indistinguishable from the wrong thing, and just as thoughts of Millie Bedden pulled him in two, so did this new impulse.

Freddie moved, or perhaps someone else moved inside him, and he leant down to pull out a cardboard box from under his bed where all his letters and writing equipment were kept. He removed the letter from Captain Meadows that he had steamed open earlier that day using George's Primus, and although he had already read it, he had to check.

"To Brigadier and Mrs Harkness,

It is with much regret that I bring to you the sad news of the passing of your son, Captain Tristan Harkness. Captain Harkness and his company had advanced through Rake's Wood but were quickly surrounded by the enemy. Unable to advance or retreat, they dug in and resisted for several hours. However, fate was against them and a heavy mortar exploded with direct force, destroying the whole area. Captain Harkness and his comrades were lost in the explosion but as death was instantaneous I am sure that he suffered no pain. A short service in memory of Captain Harkness and his men was held at Valenciennes Cemetery the following day.

I hope it will be of some consolation for you to hear that, two days earlier, during our efforts to re-take the ridge at Crow Wood, Captain Harkness showed gallantry in the face of enemy gun fire, returning on three separate occasions to help bring back his wounded comrades, who owe their lives to him. His men were loyal, devoted, and dutiful servants to Captain Harkness. He was a Son of our glorious Empire and of this you should be especially proud.

His bravery will not go unmarked. Before his death a commendation was made by his commanding officer and the award will now be made posthumously. Let pride then be mingled with your tears.

Yours in truest sympathy,
G Meadows,
Chaplain, C of E."

In more ways than one, the news of Tristan's death was in Freddie's hands. This was the letter he would no longer deliver.

They had talked and she had told him her name, Nancy, though at first Stephen didn't use it, resisting the intimacy, the connection, the memory. She was clever at breaking the ice, experienced with skittish men, and kind. After a while he forgot where he was and even who he was, calling her Nancy after all, and they talked about their lives in more detail than he would have done with anyone else. But in the end it didn't solve anything. By the time they had finished the girl had done most of the chatting and it turned out she had a story to tell of an empty, ruined life that resonated with him more profoundly than she could possibly know. When she spoke she sounded as if she cared about him, until she said that time was up and he realised it was just an act. She no longer cared at all, and he felt more alone, if such a thing were possible, than before she had reeled him in. So after half an hour he counted out three shillings, put them on the bedside chair and stood up. It looked to Stephen as if Nancy were neither happy nor sad, incapable of either, having had her soul extinguished by the ingestion of gin, morphine, and men. He wondered if he would get back to Tendring before sunrise, and whether Suhani would be waiting for him. Both things seemed unlikely. He put an extra shilling on the chair.

"Please, take the rest of the night off, Nancy," he said, and left the room, amazed, but not surprised, that she hadn't recognised him.

Replacing the dictionary on its shelf, Suhani had the urge to sleep in the library, in the chair next to the German airman. Her excuse was that he would probably wake at some point so it would be easier to help by being there with him. But in fact her reasons were more selfish. She wanted to be a mother, to remind herself what it felt like. The chair was large enough for her to curl up and rest her head on the arm, but it was difficult to fall asleep because the different ways she might break the news to Tristan about Edward kept spinning round in her head. All three brothers had been so close that they had grown up reading each other's minds before they could even read a book, so it was possible Tristan might already know. In any case Suhani thought such psychic connections, if they existed, would not be required to raise his suspicions. The fact that she had not mentioned Edward in any of her letters would probably be enough. But one thing was certain, she would not be able to hide the truth from him for a single second, he would know immediately from her fake smile, and Suhani decided that was a blessing. She cried, silently, as she did every night, for Arthur and Edward. But her tears fell for other reasons, too. Her otherness, her homelessness. England, the country of their birth, and France, the country of their death. So where was India in all of this? The Empire had eaten her up and spat her out, all for a decent cup of Indian tea.

The night was long, and she did not rest at all, but took some comfort from the fact that Manfred was sleeping soundly enough for both of them.

I will not lose him. The ominous toll of Mrs Harkness's words throbbed in Freddie's head. It was an instruction he had to follow, like a barked order from a sergeant major, so he took out another document from his cardboard box: Christopher's dictated letter to Anne. Christopher had hid the truth, giving Freddie permission to do the same. It felt like it would be the completion of a process. The letter he held in his hand was written in pencil, the new one he was about to begin would be in ink; permanent, real.

His first obstacle was the possibility that Mrs Harkness might be familiar with his own handwriting, but she'd only seen Anne's address in capital letters on the outside of the envelope, so he decided he was safe enough. Next, in an effort to convince himself the job required no emotional input – that, in fact, he was merely the messenger – he took out a blank sheet of writing paper, an ink bottle and pen, and placed them neatly on his desk, ready for business. With Captain Meadows' letter already on the desk alongside Christopher's, he had everything he needed to begin. Christopher's letter would provide the bulk of the material he needed though some things would need to be changed or left out, including the sender's address and date, which he borrowed from Captain Meadows: *Valenciennes, France, First of September, 1916.*

Freddie was thriving on the process, almost chirpy. At times it seemed as if he was looking at himself from above, through the crack in the lime mortar. Initially he was going to use his best handwriting, but then realised it was immaterial and in fact more important that it didn't look too adult or sophisticated. If he wrote quickly, it might come across as more childlike. But then there was a bigger problem and he wondered if he would fall at the first hurdle. How, actually, to begin? How does a son address his mother? Then...it came to him. Sunday under the lychgate, of course. He wrote it down, the salutation he had spied upon: *Dearest Maji.*

He referred back to Christopher's letter. The rest would flow more easily now. "*Forgive my haste, I've just a few minutes to write. I'm sorry it has been a while since my last letter, the war makes it hard sometimes. I don't want you to worry, but I have injuries that make it difficult to write. Today I have an amanuensis called...*"

Oh. Called what? He looked up at his pile of pennies and wondered which one had come from Jack. What had he called him? Billie? That would do, that would do nicely.

And so Freddie began his first forgery, his descent into the Whirlpool Rapids, putting on Billie's heavy ill-fitting shoes that would drag him under the water, and the current moved his pen across the page where the truth would be hidden by the ghostly first layer of a palimpsest.

In fact the whole exercise took him no more than ten minutes. Of course he missed out Christopher's reference to the windows, about Joseph, and obviously the passage about him missing his wife, but he felt sure it still left enough detail to be convincing, especially the crucial section about his leave being cancelled. And no fourteen-year-old boy would use the word amanuensis, much less be able to spell it. It all seemed beautifully plausible, and he was satisfied the deed was done.

But something prevented him from sealing his new letter inside Captain Meadows' envelope. What he had written was perfectly clear, and in a way it was the purity that was bothering him. His was pristine, whereas the original had some dirty smudges and fingerprints on it. So he licked his fingers, knelt down by the side of his bed, rubbed his hand into the dust that had spent years accumulating there and transferred it to the letter. He compared it to the original but was still not entirely reassured, feeling it needed more distressing, so he rubbed the letter itself into the grime under the bed, both sides, until he was satisfied it looked like it had been in the trenches. Did it? Well, it was close enough.

Time to seal the envelope. The steaming had left much of the glue behind, but it tasted of cigarette smoke and he couldn't help thinking he was licking the same glue that Captain Meadows had. He retched, but got it done and felt proud. It was a work of art only he had the skill to create.

Putting the letter down on his desk he then climbed into bed, knowing he was worn out and seconds from sleep. There was a ringing in his ears, his neck ached from sitting awkwardly for too long and his whole head pulsated with tiredness. Perhaps it was punishment for his deceit, but an undeserved one because he had no choice, like Matthew Webb.

Hours later, he still hadn't closed his eyes. He was looking up and around, at his drawings that covered the walls and the ceiling. What had he done so far? Nothing but copies. No original work, everything fraudulent, every piece of artwork a fake. Everything in someone else's voice. Suddenly he thought his forgery was madness and even if it worked how would he keep it up? But then he saw Suhani lying by her shrine – no wait, she was down on the floor, by the side of his bed, weeping, her hands up to her face to cover her black eye, and there was

Shiva on his window ledge, not the miniature bronze but the life-sized one. He must be in the library, its blue face, with the hint of a smile, granting him permission, saying sometimes people wanted to be lied to, or was that Mrs Harkness who spoke, after all Shiva looked exactly like her, and Christopher stood at the foot of his bed mouthing a word that looked like *Maji,* and Freddie couldn't hear what the despatch rider said because the engine was too loud and anyway what was Millie doing riding a motorbike and why was there a black cross painted on every bottle of her milk as if to drink from them would give you the plague?

Freddie jumped, which rattled his bed, and he knew what his dream had told him to do. Going over to his desk, still half-asleep, he picked up his piece of chalk and with three firm strokes used it to cover up the black cross on the back corner of the envelope. Then he put the letter back in his leather pouch before reaching up to take Shiva off the window ledge, putting that in the pouch as well. He thought it might help.

But sleep eluded him for the rest of the night.

25

I promised to tell you about Eddie Hunter. He's a young lad, seven years old, who lives with his mother and father and two elder brothers not far from Memory Cove. When the sea is calm, and the risks are small, Eddie's dad takes him out on their fishing boat to spend a day on the catch, filling the belly of his vessel with herring or emptying the lobster traps.

So the story goes, Eddie Hunter has never spoken. But despite his mute relationship with the world Eddie is a smart boy, content in his silences and kind too, always willing to help and happy to listen. Perhaps we could all take a leaf out of his book – you know, talk a bit less. That's why I've taken to spending long stretches of time sitting with Eddie on the harbor wall. It's where I daydream about Christopher and allow Eddie to hear my thoughts. I think it's his inability – or unwillingness – to speak that enables him to understand. Certainly, he's the only one who seems to listen.

Is this how the world will end, Eddie? In darkness? As if every breath feels like your last? The physical pain of it, the dead weight pressing down on my chest, squeezing out the air like the wringing out of a dishcloth, each breath requiring a monumental act of will, more exhausting than the last. I don't think I want to die, but I definitely don't want to live. Perhaps it's only the anger that keeps me going, the blind fury conjured up by war, and the fact that no one has ever managed to explain exactly what we're fighting about. I read the papers but they give no reasons, or none that make any sense to me. Who was this Archduke Ferdinand? If that first bullet had missed, would any of the rest been fired? Why did he matter so much that a million men might die in response, on this treadmill of revenge? What did it have to do with Christopher? With me? When one lover dies, they both do. To die and yet to live, that is war's fatal gift, Eddie. Once the numbers are totted up, will my death be counted too?

So this is how it will end: Death sitting at his writing desk, composing letters that kill those in receipt of them as surely as a bullet or a shell fired across the ocean. That which is written can never be unwritten. Soft, kind words of consolation scribbled by an Indian woman in black ink on expensive paper, from a house called Tendring in the English countryside. Words that rise from the envelope, once opened, like noxious, poisonous gas, rotting and burning your lungs until your breathing stops for ever, no matter how hard you try. Only when I sit with you on the harbor wall does the anger subside. The weight on my chest lifts a little, and the ocean settles back into its old rhythm, the fishing boats sail in and out with the tide, with my breath, as it rises and falls of its own accord, without my willing it.

You are my anchor, Eddie, but darkness stands at our shoulders, waiting. What will the fishing boats bring back with their next catch, on the rising tide?

26

Stephen had walked the long way home via Pegwell Bay and the outskirts of Sandwich, taking nearly six hours to find his way back to Tendring. Although the sun was still below the horizon when he arrived, the clouds were turning orange and it wouldn't be long before sunlight would cast its shadows over the lawn to evaporate the dew. He stood at the end of the drive between the open gates and the stone eagles, not sure if he wanted to go any further, watching a thin fog rising like steam from the grass as it warmed up in front of the house. Tendring was breathing like a sleeping dragon, waiting for him to enter its lair, but he was too drained, too worn out to resist or be fearful of it. After walking all night the pain in his hip had become so unbearable that he needed to go to his room, leaving him no choice but to take the final steps towards the house, a fifty yard journey he barely had the energy for. He thought he must look like a street beggar: dirty, dishevelled, red-eyed.

But just as he was about to take his next step, he heard the sound of horse's hooves and metal-rimmed wheels on gravel, and seconds later he had to step aside in order to let the chaise go past. It was the station Fly, bringing the two nurses from Celandine Hall. This was something he didn't normally witness, this early arrival, having always left for work by this time of the morning, if he was here at all. He watched it stop outside the front door, observed the nurses going into the house, then waited a while longer before walking up the drive, in order to avoid getting caught in conversation.

The nurses had left the front door open. By the time Stephen was in the hallway he could see by looking through the library door that they had already removed their coats and were tending to their patients, too busy to notice him standing there. He was glad he wouldn't be troubled by them. The stairs looked like a mountain to climb and his legs felt as heavy as tree trunks, so he just stood there, hoping that in a minute his limbs would recover enough energy to get him to his bed.

He was about to move when the drawing room door opened. It was Suhani, already fully dressed – prim, English, blending in – ready to leave the house, holding a small wicker basket in the crook of her elbow, and as surprised to see him as he was her.

"Oh. Welcome home, Stephen." She spoke as if they were casual acquaintances, a tone of familiarity in her voice that Stephen couldn't bear, for it was always covering up feelings of hurt or remorse.

"Thank you."

She looked him up and down. "You walked?"

"Yes I did."

"I'm going to wait at the station. Perhaps you would like to join me."

He was startled by the suggestion, tried to smile but it was little more than a flicker across his eyes. "I haven't slept. I'm going to bathe and then I'm going to take to my bed. What time is his train?"

"It could be any. I'll wait for as long as it takes. Why don't you come?" There was a tiny movement of the wicker basket in her hands. "I have sandwiches. Enough for three, just about."

There was so much else beneath the conversation, in the pauses and the gaps between the words, but he wasn't sure what it was, and couldn't work out why she seemed to be handing him an olive branch. It was almost as if she were giving him a test, or even flirting with him, inviting him to go back to the very beginning, to the moment they had first met. Or perhaps it was simply an apology, regret for yesterday. As usual he had no idea how to deal with it, though at least it no longer made him angry in the way it used to. Best to continue by saying nothing meaningful.

"Is there any hot water?"

"Not yet."

"Never mind. Cold is best. Thank you."

Several seconds passed as they faced each other. There was a generosity passing between them that was a relic of their love from long ago and he didn't want the conversation to end, fearful that if it did they would never speak again. He even considered talking about the weather, but then he remembered what she had said about his attempts at casual conversation. If he was ever going to explain himself, then now would be the time, and he would have to find a subject better than the weather. So, although he was still unsure what he was going to say, he opened his mouth and breathed in, wondering if, even at such a late stage, he might yet salvage something.

But Suhani spoke first.

"Goodbye Stephen."

Her eyes glistened and she smiled because she was about to cry. Stephen breathed out and closed his mouth. The chance was spent, if it had ever really existed, there would never be anything more to say. Their time was over and she would soon be gone. But then, to his own astonishment, he spoke anyway.

"I envy you."

Suhani turned her head down to look into the basket. Stephen presumed this was so he couldn't see her crying and when she spoke he could tell by the change of tone that she was upset.

"What do you mean?" she said.

He wasn't sure, all he could do was speak without thinking, and if he had known what he was going to say next he probably wouldn't have done so.

"Because you must love him very much."

Her eyes filled with tears, and the tears fell onto her hands that held the basket. She wiped them on her coat, one after the other. He hoped a tender word was coming, some concession to their past life, some reference to an arcade of roses. He held his breath at the possibility she might even be about to tell him that she loved him, despite everything. He desperately wanted her to.

The words cracked in her throat as she looked back up at him. But they were not what he expected.

"You look like death."

The horse outside snorted and kicked its hooves on the gravel as if impatient to get Suhani to the station. The clock made a click as it hit the quarter hour, but there were no chimes. Hannah must have forgotten to release the chiming pin. There was a kerfuffle in the library and the sound of breaking glass as someone dropped a bottle on the floor. One of the nurses rushed out to retrieve a fresh bottle of laudanum from the gun cabinet, offering a hurried, almost disrespectful good-morning before immediately going back to tend to her patient. Sometimes pain could be treated, thought Stephen, sometimes not. The sun rose above the trees and shone through the branches into the hallway, lighting up Suhani's face. Her bruise had faded overnight and for a moment Stephen thought she looked extraordinarily young, a sixteen-year-old girl on the cusp of life, a rosebud; she reminded him of Roper's daughter, Nancy, who had been destroyed by her father long before she had bloomed, but had followed a very different path, one without love. There was a cry from the library, a foreign word, someone was in pain. Someone who might live or might die, or who might have to endure some kind of existence between the two, in no-mans-land. He heard the click of the driver's tongue and the horse's hooves as the station Fly set off, and only then did he realise Suhani had left him standing in the hallway alone.

The water was freezing, which made him gasp as he tipped the ewer over his head. Standing naked in his zinc bath tub, Stephen felt the water flow down over his body, little rivulets caught in the folds of scar tissue that began with the small wound on his neck and spread like lava down his back and onto his leg, a rough topography covering one entire side of his body from shoulder to ankle. It told a story of cuts from shrapnel and shattered bones, flash-burns carved by molten shell-casing that had hit him from two yards away, and of gaping wounds roughly sewn up without anaesthetic by a surgeon in a hurry. All of it meaning he could never dry himself properly with a towel but had to dab at the fossilised wounds as gently as possible and then wait for the rest of the water to evaporate into the air.

Stepping out of the tub he walked, still naked, over to the sink and started to trim his moustache with scissors and a razor. His intention was to snip off a few stragglers in the way he did every morning, but this time he kept going until he had removed all his facial hair entirely, leaving nicotined strands floating in the sink, filthy waxed whiskers that he was glad to be rid of. His top lip felt smooth, purged. Then he covered his head in soapy water, took his cut-throat razor to his skull and over the course of the next twenty minutes slowly shaved off all his hair.

Next, he put on clean underclothes before pulling out his Major's uniform from the wardrobe, a smartly pressed livery but musty smelling from lack of use and in places moth-eaten. He laid it out on the bed and then started methodically dressing himself in it for the first time in fourteen years. It hung loosely on his shoulders and around his chest. He must have lost weight. Having removed all his hair his cap seemed loose too, and made him look and feel smaller than he was, so he took it off again and placed it on the bed.

There was a small box behind a pair of shoes on a shelf in his wardrobe, and Stephen reached inside to remove it, a presentation case with a red velour skin, its colour still as rich as on the day of the award. He brushed off a covering of dust from the lid, flicked the tiny catch to open it up and cast his eyes across the three medals inside, the colour of newly-minted pennies, neatly lined up and hanging from their ribbons attached to a copper bar. He lifted them out and without pausing pinned them to the left breast of his jacket, then checked their position in the mirror. He saw his own face again. There had been a moustache of some kind on his top lip since he was twenty, but now with its removal he looked one hundred years old.

He considered lying on the bed to try to sleep, as he had told Suhani he would, but bathing had woken him up and he thought he might as well get on with it, so he reached in the wardrobe again, this time for his shoes.

When the station Fly had exited the driveway of Tendring house, it had turned not right towards Eagley but to the left in the direction of Little Risborough railway station, where Tristan had said in his letter he would be arriving at some point in the day. The chaise got to the station at a quarter to eight and Suhani stepped down, paid the driver and walked onto the platform, installing herself on a bench to wait for the first train of the day.

It was not long before it arrived. No one got off, and no one got on. The train simply sat there, huffing and puffing, waiting for the timetable to catch up with it, and then pulled away.

"Excuse me," she said to the stationmaster who had whistled and flagged for the train to leave and was now heading back to his ticket office. "When is the next train from Dover?"

"Every two hours, ma'am, except nothing at two," he said, without breaking stride.

"Thank you."

She looked into the basket, at the sandwiches for three, and wondered if the day would be so long she would end up eating them all herself. She tried not to rehearse how she would break the bad news about Edward, but there was little else to do. It was either that or count the weeds pushing up between the tracks. Only then did she notice an elderly lady sitting directly opposite on the other platform, looking straight back at her.

Standing at the top of Bath Hill, Freddie could see smoke rising from the fields. The farmers had started burning the stubble, a destructive process that used to confuse him until he had been assured by his mother that it encouraged new growth. So he thought of Shiva in his pouch, and it began to make sense. The Indian God was following him everywhere, and it seemed to be pointing him in the direction he was going. He pushed off and free-wheeled down the hill, as he always did, having now worked out exactly how much braking to apply in case he had to stop at the place where Bath Hill met the Eagley Road.

Halfway down, he heard a metallic snap and then a rattle as something was momentarily caught in the spokes of his rear wheel. He squeezed his brakes as hard as he could, almost sending himself over the handlebars, though the braking seemed to make little difference and he found himself nearly at the bottom by the time he stopped. He climbed off to examine his bike: no chain. At first there was no sign of it, until he looked back and spotted two pieces of rusted snaking chain, halfway up the hill, lying a yard apart from each other. He wanted to walk over and pick them up, but he felt strangely dizzy and decided, for a moment at least, not to move. There was a peculiar fuzziness to his vision and he couldn't focus on anything, the result of exhaustion from not having slept, he reckoned. Looking up at the sky he almost lost his balance, but eventually his head began to clear and his frustration at the broken chain began to take hold, then turned to sudden rage as he picked up his bike to throw it as far as he could into the ditch. Glancing down at his shoes in an attempt to calm himself down, he swore, and because no one was there to hear him, he swore again.

"Shit. Shit."

He was shocked, though in a strangely agreeable way, by the sound of the word, but he was even more startled by the crunch of footsteps on the Eagley Road. Whoever it was, they might have heard him swearing. A hedgerow that curved round the corner meant he couldn't see who was coming, so he took a few steps towards the middle of the road until the figure came into view. The man was walking briskly, almost marching, and at first Freddie didn't recognise who he was, clean-shaven, bald, holding his peaked cap in his hand, and in full Major's uniform. Finally it was the limp that gave the man away. Stephen Harkness. It was him, but not him; smaller, faster. Freddie thought about saying good morning but Mr Harkness was determinedly staring ahead and it appeared he was oblivious to Freddie's presence, or was choosing to ignore him, and seconds later he had passed by. Freddie watched him march down the Eagley Road for a full minute until he was out of sight, and thought his appearance was so odd he wondered if he had imagined it. People whose faces were familiar and yet looked like someone else only appeared in dreams, didn't they? Or someone who was someone else at the same time? Had he imagined him? He felt so light-headed he couldn't decide. He pinched himself, literally, hard on the back of his hand, because that's what they did in the Boy's Own Annual when the hero thought he was dreaming. Freddie was relieved to feel the sting of it, which made Mr Harkness's appearance and behaviour all the more bizarre – and the prospect of walking to Tendring House even more ominous.

The nearer he got to it, the more he wanted to change his mind. Each step forward was heavier than the last. He was passing the orchard on his left, and the wheatfield on his right, where out of the corner of his eye he caught sight of the scarecrow. It seemed closer than usual. He looked more closely and realised it was actually Millie Bedden, who was standing there with a milk churn by her feet and her arms outstretched. She didn't seem to be coming or going. Why didn't she wave? He knew she was only thirteen, but from here she looked liked a fully-grown woman. Freddie blinked, Millie was gone, and the scarecrow returned. She had been a mirage, straight out of the Syrian desert. Perhaps that was where Mr Harkness, or his doppelgänger, had come from. His mother's warning rang in his ears: you know what happens when you don't get your sleep. Then suddenly he was at Tendring, standing between the stone eagles, and he presumed he must have literally been asleep whilst walking for the last ten minutes because he couldn't for the life of him remember how he got there.

Already there were a few soldiers sitting outside, making the most of the sun but protected by blankets from the cold early morning air. Except it was not so early. Freddie suspected it had taken three times as long to get there without his bike, and as he trudged up the driveway he sensed the house was already busy and alive with hospital business.

Standing at the open doorway, listening to the hubbub of activity coming from the library, he reached up to the lion's head and knocked, an awkward manoeuvre given the door was once again already open, before turning round for a moment to look out across the garden. His eyes were stinging with tiredness and he had to blink several times to bring the trees at the bottom into sharp-edged reality. He wondered if Suhani would answer the knock, or whether as yesterday it would be Hannah. He wanted it to be the mistress, not the servant, so he could give her the good news himself. Good news? All he had done was change it from tragic to unfortunate, and Mrs Harkness would be disappointed all the same. Still, it was better than nothing, injured was better than dead, and the best story he could tell under the circumstances.

He heard footsteps in the hallway so he took the letter out of his pouch and turned to hand it over but was thrown by the appearance of someone who was not Suhani, and not Hannah either, but Phoebe, coming to a stop on the threshold.

"Hello," she said. "You're late. Anything for me?"

He had handed the post to Phoebe many times round the back or in the kitchen, but never here. Freddie had to rethink everything again.

"Letter for Major and Mrs Harkness," he said, dropping his arm down by his side to hide the letter behind his thigh.

"Thank you Freddie."

She held out her hand but Freddie didn't move.

"Telegrams must be delivered to the addressee," he said. "It's the – "

"It's a letter," she interrupted, "not a telegram."

"Well," said Freddie, quickly trying to invent a new directive from Head Office. "It's important to...I think Mrs Harkness might..." but Phoebe interrupted again.

"Well it's of no concern to you. Mrs Harkness has gone to the station. Let me take it. I'm sure you have lots of other letters to deliver."

Freddie had run out of ideas as well as energy and had nothing left except an exhausted stubbornness.

"I'll wait, miss."

"Don't be silly Freddie."

"I'll *wait,*" he snapped, with bad-tempered tiredness.

"Well," said Phoebe, already turning to go back into the library, looking like she had more important things to deal with. "Why don't you go to the station if it's that important?"

He put the letter back into his leather pouch and then sat down on the steps of the portico, leaning his head against the side of one of the pillars. He was already almost asleep and thought Phoebe was still there to hear him when he mumbled to himself, "My bike's broke. I'll wait."

There were horse-tails and yarrow grass amongst the nettles, as well as other weeds that Suhani had no name for. She had decided to stick to counting the flowers of celandine, appropriately enough, their tiny yellow blossoms covering much of the track. Tough little rosettes that seemed to be able to withstand the boiling vapour and coal dust from the steam trains that rode over them. She day-dreamed about Celandine Hall and how it had come to be named after a weed. And why was that word used to define weakness, or cowardice, when weeds were the most tenacious of plants? She thought of Tristan coming home from boarding school, aged eight, and telling her, after much persuasion, about the bullies who had made his life a misery, nicknamed him Greenhouse because he was a "pansy". And she had let him go to war. Between the two sleepers in front of her were two hundred and fifteen celandine flowers. She had counted them twice and was about to embark on a third inventory when she was interrupted by the whistle of an approaching train.

A handful of people had accumulated on the platform. Two older women, smartly dressed, were busy talking to each other; one man, perhaps fifty years old who was in labourer's clothes, looking like he had just come off the fields; and one young woman peering anxiously down the line towards the incoming train. A wife waiting for a husband, Suhani presumed.

As the steam engine got nearer, Suhani resisted the urge to stand up and get closer to the platform's edge. If she remained sitting on the bench she might somehow be less disappointed if Tristan wasn't on the train. It might also increase the chances of him being on it, whereas if she stood up next to the nervous young woman nearby, the possibility might fade away. Normally she had no truck with such superstitious logic, but today she didn't want to take the chance.

She was getting nervous. Her heart had started to race so she tried to make each breath longer and deeper, like a sigh. The two older women and the young woman climbed aboard the stationary train and the labourer stood and waited, which was exactly the opposite of what Suhani had expected. Six people got off the train and she scrutinised them from a distance, as if any one of them might suddenly turn into Tristan. They were all men, four flat caps, one bowler hat and one captain's forage, the last one being the right age, height and build. His skin even appeared to be the same shade as Tristan's, but her heart immediately sank when he went up to the labourer to shake hands. His body language was all wrong and his features less sharp. They were obviously father and son. Hello boy, she heard the labourer say. Perhaps the soldiers were catching the sun in the trenches.

There was a whistle from the stationmaster, then a piercing reply from the engine driver, an expulsion of steam from the engine before the wheels started to grind and slip on the tracks until it settled into a slow rhythm to pull away. Suhani suddenly stood up in a panic, having the idea Tristan may have simply fallen asleep in his carriage, so she tried to scan each compartment through smoke-stained windows as it passed. But he wasn't there, nor, in all honesty, did she really expect him to be. She sat back down on the bench and contemplated another two hours of counting celandine flowers.

"Well now, the Bamfords had to wait a week. I shouldn't worry." It was the stationmaster, who was standing at the other end of her bench looking in the same direction across the tracks.

"Thank you," said Suhani, smiling up at him.

"If I've learnt anything from this war it's patience," he said. He was right, the war seemed to involve an awful lot of waiting. Sometimes, Suhani thought, waiting felt indistinguishable from praying.

Waiting. Freddie was still sat on the steps of Tendring's portico, drifting in and out of sleep. By now all ten soldiers were outside, seven spectators watching three cricketers playing a poor-man's game of cricket in the middle of the lawn. One of them made a joke about leg-before to the wheel-chaired batsman who had no legs. Freddie wasn't sure how long he'd been sitting there, but the sun was as high as it would get this time of year so he guessed he had been there several hours already.

Hannah came out, stood next to him and folded her arms. "Get yourself the sack why don't you?"

"I'll catch up. Mrs Harkness will be back soon."

"She might, she might not. Phoebe told me about your silly stubbornness. Give me the letter Freddie."

He took his leather pouch, hugged it to his chest and looked directly at her. He had taken enough from Hannah and barked, "Leave me alone!"

He could see that Hannah was taken aback by this harsh reply and even that she felt hurt by it. She unfolded her arms. "Well. You know best, don't you Freddie."

Still half asleep, he thought he probably did. He looked away, closed his eyes and heard Hannah walk back into the house. It was true, he might get the sack and he imagined George Franklin would be furious, at least between varying states of unconsciousness, but not only did he not care, he liked the fact that he didn't care.

He watched patches of orange light drift slowly across the insides of his eyelids until he started another dream, one where Millie was running up the drive, holding a baby.

"Can someone help?"

Freddie opened his eyes again to see a young girl standing right in front of him, holding a bundle of something wrapped in an old flour sack. He felt as if he'd been asleep for hours again, but in reality it must have been no more than ten seconds.

"You got nurses here haven't you?" said Millie, holding out a lifeless baby in her arms. Freddie could tell from the melancholy lilt in her voice that she felt it was already too late. "I don't think he's breathing. I tried everything I know." There was a cry of Howzat from the match on the lawn as Freddie stood up with no idea what to do next, feeling a heady mixture of being suddenly wide awake and yet still in a dream.

"Everyone's out in the fields," said Millie with a look of desperation as she offered Freddie the bundle for him to take. It was then he was able to see that it wasn't a baby after all but an animal of some kind, a puppy, and probably no more than twenty minutes old, the time it would take to run from Bedden's Farm to Tendring. He didn't want to take the bundle from her, didn't want yet more responsibility for another life, but Millie's obvious despair made it impossible to refuse. So he gingerly took the puppy and said, "They'll be someone in the library. Come on."

Freddie, Millie, Hannah and Phoebe all stood in a circle around the nurse who was holding the puppy and rubbing its back. The nurse's face suggested she was not hopeful and then she proceeded to say as much.

"I'm sorry. It won't be long before he gives up. How many others did the mother have?"

"Three."

"How old are you Millie?"

"Thirteen."

"And you live on a farm, don't you."

"Yes miss."

"Well then, this should come as no surprise. The best thing you can do is go home and look after the other three, and their mother."

Millie looked broken-hearted. "I suppose." Everyone stood still, waiting for the inevitable, until the nurse turned to face Millie directly.

"Do you want to take him home, or leave him here with us?"

But before Millie could answer, Hannah interrupted. "For goodness sake! Freddie, go into the kitchen, there's some rat poison in the cupboard over the sink. Quickly now!" She took the bundle from the nurse and wrinkled her nose as if searching for fleas in its fur. Millie started to cry and everyone else looked at Hannah incredulously. "Well go on!" she snapped impatiently, but Freddie remained glued to the spot, her sharpness having the opposite of its intended effect, so she had to repeat herself with a growl he could no longer resist. "Go on!"

Freddie flinched at her voice and then ran out of the library, past the stairs and through into the kitchen, wondering if he would recognise rat poison if he saw it. But when he opened the cupboard over the sink there was no mistaking it, a bottle with the word Poison printed on the label, a skull and crossbones, and a picture of a rat. Two other words on the label meant nothing to him, Strychnine Sulfate, but the strangulated sound they made in his head suggested they would be enough to efficiently put the puppy out of its misery. At least that was what he hoped. He grabbed the bottle and ran back into the library.

There was no time for Hannah to say thank you when Freddie handed her the poison. Instead she spoke directly and hurriedly to Millie. "Sometimes it works, and sometimes it doesn't. Such is life. Will you let me try?"

But the nurse interrupted before Millie could speak. "What do you think you're doing?"

"My Pa used to do it," said Hannah who, unimpeded by the puppy she was holding, was already opening the bottle. "And the midwives, so they say. There's nothing to be lost, is there Millie?"

Millie nodded because she was too nervous to speak. All the while Freddie was watching, trying to work out what was going on, and began to realise that Hannah was not ending the animal's life but attempting to revive it.

Hannah quickly handed the puppy back to the nurse, then licked the end of her little finger and carefully inserted it into the top of the bottle. "You don't want to get this on your clothes, let me tell you now." She removed her finger to reveal a tiny spot of white powder on the end of it, the size of a peppercorn, before slowly putting the top back on the bottle. Then she said to the nurse, in a gentler tone, "Hold the little mite up a bit so I can get this in." The nurse looked suspicious but did as she was told and Hannah inserted her finger into the puppy's mouth, as far down the back of its throat as it would go, leaving it there for a few seconds before withdrawing it.

"There. Keep it warm. We'll know in a few minutes." She started to walk towards the door. "Phoebe, come and open the doors for me, I need to get this off my hands. We don't want poison on the door handles do we now." Phoebe obeyed and followed her out into the hallway.

The nurse held the puppy close to her chest as Freddie and Millie watched and waited for several minutes, but it remained lifeless. By now two of the soldiers had come in from the lawn to see what was happening, more interested in this spectacle than the cricket match outside, and then Hannah and Phoebe returned moments later. Everyone gathered round the nurse to examine the inert sack in her arms.

A feeling of despondency came over Freddie. Life was life and death was death, and only one direction of travel from one to the other. It seemed there was no room for miracles in this world. Millie was getting distressed and Freddie realised that at some point she had grabbed his hand. He had never held a girl's hand before. It was hot, her palm was wet with sweat, the skin hard and rough from years of lifting milk churns and tugging at udders. The feeling was not at all what he'd expected, not romantic or tender, not soft or poetic. It was a hundred times better than that.

The sound of laughter filtered in from the cricket match outside, the thwack of bat against ball, a yell of Catch It! and a groan of disappointment. Then the puppy began to fit. It shivered like it was unbearably cold and its legs twitched, running in its dream towards life. Millie let go of Freddie's hand and looked at Hannah, who cautioned, "We'll see." They kept on watching it for another minute as the little creature continued to spasm in a way that alarmed everyone except Hannah. "It'll calm down," she said. "Don't you worry now. Give the little mite ten minutes and then we'll know for sure."

And so they waited patiently as the convulsions began to dissipate and the breathing became more regular. Freddie made a calculation in his head: a life had just begun that might last fifteen years, longer than he had lived so far, and the whole of it depended on a fingertip of rat poison. It reminded him of something he had forgotten about since Millie had woken him up on the steps – the letter in his pouch. The words he had committed to the page using the curves and lines of the forger's pen, Tristan's letter written, with Christopher's unwitting guidance, in the lengthening shadows of Freddie's fitful night. They were only words, not poison, but still, he would put his own measure of Strychnine Sulfate down Tristan's throat, bringing him back to life.

As the puppy came to, the soldiers began to clap and cheer.

Another train had arrived and departed, but no one came for Suhani. One soldier had disembarked but no friend or relative was there waiting for him, he just stepped off the train, lit a cigarette and strode away down the platform. They had smiled at each other as he walked past, a knowing smile, a craving for her to have been waiting for him, with a brief flicker of sadness that it was not to be. She watched him until he reached the end of the platform where as he turned to exit he threw her another glance, and then he was gone. If Tristan wasn't coming home, she imagined taking this one instead, such was her desperation to be a mother again. She smiled at the idea. The lengths people will go to, along this reckless road, to be loved.

She sat on the bench examining her sandwiches but had no appetite. The old woman on the opposite platform was still there, and still seemed to be watching her across the tracks. Meanwhile the station-master brought Suhani a cup of tea which she sipped out of politeness only. There would now be four full hours before the next train from Dover which would in theory give her time to go home and come back. Perhaps her presence on the platform was preventing his arrival, she should walk away, let the kettle boil on its own. But she felt no inclination to move, because...you never know.

Indeed, there were two other trains, but they were from Ramsgate, not Dover. Even so, her heart fluttered with expectation. Anything was possible because of the war, plans were often changed at the last minute, soldiers could be sent to one place and end up in another, and everyone had learnt to be sure of nothing until the person you loved was physically in your arms. So it would be no surprise if Tristan didn't arrive today. There might be a letter waiting for her at Tendring saying he had been delayed until tomorrow, or Friday. Or next week.

But she carried on waiting, because she believed with all her heart that he was coming. His letter said so.

27

Normally Stephen would walk into the village and then catch the omnibus from there to his place of work, but this was not a normal day. He felt no desire to sit next to other people or be subjected to their idle gossip, and especially not their silent scrutiny of his Major's uniform or shaven head. Without knowing how the day would end, but only that it would, he had instead chosen to walk the eleven miles to the munitions factory. To avoid any chance of being seen he had taken the long way round, along the bridle path past the church and through several fields, only occasionally stepping on to the road when he had no choice. He met no one except the postboy, and marched past him brusquely, ignoring his gaze in the child-like hope that by avoiding eye-contact he wouldn't be seen.

By the time he was standing at the final crossroads that led to his factory, half a mile away, he had been walking for three hours since leaving Tendring and he suddenly felt as tired as he had ever been, more exhausted even than during the worst of the battles in South Africa. He was aching all over his body and it was only now he realised why: he had not slept for at least forty-eight hours and had walked more or less continuously for half of them, on a journey that felt as if it had taken in most of Kent. Yet although he could barely stand he felt in other ways wide awake, his senses more acute, the smell of trampled grass mingling with the fumes from the factory, and the dark clouds above it growling in the sky like molten lead.

He looked out across the marshes towards his factory, a purpose-built collection of oblong blocks that were serviced by a steady flow of petrol-powered trucks and horse-drawn vehicles bringing both staff and supplies. Presumably his assistant manager was running the factory perfectly well without him. He was a pompous little fellow who would delight in taking over the job in the belief that he could do it better. He was welcome to it, Stephen thought, and would have smiled dismissively except for the excruciating pain in his hip.

He wondered if he would get to the factory before the rain clouds broke, and then he pondered why he was there at all. If someone had been standing next to him to ask what he was thinking he would not have been able to say. His intentions had no shape or form, dwelling not in his head nor even inside his body, but were instead an external impulse as if from the clouds above, which, he had an inkling, were about to propel him to walk the last half-mile of his life.

Jacob Pennington was indeed running the factory perfectly well because essentially he ran it anyway, whether Stephen Harkness was there or not. After all, he had worked there for a full year before and had taught Stephen the ropes, and would have got the job himself had he been of a higher rank or social status. But that was not the only reason he hoped that Stephen would stay in jail and be locked away for good, and he'd said as much to his wife as he left for work earlier that morning. "Always thought there was something not right about him," he declared as he put on his coat to leave. "You never know where you are with that man. He'll get what's coming to him, I reckon."

When Stephen entered his office Jacob didn't recognise him. The shaved head gave the impression of skin having been tightly stretched over his skull, the contours of his cheek-bones casting shadows into his hollowed-out cheeks, and the missing moustache revealing a mouth with lips so thin and tight that they drew one slender line across his face. The Major's uniform completed the disguise to such an extent that Jacob actually said, "Can I help you?" only realising when Stephen limped into the office who he was.

"Oh. What are you doing here?"

Stephen looked at him but didn't speak, instead walking with slow and precise steps straight past him, ending up with his face almost touching the glass of the large window that looked out over the factory floor. His appearance was so bizarre, so shocking, that Jacob had no idea how to respond. All he could offer up was a forlorn request, "Do you want some tea?" to which he didn't expect an answer, though he persisted with speaking to Stephen's back simply because it felt less uncomfortable than silence.

"I've just made a pot."

Jacob thought he saw a slight movement from Stephen's head as if he were about to reply, but nothing came. He tried a different tack, thinking he might have better luck by pretending to be his ally. "They let you out then. Always thought it was a load of nonsense." It was the exact opposite of what he had said to his wife, but becoming factory manager would require some sophisticated manoeuvres.

His words had an effect, but not the one Jacob had intended. Stephen raised his hand and placed it against the window. His voice was barely audible to Jacob, who thought Stephen was talking to himself.

"If we all just decided to stop, then that would be the end of it, wouldn't it?"

"What?"

"It's a funny business don't you think? It only takes one man to pull his trigger and then the rest of us fall like dominoes." He turned round to face Jacob. "Never mind. We'll just carry on I suppose, until we run out of bullets. Or people."

Jacob thought it best to agree. "Yes. I suppose so." He noticed a different air about his boss, besides his appearance, some change in his tone of voice, a strange music, a pitching and rolling he hadn't heard before. Stephen's brief incarceration seemed to have fundamentally changed him. In the past there had always been the fear that at any point Stephen Harkness, Major, might fly off the handle, so everyone would keep their distance, say no more than was necessary, and choose carefully the words they did use in order to avoid any confrontation or misunderstanding. That was how it was in the office and on the factory floor. Jacob knew that Stephen had ruled with fear because he had no other tools at his disposal, but this appeared to be no longer the case. Stephen's anger had been left in his prison cell and it was possibly this, more than his actual appearance, which made him unrecognisable. He seemed contented, even happy, though this new peacefulness didn't make him more approachable. On the contrary, Jacob found himself recoiling, feeling that he was in the unsettling presence of a shaven-headed madman.

"What are you doing here Stephen? Go home and get some rest. Come back tomorrow."

"Tea? What sort of tea?"

It was an unnerving non sequitur. Stephen was clearly not in control of his thoughts. Jacob felt the need to make a more drastic move and picked up the candlestick telephone from his desk. "I'm going to call Bill. He'll come and get you."

"Please, not Tetley's. We blend our own at home...Well, my wife does..."

"Sit down Stephen, while I make the call."

Stephen walked towards the chair as if he were going to comply, but he kept going towards the far wall and placed his hand on a large lever that was labelled Evacuation Alarm. He removed the locking pin.

"What the hell are you doing?" asked Jacob, phone in one hand and earpiece in the other, leaving both suspended in the air. A voice from the earpiece was just audible: *"What number do you require?"*

Freddie was sitting back on Tendring's front steps, holding his knees up to his chest and resting his chin on them. He rubbed his temples but failed to soothe them; it was impossible to think a single coherent thought, despite the fact his mind was racing.

Tendring had settled into a stillness with barely a murmur coming from the house. Millie had left with the puppy in her arms, stroking its head while it stretched itself with a yawn as if the whole business had been a fuss about nothing. The cricket match had long since ended, though the three stumps had been left stuck in the middle of the lawn, and all the soldiers had drifted inside as the afternoon got cooler. Freddie counted the small triangular flags that made up the bunting surrounding the portico. Thirty-six. The sun's position, vague though it was behind the clouds, suggested it was now late afternoon, and he began to fear Suhani would not show up. Freddie wondered why she was waiting so long at the station, but then just as quickly realised that of course she would hold out for the last train, in which case he would have had enough time to walk all the way to Little Risborough station to deliver his letter there. But that would have required a crystal ball. In any event he simply didn't have the energy and if they had crossed each other on the road he would be in a worse position than ever. So it seemed waiting was his only option, and the longer he waited the more he felt stuck to the spot.

But he would have to leave soon otherwise his mother would worry, and if the last train was later than seven he would have sat there all day for nothing, losing his job to boot. His thoughts piled one on top of the other until they were drained of any meaning, and he just sat there, no longer caring about the consequences.

"Are you cold?"

It was Phoebe, holding out a blanket. Now that she mentioned it, he realised why he was hugging his knees, so he took the blanket and wrapped it around his shoulders. She sat down next to him.

"It doesn't look like he's coming today, does it? You get used to it." There was a melancholy to her voice. Freddie examined her profile and noticed that a thin layer of tears had collected around the bottom of one eyelid. Perhaps it was just the cold air. He wanted to answer her wisely, find some way to lift her spirits, but was unsure what she had meant so came up with a question of his own.

"Do you know when the last train is, miss?"

"Six."

"What's the time now?"

Just as he said it, the sound of chimes came from the hallway.

"A quarter past five," she said.

"Well, a watched kettle never boils, miss." He thought that might cheer her up, but she seemed to shrink further into her own world, then stood up to stare out across the lawn and, without thinking, put her hand to the bump of her belly.

"Sometimes they do."

Freddie expected her to walk back into the house but instead she just stood there for a full minute, staring beyond the lawn and the trees. It was only when Freddie thought she might never move again that she turned to speak to him in a voice so quiet he could only just hear her.

"I know what's in your letter, Freddie."

The blood rose up into his face. He looked directly at her for the first time, unable to turn his head away, and swallowed hard. How could she possibly know what was in his letter? He had only written it the night before. And what was her interest in it? She might think she knew, but she didn't. He was about to say words to that effect but was saved from it when Phoebe swung round abruptly with no intention of listening to his excuses, and went back through the front door, closing it behind her. Freddie heard the throw of a bolt echo down the hallway behind the shut door and for the first time that day he felt he didn't belong there, that he was violating the steps he sat upon, his presence resented, the cause of all their troubles in Tendring. She had closed the door not just to keep out the verminous foxes, but the postboy too, and the letters in his pouch. Beyond that, it was as if the house itself was rejecting him, the bricks and mortar no longer wanting deliveries of post. He closed his eyes, not for sleep this time, but to deny the possibility of Suhani ever returning.

A mother and her small child had entered the station and were now standing on the platform in front of the bench where Suhani was sitting. It looked like they were waiting for the six o'clock arrival and the mother checked the railway track left and right in nervous anticipation. The little girl, however, had turned to stare at Suhani. They both knew why. Suhani took a sandwich from her basket and held it out as an offering to the little girl, but she refused, snuggling shyly into her mother's dress. With a gentle smile Suhani returned the sandwich to her basket. There was the distant sound of a train whistle and she looked away down the track towards it.

The little girl tugged at her mother's dress. "I'm hungry Mummy."

"Not now Poppet."

Suhani smiled at her again, but the girl remained as coy as a kitten. She tried once more with the sandwich. After a moment's thought the girl let go of her mother's dress, and Suhani knew that it was not only her hunger that had animated the girl but also curiosity about her skin. Suhani was used to it, it was often children who pointed and she accepted their inquisitiveness. She was, after all, an unusual sight in the lanes and villages of Kent. The little girl took a step nearer and was within an arm's reach of the sandwich when the mother suddenly noticed and snapped, "Lily! Get away!" She grabbed her daughter and dragged her a few yards further down the platform angrily murmuring something about the sandwich being filthy. As she did so she looked back with a vicious stare and Suhani saw a deep-rooted hatred that presumably would be passed on like a virus from mother to daughter before the little girl could possibly know better. What would ever break this endless cycle? Suhani had kept herself to herself for many years, felt forced to, yet perhaps her self-imposed solitude only made things worse, amplifying her otherness, ironically drawing attention to herself. Whilst it was always there in the background, Suhani could go days or sometimes weeks without needing to think about these reactions to her, but now she felt the old doubts swell up inside. What did anyone really think of her? Was she even accepted in her own home, by the people she gave a living to and was immeasurably fond of? What about Hannah? She was her confidante, and another outsider, but her skin was still white.

The train pulled up with another whistle, this time in ear-splitting proximity, and Suhani stood up to get closer to the platform's edge. About a dozen people disembarked, making it the busiest train of the day. Three of the passengers were in army uniform and little Lily ran to one of them, a soldier, who picked her up and swung her round, laughing "Hello Sausage!" The family walked past as they headed for the exit and the little girl, held in the arms of her father, looked at

Suhani, still unsure what to make of her. Once more Suhani smiled, and once more Lily looked away. The mother glared, but the father smiled back. Perhaps he had left his animosity on the battlefield, Suhani thought, or had it shot or blown out of him; or was sick to death of hating for the sake of it. Or perhaps he was just being kind, regardless of the war. There were people like that, too, she knew, and felt a trace of hope for Lily after all. Then they were gone.

The disembarked passengers streamed past Suhani, mostly young men. She desperately scanned the suits and uniforms, each one momentarily worn by Tristan, each one a fleeting possibility, until her eyes disabused her of the illusion. One placed a top hat on his head, the rest flat caps, and they all wore a tie, even the poorest amongst them, a threadbare gesture of respectability. Although they were still many yards away it was clear that neither of the two remaining soldiers were Tristan, and Suhani felt emptied out of energy and hope.

"I apologise for that dreadful woman."

The words had an upper-class clip to them and Suhani turned round to see an elderly lady, smartly dressed as if it were a Sunday, facing her. Then Suhani recognised her as the woman who had been sitting on the opposite platform since first thing that morning. She reminded her of someone from her past, a call from across the years, but Suhani couldn't place her.

"Thank you," said Suhani. "It doesn't matter."

"I've been here all day too, you know, on the other side. It's a lonely business, waiting, I thought I'd come and talk to you if you don't mind."

"I'm so sorry, I'm about to go. That was the last train."

The woman smiled kindly. "Ah well. Never mind. Another time perhaps. You'll be back I take it."

"Yes I imagine so."

The woman stared intently into Suhani's eyes. "Forgive me, you're from the house aren't you?"

"Tendring?"

"Yes, that's the one. I remember it from well before your time. Always thought it was a handsome place. Anyway, wouldn't you know, I lived in India for thirty years. I don't know about you but I miss it. Not the heat so much, mind. We must swap stories, when we have time."

"Yes we must." In her hurry Suhani thought she had sounded curt, so she added, "I'd like that."

The woman took a moment to look down the track. "I know who you are and I know what you've lost. My mother used to say if you believed in something hard enough it would come true. Nonsense of course, but I still find it helps, in a funny sort of way." Then she put her hand on Suhani's arm. "You must never give up hope, my dear." With that she walked away, raising her hand as she went, in lieu of a goodbye.

But Suhani couldn't let her go. There was more to say, not later, but now. She called out "Excuse me?" and briskly walked the few steps to reach the woman, who turned round with a look of delight on her face.

"My dear?"

"I wondered...If you don't mind...Who are you waiting for?"

The woman kept her eyes fixed on Suhani and seemed to be deciding how best to answer.

"Well. I come here once a year. An anniversary of sorts." Then she added with a chuckle, "I'm afraid I may not have many more left in me." Once again she turned to wend her way down the platform, talking to herself as much as to Suhani. "We'll see about that. But I'm not waiting for anyone anymore. I just like to watch the trains. They are very reliable you know."

Walking was clearly uncomfortable for the old woman and she had to take her time to reach the end of the platform where eventually she turned right, taking the exit out of the station. Suhani watched her until she disappeared, leaving her alone on the platform to stare at the empty tracks.

What was grief except a permanent state of waiting? The old woman's entreaty to cling on to hope had left Suhani feeling that hope was all there was, that it replaced the thing you were hoping for, long after it had passed out of reach. Tristan was not coming home today. He might simply be delayed, or, even more simply, he might be being eaten by rats in French mud.

28

Inspector Roper and Jacob Pennington stood five hundred yards away from the factory, listening to the whine of the evacuation alarm and the frenzied chatter of the crowd of factory workers who had gathered at a safe distance.

"Where is he?" asked Roper, breathless, having just arrived.

"I left him in the office. It's at the far end of the main hall."

"Is it safe?"

"Safe enough, but I'm not going back in, if that's what you mean."

"Can I turn that noise off?"

"On the wall behind my desk."

Roper squinted in an effort to see the factory more clearly. "How did he seem?"

"Well now, I didn't recognise him at first. Strange. Shaved all his hair off. Looks like a breakdown of the nerves to me."

"What's the best way in?"

"That fire escape on the far left? Go up there. Inside there's a gantry that will take you straight into the office." Jacob passed Roper a hand torch. "You might need this."

Roper pushed open the office door. The alarm was deafening inside the factory and it was beginning to cause a physical pain in Roper's ears, so he quickly found the handle to shut it off. Jacob's earpiece was still off the hook so Roper leant across the desk to replace it. He must have left in a hurry. But there was no sign of Stephen, except a pot of tea, still warm to the touch, and a fug of tannin hanging in the air.

The ticking of a mantelpiece clock and the ringing in his ears fell into a black hole of silence. As he walked out of the office, down the iron steps and across the factory floor, the smallest of sounds filled the vast space, the scraping of his shoes echoing up to the ceiling and his husky breathing bouncing off the walls. The air smelt sickly sweet and he blew out a lungful of air through his pursed lips to try to get rid of it.

He had no idea where to look next. There were several doorways on both sides of the factory floor and he imagined he would have to methodically check them all, one after the other, until one in particular caught his eye: *Strictly no admittance. Keep locked at all times.*

If it was locked he could eliminate it. If it wasn't, it would be because Stephen had a key. As he got closer he saw that the door was slightly ajar by half an inch and Roper knew that if Stephen was in charge of doors that were meant to be locked, they would be locked. He pushed it open to reveal a stairwell with a wrought iron spiral staircase and leant over to look down the centre of it, but could see nothing into the darkness beyond the first few steps. He pulled out the torch, switched it on and called out: "Stephen?" The long reverberation suggested that the steps led down for some distance. Roper held on to the outer metal bannister, cold and scratchy from rust, as he began to walk down, using his torch to illuminate each carefully negotiated rung.

The passageway at the bottom was dimly lit by a string of electric lights so he switched off his torch and began walking, getting the sense as he progressed that it was becoming more of a tunnel, much longer than he first suspected, taking him away from the main factory and leading into a central hub from which several spokes of paved pathway radiated out to their own opening in the walls. He must have walked a hundred yards or more to get to this point and was breathless from the exertion and stifling air. The cavities themselves were in darkness, so he switched his torch back on and tried again.

"Stephen?"

There were six doorless alcoves that felt more like dungeons, though they appeared recently built, the brickwork clean and painted white with lime, reflecting back his torchlight. The first one was entirely empty. Roper pondered the possibility that all of them would be like this and he was on a wild goose chase. There was the same sickly smell, almost like sherry, and mixed in with the whiff of dampness it made him think of Holy Communion, of singing in the choir aged seven, and the repulsive, intimate smell of Canon Lummis's breath as he stood alone with him in the vestry.

Shining his torch into the second alcove he could see the walls were lined with shelves stacked with large glass jars. He looked to his left to examine them more closely and read one of the labels: *Lyddite.* On closer inspection he could see yellow crystals covered in a layer of what was either water or oil and he started to breathe heavily again, but now for different reasons. He knew what Lyddite was, everyone did, a high explosive that was bound for the Front, and he began to feel trapped and claustrophobic. His ability to think clearly under pressure was what had enabled him to rise to the level of Inspector, so he was unfamiliar with the anxiety now enveloping him, a feeling he feared might soon turn to panic if he didn't pull himself together.

Then he jumped. Someone spoke.

"Is that you Jacob?" It was unmistakably Stephen's voice coming from one of the other alcoves and Roper gingerly walked towards it.

"It's Bill," he replied, scanning the various open entrances with the beam of his torch.

When he found him, Stephen was facing the wall, his back to Roper, and at first Roper thought it was someone else, just as Jacob had. The uniform, the shaven head, the pathetic slope of his shoulders. He was surrounded by small wooden chests labelled TNT and Stephen seemed to be doing something with his hands, although Roper couldn't make out what.

"Is that you, Stephen?"

Stephen half-turned, enough for Roper to see him opening one of the glass jars.

"It's safe enough under water, but if you let it dry out it becomes rather volatile. Well, that's an understatement. A spark will do it, or sunlight, or even just dropping it." He poured the water out onto the floor by his feet, using the lid to stop the crystals from escaping. He seemed so unconcerned by the obvious danger that he could have been making another pot of tea, Roper thought. He started to perspire. Keep a clear head, he told himself. "Why don't we sit down and have a chat?"

Stephen glanced at him momentarily but returned to the jar and began pouring the crystals out onto the top of a case of TNT that was level with his knee. "It's hard to say how quickly it will dry out. It's quite damp down here."

Roper took a step back towards the open doorway, as if that were safer, and began the arthritic process of sitting down on the floor, grunting from the effort. "Why don't you sit down with me? I'm going to sit down Stephen. I think you should do the same."

Stephen carried on pouring the crystals out, slowly and carefully, until the jar was empty. He replaced the lid and then used his fingers to tidy up the pile, making a perfect pyramid of yellow, salt-like granules. His movements seemed precise and calculated, making Roper more nervous than ever. Finally Stephen sat down to face Roper, six feet away.

"Actually I'm glad it's you," said Stephen.

Roper didn't like the sound of that. There was an ominous ring to Stephen's words, so Roper decided to try and make the conversation seem more casual. He shone his torch at Stephen's medals hanging from the left breast of his jacket.

"I've not seen those before."

Stephen twisted his head in order to see them and pointed at each one as he spoke. "No. I've never worn them. This one for cowardice. This one for murder, and this one..." he paused to emit a small snort of derision, "attempted suicide I suppose." Then he fished into his jacket pocket to take out a packet of cigarettes and a box of matches. Roper felt the panic rise and he instinctively wiped his brow with his fingers.

Stephen continued as he took out a match. "Why is suicide a criminal offence do you think? I've never understood it." He rolled the match between his fingers.

Roper's eyes flicked between the match and the Lyddite which was behind Stephen, less than a foot away from his friend's shoulder. "You don't want to do that Stephen. Put the matches away and let's have a chat you know?"

Stephen was looking straight into Roper's eyes as he took a cigarette out of the packet and gripped it casually in the corner of his mouth. It was an uncharacteristically vulgar pose. "It's the perfect crime isn't it. You can never catch them, never charge them, never string them up. They do that for you. Must be very frustrating."

Roper reached forward. "Stephen. Put the cigarette away. Give it to me."

Stephen removed the cigarette from his mouth but held it close up to his face to read the minuscule text printed along the edge.

"Christopher Ellis asked me to help him and I decided to do so. It wasn't difficult, though getting him up that tree was. I suggested a heavy dose of morphine but he wanted to make sure you didn't blame the nurses. Some drivel about life insurance too. I suppose he'd had a lot of time to think about it. In the end I did both, morphine first, then I winched him up, just to be certain, and because that's what he wanted. I know you'd call it murder, but it didn't feel like it. He thought it was better for his wife and I'm inclined to agree. And I think it was the only way I had left to tell my own wife that I loved her. That I still had courage. That I was still capable of... well, whatever it is men are required to do. A valediction I suppose. I'm sorry that she'll never find out. Christopher will get away with his crime, and so will I."

Inspector Roper was too petrified to move and had let the sweat drip into his eyes. The stinging blurred his vision and his thinking. If he jumped quickly forwards he might be able to subdue Stephen, but his seated position made any quick movement impossible. That had been a mistake. Then he thought about Stephen's final remark. It didn't make any sense.

Roper said, "Get away with it? But you've just told me."

Stephen put the cigarette down and began to examine the match instead. Roper suddenly realised it made perfect sense after all. Stephen was going to take him with him. Panic overwhelmed Roper, and then was horrified that he'd begun to lose control of his bowels as he tried to get up but couldn't find a way to lift his fifteen stone frame. So he began to crawl slowly backwards out of the alcove, thinking these might be the last few seconds of his life.

"Just...Don't do anything silly, Stephen. I'm going to get some help." He hoped it didn't sound like the lie it was.

"How's Nancy?" said Stephen, still fiddling with the match in his fingers.

Thrown by this change of tack and mention of his daughter, Roper froze. "Nancy? What's she got to do with anything?"

"I suppose you wouldn't know how she was, would you. You haven't seen her for years, have you."

"You know I don't know where she is."

"That's because you haven't looked, or listened to the rumours. It turns out she's not far, actually. I found her almost without looking."

Roper made some quick calculations, sensing another devastating blow was coming. "How? Where was she?"

"Ramsgate. Rosary Road."

"Did she say anything?"

Stephen lit the match. "Yes, she did, actually." The flame illuminated his face with a deep orange glow. "So yes, I'm glad it's you. Good luck, Bill."

Roper looked horrified, scrambled to his feet calling out "Don't! Don't!" then stumbled out into the hub and back down the tunnel, tripping and badly cutting his hand on something sharp in the darkness. He picked himself up and as his lungs started to burn from the effort of running he wondered how far he would get and if he would hear the explosion before it killed him.

Suhani thought the horse pulling the Station Fly was resisting every step, probably knowing it was going in the opposite direction to its stables and therefore taking longer over the return journey than it should. The holes in the road seemed deeper than normal, throwing Suhani from side to side and making her feel queasy. The driver sitting next to her had attempted polite conversation about the lack of rain over the summer months and how hard the roads had become, but that thankfully there might be some tonight. Suhani had replied with such short, empty phrases that he soon gave up, which was the effect she wanted. Hopefully she wouldn't have to talk to anyone when she got to Tendring and Hannah would have everything under control. It might even be possible to slip up the stairs without being seen.

The sun was low, below the clouds, an hour before setting, and shone through the branches that hung over the road, the light flashing directly into her eyes, making them water. She shaded them with her hand but the intense brightness still penetrated through her fingers and began to give her a headache. She looked away and crunched her eyelids, but instead of seeing blackness she imagined rats scuttling through the trenches and nibbling at bones, until the rocking of the Fly began to make her feel light-headed.

"Please, I'd like to walk now."

"We're nearly there ma'am," protested the driver.

"Well, exactly," she replied, as kindly as she could. "I just need a bit of air, the road is a little too bumpy. I'd like to walk now please."

"As you wish, ma'am," he said, though he seemed put out. He pulled at the reins, the chaise came to a halt and then he offered to help her climb down, but she refused him with a polite wave of her hand.

"Thank you, I can manage," she said, but as soon as her feet touched the ground she had to stand perfectly still in order to take in a deep breath of fresh air. A bubble came up from her stomach, tasting of acid and bile mixed with Tetley's tea.

"You all right ma'am?" asked the driver from his lofty position on the carriage.

She removed a lace hanky from her sleeve and wiped her mouth. "I'll be fine thank you. I'm feeling better already."

"Why don't you let me take you home? I can't turn round here anyways."

Suhani replaced the handkerchief and took another deep breath. "Please, Mr Martin, let me walk."

He reluctantly took the hint. "Very well, ma'am, you be careful now," and with a flick of his reins he was off.

Suhani watched him until he was lost to view. It was only half a mile for her to get back to Tendring, but she began to wonder if she would make it, her stomach churning with each step. Perhaps she should have stayed on the carriage after all.

There was an unexpected gust of wind that sent a chill through her body. Her hands began to shake, and then she trembled, as if freezing cold. Her gut felt tender, but she suspected there was more besides hunger and tiredness making her feel this fragile. Then she worked out what it was. To live in permanent fear was a mother's lot; to grieve ahead of time, just in case the rats of France were chewing through her son. She suddenly came to a stop in the middle of the road and found herself listening to the quickening breeze in the treetops. If she thought of nothing but the next step she would arrive home soon enough, or if she kept her eyes closed Tendring might come to her.

The approach from Risborough had trees on both sides making it impossible to see the house from the road. It was not until Suhani passed the leftmost gate to stand between the guardian eagles that the house came fully into view, though she found to her dismay that her vision was blurred and she could make out no details. The long day had knocked her out. Tendring shimmered like a house reflected in water, an image from a country far hotter than this one. She blinked heavily and looked down at her basket in order to focus on an object nearer her eyes, but she only succeeded in catching a whiff of sweaty egg sandwiches. She thought she might faint, and looked back up at the house in order to stabilise herself. The building seemed more solid now, clearer, but there was still some movement, more specific, that was now becoming discernable. A figure under the portico appeared to be waving; a chaiwala perhaps. But when she squinted to see more detail she realised he wasn't waving at all but standing up and putting on his shako hat.

What was Freddie doing here? What was the postboy's message, so late in the day? What news could be so important that he was still here at half-past-six? She saw the edges of his uniform sharply defined against one pillar of the portico, and the white flash of the envelope in his hand from fifty yards away as distinct as if he had held it up to her face. The harder she tried to clear her thoughts, the more fanciful they became. Here was the postboy who she knew understood the sign of the black cross, could smell the gunpowder on the envelope and feel the grit of French soil under his thumb. She began to shake at the thought of it, of rats in the trenches. That was why he had waited for her return, and why she had waited for so long on the station platform. Tristan had not climbed aboard the train because he had gone over the top and never returned. The letter would tell her why, and a package of his belongings would follow in a few days. The unfinished triptych was now complete, the universe destroyed, never to be put back together. What little was left of her heart would be broken, and no matter how loudly she wailed into the sky no one would hear, except the crows and the clouds.

Still fifty yards apart, they stared at each other, Freddie and Suhani, waiting for the other to move, until finally Freddie took the first step towards her. She dropped her picnic basket onto the lawn by her feet and wondered what she would do next. Perhaps she would run to the church and hide amongst her children, as she so often did, but then beyond, to the hills where thunder might roll in so that no one could overhear her futile dreams. And she could go further still, into the future that had been denied her, where the paint on the canvas was still wet, the guns were cold, the medals were wrapped in a woollen sock to be put away in a drawer, until the day came when there were sons and daughters to proudly show them to, Suhani's grandchildren were held by their mothers to the breast, and the bunting still fluttered in the wind.

29

Suhani raced from Tendring towards the Eagley Road. Freddie was calling out her name and was gaining on her, so she hitched up her dress in order to move her legs more freely. If only she had been wearing her sari instead of this ridiculous English garment. When Freddie called her name again – Mrs Harkness! Mrs Harkness! – Suhani cried out in reply a desolate, wordless lament to the rhythm of her running that must have sounded like the song of a wild animal in distress, chased by dogs, howling its own requiem in anticipation of the kill.

As she turned left down the bridle path towards the church her dress snagged on some thistles and she snatched it away, leaving behind frayed rags hanging on the thorns. The delay allowed Freddie to get closer still, so she kicked off her shoes and ran more freely along the path, unable to feel the sharp saplings scratching at her legs or the stones grazing the soles of her feet. Why did Freddie persist? The longer the chase went on the more ominous the letter became, and all possible meanings fell away except one, as if there had ever been any doubt. But her bare feet meant she was running faster than Freddie, and pulling away.

The church was still a mile off but it felt like a hundred. Her desire to run forever was no match for her burning lungs, and her light-headedness returned, worse than ever. She could not go on. Her running quickly deteriorated into a stumble and then she found herself standing still, struggling to breathe. She put her palm to her chest, feeling the rise and fall of her own breath, a quick, painful gasping that felt like drowning. Between the black clouds and the horizon below them the sun was setting and her race with Freddie was finished. He would catch up with her, the hunt would soon be over, with the truth not far behind.

Out of nowhere a rabbit ran across her path into the field to her right, hopping over and around the short cropped stalks of wheat that glistened in the last of the day's sunlight. Without reason or care, Suhani stepped slowly into the open space of the harvested field where the stalks cut with a burning sensation into her feet. It would at least give her a few final seconds to be alone. Eventually she found her way to the very middle where she stood still and closed her eyes, allowing her breath to recover, until at last she felt becalmed. Only then did it occur to Suhani that Freddie might have lost her, because for several minutes she didn't hear him nor had she looked round to see if he was following. She turned to do so now, but all she saw were wheat stalks painted with delicate touches of blood; no sign of Freddie. Finally she understood this was not her final destination and if she kept going she might never be caught. Then it dawned on her where she was headed.

The sun had now set, leaving streaks of black and orange cloud to illuminate Suhani's path as she approached the monument. The fifty foot tall obelisk stood on the highest hill in Kent, which wasn't to say very much, but nevertheless it was a place where you could see for many miles in all directions. Her memory of the day it had been erected, in

1904, was as bright as the evening light that now surrounded it. Then another memory, a sad and confusing blur which she had set aside all those years ago but came back to her now like wiping condensation from a window, of how she had gone to the grand unveiling but Stephen had not, locking himself in his room with the excuse of a bad cold. She stood to gather her breath, looking down at the bronze plaque at the foot of the monument to scan the list of names, men of Kent who had fallen in the second Boer War, above which was the title: *South Africa 1899 – 1902.*

Suhani's bare feet were stinging, and sticky with blood. This was the end of her journey. She couldn't move, nor did she want to. All day she had wanted the waiting to end, now she wanted it to go on forever.

At first she thought she could hear thunder, just as the driver of the station Fly had predicted, but it sounded more like explosions. She wondered if it might be the guns from France, but there needed to be an easterly wind to hear their pounding thuds, and the sound was definitely coming from the west, where the sun had set, where the factories lay hidden in the marshes. After a moment of silence, there came an almighty rumble that hit her in the chest before it reached her ears, a wave of sound unlike any she had heard before, like the tearing apart of the earth under her feet. It shook the trees and even the monument before her seemed to visibly vibrate under its force.

Then it was over, its ending as surprising as its beginning. Nothing had changed, except the woodlarks and blackbirds had stopped singing, and her breath seemed to be outside of her body – until she realised it was not her breath at all but someone else's, and she was no longer alone.

"What was that noise? Was it France?"

He was standing behind her, the sorcerer, the bringer of letters, the winged messenger, destroyer of worlds; yet all Suhani had heard was the emptiness left behind by the explosion, not his words. He had found his silent way to her, and in the end she felt relieved to have been caught, like an institutionalised prisoner returning to her cell.

"It was too close for that," she said, turning to look at him, knowing the game was up, the hunt finished. "France is in the opposite direction."

Her eyes began to overflow with tears as Freddie stood there offering the letter to her, and which, finally, she took. Another memory resurfaced, from India, of a time before Stephen, of the white English woman she'd lived with and looked after – yes, of course, that was who the old woman on the station platform reminded her of, the one who had been as good as a mother to her, the one who had said on the day of Suhani's leaving: if you need kindness, be kind. So she looked hopefully into Freddie's eyes and said, "Won't your mother be worried about you?"

"You'll be all right, Mrs Harkness. It's a good letter."

He was so innocent she thought, he couldn't possibly understand what it meant to lose one son, never mind three, but he seemed so certain that for a moment she accepted it. She really would be all right. How long would it take for her universe to be recreated? There was nothing left now in her life but the letter he had handed her, no Tendring, no Hannah or Phoebe, no Stephen any longer, no more of life itself, so she opened the letter and began to read.

Jacob Pennington stood and watched his factory burn. The worst of the explosions were over, though a few rogue shells still burst with a crack into the sky, and after a while he observed the show dispassionately, as if it were a firework display. A hundred factory workers were lined up with him, almost all of them women, young girls really, the glow of the fire reflected in their astonished eyes, the war made real, the battle finally come to rage in the garden of England.

Jacob tried to calculate which buildings had been lost and which had survived, or which were salvageable. The main block still stood, but a fire was eating its insides and would soon devour the walls. He suspected the whole enterprise was done for and he wondered what role he would be given in its resurrection. In a few months time, after a rapid rebuild, he might be Manager, and would have tea made for him, not the other way round. He imagined Stephen Harkness making his own pot of tea before blowing himself up.

Then a figure approached, a limping silhouette, and Jacob's heart sank, thinking for a moment that Harkness had made it out. But then as the man got closer he saw that it was Roper, damaged in the blast with blood running from a gash in his leg, but definitely Roper.

The first few drops of rain fell from the sky and another shell exploded, weaker now, like an afterthought: the last he or anyone would ever hear from Stephen Harkness.

Suhani couldn't believe it at first, couldn't understand why a letter of condolence would begin so informally, and it felt as if Tristan, not Freddie, was standing there, or some strange union of the two. She held the letter out to try to find the last vestiges of light, and with each word she found herself coming back to life, and Tristan too. There was no condolence, because none was required.

Dearest Maji, Forgive my haste, I've just a few minutes to write...

Overcome with a sudden, perfect happiness, it didn't remotely occur to Suhani to question how Freddie already knew what was in Tristan's letter; or why his smile had the sheepish look of a guilty man.

30

Dear Mrs Ellis,

Forgive my revisiting your loss but I will come straight to the point if I may. You will remember I promised to let you know where your husband's body would be interred. It is in Holy Trinity Church, near the village of Eagley, in Kent.

The church lies at the end of a shallow dip, surrounded by fields and woods, and it is the most beautiful and peaceful place you can imagine. With your blessing, I have taken the liberty of leaving a small posy of flowers on your husband's grave, whenever I am passing that way. I stop there often these days.

I hope this will give you some solace, Mrs Ellis. Rest assured you and Christopher are separated only by distance.

Yours sincerely,

Suhani Harkness.

Suhani didn't like to mention that he was buried next to a German airman. But as she wrote down Anne Ellis's address, obtained from Nurse Collins, she thought it strange, and beautiful, how the war was sprinkling English churchyards with the bodies of foreigners.

Part Three

31

Winter

The preparing of food, the washing of clothes, working in my mother's shop, these things are all I have to prevent myself from losing my mind. It allows less time for my depression to envelop me, though when it does I wear it like a woolly coat. It is never far away, close enough to reach out for whenever I want, wrap myself inside it, and be weighed down by its warmth. When my mother sees my shoulders droop, she gently tells me to sit up straight. She means don't wallow, but it's hard not to.

Christopher is buried in a churchyard in a small village in England called Eagley. I now have another letter from the woman called Suhani Harkness – my mother thinks it might be an Indian name – the first one, the one I read on the beach, tells of how she looked after him at the end, and the second describes the church and the graveyard. It sounds very pretty, and I'm grateful that there is a grave to tend, but I wonder if I'll ever see it. Money is scarce, people seem to be buying less in the shop with cheaper alternatives setting up in the town. We will see. Mother and I are setting aside a small amount each week so that I may one day be able to visit. Christopher would have liked to have been able to hear the sound of the sea, but at least he is somewhere – Mrs Henny's son was Missing Killed In Action, and everyone knows that's a euphemism for mincemeat.

So I keep myself busy. Mother means well, she says each new day will carry less pain than the last, but I find time flies more like a swallow than an arrow. Today is harder than yesterday, tomorrow may be easier, no rhyme or reason behind the direction of flight. The feelings come unbidden at moments you least expect and can't prepare for. That is, all except one, a painful memory I force upon myself yet brings me some comfort simply by dint of its regularity. Every evening I take a few moments by the garden gate, where you can stand and watch the sea, something Christopher and I did together so often. After all, you have to hurt in order to recover from the pain, don't you? Poison is medicine, in small doses, so they say.

Joe drops in every day. He is very kind and loves to talk about the weather. I feel bad that sometimes I don't want him here. Anyway, he doesn't usually stay for long, and once he has left I am grateful for his visit. Alone, I feel less lonely.

32

No newspaper reported the explosion at Milbridge Munitions Factory and there were no funerals, because there were no bodies, though the people knew what had happened and filled the church for Major Stephen Harkness's memorial service. There was talk of Harkness having gone insane and blowing himself up, though not everyone believed the story and thought it more likely some act of incompetence was being covered up. They were not mourners in the pews but gossip mongers, gawping at grief, trying to catch a glimpse of the sad, mysterious Indian wife who lived in the manor house outside Eagley. But Suhani gave nothing away, put on her best English façade, and the people were disappointed.

Because the truth was that Suhani was not grieving, not for Stephen, and the times when she did feel a sadness were for the life he had lost not in the explosion but long ago in South Africa, for reasons she would now never fully understand. Sadness too for a marriage that had been a ghostly imitation, a forgery, for the lost years and the silent bedrooms, for the man who never came home. She had done her grieving for Stephen in 1902, and could not revisit it, not even for appearance's sake.

Suhani had thought that Tendring would come alive with Stephen gone, but to her surprise the opposite happened. There was less post because there was no more contact to be had with the factory, nor with the Masons, nor with the medical staff at Celandine Hall. That, combined with Suhani's lack of any kind of social circle, meant sometimes Freddie didn't deliver to the house for several days. The beds were still in the library but they were unoccupied and all their bedding removed, their skeletal frames awaiting collection. A new annexe had opened up at Celandine and Nurse Collins had decided it would be more efficient to have everyone in one place, so Tendring now felt acutely empty. The ringing of footsteps had begun to seem more noticeable, so much so that Suhani moved a carpet from an upstairs bedroom into the hall in order to absorb the sound, though it seemed to make little difference. The extra nurses had departed with their patients and Suhani was left alone with only Hannah and Phoebe for company. There were letters of condolence at the loss of her husband – some of them even appeared to be sincere and kind – and letters of reply to and from the new widow, but they faded quickly over a matter of a few days. She finally wrote to Mrs Ellis as she had promised she would, and she wrote once a week to the hospital in Valenciennes where Tristan was recuperating, though so far she had received nothing but Field Service Postcards in reply. There were administrative and financial issues to deal with and Suhani delved into the detail with some reticence, discovering things about Stephen's finances that left her worried for the future. There was an Army pension, but it would not sustain Tendring forever. At least there were no relatives to complicate matters further. His parents long dead, Stephen had once mentioned a brother, but they were estranged and Suhani wasn't even sure of his name, much less his whereabouts. Sometimes she thought Stephen had willed loneliness upon himself, and the explosion was its natural conclusion. She put the papers away in a drawer thinking she would revisit them in the New Year.

So although Suhani was not grieving for Stephen, she missed him in a different way, the man she had known since she was a child in India. Sometimes she sensed his presence, like the amputees in the library who used to say they could still feel their arms or legs.

It was only when Freddie's visits had dwindled to two or three a week that she realised she was missing someone else too, though why that was she couldn't quite say. It wasn't so much the postboy himself but some shroud he wore, some mystery he brought with him that would not reveal itself to her. He had always been quiet and taciturn, which had brought out the protective mother in her, but he now wore another layer, a prickliness, ensuring he didn't linger for a second longer than necessary. She wondered if she had in some way upset him or let him down, though she couldn't imagine how. On top of that, he simply didn't look well. Perhaps there was a problem at work or at home that he would like to talk about but couldn't bring himself to. She resolved to try to have that conversation with him when he next delivered the post. Stephen, though he hadn't known it, had taught her never to take silence as an answer. There was, however, an urgent need to have a more important conversation with someone else first.

Suhani was standing in the hallway having just returned from lighting the candles at her garden shrine. It had been dark and cold outside, winter having set in, only the glass cages protecting the flames from the freezing air, and so, shivering herself, she shut the front door behind her as quickly as she could. Thinking she could hear some knocking coming from the kitchen, she walked past the stairs and through the open kitchen door, but no one was there. The connecting door to the laundry was open too, and this was where the noises were coming from. It must be Phoebe finishing the last of the sheets that were to go back to Celandine. It was Phoebe who she wanted to talk to, and now was her chance.

"Phoebe, you're working very late," said Suhani as she entered the laundry room, but to her surprise it wasn't her.

"Phoebe's resting ma'am," said Hannah as she continued to pull sheets off the overhanging airer, causing it to swing and knock against the wall.

"Let me help you then."

"It's nearly done ma'am."

But Suhani helped anyway, taking a sheet for herself, folding it up and dropping it into a basket by their feet. "I imagine she needs her rest," she said, deciding that if she couldn't yet raise the issue with Phoebe then it might be helpful to get something out of Hannah. "I should have seen it sooner I suppose. But it's been difficult to see anything clearly these last few weeks."

"What would that be, ma'am?"

Suhani gave Hannah a knowing look. "How long have you known?"

Hannah looked away, using the folding of another sheet as an excuse. "Known what, ma'am?"

"I may have been blind but even I can see the bump in her belly."

Hannah stopped folding and sighed. "Well...Since about June I suppose."

"You should have told me."

"I told her to get rid ma'am, but she wouldn't hear of it. You wouldn't know to look at her but she's an obstinate mule and make no mistake. Now it's too late. There's no bigger fool than a stubborn one. But then...I do believe she knows what she wants. She says the little mite wants to be born. I suppose we all want that, when you think about it."

Suhani took another sheet and began folding it. "Is she happy?"

"Hard to say, isn't it," said Hannah. "I think she is, and I think she isn't."

"Do you think I should go up and see her?" asked Suhani. Though it was a question, her mind was already made up.

"Well don't bother if you expect to change her mind, ma'am."

"That is not my intention. She just needs to know she's safe here."

"Very well, ma'am. I'll keep my nose out. Kitchen needs a tidy I wouldn't be surprised."

Suhani dropped her sheet into the basket. "Hannah. What on earth happened? Except for one trip to the theatre, and that was with you, I don't think I've ever seen her leave the house."

Hannah reached for the pulley to raise the airer. "I don't know ma'am. Perhaps you've been blind for longer than you think. If you don't mind me saying so ma'am."

Hannah's words troubled her the more she thought about them, and as Suhani climbed the narrow wooden staircase that led to Phoebe's bedroom at the very top of the house, the more their meaning changed with each step. The implication that she had been blind to Phoebe leaving the house was not, perhaps, what Hannah had meant. There was another possibility that made Suhani blanch: that Phoebe would not have needed to leave the house in order to get pregnant. Suhani swatted the thought away, literally with her hands as if annoyed by a wasp, before reaching Phoebe's bedroom door. She knocked.

"Come in?"

It sounded like the voice of a child, but then it was not so long since she had been one. Suhani opened the door to find Phoebe sitting in a chair embroidering a lace camisole.

"Ma'am?" Phoebe looked startled by her visitor and began to stand up, but Suhani gestured for her to stay where she was.

"Phoebe. I'm sorry to disturb you so late at night. May I sit?" But Suhani was already perched on the edge of Phoebe's bed before Phoebe had a chance to answer. "I'd like to talk to you."

Phoebe looked apprehensive. "Yes ma'am?"

Hitching herself sideways onto the bed, Suhani leant back against the wall and crossed her legs. She knew her informality would disconcert Phoebe, but would also enable her to gain Phoebe's confidence. She looked around the tiny room, at the hard, thin double bed she shared with Hannah, the sink at the window, the drab curtains, all illuminated by one candle.

"I was younger than you when I started in service. It was hard, but my mistress was kind. I hope I look after you well."

Phoebe seemed confused by the question. "We look after you, ma'am. That's the point isn't it? I'm very happy."

"Good. I was happy too. But it didn't stop me wanting to escape."

Phoebe spoke quietly, clearly finding this conversation of equals awkward. "There's no point dreaming ma'am. There's no escaping, is there. You can't run away without somewhere to go."

Suhani glanced at Phoebe's handiwork. "Life is not embroidery, Phoebe. You don't have to know what it will look like before you start. What is it? Do you have enough light?"

"It's a Rose Stitch, ma'am. It means it will look a bit like a rose." She looked embarrassed. "If I do it right."

Reaching across to pat Phoebe's hand, Suhani said, "You'll do it right." She leant back again and spoke into her own lap. "You'll probably find it hard to believe but Stephen was fond of roses. Passionate, even obsessive, you might say. He grew them every year in India until... well... his favourite was called Frau Karl Druschki, it was the purest white, and when he was not in uniform he loved wearing the bud of one in his buttonhole. He had a rose-walk built which was his pride and joy, a hundred yards long, an iron-framed arcade over which he grew climbing roses. He used to walk it alone, and I used to watch him from the house. And then, later, secretly, we used to walk it together, late at night."

Suhani looked up momentarily to see if Phoebe was watching her.

"Then one year the monsoon failed. Water ran short, so an appeal was made to conserve supplies to prevent people dying of thirst. Stephen had the watering of the roses stopped, and as a result every rose in his arcade died. It was a devastating blow to him. He had the whole arcade dug up, the ironwork removed, and put a hedge in its place. Now that I think about it, he was never quite the same after that."

Suhani shifted her weight on the bed in order to get more comfortable and then stroked the top blanket with her palm.

"Anyway, things changed in more ways than one. Our first child was due."

Phoebe dropped her head, but Suhani was determined to continue.

"We were not married." She wanted to check Phoebe's reaction, but with her chin on her chest and her eyes down it was impossible to judge, though Suhani suspected she was listening intently.

"It was very difficult. Everyone thought I'd been taken advantage of, but that was not the case. I knew my mind more than he knew his. But he stood by me and we were married later that year. In those days he was an extraordinary man."

Phoebe finally looked up. "I'm sorry he died, Mrs Harkness."

Suhani could only acknowledge her with a smile, knowing there was no unambiguous reply, no way of simply agreeing with her. She let a few moments pass until she could no longer avoid the question she had come to ask. "So who is the father of your child, Phoebe?"

Phoebe picked up her embroidery as if it offered some protection and began working on it again. "I can't say."

"You mean you don't know?"

"No, I mean I can't say."

"Has he abandoned you?"

"Not in the way you mean."

"In what way then?"

"I can't say."

Suhani breathed in, held it, and then sighed.

"Did you love him?"

Phoebe looked up and Suhani could see a change had come over her. "I still do. I don't want to answer any more questions, ma'am." She tried to push her needle through the lace, but couldn't see what she was doing because her eyes were filling with tears, and she pricked her finger. "Blast!" she hissed.

Suhani lifted herself off the bed, took the small hanky from her sleeve and wrapped it around Phoebe's finger. "You know this will be very difficult on your own, don't you."

Phoebe put her other hand to her unborn child, quite deliberately, and said, "But I won't be on my own, will I."

There was a sound of defiance in her voice that Suhani admired, a quality she recognised in herself, and as she looked at Phoebe she saw a silhouette of her own life dancing in the shadows on the wall behind Phoebe. She held Phoebe's hand more tightly. "Well, so be it. A rose it is." She unwrapped the hanky from Phoebe's finger and dabbed at the pinprick. "One minute of cold water, that should do it." Then she lifted up one corner of the camisole between her forefinger and thumb. "Show me when you've finished. I'd like to see it."

"Yes ma'am."

When Suhani left the room, she stood outside the door for a moment, wondering how she might protect Phoebe from the staring and the gossip and the crossing of roads that was about to come, and the war she would have to fight long after this one was over. At least, in her different ways, Suhani had experience of such things, and could help Phoebe hold her head high. She might even be some kind of step-grandmother or aunt, and for the first time in many months, Suhani could feel the unfolding of hope.

33

"You're not too old for me to tan yer hide Freddie! You don't eat your porridge, you pick at your meat pudding and now there's toast in the bin. This is a right carry on."

"Yes Ma."

"Yes Ma's not good enough. Getting fancy ideas from those fancy houses aren't you! You need to go to bed and sleep like a normal boy, not shuffle about in the small hours like a thief."

"I'm sorry Ma."

"You will be if you don't get that porridge down you in the morning. I'm not throwing it away. You can have it cold, day old or not."

The floorboards outside his room creaked. She was already walking away from Freddie's closed bedroom door as she spoke her final words. It was a long time since Freddie had known his mother to be this angry, and the fact that she had not wished him goodnight suggested she was disappointed too, which hurt him even more. She had never done that before. He called out goodnight, but there was no reply.

Perhaps she was changing because he was. He knew in the last few months he had grown taller, the bottoms of his trousers no longer touching his shoes, yet at the same time his uniform seemed to have become baggier. And the change was not just physical. The fact was, he found it difficult to eat, and when he did he often threw it up again. Eating made him feel sick and not eating meant incurring the wrath of his mother. He wobbled between the two states, like a spinning penny, and the exhausting balancing act took up what little appetite he had. His post round seemed to be taking longer, even though Tendring was not often on the route, and he was sure his bike was getting heavier, the muscles in his legs and arms aching from the moment he got up to the moment he went to bed. The only time he was unaware of his limbs hurting was when he was asleep, which was hardly ever, and when he did sleep it only lasted until he woke from his dreams, twitching.

Of course he knew he had to force something down or else he'd be dead from starvation, but he found it best to swallow fragments of food when he wasn't thinking about what he was doing. There was a tightening of his stomach that meant he was always on the lavatory, emptying out what little he had inside him with what looked more like beer than shit. On one occasion he got there only just in time, some of it splashing on his shoes, and after a while he became conscious that he might be constantly smelling of excrement. He had decided to drink less so that it would be less runny, cutting down to one glass of water a day, last thing at night. But it didn't make any difference, except once in a while the exact opposite happened and he couldn't go at all, no matter how hard he pushed or red-faced he became. His pee, he noticed, was dark orange and stung when he forced it out. At least the colour looked healthy. Sometimes his head hurt so much he thought his brain would burst out of his ears.

But there seemed to be one solution to his loss of appetite: putting pencil to paper. Often all he had to do was imagine the act, which was usually enough to enable a bowl of porridge to stay down. But occasionally visualising it was not sufficient and he had to go through with the performance. Like George Franklin knocking back his hip flask and the gin making his decisions for him, there was an inevitability about the pencil dragging Freddie's hand across the postcard. It didn't matter that it was shameful, it was the next five minutes that were important.

So Freddie knew what was coming and took out from his pouch a small parcel, an official looking package with the sender's address printed on the back: War Office. He observed himself doing it, watching himself taking out the topmost postcard, as if his left hand did not belong to him. Already he felt better, less anxious, and was somehow able to ignore the wrongdoing just as he could ignore the stains on his shoes. It felt like someone else was reading what was printed across the top of it in bold black capital letters: FIELD SERVICE POST CARD. The amanuensis had come to protect him, another version of himself but as yet without a name, standing at his shoulder, guiding the strokes of his pencil. Always, it seemed, he was watching from above.

The instructions on the extreme left of what was otherwise a blank side of the postcard were blunt and precise:

The address only to be written on this side. If anything else is added, the postcard will be destroyed.

Freddie wrote down the address in the handwriting of Tristan's amanuensis. He read it over, but then the twists in his stomach returned. Perhaps he should have used his left hand for this. Tristan would do that, wouldn't he, for so few words, no need for outside help? He wouldn't need an amanuensis to write a simple address. Next time. He would remember for next time. Tristan's recovery would have to be gradual. And when he was eventually recovered, Freddie would have to send him back to the front. But right now he didn't want to think about that.

He turned the card over to see several lines of text that involved simply crossing out various options to leave a simple message: the first line was *I am quite well* and Freddie drew a line through it. That much was obvious, Tristan was not well. The next line Freddie left untouched: *I have been admitted into hospital.* Mrs Harkness knew this already but there was no option on the card to describe someone continuing to convalesce. It would have to do, as it had done on the three previous Field Service Post Cards that Freddie had already forged and delivered. He crossed out *sick*, which left the word *wounded* as part of the message. Next he dragged his pencil through *and hope to be discharged soon*, to leave *and am going on well.* This was the fourth time he had chosen the same options and each time he hoped it sounded neither too negative nor too positive.

Finally there was a blank space for the date. He put his pencil on his desk, leant down to pull out his box from under the bed and took out four letters from a pile of twenty or more. So many letters, they filled his room like autumn leaves. These four were from Mrs Harkness to Tristan. It would have raised the alarm if he had allowed them to be delivered so Freddie had intercepted them all. It meant, having read each one several times, that he was aware of other information too: Tristan would now know about the death of his father and his brother. Suhani had broken that news in the first letter, and its restrained mournful rhythms were confirmation, if Freddie needed any, that he was doing the right thing now. It also told him that his endeavours to prevent Mrs Harkness from grieving again were working, and it felt like the Field Service Post Cards were a gift, making the deceit as easy as falling off a log, irresistible...and he still had a handful left from the pile he had taken out of George's overflowing return-to-sender drawer. There was no time limit on this exercise of deception. He checked the date of the most recent of Mrs Harkness's letters and picked up his pencil again to fill in the final blank that came after *I have received your letter dated...* Freddie signed and dated the postcard, the seal of Tristan's amanuensis, then stamped the date for two days ago before gathering everything up – the rubber stamper, the ink pad, his pen and ink bottle, a pencil. He then returned everything to his box before sliding it back under the bed. The process of tidying up and clearing his desk had made his head clearer too, his thoughts more manageable, and his heart slowed so that the thumping in his ears felt more like a gentle rocking. He picked up the package that still contained nearly fifty blank postcards and, together with his forgeries and Mrs Harkness's four letters, returned them to his pouch. He no longer felt like leaving things under his bed. In some way, he thought his father might be watching. He wondered if his pouch bulged suspiciously. Forgeries came gift-wrapped in paranoia.

There was now only one more act to undertake and Freddie crept downstairs to do it. The porridge was stone cold, but Freddie spooned it in without it touching the sides. He relished the feeling as it slid down to fill his stomach and he had no doubt that Mrs Harkness would be grateful. Each spoonful not only kept Freddie alive but Tristan too, and it was almost as if he was feeding Mrs Harkness's son as well as himself.

But suddenly the satisfied feeling twisted in his stomach like off-milk, and the black fire in his belly returned. He ran outside to the lavatory, first to stick his fingers down his throat, then to sit and allow his guts to empty their watery contents again. He looked down at his crumpled pyjama bottoms, held his head in his hands and suddenly wept, wanting to die. He hated having eaten the porridge because, despite the best efforts of his bowels, it kept his heart beating and his lungs taking in oxygen, which was, at that moment, more than he could possibly bear.

On his way to Tendring the following morning, Freddie stopped by the apple tree and rubbed the postcard into the mossy bark at the base of the trunk. This was his new method of ageing his letters from the trenches. It was quicker and probably more convincing, more earthy, than house dust.

When he turned the corner at the bottom of Tendring's drive to pass between the stone eagles he could see a horse and cart waiting by the portico and a flat-capped labourer loading it with redundant iron bedsteads from the library. The work was being overseen by Mrs Harkness, who stood on the steps. The sense of change, of moving on, unsettled Freddie. He needed everything to stay the same, for every day to be indistinguishable from the one before and the one to come. Even the cooling of the air and the shortening of the days troubled him. Every part of his body was aware that the passing of time would be his eventual undoing. Except for in his head, where he continued to ignore the possibility.

As Freddie approached, Mrs Harkness spotted him. She went into the house and returned a moment later holding a letter. The labourer was throwing the iron frames unceremoniously onto the back of his cart as Freddie arrived and dismounted, balancing his bike against one pillar of the portico. By then Mrs Harkness and the labourer were in the middle of a conversation so he had to wait his turn.

"...Forgive me ma'am," the labourer was saying, throwing another frame onto his cart, "it's none of my business but people are talking." He brushed his hands together to purge them of dust and turned to face her. "You need to get rid. I can't be seen coming here no more. I can't be doing with... with bastards, pardon me for saying so. It's hard enough as it is with Mr Harkness gone, if you catch my drift. I'll get the last of these and that'll be that." He attempted to walk back through the front door and into the house, but Mrs Harkness refused to step aside.

"I was hoping you could help on Sunday, Mr Lawes," she said.

Freddie watched Mr Lawes studiously avoiding eye contact with Mrs Harkness. Then, even worse, he looked directly at Freddie.

"Word gets around, I'm sorry to say, ma'am."

"Perhaps people should find something more interesting to do than gossip."

"That's as may be, ma'am. I've got my own reputation to think about, is all I'm saying. If you don't mind..."

Freddie suddenly blanched. He thought they were talking about him. Mr Lawes had called Freddie a bastard, within earshot. He looked down at the water marks on his shoes where he had tried to clean them. Perhaps his own visits to the house were being questioned in some way? It looked like Mr Lawes didn't want to be seen anywhere near him and didn't care that he could hear him say so.

"Well I'm sorry you feel that way, Mr Lawes," said Suhani as she handed him a shilling. "We'll have to manage without you. I'll be sorry not to see you again."

"Yes ma'am, likewise," he said, side-stepping past her in the doorway to go back into the house to retrieve the final section of bed frame.

"Hello Freddie," said Suhani. Freddie sensed a false ring to her cheerfulness as she continued, "I have a letter for you. Anything for me?"

He put his hand in his pouch but left it there as he looked at Mrs Harkness. It was rare for him to say what he was thinking, but today he was too tired and hungry to care about the consequences, and since Mr Lawes had gone into the house, now was his opportunity.

"Have I done something wrong?" he said.

"You? Why?"

"Why were you talking about me?"

"What?"

He saw that she looked genuinely confused. "It sounded like Mr Lawes wanted to get rid of me." As soon as he said it he saw that he had misunderstood, thinking his forgeries hung so heavily around his neck they were visible to everyone.

"Not you Freddie," she laughed. "He wasn't talking about you. I can't imagine you doing anything remotely wrong. In fact no one's done anything wrong. It's just silly gossip. It's a sad thing when other people's lives are more interesting than one's own, but there we are."

Mr Lawes came back out of the house with the last of the sections of bed frames and threw it on to the back of his cart. "Thank you ma'am," he said as he climbed up onto the front of the cart and twitched the reins with a click of his tongue.

"Thank you Mr Lawes," she replied as he pulled away. Freddie watched the cart turn and head down the drive and would have kept watching until it disappeared through the gates, except he realised Mrs Harkness was speaking to him. He turned to see her holding out her letter, eager to swap it for his. "So, Freddie. What have you got for me?"

He removed the Field Service Post Card from his pouch and handed it over. When she recognised the postcard for what it was she sighed, her demeanour changed, her voice softened and for a brief moment she became distant, talking to herself.

"Oh. Another one of these. That's four now."

Freddie felt the need to explain, had to think quickly and managed to dredge up another of his boss's words of wisdom. "Mr Franklin says the censor won't let you say anything worth saying," and then he needed to quickly change the subject to avoid further scrutiny. Watching Mr Lawes drive away with his cart load of bed frames gave him his cue: "Where are the beds going, Mrs Harkness?"

She was examining the postcard, turning it over repeatedly to read both sides more than once, only partially attending to Freddie's question. "Oh. Celandine Hall. They opened up the Trophy room." Then she looked directly at him. "They were good men, I'll miss them, but it's better for everyone this way. The Army look after their own you see, now with Stephen gone... On Sunday afternoon we'll restore the library to its former glory. With or without Mr Lawes." Then she gave Freddie another of her winks. "We'll put Shiva back on his pedestal, shall we?"

"Yes ma'am." Freddie nodded. "Goodbye ma'am..." He did up his pouch, straightened his hat and mounted his bike. But there was a sense of unfinished business, and his sentence had trailed off unsatisfactorily, a cold porridge of a goodbye. Sunday was his half day off and perhaps this was an opening for Freddie to gain approval from Mrs Harkness, a bargain with the future to push back the inevitable, even for a minute. The more he could get her to like Tristan's amanuensis, the more she would forgive Freddie. Or was it the other way round? He didn't know who he was, and his head spun; he wasn't sure he was anybody at all. He wondered if she could see right through him, literally, as if he were made of glass, or smoke, or fine rain. Without any intention or plan his arm lifted itself to put his fingers up to the small scar on his forehead, not only to check if it was there, but to see if the rest of him was too. It was a way of restoring some hard ground beneath his shoes, to stop him keeling over. Instinctively he spoke, the words being as new to his ears as they were to hers.

"Can I help?" he said, still rubbing his forehead. It sounded not like a question but a declaration, and made him feel solid again, anchoring his feet to the ground.

"Help?"

"Half day on Sunday."

"Oh I see. That's very kind Freddie. But we can manage. Wouldn't you like to spend time with your family?"

He was already working out how he would explain his absence to his mother. Normally he would take her for a walk, if he went anywhere on a Sunday afternoon. He would think of some deceit, he always did. "I always go out somewhere, ma'am."

"Well, if you'd like to. Thank you. We'll have scones and jam shall we?"

The sickly suggestion was enough to trigger his nausea again, not that it had ever really left him. Perhaps another Field Service Post Card would restore his appetite, and his stomach seemed to settle at the mere thought of it.

Suhani glanced down at the postcard again. "Perhaps you will have a proper letter for me next time."

He leant forward to put his hands on the handlebars, preparing to leave, and absent-mindedly tested his brakes. "I'll see what I can do for you, ma'am."

The amanuensis whispered in his ear like a dream, with a better answer. Some new, improved scheme was coming.

It was only later that morning, when Suhani was sitting alone in her bedroom at Tendring, as she so often did these days, that she realised she had forgotten to ask Freddie how he was, ask him properly, directly, about how pale and tired he looked. The conversation with Mr Lawes and the card from Tristan had distracted her. But perhaps it would not have been an easy subject to bring up. If Freddie came on Sunday that might be a better opportunity as he would be out of uniform and would feel freer to talk. Or perhaps at church, if she was the last one out. She would like to help, if she could.

Suhani turned to the four Field Service Post Cards that she had laid out on her dressing table. They looked identical, all with the same erasures and default message, and the same signature from Tristan's scribe. Only the dates were different. Why was he still in hospital in France? If he was not improving they would send him home, and if he was getting better he'd go back to the front or else be given leave to find his own way back to Tendring.

Whatever it was, there was something Tristan wasn't telling her.

34

That same day, Freddie had a letter for Bedden's Farm. In his four months on the job it was the first time he had delivered there. Millie had never gone to school, instead was put to work on the farm from the age of five, and Freddie doubted she had ever learnt to read. It was more than likely her mother and father were illiterate too, so whatever was in the letter they would have to ask him to read it to them, as several households in the village did.

The path to the farmhouse was too rough to cycle on so he pushed his bike towards the front door. An old brown Labrador with greying eyebrows came waddling up to him for a sniff of his crotch and he patted her on the head to push her away.

Freddie knocked. Another dog growled from behind the door, younger, more protective. He had become an expert at determining the mood of dogs. While he was waiting he took the letter out of his pouch to glance at the postmark. Exeter. Who did the Bedden's know there?

It was Millie who came to the door. She was holding the puppy in her arms, feeding it milk with a glass nursing bottle, which the puppy gnawed as it tried to extract the last few drops from the rubber teat.

"Want to come and see the others?" she said, proudly.

He was uncertain, but said, "All right."

He followed her back inside the house as far as the kitchen, where the smell of wet dog mingled with freshly baked bread and new milk. Another labrador was lying patiently on a blanket in the corner, nuzzled by five thirsty puppies.

"She don't want to know this one," said Millie, rocking the puppy in her arms. "I want to give 'em names but I can't really tell 'em apart yet. Except this one. You can stroke him if you like."

Freddie obediently ran his hand over the top of the puppy's head but accidentally touched Millie's arm. He quickly withdrew.

"Do you want to hold him?"

To his surprise, he did. There was something comforting about its innocence, something about the world that lay ahead of it that he envied and was not unlike the future he himself had known only a few months ago. One without wars, letters, or grown-up girls. He held out his arms to take the puppy and Millie carefully handed it over. It wriggled and looked directly into Freddie's eyes, but the moment was short-lived – Millie's mother had come into the kitchen, wiping her hands on a cloth. She was a large woman and although she was not old she seemed to have difficulty walking.

"What's this?" Her abrupt tone made Freddie feel like a trespasser and he guiltily handed the puppy back to Millie.

"Morning Mrs Bedden," said Freddie cheerfully, over-compensating for Mrs Bedden's mood, as he dug out the letter for her to take. She looked at it dismissively, still drying her hands, and peered at it as if he were holding out a dog turd.

"You're goin' to have to read that."

The opening, the reading, the illegal act, it was the rule every postboy in the country had to break. As he used his finger to tear open the envelope he was desperately hoping it would not be bad news. There was no black cross, but that was no guarantee. Millie had no brothers as far as he knew, so it was unlikely to be a communiqué from the front. In any case the letter was from Exeter. When he unfolded it, a second separate sheet of paper fell out, which he managed to snatch from the air just before it reached the floor.

"Who's it from?" asked Millie, nervously.

"Just let the boy read it," said her mother.

Freddie found it difficult to focus on the writing, a reminder of just how tired he was. The centre of his vision was blurred and a shiny ring of metallic reflections slowly drifted from left to right, accompanied by a sharp, localised pain on the top right of his head. He squinted, which seemed to help, and when the writing finally came into focus it turned out after all to be easy to read. In fact he thought the style was almost childlike with uneven lines and letters that were mostly not joined up, making words that were often spelt incorrectly. The writer was presumably themselves only semi-literate. Freddie cleared his throat as Millie and her mother watched him. He began to read the letter out loud.

"Winnie dear. How are you getting on? We are still taking in the overflow. Dick is home but on duty most of the time so he's no help. The regulars don't like it but it makes money. We are expecting Millie on Sunday as arranged."

Freddie stole a glance at Millie whose eyes glistened with what seemed to be excitement, but her mother just folded her arms, waiting for more detail.

"Give the letter from the War Office to Millie then she won't have to buy a ticket. Dick will pick her up from St Davids. I'll send a shilling a week. Hope you are all well. Yours, Olive."

Millie's mother held out her hand to take the two pieces of paper from Freddie, but her eyes were on her daughter. "Don't hang about, Millie. You're not worth a penny yet, never mind a shilling. Cows to milk."

Freddie handed over the letters while Millie replied, "Yes Ma." Then she turned to Freddie and handed the puppy back to him again. "Come and see Primrose."

The cowshed smelt sickly sweet from milk and dung. Primrose was honey brown with wary, tired eyes that blinked away the flies, and sharp bones that stuck out of her back so much that Freddie thought they might burst through the skin. Millie sat on her milking stool pulling at Primrose's teats, attempting to fill a bucket with her milk.

"Can't get much out of her right now," she said. "We think she's ill but we don't know what's up. That's why she's away from the others. Still, she gives us a pint or two, don't yer my girl."

Freddie looked around the cowshed as Millie was talking. There were holes in the roof where the tiles had slipped and shafts of light split the ceiling, striking the floor like torchlight. A bale of hay was propped up in front of Primrose's nose but the wretched animal did nothing more than sniff at it. Above that, hanging from the wall, was a framed picture. An odd thing, Freddie thought, to have in a cowshed, all the more so because of its subject: a young man with long hair, expressionless except for his eyes that stared directly out. Freddie wondered if it was an engraving of Jesus, though there was no religious symbolism, nor did the face look masculine enough, neither man nor woman. In any case, it couldn't be Jesus because the name of the person was written around the top of their head like a crown: Sinistra. If anything it sounded like a girl's name; so perhaps it was. What was such a thing doing in a cowshed?

He turned his attention to Millie as she leant sideways to milk the cow, catching sight of a small birth mark that was exposed on her neck as she tilted her head, and some strands of dark hair, wet with sweat, that were stuck across it. Millie seemed oblivious to the silence but after a while Freddie felt the need to break it. "You getting on the train on your own?"

"I'll be all right," she replied, straining to reach Primrose's udder. "I got my documents haven't I."

Given that Millie was thirteen, a year younger than Freddie, he was amazed by her confidence, her fearlessness for life, and how she managed to sound like a woman ten years older. Somehow age seemed to have nothing to do with the passing of the years, and he was envious, wishing he could run headlong into the time that lay ahead of him.

Another minute went by without either of them speaking until Millie squeezed out the last few drops of milk. She stood up, wrapped her arms around the cow's neck and kissed it on its ear. "I'll miss you," she said, before turning to face Freddie. "Do you want to look after Lester while I'm gone?"

"Lester?"

She nodded at the puppy Freddie was still holding.

"Oh," said Freddie. "No thanks. I mean, I'd like to, but... I wouldn't know what to do. And Ma said she'd never have another dog after Jip."

Millie suddenly stepped forward to kiss Freddie on the lips, squashing the puppy between them. The speed of her attack meant there was no time for Freddie to feel anything except astonishment. It was an earthquake of an event he had waited so long for and had dreamt so much about that he had always assumed it would never happen. Her lips were weather-worn, rough round the edges, though just as he was beginning to detect some softer flesh nearer the middle of her mouth, she withdrew.

"Dad wants to drown it." It was as if the kiss had never happened. "You could come here and feed it. On your rounds."

Freddie sensed there was a bargain being presented to him: in return for looking after Lester, a kiss. It might be worth it. She leant forward again to double the offer and for a moment Freddie was tempted, but he pulled back.

"I don't want to look after your dog. I can't."

She looked hurt, though Freddie also detected a twinkle in her eye. "Then I might as well drown it myself," she said, taking the puppy from Freddie's hold.

The metallic ring that seemed to float inside Freddie's eyes had got wider and had drifted to the extreme right where it was difficult to follow. His head could barely contain the rhythmic stabbing that had increased its rate, along with his pulse. He couldn't think straight.

"How long are you away?" he said, squinting again, trying to force his thoughts into focus.

"Don't know. A month or two probably."

"Well..." he began, but he could feel himself losing his balance and thought it best to sit down before he fell down, planting his backside on the ground by the door. He removed his leather pouch and tossed it to one side then leant back and closed his eyes, suddenly feeling intolerably tired. What was he about to say to Millie? He couldn't remember. Why was he even there? His head pounded, but sleep was irresistible, and even before he closed his eyes he was dreaming of George Franklin – except it wasn't quite George but more like the man or woman in the framed painting above Primrose's head. And the shadowy figure was handing him a letter.

When he opened his eyes again, the first thing Freddie saw was Sinistra looking down at him, until Millie leant over, obscuring the picture with her own face.

"You all right? I thought you were dead for a minute."

"I'm fine," he croaked, and in a way he did feel better, his headache a more general discomfort like a very tight hat, and the shining ring of metal gone from inside his eyeballs.

Millie helped him sit up against the oak-beamed door frame of the cowshed and then sat down next to him. They both watched Lester inquisitively navigate his way under Primrose's legs and Freddie panicked that the puppy might get trampled, but he felt too weak to say anything. In any case he suspected that all life on the farm was precarious and it was not for him to interfere.

"You look terrible," said Millie.

"I'm all right," he said, grunting with the effort. "I should get going. How long have I been here?" He started to roll to one side in an effort to stand up, but it caused a sudden loud bang inside his head, the scintillating ring of silver liquid immediately returned and he rolled back with a groan, putting his hands up to his temples.

"I've milked ten cows while you've been asleep," said Millie. "And delivered some of it. I'd go home and get to bed if I were you."

"Ten?" He rubbed his face in despair. He must be hours behind.

Millie handed him a handful of blank postcards. "These fell out of your bag when I picked it up," she said.

He took them from her and tried to sound indifferent to their significance. He even feigned a yawn. "Oh. Those."

"What are they?"

He wanted to keep her away from the subject of Field Service Postcards, but on the other hand he found he couldn't resist her interest, feeling a rush of manhood triggered by knowing something she didn't. To explain the workings of the postcard, to unravel the mystery for a girl, made him feel like a man, borrowing some of her extra years to use for himself. Perhaps it was the kiss that had changed everything, some magic had been transferred from her mouth to his and their life would most likely take a new direction now. He no longer felt invisible and slipped effortlessly into a world where he and Millie would get married at some point in the future.

"Soldiers send them back from the front. You cross out what you don't want to say, leave what you do."

"What you doing with 'em?"

Freddie looked at the face on the wall. What indeed? It had been four months since Freddie had put the parcel in the drawer labelled *Received in Error Return to Sender* and had forgotten all about it until the moment had come, a few weeks ago, when he had needed to remember it again.

"Well, things go astray." He thought about the box he kept under his bed. It was full of things that went astray.

Millie seemed to understand, or pretended to. "How do they work?" she said. She was flirting, Freddie knew it, and was secretly thrilled by it. He pointed at the first line of text on the card. "This says *I am quite well*. If it's true you leave it. If it's not you cross it out. This says *I have been admitted into hospital.* Same thing. And so on till you get to the end."

"Why don't they just write letters?"

Freddie had asked that question himself when he'd first seen the postcards and had taken a while to work it out, but now he tried to make his answer sound unprepared, as if thinking impressively on the spot. "I don't know, sometimes they don't have time I suppose. Or they don't know what to say. Or the censor stops them...or..." he glanced up at Sinistra, "they can't write so they get someone else to do it."

For the first time in his life, someone was interested in what he had to say. Up until now his growing up had been thwarted at every turn, his job as a postboy seemed only to give everyone permission to treat him even more like a child than they had when he was at school. The uniform was nothing more than a costume for play-acting, the shako hat designed to make him look merely comical. But Millie looked at him differently, and he wondered if he told her about the lies and deceit, the forgeries, whether she might understand. She might even approve. They might be in it together. Partners. The engraving had changed its expression too, its eyes seemed wider, its mouth poised as if about to speak, and Freddie had the strangest feeling the amanuensis had acquired a face.

So he decided. His deception required energy he no longer had; always hiding, never seeking. His body ached all over, his head swam and his blood grumbled in his ears. Whatever the consequences, keeping it all to himself seemed impossible now.

She put her face up close to his. "If I give you another kiss, will you look after Lester?"

Freddie looked down at the Field Service Postcards he was holding in his lap. He had a better bargain in mind.

"If I look after Lester, will you keep a secret?"

When Freddie broached the subject of the puppy to his mother she was more amenable to the idea than he had expected. As long as it was not for good, she said, she would look after Lester while Freddie was out at work, and wouldn't mind having the company. The story of Olive Bedden came up too, and Freddie's mother knew all about her, of how she had met a Threlfall's salesman two years earlier and with whom she had left for Exeter to run a boarding house. They had caused quite a stir because no one was aware they had ever married, though Olive Bedden had miraculously become Olive Carter overnight. Despite this, Freddie's mother said she liked Olive, not least because she didn't go to church, and was sorry to see her go. Some people were wanderers, she said to Freddie, and some stayed put like limpets, whilst some didn't get the choice whatever they were. One day, his mother said, she'd like to go to the seaside because she would like to know what the sea sounded like. Her milky eyes meant she judged everything in terms of sound. It suddenly occurred to Freddie that until his voice broke at some point in the future – hopefully soon – he would continue to be six years old in her mind's eye. It had been a long time since his mother had used her hands to see his face.

He explained that after helping Mrs Harkness clean the library on Sunday he would collect Lester from Bedden's farm. He wondered who would deliver the milk while Millie was gone. Someone who was paid less than a shilling a week, no doubt.

He wished his mother goodnight, and then tried to remember the last time he'd had a proper conversation with her that wasn't muffled by his closed bedroom door between them.

Freddie had not drawn anything for weeks. The desire had left him, replaced by Field Service Postcards. But in the anaemic candlelight of his bedroom he took out a fresh sheet of paper and although he knew he was unskilled at drawing from memory he fancied attempting to replicate the engraving from the cowshed. If he could bring it to life he could then erase it again by screwing it up into a ball. But his pencil wouldn't move. It felt as if it was waiting for permission from the face he was about to draw, for a blessing that would never come. The paper remained blank, his hand hovering over it, motionless.

Then, without thinking, he swapped the pencil from his right hand to his left, and another force, or person, took control, his left hand compelled to move beyond his own influence, or so it felt. Miraculously he began to draw. The result was frustratingly naïve, a slow accumulation of lines and curves that bore only a childlike resemblance to the subject, the work of a new student of art, a first attempt, a drawing that would have to be thrown away. But the innocence was precisely the point, that was why he was dragging his left hand clumsily across the paper. It wasn't about the drawing itself but about being given permission to take his forgeries to the next level, and how to go about it. He had been pondering what he might write from the moment he'd departed Tendring with his promise of a proper message for Mrs Harkness, and even more so since leaving Bedden's Farm, how he might promote his forgeries from postcard to letter. Having swapped his pencil for a pen and his right hand for his left he now felt confident he had a convincing first line from Tristan.

The pen moved, and he began to write: *Dearest Maji, forgive my poor handwriting, my left hand is the only one that works right now...*

He was out of the woods, but to continue he would need help from several other letters he had recently acquired... intercepted... stolen, if truth be told... that had been destined for the mothers and wives of Eagley and Little Risborough, and which now lay open on his desk. Solitary words and turns of phrases like *God's help, Confined to barracks,* and *the kind Surgeon Captain Larrey* gave his own writing the ring of authenticity as he watched the letter from Tristan to Suhani form in front of his eyes, flowing from another heart, pouring out of his pen without him having to think or feel responsible for their meaning. He was merely an amanuensis, wasn't he?

The letter wasn't long, half a page, a stunted text which Freddie thought might not be convincing. Perhaps the reason for its brevity could be that Tristan would have to rush to catch the post, so he added a postscript to that effect. When he sealed the letter up and franked it with his stolen rubber stamper, Freddie hoped that Mrs Harkness would be proud of her son.

As he packed his forgery tools away, he was overcome with a familiar desire, suddenly feeling enormously hungry. He thought he might go to the kitchen to empty the bin of the bread and jam he had secretly discarded at teatime when his mother hadn't been listening. But he had only got as far as the top of the landing when the dizziness returned and he was unable to stop himself from falling forward. As his body rolled down the stairs, and just before he lost consciousness, he was consoled by the thought that a broken skull might be a more permanent solution to all his problems, and a shorter route out of the woods.

35

When Freddie woke up in bed, he thought at first he was in a cathedral. Vaulted wooden beams stretched high above his head and stained-glass windows were casting spots of green and red light onto his bed sheet. Then he corrected himself. Surely he was in the library at Tendring because when he lifted his head he could see a hundred berths all lined up in four rows, each occupied by a wounded soldier. But that couldn't be right either, this space was vast in comparison, and the echoes of nurses footsteps as they patrolled the lines and the quiet methodical chatter as they stopped at the ends of the beds made it sound like an alien world. None of the soldiers spoke, instead they just lay there, many of them smoking, as if they were banned from talking until they got better. Maybe he was in heaven and these were the rules: a dull, relentless lingering where if you had died from your injures then that was what you were eternally stuck with. A waiting room. It was, at least, peaceful.

"Hello Jack."

Jack? Freddie looked at the figure standing over him and thought for a moment it was his father, though he couldn't be sure as he was still struggling to focus his eyes. Not that it would have helped – he was unable to remember what his father looked like. The figure held a jug in one hand and a glass in the other and asked, "Water?"

Freddie blinked, finally recognising the man's face but unable to place him or recall his name. Why had he called him Jack?

"The nurse says you've got to drink."

Gabriel. That was it, the one who always seemed not quite there. Freddie noted that Gabriel had no wings but wore a white coat that seemed just as ethereal, as did his quiet, quavering voice.

"And eat. Dinner's in half an hour. We can sit together again." Gabriel appeared nervous, shaking as he poured the water into a glass, diligently avoiding eye contact. The dryness of Freddie's mouth and the stale smell of his own breath made Freddie suddenly realise just how thirsty he was. He grabbed at the glass before Gabriel had finished filling it and then drank so quickly that some of the water spilled down his chin. Handing the glass back with a gasp, Freddie hoped for more of the same, but then a hazy memory of rolling down the stairs, or at least the beginnings of it, caused him to pause.

"Are you a doctor?" asked Freddie. Somewhere in his head, some untouchable memory, he knew that Gabriel was not a doctor, it was simply that the white coat made him look like one.

"No," confirmed Gabriel, filling up another glassful and looking around as if he were fearful of being caught doing it. "Patient. I help out. Part of...my recovery. Good for treating my nerves, I'm told."

Freddie's head was still clearing as he continued to try to work out where he was. He felt disorientated and light-headed, and it frightened him. "Were you shot?"

Gabriel paused, the glass still only half full, and winked, not at Freddie but at the air in front of him. "We were shot at, many a time, weren't we Jack."

Freddie didn't understand what he meant. Looking up at the high ceiling again he noticed some painted coats of arms where the roof beams joined up, and then, where the roof met the high walls, some carved wooden figures that looked like knights but had the countenance of angels. If this was the after-life, its austere and unwelcoming aura would take some getting used to.

"Where are we?" asked Freddie. Of all the answers Freddie might have expected, Heaven would have sounded more likely than the one he was actually given.

"Boulogne."

Freddie knew where that was. France. Surely he had misheard.

"Hotel Christol," Gabriel added, but the clarification didn't help. If he was in a hospital in France he must have volunteered as a soldier and lost weeks or months, or perhaps a year, of his life.

"Have I been shot?" The question sounded ridiculous, yet why else would he be there?

"You're here because your mother couldn't wake you. I told them your mother was in England, but they don't listen. It was a bang on the head but you'll be all right. They want the bed back."

It was the first thing that made any sense. This was not Boulogne. He remembered falling down the stairs and expecting it to hurt, but he had no memory of pain, nor did he feel any now. Gabriel still refused to look at Freddie as he handed him the glass of water, but Freddie's thirst now seemed less important than a hundred other emotions that were troubling him, all indistinguishable from one another, merging and overlapping, floating in front of his face just out of reach. As he tried to sort them out, Freddie murmured Gabriel's words back to himself, "You'll be all right". Always he would be all right, and yet he couldn't recall the last time he had been. Then, as he attempted to sit up, he suddenly remembered who he was. Postboy.

"What day is it?"

"Saturday."

Saturday. Freddie sipped at the water and tried to work out how much time he had lost, groping for any memory that might give him a clue. Only when he closed his eyes did an image float to the surface: Millie's kiss. He was delivering a letter of course, that was it, to Boulogne's Farm. No, no, Bedden's Farm. Which day was that? And who had done the post since? He supposed George Franklin might have taken it out himself, or they might have sent someone from Little Risborough, someone who would do a better job and be given it permanently so Freddie would end up scrumping and begging for the rest of his life. He scratched his head. Which day had that been? If he had rolled down the stairs on Thursday night he would have lost not a year but only a day and a bit. Of course his mother was in England. Where else would she be? And how had his mother got him here, wherever he was? Perhaps she had commandeered a horse and cart, perhaps from Alfred Ambrose next door, or from one of the Lings opposite. Why wasn't she here now? Then another thought pushed aside the previous one even before he had finished it, one that turned out to be the most troubling of all: had he left Tristan's letter on his desk or put it away?

There was a sudden crash and a cry of frustration. Lifting his head from his pillow Freddie tried to sit up to see what the commotion was – a nurse had dropped a metal tray on the floor at the far end of the hall, but even before the sound of it had died away there was another crash, much closer, of shattering glass. Gabriel had dropped his jug on the floor by his feet. He immediately fell to his knees, scrambling like a wounded animal under Freddie's bed, cutting his hands on the fragments of glass. Freddie's reaction was to climb out on the other side because he might be invading Gabriel's space. Aware for the first time that he was still in his own pyjamas, he stood there looking at the empty bed, feeling guilty that he had in some way caused the disturbance. Certainly, everyone seemed to be looking at him, and when the nurse who had dropped the tray came hurrying in his direction he felt sure it was his fault. She came to a stop by the broken glass on the floor but ignored Freddie, instead carefully kneeling down to look under Freddie's bed.

"Gabriel?"

Freddie watched as she reached towards Gabriel with her hand and then repeated, more softly, "Gabriel?"

"I want to talk to Jack," he mewled, the sound muffled by the bed-frame and mattress he was hiding under.

"It was a tray, that was all," said the nurse. "I just dropped it. Nothing to worry about. It's safe to come out."

Freddie could hear Gabriel's breathing, fast but shallow, and then another whimper. "I want to talk to Jack."

"You know what to do," said the nurse, lowering her head further until it touched the floor. "Take some slow, deep breaths."

There was a moment of stillness, only to be broken when Gabriel suddenly snapped at her, this time screaming: "Jack!" His voice echoed throughout the hall, silencing everyone else in it. The nurses stopped what they were doing and a number of soldiers held their frozen cigarettes an inch from their mouths. One in particular, two beds down, slid his eyes to one side to watch what was happening, his gaze alighting finally on Freddie. The soldier's features reminded Freddie of the engraving in the cowshed, an expressionless face that could mean anything you projected onto it. The cowshed, thought Freddie, Millie's kiss...

"Jack's not here, Gabriel," said the nurse. "I'm sorry."

"He's in the bed. I saw him."

The nurse pulled her head and shoulders out from under the bed, sat back on her heels, gripped her hands in her lap and sighed heavily. She looked up at Freddie.

"Do you want to try?" she whispered. "He thinks you're his friend. If you go along with it he might come out."

Freddie thought the nurse's whispering was pointless. There was no way Gabriel wouldn't have heard. Perhaps it was just to show respect. Or perhaps the deception would work better precisely because Gabriel could hear it. Once again Freddie would have to pretend to be someone else, to wear a different skin, to be dressed up in one of his assorted uniforms. He was sick of it, sick of pouring himself into a vessel that was Freddie by name only, except now he couldn't even be Freddie and instead he would have to answer to the name Jack. Jack, the man who had called him Billie. Freddie almost laughed at his ridiculous assortment of names.

"What do you want me to say?" he asked the nurse.

"Just talk to him. Ask him to come out."

Freddie glanced up at the ceiling for some advice, but none was forthcoming. The carved knights gazed down on him dispassionately: you decide and we will judge, they seemed to say. He rubbed his face with his hands to bring the blood back to his cheeks, then knelt down by the bed on the opposite side to the nurse and leant forward so that the side of his face rested on the floorboards. Gabriel lay with his back to Freddie.

"Do you want to come out?" said Freddie half-heartedly, his words sounding ineffectual and disingenuous, merely following instructions. Gabriel was slowly rocking his body and had started moaning in time to his own movements with a sound that seemed to come from deep within his chest.

Freddie tried again, a little louder. "Do you want to come out?" He wasn't sure if he was being deliberately ignored or if Gabriel had drifted off into a world of his own. Either way Freddie felt the need for a different approach, a new question, perhaps one that might make him sound more like Jack. Then he realised that the noise Gabriel was making was not a moan at all but the beginnings of a song, wordlessly humming a tune that Freddie recognised. He sat up and looked at the nurse.

"I don't know what to do."

She smiled and raised her eyebrows in a way that suggested she was out of ideas too, but then she said, "Sing with him."

The nausea returned, though it was no longer to do with the lack of sleep or food but with having to entertain an audience of a hundred soldiers and nurses, all listening attentively, and the Knights in the roof judging him, just as he had feared. He stared at the nurse and wondered if this would be the first time in his life he would not do as he was told, but before he had the chance to disobey she added, "I'll sing it too."

And so they did, two choruses about how your troubles could be packed away in an old kit bag and how a smile would solve everything. Freddie sang under his breath in the hope that no one but Gabriel would hear him. In the end his embarrassment receded because some of the other soldiers started to join in, but the tempo was slow and the melody a mournful litany of out-of-tune vowels, as if they didn't believe a single word of the song's sentiments... smile, boys, that's the style. Though no one did. The singing reverberated through the hall, once more giving Freddie the feeling he was in a cathedral, a place where the melody acquired a terrible beauty, the sound of loneliness bouncing off the walls. In a room of a hundred people, he felt quite alone.

The soldier two beds down, the one who appeared fixated on the proceedings, seemed determined not to join in, instead stubbing out the remnants of his cigarette before pointedly lighting up another. When the song was finished Freddie heard him murmur, "Fuckin' shite." Freddie was more startled than hurt by the soldier's needless observation, but like him he was certainly glad the concert was over and looked to the nurse for further instructions.

"Tell him who you are," she said.

As they knelt either side of the bed, looking across at each other, he knew what she meant and what he had to do, which forgery needed pulling out of the drawer today. More deception. He leant back down again to look under the bed to see Gabriel had curled himself into a ball and was clasping his hands above his head. Freddie could see blood dripping from the shards of glass still embedded in them.

"It's Jack," said Freddie. "Do you want to come out?"

"You said you'd look me up." Gabriel shifted his weight slightly to match the rhythm of his words and Freddie wondered if the lack of eye contact was the one thing that enabled Gabriel to speak, albeit in a husky monotone.

"You said if I promised to say what you told me to say then you'd come and get me. I could have your spare room in Rye. You said you'd write and let me know. Why didn't you come?"

"I'm here now," said Freddie.

"Nah. It's not you, I'm not stupid. You're lying. You're one of those demons, following me wherever I go, like in the other house. Making me say things I don't want to say and crossing the lawn in the middle of the night. You said it was Harkness, but I saw a demon, didn't I?"

What had Jack told him to say? Freddie wanted to ask him what he meant but was interrupted by the soldier two beds down who swore under his breath again, the same two words, then put his cigarette in the ashtray by his bedside, stood up and walked over to the nurse. He was wearing his army jacket with its buttons undone, over his pyjamas, all hanging loose around his emaciated body. "What's his name?"

"Gabriel."

"Last name I mean."

"White."

"What rank is he?"

"I don't know. I'm not sure."

"Well, let's think of something shall we?" and with that he went to stand at the foot of Gabriel's hiding place, put his hands in his jacket pockets and tilted his head to one side. Freddie expected him to say some wise words, a verbal brushstroke of kindness to release Gabriel from his self-imposed prison, but everyone jumped out of their skin when the soldier suddenly shouted, "Look lively Private White!"

Immediately there was the sound of shuffling from under the bed and Gabriel appeared, urgently standing to attention and saluting with his shaking right hand.

"Stand at ease, Private." Gabriel obliged, and the soldier looked him up and down. "Get your hands seen to. We don't want any gangrene round here." Then he returned to his bed and his cigarette, and after the first long drag he said, to no one in particular, "Usually works."

The soldier's crude but efficient treatment of Gabriel had affected Freddie too. Finding everything around him appeared sharper and at the same time more mundane, he decided finally that the Knights were not angels, were made of nothing but carved wood, and he knew exactly where he was. Celandine Hall.

There was a canteen in the west wing for those patients who could walk, which, it turned out, was a good half of them. Freddie sat with Gabriel to eat but they didn't speak, except for one attempt from Freddie to raise the subject of the pock-marked potatoes he was pushing around his plate with his fork. Gabriel met it with a grunt and a pointed avoidance of eye contact, which seemed to add to Freddie's sense that his impersonation of Jack had been a failure. Their earlier connection had been a temporary respite for Gabriel who had now withdrawn back to the hollowed-out trenches in his head.

What struck Freddie most as he glanced around the canteen at the scores of faces seated in front of their dinner plates was that you could divide them into two distinct categories: those who seemed perpetually cheerful, smiling, joking, chain-smoking, eagerly stuffing their faces as if they were at a children's party; and those who were silent, expressionless, chewing slowly and thoughtfully, if they ate at all. Freddie wondered what made the latter look constantly haunted and he examined them on the sly for several minutes until he worked out what it was. They never seemed to blink. Not even cigarette smoke could trick their eyelids into moving. He wondered if the two groups had evolved distinct strategies for dealing with the same problem, and what the difference was, really, if anything. Perhaps the cheerful ones were better actors, that was all, but when the sun went down they would all partake in the same collective memory of war, whilst each one of them would take it, alone, to the grave.

It was George Franklin who arrived in the evening to collect Freddie from Celandine. He seemed put out as he handed Freddie a bag of clothes for him to wear, probably he wanted to be in the pub instead, and then Gabriel and Nurse Sarah – they used first names at Celandine – stood at the enormous front door to wave them goodbye. Freddie's headache was so constant that he had ceased to notice it most of the time, but the rough ride in the horse and cart brought back the shooting pain and flashing light behind his eyes that made listening to George almost impossible.

"A lot of catching up to do, boy. I'm lucky you didn't break your neck."

Freddie kept quiet, feeling he was being accused of falling down the stairs deliberately.

"You'll have to put in a day's shift tomorrow, I'll come in myself to help out, then we should be square."

Tomorrow. He thought he had a previous appointment on Sunday but he couldn't remember what. There was Tristan's letter of course, he had to deliver that, but he was sure he had agreed to something else as well. Then he remembered Lester, that was it, he had arranged to collect Millie's puppy. Lester, Millie, Tristan. They danced around his head in a carousel. Had he confided in her, told her about the letter?

His memories seemed real, but he couldn't trust them. And the job before going to Millie's farm? He hacked his way through a jungle of disconnected thoughts until he arrived at the library. Yes, he had offered to help clear the library at Tendring.

As the juddering of the cart shook Freddie's brain inside his skull, he closed his eyes and tried to work out how he might contrive to be at both Tendring and the Post Office at the same. He decided not to worry. He always came up with something. His gift was not drawing, but duplicity.

36

The sandwich Freddie's mother had made him on his return that Saturday evening had looked so unappetising he left it uneaten on the kitchen table. Later she had put it outside his bedroom, telling him through the closed door that she had done so, this being the only way left for them to communicate with one another. Her words had sounded feeble, like an apology. He wished they could talk properly, and he sensed she wished it too, but the best he could do was wait for her to go back downstairs, take the sandwich in and hope she would think he had eaten it. This was the limit of their conversations these days, and dishonesty seemed to permeate everything he did. As usual, his sleep was fitful, and tedious.

Now, Sunday morning, Freddie decided he could save himself time by missing Matins. He'd catch the congregation on the way out. In addition, he thought if he managed to persuade George that he could save an hour or two by combining three separate routes into one he would succeed in catching up on all his deliveries. It was possible the penny might drop for George that this would be an efficient way to deliver the post as a matter of course, every day. But Freddie doubted it, the old system would prevail in the end. It was of no consequence – the new plan gave him the reason he needed to be out all afternoon, the time to run his extra errands, that was the point. The post itself, well, in reality he would have to spread it out over the next couple of days, but no one would notice. Wartime post was always erratic and this would make little difference. His leather pouch bulged not only with his forgeries and Field Service Postcards, but now also with the extra letters from the amalgamated rounds. He mounted his bike and pedalled away from the Post Office.

He stopped at the top of Bath Hill, as he often did, to take in the view and empty his mind of thoughts. But this morning he found he couldn't, and was instead recalling his first day, a time that could have been a hundred years ago for all the changes that had slipped by. Although the passing of time was almost invisible, like the turning of the hands of a clock, there were occasionally days like this one that chimed the hour, and the trees that lined the edges of the fields looked utterly different from the day before. Autumn had become winter overnight as suddenly as the sounding of a bell. And just as the seasons crept up on you, exactly as Mrs Harkness had said they would, so had his own life. He had grown up, unnoticed, and was no longer the boy who had stood there looking out across the fields and woods only three months ago. He was the beginnings of a man, his own assassin, another version of himself trying to break out, a butterfly bursting out of its chrysalis. Except no, not that, this changeling required a bleaker metaphor, less elegant, without beauty. In his mind's eye he turned the pages of his Boy's Own, looking for a better comparison, for a creature that could not fly. That was it, he was a snake shedding its skin. He stroked his top lip and pushed the soft, tiny new hairs against the grain. There was no going back to the world before Millie's kiss. And something else had changed: he realised for the first time in weeks his head no longer ached.

The only thing that appeared unaltered was Tendring. As Freddie looked down into the shallow valley in which it nestled, he held out his hand to cover the house from view, trying to imagine a world without it. But even if he shut his eyes it still lingered, the one dependable feature in the landscape, an unchanging presence on which the trees and hedgerows hung their cloak of evolving colours, the seasons spinning round it, becalming Tendring in the centre of a storm. Every road or path to Tendring was downhill though it was not the vortex of gravity that constantly pulled him in but an overwhelming desire to change the past. He wondered how different his life might have been if the black front door, on that first day, had not been open.

He dropped his hand so that the house became visible again. He had to resist the pull of Tendring a while longer, however, as it was not first on his itinerary. The sound of bells reminded him he had to get to church before eleven, chucking out time.

As the congregation filed out, Freddie was waiting for them, his post already sorted in the same order that the multitude exited from the church. The village hierarchy was fixed and if anyone found themselves further ahead than expected they would make some adjustment, an inspection of the flowers along the side of the path, or of the hands of a pocket watch, or, if all else failed, an examination of the sky so they could pause and slot in to their designated place in line. It hadn't occurred to Freddie until now that the pecking order was determined by wealth, the well-off at the front, the poor bringing up the rear. When Mr Harkness had walked beside Mrs Harkness they had usually been first in line, or near to it, but today she came out last, with her servants, wearing a sari. Freddie presumed she was no longer rich. As the queue filed past he handed out ten letters in quick succession, mostly to the men, many of whom passed the letters to their wives for safe-keeping.

But then his scheme fell apart. Mrs Harkness paused to talk to him, letting Hannah and Phoebe walk on. This was not part of his plan. Damn it, he hadn't thought it through.

"Are you all right, Freddie?"

"Yes ma'am."

"I heard you were taken ill."

"No ma'am. I fell down the stairs. No harm done."

"I seem to remember hearing that before," she smiled. "Well, all the same, you've been looking very pale recently. And thin. Nothing that scones and jam won't fix, mind you."

"Ma'am?"

"You're still coming this afternoon?"

"Yes, yes of course."

"Good. I will see you later." Freddie felt relieved when he saw she was about to leave, but then she stopped with an afterthought. "Is there any post?"

Freddie didn't know how to answer. Things were unravelling. Of course he had Tristan's letter with him but there was a risk she would open it there and then. Was there a risk? After all the letter had been expertly crafted and she would be eager to believe it. He now fully understood that lies worked best when they were what people wanted to hear. Giving it to her now would get it over and done with – until the next time that is, which was something he was already working on. What was it, some message about being sent back to the front? Yes, he remembered now.

"No ma'am." Once again, it was the exact opposite of what he had intended to say. The shooting pain in his head...the drifting silver ring of light...they had come back, suddenly, worse than ever. Freddie had been over-ruled by the amanuensis. It was more than he could stand and he couldn't stop himself grimacing, which he tried to hide from Mrs Harkness but without success. He could see her concern and to his immense embarrassment she put her hand up to the left side of his face and held it there, her countenance changing, speaking under her breath so that no one else could hear.

"You must tell me the truth Freddie."

Freddie swallowed hard. He was afraid he might actually cry with the pain in his head, and even more afraid that Mrs Harkness would misconstrue it for guilt, or the precursor to a confession, so he fixed his expression to hold the tears back.

"What do you mean ma'am?"

She put her other hand up to the right side of Freddie's face and took a small step nearer to him. It was the kind of close contact normally reserved for mothers. "I can see you're not happy, Freddie. The silent one speaks with his eyes."

He remembered the feel of his mother's touch on his face. But this was different. Mrs Harkness's hands were cold and her fingers seemed to be reaching inside his head for his thoughts.

This was his chance. He could tell her everything here and now, the truth, he didn't care what her reaction might be, all that mattered was that it would be over. But he couldn't do it, instead he took a step back, withdrawing his head from her hands more aggressively than he had intended and snapped at her not because he was angry but because of the pain, shouting, "For God's sake it's just my head! I'll be all right!"

Some heads had turned, Hannah and Phoebe amongst them. No one ever raised their voice in the graveyard. Mrs Harkness dropped her arms down by her sides and Freddie glanced into her eyes, seeing hurt and disappointment in them.

"I'm sorry," she said. Then she smiled at him and he tried to smile back. He could see that he had crushed her.

"It's all right," said Freddie. "No harm done." But he knew that there had been.

37

Two trains from opposite directions pulled into Little Risborough station at the same time, the first from Dover, the second from London. The drivers waved as they passed each other and applied their brakes, the grating sound of metal on metal resonating under the station canopy like swords being sharpened. Both engines sighed as they pulled up, battle-weary, expelling steam onto the platforms with a misty embrace for the waiting passengers. Fewer trains on a Sunday meant more travellers for each individual journey, and both platforms were busy with departures and arrivals, farewells and open arms, with everyone dressed up to the nines.

The first to step onto the platform was a soldier, a Captain, young and skittish, calming his nerves with a cigarette. As the carriages decanted people around him he remained standing on the spot to watch them slowly disperse, then threw down his unfinished fag onto the ground in front of his feet and extinguished it with a single twist of his boot. He tapped his right breast pocket with his left hand to check something, then walked towards the exit.

He could take the station Fly, or he could walk, there was still time.

Part of him wanted to get to Tendring House as soon as he could, but a hushed, more insistent voice spoke of fresh air, peace and quiet, and the collecting of thoughts to rehearse his opening lines, so the walk would be best, he decided. Besides, by the time he was standing outside the station the two spaces for horse-drawn carriages were now empty so there was no longer any choice in the matter.

The road to Tendring varied between smooth flat surfaces as old as the wheel, and gravel-topped stretches that crunched under his boots, though the variation made no difference to his pace, one hundred and twenty beats per minute, like all army regulations hard to shake off. Apart from stopping when a car pulled up to offer him a lift, which he declined, his pace remained constant.

It was cold but sunny, his favourite combination, and he found his thoughts drifting back across the Channel to wonder what the weather was like there. For the umpteenth time that day he again pressed his left hand to his right breast to check that the envelope was still in his inside jacket pocket, which of course it was. The letter of commendation, and the Military Cross itself, for "conspicuous gallantry and devotion".

Freddie had been assigned the library windows, to clean them inside and out with soapy water. The four enormous sashes were going to keep him busy all afternoon with their sixteen individual panes and several trips to the kitchen to change the dirty water. The top sashes required a ladder so Mrs Harkness asked him to bring in the one that seemed to otherwise permanently lean against the portico outside. Even though he had seen the ladder every day, and sometimes even examined it as he had waited for his knock on the door to be answered, this afternoon he'd had to think hard where it was. It had been leaning there since Freddie's first day and had blended in to such an extent no one noticed it any longer. It was a kind of sorcery, he thought, that you could look but not see; things only existed when you wanted them to. And from there it was only a small step to the even stranger, dark magic of Tendring: when you needed something you could will it into existence. He tapped his right breast pocket to check that his letter from Tristan was still there.

Freddie climbed up to the top of the first window, hoping his swirling head would not make the climb too precarious. Then with his damp cloth he set about wiping away three months of accumulated grime from the left uppermost pane. At the same time Mrs Harkness and Hannah cleaned the bare floor while Phoebe knelt to polish the brass fender around the fire place. They all carried out their work in silence save for the sound of Hannah humming the same tune over and over for a whole hour. Sometimes when Freddie stopped to rinse out his cloth in his bucket he took the chance to watch the work that was being done around him. The beds were gone but the furniture was yet to be returned to the library, which made it feel empty, un-lived in. It was as if he had never stepped foot in it before, and everything that had happened in this hospital annexe, from birth to death, was consigned to memory. And memories could be forgotten. Things could be willed out of existence too.

"Freddie?"

He was still at the top of the ladder when Mrs Harkness called up to him, her head just below his feet. "We need your help to bring the tables in." And then she smiled, adding, "Somewhere to put the scones." He felt regret for shouting at her in the churchyard, but her smile suggested she had forgotten all about it. He had never known anyone else with such infinite kindness. If anyone deserved to be happy, to be protected from pain and heartache, she did.

There were three tables of different shapes, square, round, and octagonal, though in all other respects they seemed to come from the same family. Mahogany inlaid with mother of pearl in the shape of elephants, Freddie guessed they must have originally come from India. Phoebe stood up to help but Freddie saw Mrs Harkness discreetly raise her hand and shake her head. Surely it would be easier and quicker with four pairs of hands, Freddie thought, but it seemed Phoebe was excused. Only when she knelt back down on the floor did he notice her bloated belly and made some connection. These kinds of girls were always treated as fragile objects, though he didn't fully understand why.

So he helped Mrs Harkness and Hannah carry the tables through from the different rooms in which they had been stored around the house. But it turned out the smallest table only required two people to carry it, so Hannah stayed behind in the library to help Phoebe set out the tea service as he and Suhani ascended the stairs. It was the first time Freddie had been upstairs in Tendring and the atmosphere was different, unlike the reverberant spaces downstairs. Yet its very dryness made it eerie and unwelcoming.

"This is Tristan's bedroom," said Mrs Harkness, lightly.

It barely needed to be said. Someone had made an attempt to tidy the tubes of paint, palates, and collections of brushes that stood in bottles of turps, setting them to one side on the window ledge and the mantelpiece. But the room still felt cluttered and messy, not so much a bedroom, more a room with a bed, and in some ways it reminded Freddie of his own at home. Between the bed and the far wall was the painting of the three brothers Freddie had first seen in the library, too big for the space it now occupied and resting on its easel awaiting completion. Even though it must have been the case that Tristan had not set foot in the room for months there was still the unmistakable smell of oil paint, as if he had just left his studio and would return at any moment to finish the portrait. If Mrs Harkness was sensing it too, it would surely make Freddie's delivery easier.

As he helped Mrs Harkness with the small round table, Freddie became aware of that familiar but unwanted feeling of anxiety. The pungent smell of paint had triggered the flashing metallic ring once more to drift slowly across his vision, just as it had on his first day, and then another of those frightening bangs in his head went off like the crack of a whip, so he had to put his side of the table down. It was panic now, and along with it came its twin, that sudden, enormous, enveloping hunger. The scones would go down very smoothly he thought...and would come up again more easily still.

"Are you all right, Freddie?"

"It was just a bang on the head."

"I'm sorry I upset you earlier. It's none of my business."

"I'm all right." His voice dropped an octave halfway through and Suhani tried to hide a knowing smile, but Freddie spotted it and blushed. "I'm fine..."

As he grabbed the edge of the table again to lift it up, he caught the pencilled outline of Tristan's eye, but immediately pulled his gaze away from the triptych, fearful that if he returned to it the painting would miraculously be complete. It was then he decided to deliver his letter to Suhani at the last minute before leaving. That was it, pretend it was an afterthought and avoid any awkward questions. The less time there was to lie, the less of a lie it would be.

On his walk from Little Risborough station the soldier passed Bedden's Farm, but there was no sign of life. They must be out in the fields, even on a Sunday, he supposed. His boots were a size too small, they'd got muddled up weeks ago with those belonging to another soldier who had then, only an hour later, got himself blown to smithereens, so there was no chance of swapping them back. Nor did there seem to be any mechanism available at the front to acquire a fresh pair that fitted. Back here in England his complaints fell on deaf ears, which he took to mean that it served him right. Callouses had developed on his toes and on the backs of his heels that now prevented blisters, but the boots were still painful so there was nothing else for it but to rest his weary feet. He sat down by the side of the road wishing he could loosen his boot laces, though this was not possible without also removing his neatly wrapped puttees. He thought about it but decided he couldn't be bothered so he let his feet throb and lit a cigarette. He had to strike three matches – the wind was picking up.

He felt immediately calmer. It was an accepted, if unspoken truth that in the trenches the most important piece of kit was the cigarette. To go over the top required some form of sedation. It wasn't that the nicotine made anyone less terrified, it was just that it took away the smallest scintilla of...what was it? A different sensation that lay deeper in the gut, the loss of self, an indifference to it, just enough to be able to lift up one's feet and walk into no-man's-land. He had done it three times, and in the hour of waiting before each attack he had smoked his way through a pack of ten, each cigarette pushing away the fear of dying by a fraction of an inch. But there was a curious, unwanted trade-off for him, his anxiety replaced, or covered up by, of all things, a stutter. He had developed it in the trenches and on every drag of smoke it had deteriorated further, slowly but inevitably, so that in his moments of highest stress he could barely speak at all. He hoped that would not be the case when he got to Tendring. Perhaps he should resist sneaking in another fag before his arrival. The one he was currently smoking was now finished so he flicked the butt into the middle of the road, stood up and began walking, disappointed that, if anything, his feet felt worse.

Phoebe had lit the fire and the wintry smell of burning wood tingled the nostrils and stung the eyes. Mrs Harkness and Freddie shared the octagonal table, whilst Hannah and Phoebe each had their own, creating an odd lack of communality for a scones-and-spiced-tea party.

Although Mrs Harkness did her best to ensure that afternoon tea proceeded without hierarchy or ceremony, Freddie still felt uncomfortable, way out of his class. He had no idea what the rules were supposed to be so he sat hunched over his plate in an attempt to go unnoticed. Suhani had released a catch underneath their shared table which meant it was free to spin on its central pedestal and the plate of scones could be presented directly to Freddie. He had been so surprised the first time she did it that for a split second he thought it was the world turning beneath the tabletop, an effect that magnified the dizziness he already felt. The feeling was now so familiar to him he thought little of it, even welcomed it as an old friend – any purging that might follow would make him feel better and enable the amanuensis to do his job. There was an exotic, spicy perfume coming from the teapot that Freddie had never smelt before and that, too, made him heady, so he decided to line his stomach with the first scone as quickly as he could, taking a second bite before the first was swallowed.

"Steady on," said Hannah. "You'll bite your own fingers off if you carry on like that."

Freddie paused and looked up, embarrassed. His left hand took the half-eaten scone from his right.

"We have lots more in the kitchen," said Suhani, smiling kindly across the table. "You can take some home with you if you like."

He was already caught in a vicious cycle: eating made him feel ill, but he ate more to feel better. He knew how this would end and half of him was looking forward to it. Not knowing where the toilet was or even if there was one on the ground floor, he decided he would have to think of a reason to go outside. Fresh air was the obvious excuse. How many scones would it take? He was going as slowly as he could but was already on his second one when Suhani started talking about the masala chai.

"...Cardamom and ginger, mainly. Cloves and black pepper. I like to put saffron in it but we haven't been able to get that since before the war. Milk and sugar, lots of it. What do you think, Freddie?"

Freddie was in the middle of sipping it. He could feel the chewed, acidic remnants of scones rising back up his gullet and swallowed hard to try to push them back down, but the sickly taste of the masala chai just made things worse. "I think I need some fresh air, ma'am," he said, already standing up before he'd finished his sentence and rushing for the door.

Suhani called out behind him, "Are you all right?"

But he was already running out of the library and seconds later throwing up between the pillars of the portico and onto the grass. As he spat out a slimy currant and the final globule of sick, his mind miraculously cleared, purged of fear as easily as his stomach had of vomit. This was all part of the plan, a plan that was superficially his and yet really belonged to someone else: his better half, the amanuensis.

A breeze was picking up and the chill air bent the tops of the trees. Despite this the soldier was beginning to feel too warm inside his woollen uniform, marching himself ever nearer towards Tendring. Compared to the desperate misery of the trenches this discomfort was trivial and he should not be complaining, but he wished he was allowed to loosen at least some part of his uniform. Perhaps he would, no one would know. So without breaking stride he loosened his belt and undid the top two buttons of his jacket. His ingrained army discipline fell away and the marching turned into walking, a more casual gait that cooled his neck and even, to some extent, made his feet hurt less.

As he rounded the next bend he spotted smouldering fumes in the far distance being blown sideways by the increasing wind, and wondered if it might be from the chimneys of Tendring. The smoke made him consider firing up another cigarette, but because he would soon be required to speak and had no desire to do so with a stutter, or worse with a crippling inability to say anything at all, he would have to live with his uneasiness and the cigarette would have to wait.

He quickened his pace again. The Military Cross was burning a hole in his pocket and he was eager to share its story.

"But I haven't done the outsides yet," protested Freddie as he walked alongside Suhani in the rose garden behind the house. Suhani had hoped the cold air and a change of scene would restore Freddie so that she could speak to him more candidly, away from the others.

"You must go home," said Suhani. "The windows can wait. I'll arrange for Doctor Herring to call on you this evening."

"I'm all right. I feel fine now."

"If you ask me, you've not been fine for weeks. You can have some water and rest here first if you like, then you must go home. Hannah will go with you."

"I don't need any water. Don't touch it during the day."

"I'm not sure that's wise, Freddie..." but Suhani had detected irritation in Freddie's voice so she tried a different tack.

"Have you ever seen one of these?" she said as she held out her hand to touch the baked branches of a Bay tree. "I thought the dry summer had killed it. The leaves turned to rust in July, but now to my surprise there are some green shoots. Some would say it's come back from the dead."

"What would you say?"

"Well, I would say we all need our sleep." She plucked three scorched leaves from the tree and held them out for Freddie to take, but he looked sceptical. "Put them under your pillow," she said. "They promote good dreams."

"Even the dead ones?"

"Well, they're all dead once they're plucked, aren't they? But they still have an aroma." She delicately placed one of the leaves under her nose and sniffed it, then held it out for Freddie to do the same, so he pushed his head forward slightly.

"Is it Indian?"

"The leaves of the Indian Bay are larger, and actually have an entirely different flavour. But we sometimes use these anyway."

"Well, there's a war on."

"Quite."

Suhani felt the informality was finally having an effect. Freddie had conspicuously dropped the use of *ma'am* and had smiled at her for the first time in what seemed like weeks. In fact she wasn't sure if she had ever seen him smile at all, until now. He had begun talking to her as if they were equals and this was her chance to probe further. They started walking again around the back of the house, a slow meander but with Freddie always a yard behind.

"Is your father in the war?"

"Pa's dead. I don't remember him."

She thought about saying she was sorry, but Freddie's tone suggested he didn't want her to, nor needed her pity.

"Do you have any brothers or sisters?"

"Just me and Ma... I'll go and fight, when I'm old enough."

"I see. How old are you, Freddie?"

"Fourteen."

'Do you think there will still be war in five years time?"

"They don't always check your age."

"I think if there are five more years of war there'll be no men left to enjoy what they are fighting for."

"We have to stop the Hun."

She turned to face Freddie. "Yes, I suppose we do. Sometimes I wonder why though. No one seems to tell us."

He looked down at his shoes. Suhani caught sight of the faded scar on his forehead as she waited for his reply.

"Well, for one thing, the honour of the British Empire."

She nodded at Freddie with a wistful smile. "Ah yes. That's what the posters say, isn't it." She began walking again, with Freddie still one step behind. "What would your mother say if you went to fight in the war?"

"I don't know."

"And what would she say if you didn't come back?"

"Well..."

Suhani allowed the silence to linger for Freddie to come up with an answer.

"Well, I'd make sure I did."

She stopped again to face Freddie and took both of his hands to cradle them in hers. Sensing resistance, she gripped more tightly. "Please, don't leave your mother. Go home and tell her that you love her."

Freddie appeared to think about it, but then pulled his hands away from Suhani's. "I can't do that. I've never done that."

"Well, Freddie, you don't have to use words." She began to walk back towards the house, dragging her fingers along the top of the low-cut golden privet. "But there will come a day when you'll regret it if you don't."

They stood in the middle of the library. Suhani had her back to the open door and was wrapping a scarf round Freddie's neck. "What you need," she said, "is a square meal, and a good night's sleep. And don't forget what I told you." She nodded at Hannah who was standing in her hat and coat, ready to escort Freddie home. "Hannah will go with you and then she'll call in on Doctor Herring. Stay at home until he visits and do as he says."

"I have to go to work. Mr Franklin says I've got some catching up to do."

"Freddie, listen to me. Your eyes are as black as lumps of coal. Your hands shake when you eat, and then you sick it up. You're not well. I can't help you if you won't help yourself." Then Suhani tucked one end of the scarf inside the other to signal an end to the discussion. Phoebe came in holding a glass of water, stopping next to Suhani and holding it out for Freddie to take, but he ignored her, aware of the effect too much water had on his digestive system. "I'm not thirsty."

"Come on, Freddie," said Hannah. "I haven't got all day." Then she swapped a glance with Suhani. "If you don't mind me saying so, ma'am."

Freddie grimaced. The endless cycle of headaches was now on a bad run. His vision blurred and briefly he wasn't sure who was standing in front of him so he took the glass of water, if for no other reason than to give himself time to think. He took one sip, making the smallest amount last as long as he could, and then handed the glass back to Phoebe. Nobody spoke. The silence was short, no more than an intake of breath, but it had already become too long, and suddenly Freddie was confronted with a stark choice: to leave, or to deliver the post.

So he just did it. After all, that was why he was here. It was simple, in the end much easier than he had expected, the effortless act of doing his job, putting his hand in his breast pocket and taking out the letter, as easy as on his debut when he'd delivered Captain Hurley's telegram from Celandine Hall. He remembered it, that first day of innocence, which had also turned out to be his last. Freddie held out the letter to Suhani and said: "I forgot."

She raised her eyebrows but took the letter from him, saying, "You see. You're not yourself."

He scrutinised her face for any signs of doubt as she scanned the envelope, but to his relief detected none. On the contrary, she sounded happy.

"Ah, I think it's from Tristan," she said, her tone uplifted by the possibility. Freddie saw Phoebe hold the glass up to her chest with both hands as if it offered protection. Or perhaps she was praying. He thought it was an odd reaction.

"A proper letter," said Suhani as she pulled out the folded letter from its envelope and winked at Freddie. "Clever boy."

Suhani's Indian accent had become stronger, perhaps reverting to some happier time from her past. So far so good, Freddie thought, but his heart was racing and he wanted to escape. The air was cold yet as stifling as the hottest summer's day and he desperately wanted to remove the scarf that was itchy and constricting, making his neck flush, like a noose. He thought of Christopher. Trapped and unable to move, Freddie was overcome instead with the sudden inexplicable urge to call out, or even to break something. He flicked his eyes around the room for an ornament or book to pick up and examine, perhaps even to throw across the room, but nothing was within reach. Standing there, frozen, he knew that of course he would do none of those things, that they were substitutes for needing to run, to flee the library. But he couldn't. Suhani stood in his way.

As she opened the envelope Freddie waited for her to read the opening lines, but then lost his nerve and said, "I have to go."

"Please," said Suhani. "One minute."

Freddie tried hard not to sound desperate. "Please, let me pass," he said, the formality suddenly freeing up his paralysed muscles so that he was able to take a step forward. But Suhani didn't move and still he couldn't get past. Instead she just stood there. The sun went in, and the temperature dropped further.

"I don't understand," she said, looking confused.

He knew he was in trouble and tried again to step past her. "Please, let me pass." His voice cracked. One more reason to be stared at.

Frowning at the letter with the air of someone solving a puzzle, Suhani held out her hand to stop Freddie from passing. Then, with her eyes still fixed on the words that she was reading, she slowly turned round, took the few steps towards the library door, and slowly, but firmly, closed it, the way Mrs Mawby used to shut the classroom door when about to deliver some punishment. The click of the latch bounced around the library walls. Suhani stood there, poised to move, but not moving.

"He says he's writing this with his left hand."

Freddie swallowed hard. So far each lie had kicked up enough dust to cover the footprints of the previous one. Could he do so again? What was Tristan's story? For a terrifying moment he couldn't remember what he had written, but then it came to him just in time.

"His injury."

He waited for his words to have the desired effect but none was forthcoming. The only thing he detected was Hannah alternately looking between Phoebe, Suhani, and himself, as she tried to understand what was going on. Freddie felt he had miscalculated somewhere, missed a trick, but couldn't work out what.

The crows cawed and circled outside on the lawn.

And then they came, Suhani's bitter words, as cold and sharp as army steel.

"But Tristan is left-handed."

A drip of sweat stung Freddie's eye.

Then, out of nowhere, there was a new sound, the crunch of boots on gravel coming from outside. Suhani seemed oblivious to it, touching her forehead with her fingertips, but Freddie could hear it well enough, as close as if they were his own footsteps, and he looked up towards the sound where he saw he had left one of the top library windows ajar.

"It's a mistake," said Freddie. "That's all." Then he had an idea, a remote memory of his conversation with Jack, two words that offered a means of escape. He piped up, too cheerfully, "Shell-shock."

Suhani continued to rub her forehead, briefly lifted her eyes up to Freddie's and then dropped them back down to the letter again. He could see she was attempting to reconcile what was being said with what it meant. The mute stares had locked onto his face and Freddie's stomach began to constrict, as did his ring of accusers, until the silence was broken by another noise, this time loud and abrupt. It made everyone jump, a knock at the main front door. Two resonant thumps that could be felt as much as heard, perfectly timed to nail down Freddie's last two words in affirmation.

Shell. Shock.

Hannah jumped to it. "Who in God's name?" she gasped as she walked impatiently up to the library door, pulled it open and disappeared into the hallway. Suhani looked towards the sound and seemed to resent the intrusion, but Phoebe continued to stare at Freddie. He noticed the muscles in her jaw twitching unnaturally quickly. What was any of this to her?

"Well it's odd, Freddie," said Suhani, returning to the letter, an entirely new tone in her voice that was perceptive, sly, suspicious. "I encouraged him. Left is left and right is right. Why would he tell me he was writing with his left hand?"

Freddie had now run out of ideas, panic rose further, bringing the acidic taste of undigested scones with it, and the best he could do was find a different way of saying the same thing. He sounded almost angry, as if trying to stamp it out.

"Shell-shock! You know what it can do."

There were voices coming from the hallway but Suhani ignored them. Instead she read again from the letter, quoting directly from it.

"What is this? *I am very sorry to hear about Father.*" She couldn't take her eyes off the page. "What does that mean? These words are empty. He always called him Papa..."

"Shell-shock. That's it."

Hannah reappeared, standing in the library doorway. "Ma'am?"

Behind her stood the intruder, a young soldier in smartly pressed uniform and thick-rimmed spectacles. He looked intelligent but fragile, unsure of himself, and Freddie felt momentarily protected by the presence of a kindred spirit. It might also be the distraction he needed. Suhani and Phoebe both turned to look at the visitor. Both seemed put out.

"Who are you?" snapped Suhani.

Her sharp tone was a shock to Freddie, but the diversion might be useful and triggered a fleeting, idiotic notion that he could try walking out of the room unnoticed. Or he could just run. He removed his hat in preparation. But he knew it would not be possible, not now. He ran his fingers through his hair, the bumps on his skull feeling unnaturally prominent, as if the pain was trying to push its way out, and the flashes of light were worming their way into his vision again with all the colours of the rainbow. An image that ought to have been beautiful but was the opposite, a sinister, ominous, expanding silver mist drifting from left to right. The soreness it brought with it would have made running unendurably painful.

The soldier struggled to get his first word out. "M...Mrs Harkness?"

"Yes?"

He put his hand inside the left breast pocket of his jacket, searching for something. "I have a letter f...for you."

Suhani glanced down at her own letter that she was gripping in her hands, then looked at Phoebe, at Hannah, and at Freddie, as if nothing was in its rightful place.

"It is a letter of...of...of commendation from your son's commanding officer. I have the m...medal with me." He was still rooting inside his jacket, then changed arms to search the pocket on the other side. "I also have a letter of condolence from B...Buckingham Palace." Finally he pulled out the letter and held it out for Suhani to take.

"Condolence?"

"Yes ma'am."

Again she looked around with horror at every face for validation. "But I have a letter here, from my son. Written two days ago."

"T...Tristan Harkness?"

"Tristan Harkness."

"There must be some m...mistake."

"There must indeed. He's been in a French hospital for several weeks. He has written to me four times."

Her fingers had been touching her forehead all this time, but now she dropped her arm and turned to face Freddie. He witnessed her face turn cold, and he saw that, beneath her confusion, she was beginning to understand his treachery. She took a step nearer, close enough for Freddie to smell her rose perfume and see the tiny red veins in the corners of her eyes.

"He has written to me exactly four times, hasn't he...?"

Freddie was not sure who she was talking to, the soldier, or himself. Suhani looked down at the letter and began to read it again. Phoebe was glaring at Freddie and he saw a tremor rise up through her body until it reached her lips, wet with her own tears. For she had begun inexplicably to cry, weeping not with sadness but with incandescent anger. Freddie wondered once more what this had to do with her.

"Hasn't he, Freddie..." repeated Suhani, her tone as dull and empty as a freshly dug grave. The ghost of Mrs Mawby returned, admonishing him at school for taking all day over learning nothing, how it cut into Freddie's heart, how he had let his favourite teacher down. Except this was infinitely worse.

"He has written *four times* from a hospital in France. Hasn't he." Her words came from further back in her throat now, gutturally wrapping themselves around him like barbed wire, and she stood close enough for him to feel the hiss of warm air blow across his face. Freddie glanced at Phoebe who was using her fingers and palms to wipe away the wetness on her cheeks, whilst Hannah put her hand to her mouth to stifle another curse.

Then the clock in the hallway chimed, three strikes that seemed to take forever, soaking up the passing of time until it seemed to come to a stop.

"Commendation for what?"

Suhani was talking to the soldier now, though she hadn't moved from staring hard into Freddie's eyes and he could smell her breath, sickly sweet from scones, saliva, and sweat. She was also beginning to cry.

"The Military Cross," the soldier replied, his boots scraping on the wooden floor as he shifted weight. "As next of kin you would have been notified immediately, three weeks ago or more. The letter is signed by the...by the...King himself. You must be very proud?" The uplift made him sound desperate. Over Suhani's shoulder Freddie could see the soldier delve deeper into his pocket to pull out a velour case, which he opened to reveal a medal, the colour of tin.

But Suhani remained undistracted. Her eyes were penetrating deep into Freddie's, she blinked heavily, some of her tears falling onto the letter in her hands.

"But I have a letter from him." Her words were now a whisper, a freezing, icy sotto voce. "Written two days ago. Don't I Freddie."

He thought for a moment she was going to hit him, even hoped that she would so that it would make everything easier, all be over, but she just stood there, her face a foot away from his. Only then did he realise he was crying too. Perhaps he had been for some time.

"Don't I," she repeated, with a vicious growl, "have a *letter* from him."

Freddie wiped his nose with the back of his sleeve. He knew the truth was ready, its still-born arrival inevitable. Now that he had no choice, it was simple.

"No ma'am. You don't."

When the reaction came, it was not a surprise to Freddie, the swipe of a hand across his face, a stinging of his cheek and a crack in his ear that rung so loudly through his skull he could barely hear Suhani's wailing and Hannah's blasphemies above it. But the shock was that it had not been Suhani who had thrown the blow, but Phoebe. Phoebe the quiet servant girl, pushing Suhani aside and swinging at Freddie with such force it had knocked him sideways.

"Liar!" she cried, as she hit him again, the violence of it throwing him back over his own feet. He tripped, almost fell, and put his hand up to his burning face in disbelief. Did she mean his letter was the lie, or his confession? But then he wasn't sure which it was himself. He tried to regain his footing but Phoebe was upon him again, "Liar!" she repeated, screaming, hitting out again, this time connecting her outstretched palm to catch the back of his head, driving him towards the library door. He started to run but fell over, catching his side against the pedestal supporting the statue of Shiva, which wobbled indecisively until it finally toppled down, landing on the floor and breaking into several large pieces of dusty, bone-white plaster. Hannah was attempting to restrain Phoebe from landing more blows by wrapping her arms around her from behind, but Phoebe was having none of it and tried to wriggle her way out of the hold, continuing to scream the same word repeatedly, two syllables merging into one, until the word disappeared to become just a sound: "Liar! Liar!"

Freddie sat collapsed on the floor trying to push himself away from

Phoebe but his shoes lost grip on the polished wooden boards. The letter was by his feet, Suhani must have dropped it, or thrown it to the floor. He looked up at her but she had turned away with her face buried in her hands, standing perfectly still yet with one foot in front of the other as if she had begun to walk away and then changed her mind. She howled, repeating words that Freddie couldn't understand, a tremulous, drawn out, pulsing noise that became increasingly muffled as she suddenly dropped to her knees with a crack, buried her head even further into her hands and body, and began to rock back and forth in a rhythmic sway of eternal grief, in time to her moaning.

Then to everyone's surprise Phoebe turned her sights on Suhani, and although Hannah's restraining embrace must have squeezed out Phoebe's last breath, the young girl managed one final, rasping footnote of contempt: "*You* let him do this."

Everyone stood condemned by Phoebe's words. Then came some imperceptible movement: Suhani's quivering body, the head now raised in protest, the flow of tears damned by Phoebe's declaration. Hannah loosened her grasp, allowing Phoebe to drop to her knees beside Suhani. The clock ticked and the pendulum swung as they held on to each other, accusation followed by forgiveness: no choice left.

A gust of wind rattled the open library window and Freddie got up from the floor to wait for words to be said, knowing they would never come. No longer was it Freddie's crime, thought the amanuensis, but Suhani's. Yes, that was it, Mrs Harkness made him do it, gave him no choice. Phoebe was right.

He got up and walked around the soldier's static body to reach the door, watched but unnoticed, his shoes crunching down on the broken fragments of Shiva that lay scattered across the floor. He left the three women to their icy vignette, one of whom he now realised he loved more than his own mother. But it was too late. He left the library, left Tendring, an abrupt and unexpected parting, unfinished yet final, and walked out across the lawn, through the gates and between the eagle's wings, towards Bedden's Farm.

38

On the hills that rise up behind Memory Cove, where the horses run wild, lives the most beautiful creature I have ever known. My world would be forsaken without him. He lets me approach so closely that I can see my own reflection in his eyes and stroke his pure white mane as it catches the wind. I have taken to visiting him every day on Rainbow Hill, and he has taken to me, his hot breath warming the cold air around my face. When I lose sight of life, as I often do, his naïve power casts a light along my path so I can find my way back, as safe as the stars.

The young horse stands a year old with more growing to do yet, already possessing the fragile majesty of the ghosts of his fully-grown ancestors that run the fields up to the top of the hill. Joe told me horses grow much more quickly at first, before greatly slowing down. This one won't reach full adult height until he is four years old. Joe says we can't break him until he's three but I don't want him broken at all and I sense he doesn't want to be either. He is healing me and there's a bargain to be had in it. His name is *Anuun*, which means *Free,* and when I call him he comes running. We are like lovers, there's no other word for it.

I talk to him and he understands. Not the words of course, but my sadness and my happiness running through them. We could all do worse than learn to listen to each other in that way. When I speak of Christopher his breathing slows down and he barely moves, and when I talk of Eagley, of how it is on the other side of the world, I wrap my arms round Anuun's neck, close my eyes and dream he might sprout eagle's wings and fly me across the ocean. In that moment it's as good as doing it. I am certain there is magic in his heart.

A few days ago Mother, Joe and I drove the ten miles into Halifax for supplies. Eddie came too. There is a library there, the most impressive building in the street, grey stone walls and white painted windows facing the sea. I begged Mother to give me time to visit and she said I could have half an hour, without asking me why I wanted to go there. She knows from experience that grief needs no reason except itself. Joe stayed with her to help load the truck, and because they knew I'd prefer to be alone.

I was looking not for words in the library but for pictures of English villages, perhaps even a church. Not Eagley itself, that would be too much to expect, but some impression, some reflection, of Christopher's adopted home. The woman behind the counter suggested Chambers's Encyclopaedia, but it seemed to say little more than that a village was a village, and there were no helpful illustrations or photographs. I had given up, my half hour run, and was already standing on the steps leading out onto the road, a place where it is just possible to see the cargo ships in the harbor, when the librarian came up from behind holding a book and trying to hand it to me. They were poems she said, better than pictures, and was sure they would give a fine impression of English villages. I could keep it for two weeks. When I said I wouldn't be back for a month, she smiled and said to make sure I spoke to her, no one else, when I returned it.

I sat in the back of the truck amongst the cases of provisions, being thrown from side to side by Joe's rough negotiations of the bumps and pits on the road back to Memory Cove, with the book of poems open in my lap. The poetry was hard to decipher, I was not experienced in it, and in the brief moments of clarity that did rise up from the page there seemed to be no descriptions of rural life, no village talk from England, no reason for the librarian to have given the book to me. By the time I reached *The Milkmaid,* halfway through, I had given up on finding the countryside and was beginning to realise instead almost every stanza was about war, or loss, or sometimes both. I had never explained to the woman behind the counter why I wanted to see pictures of English villages, and perhaps she had got the wrong end of the stick.

I have now read the anthology twice. The second time I sat at the piano reading the poems out loud and some of the strings softly vibrated to my words in such a way that an untuned chord hummed continuously in the air. The sustain pedal is stuck open and needs repairing, it seems. Now I read the poems in the way Anuun reads me, beyond the mere comprehension of words, beyond even understanding. The librarian was right, village life is there after all, found behind the written word and deep within the sound of them, in the humming of the chord.

Anuun lowers his head to make it easier for me to cling on. I hold on more tightly as we fly across the ocean, back home to Memory Cove, so high in the sky I can see my future laid out before me.

I will never go to England, because I am already there.

39

The wind had picked up and Freddie had to lean into it as he walked the uneven track up to the front door of Bedden's Farmhouse. Perhaps it was because the weather was casting a dreary pall, but he hadn't noticed until now that the building was in grave need of repair, grey paint peeling from the windows and cobwebs hanging behind the glass as if no one had lived there for years. The house felt unoccupied even before he raised his hand to knock on the door and somehow he wasn't surprised when no one answered. More than that, he felt relief. He was there to collect Lester but it was the last thing he wanted to do. The extra burden of looking after a puppy dog filled him with dread. He didn't want to be there, but he didn't want to go home either. His mind and body were beyond tiredness and he felt as heavy and useless as wet straw. If he was asleep or awake, or even dead or alive, he didn't care, nor did he imagine that anyone else would.

The barn was fifty yards away to the side of the farmhouse and he found himself headed in that direction. He knew the barn door would be open and it would be somewhere to lie down, somewhere that reminded him of being young and of a time before his voice had started to break.

Primrose was not there. An empty bucket had been left in its usual place, untouched, still ready to receive milk, still smelling of it with a thin coating of pink, cloudy wetness covering the bottom. It looked like the bale of straw that Primrose had poked at with her nostrils last Thursday had not been touched since.

Freddie sat down against the far wall, collapsing in a pile of unwanted limbs, and looked at his hands to check they weren't rotting away, then wondered where such a strange thought came from. His left hand trembled, it was cold with the barn door wide open, but his right seemed fit, ready and waiting, quietly in charge.

Primrose must have recovered, thought Freddie, and been taken back to the other cows. But then he looked back at his shaking left hand and thought the opposite. The empty house, the empty barn. Freddie put two and two together, remembered the shooting of the horse from long ago, and wondered how long he would have to wait for the sound of a single gunshot to ring out from the field behind the house.

It was not a gunshot, however, that woke Freddie, but a voice.

"What you doin' in here?"

He kept his eyes closed, his dream lingering in his head. He had been delivering not post but coal and Mrs Mawby had burst into furious tears because he had dropped a sack by her front door and it had ruptured, spilling lumps of coal onto her doorstep. When she slammed the door shut in his face, the wooden panels split down the middle with a loud crack. Perhaps there had been a gunshot after all. He wasn't sure.

"I were beginning to think you weren't comin'," she said with a delicate shudder in her voice. Whoever this person was, they were either sad or nervous. Then the dream receded to nothing and Freddie remembered he was in the barn at Bedden's Farm. Squinting through one eye at the silhouette of the figure in the open doorway, he pushed down with his arms in an effort to sit up, having slumped onto his side in his sleep, his eyes slowly growing accustomed to the light. It was Millie who stepped in. Of course it was. His confederate. But there was an unusual shape to her and at first he couldn't work out what, until he saw that she was wearing her best coat, gloves and bonnet, and carrying a small tattered suitcase. Finally he remembered why.

"What time's your train?" His voice cracked, the last part of him to wake up.

"Four o'clock." It sounded like she was trying not to cry. "But I don't want to go."

Millie had always been older than him in his thoughts, and in his dreams, but now a new reality possessed him, her over-sized Sunday-best not concealing her true age but revealing it. She was just a girl, younger than him, someone who was not his saviour but in this moment faint of heart, in need of some fingertip of rat poison that might one day pass through his skin into hers.

"How come?" he said, making it sound flat so that he didn't upset her further. But it sounded like he didn't care, so he added, too late, "I'm sorry. I thought you wanted to go."

"Only when my ma and pa are listenin'. Dad got angry. He does that sometimes."

"With you?"

"With my ma. Don't make no difference though. He'll swing at whoever's nearest. Can't afford a runt he said. Don't know if he meant Lester or me."

Freddie couldn't think what to say next. He understood that farm life was as much about death as life, then thought of Primrose discovering such a thing to her cost and remembered the sacrifice of the horse he had spied on all those years ago. There was a balance between the two, life and death, that refused to be swept away from the barns and fields. So he just let the moment pass in silence. Millie wiped her nose with her sleeve, stopped crying and stared at her own feet spread out in front of her.

"That's why I got to go. Earn proper money Dad says. But I got to go on my own and I'm frightened about it."

Freddie wondered what Exeter might be like. Just a bigger version of Eagley, he supposed. "You'll be all right." He sounded like George Franklin, that useless man. It had never worked on him, the trite notion that things would be all right, so he fished out another apology. "I'm sorry you're leaving though."

Millie sat down beside Freddie and placed her suitcase between them.

"I don't mind about Primrose," she said, carrying on as if she had been asked about it. "Not so much. She was hurting. Can't drink milk with blood in it. It's what we do, Ma says, end life at the right time. But Lester's not in pain, he's happy. Makes no difference though. Dad says he'll drown him in the river. Should've just let him die in the first place I suppose. You'll still take him, won't you?"

Millie pulled up her knees to place her folded arms on them, then rested her head sideways in order to look at Freddie. He couldn't answer her, couldn't say yes or no. He thought he was done with lying, and she seemed to know it, so she gave up waiting for an answer and forced herself to stop crying, which Freddie thought made her look older again, back to being more than her years, and his role as protector was already done with. How sudden the transformation had been, how well-practised she was at pretending to be an adult. He looked at the cracked skin in the corner of her mouth and the freckles on the bridge of her nose, left over from the summer, some of them as large as grains of wheat. Her skin was still tanned – or it might have been just grime underneath her skin – and a soft white down of transparent hairs was glistening in the light by the sides of her ears. He had looked at people's faces before, but not in this way. He realised she was letting him look at her; inviting him to do so. More than that, he could see she was trying to earn his favour.

"I got found out," he said.

"I didn't tell no one."

"I know you didn't," said Freddie. "I told her myself. Well, I made a mistake and she made me tell her. I don't know what to do now. Can't go back, can't go home. Can't show my face anywhere. Don't know where to go."

Millie looked down into her lap, became remote, lonely. "I wish you could come with me."

He thought about contradicting her, but something stopped him – an alternative future he was not yet quite ready to dismiss. It was always the impossible things that were most attractive. Then Millie stood up, quickly, sending a gust of air across Freddie's face that blew away the words she had just uttered. She wiped her nose again, this time with the back of her hand, and smiled at him. "You'll look after him, won't you."

It was no longer a question, and it gave him no choice. Then it washed over him again, feeling sick and hungry at the same time. It was an old friend now. "Of course I will."

"He's in my bedroom. I'll go get him. Do you want to come with me?" But before Freddie could answer, Millie emitted an unsmiling laugh. "Except my dad's still got a gun in his hand, so you'd better stay here." Then she left the barn, too cheerfully, turning in to the wind that was stirring up some leaves in the front yard.

Freddie breathed out heavily. He was cornered, nowhere else to go, his future decided, set in stone. Millie would give him Lester, and Freddie would take Lester home where he would then confess his forgeries to his mother. His mother would be angry, though she would express it with silence and nothing would change, the lies would still be lies, his head would still ache and the pain would be so bad he would have to bury it in his pillow to muffle the screams. Suhani would tell George about his forgery, Freddie would be fired, and Inspector Roper would come knocking. He wondered if anyone would write to him in prison, if it was allowed, and if so who would deliver the post.

He pushed Millie's suitcase to one side, trying to give himself room to think. All he had ever done was write down other people's stories; stories that they told and stories that they wished to hear; stories that lay folded up in the dark pocket of his leather pouch. Then he heard someone speak, though he knew it was from inside his head: *You just do your job.* The words were uttered not by George Franklin, however, but by some other voice. His own but not his own. The amanuensis was speaking to him.

He wondered how long Millie would be gone. Perhaps she had to get into the house past her dad without him noticing, and then out again. He thought about scribbling a quick note to her and then running home because he felt there might be something he wanted to say but couldn't do so out loud. He knew what husbands wrote to wives, sons to mothers, and mothers to sons, he'd read that sort of thing many times. But a boy to a girl? He could slip it inside her suitcase. It was an idea that empowered him, made him her guardian again. Of all the letters he had written this would be the first in his own voice. But then he remembered that of course she couldn't read, and immediately he felt like a fool.

The wind caught the barn door and pushed it to, with a creak. No, Millie couldn't read, but some part of the plan still persisted, refusing to die. There was a crawling sensation in his left arm, a twitching of its own accord. He unfastened the suitcase, two latches that easily popped open to release the lid. Only then, upon examining the contents, did he realise why he had really done it.

He recognised the letter. It was the one he had delivered the previous Thursday, and tucked inside it was another, the one from the War Office, permission to travel. It was as good as a ticket. If he sat on the train wearing his postboy uniform he would probably blend in with the war effort, no questions asked. Little Risborough to Exeter St Davids, Sunday 12th November, it said, for Millie Bedden.

Damn it! He hissed the words out loud. It was her name, not his. That was a problem.

But not, the amanuensis reminded him, an insurmountable one. He put his hand down into his jacket pocket and groped around until his fingers found a familiar object, its powdery dryness putting his teeth on edge. A one-inch stick of chalk that, combined with a smear of spit and a standard issue soft-grade pencil, meant he could change the letter M into a B. He was now an expert forger and could make it blend almost perfectly, certainly good enough to fool the cursory glance of a ticket collector. He thought of his mother and felt a strange sadness, not least because he was all too easily able to dismiss her. Jimmy Gardiner had run away and left his family, was not the first to do so, so why couldn't Freddie? It's not as if he'd be gone forever. With luck Millie would explain. He quickly scribbled her a short note after all, in the desperate hope she'd find someone to translate it.

Signing up. Give Lester to Ma.

There was no time for more, he had to hurry now, she'd surely return any minute, so he slipped through the half-opened barn door, looked around to check he was not being watched, set his face against the wind and began the long trek to Little Risborough Station. He had no idea what the time was and therefore would need to run to make sure of catching the four o'clock.

With each breathless step he pulled away, heading for Exeter, escaping Tendring and its haunted trenches of broken souls, leaving Freddie Lovegrove behind, shedding his loathsome skin. And finally the amanuensis had a name. Billie Bedden.

Part Four

40

February 1917

In the six months that followed, winter passed with just three occupants in the house, a cold and rainy season without the comfort of snow, nor the expense of a lit fire. And then a baby was born in February. The birth had been difficult, a day-long crescendo of moaning and screams that filled the empty hallways of Tendring and could almost be heard in Eagley village. But in their different ways Suhani and Hannah had experience of bringing children into the world, as well as mothers back into it, so Phoebe and her baby were both delivered as healthy as ripe tomatoes.

Every day Suhani sat at the library window for an hour or more, drawing some comfort from the solitude and repetition, waiting for a new season to be born in the hope her mood might lighten with it. On this day she watched the forks of frost slowly retreat towards the edges of the window frame, away from the heat of the sun. In the days before the fall, and on such a freezing morning, Hannah or Phoebe would have brought her breakfast by now, but this was a new normality that both girls understood and which meant they would need to keep their distance until Suhani decided to rise from her seated position. It was a leather wing chair that was big enough for her to sit sideways with her feet tucked under her body, allowing her full black dress to cover all of her limbs and much of the chair itself. Sometimes she felt like she was a large black cloud that had floated down from the ceiling. Other times, swirling, breath-defying smoke that had risen up from beneath the earth.

In her lap she held a broken shard of plaster, white on one side, blue on the other, with the corner of an eye painted on it. Behind her was Shiva, now partially restored, most of its pieces glued together, though the extremities of its arms and head were yet to be completed. This was the only time and the only place where the weight on Suhani's chest seemed to lessen, where she was able to empty her thoughts out across the lawn, where she could pick up individual pieces of her shattered life and pretend to glue them back together. But it was an illusion, a temporary reprieve that gave her just enough desire to live for one more day, with reminders every fifteen minutes from the clock in the hall that just as there was no going back in time there was no going forward either. The seasons would change but she would not, and she would simply have to wait until the moment repeated itself the following morning, and every morning. She wondered how she would keep herself alive once Shiva was fully restored.

Sunlight was turning the frost on the windows into a veil of condensation. Today was to be one of further loss, though no one would die. Hannah was leaving, heading back to her homeland across the Irish Sea, for reasons that were spoken and reasons that stayed hidden, which made Suhani think of other extremities of the British Empire as she rolled the piece of plaster between her fingers. Perhaps she would return to her own homeland's lush fields, greener than England, though she knew in her heart she would not. For all its shadows and ghosts, Tendring was her home now. More than that Phoebe needed looking after. Suhani looked into the empty crib next to her chair and contemplated the forked and unsigned road a mother had to walk every moment of every day. She would shine a light along the path. Phoebe was barely more than a child herself and besides, the newborn was Suhani's own flesh and blood too, more than mere consolation. A baby with Tristan's eyes that, like those of Tristan himself, reflected back their mother's adoration. In which secret corner of the house had the miracle occurred, Suhani wondered?

"Phoebe is asleep ma'am. For a hundred years I wouldn't be surprised."

Hannah was speaking from the library doorway and Suhani presumed she was pushing her gloves on and adjusting her hat, but did not turn to check, preferring to watch the shadowy shapes of crows on the lawn that were vaguely visible through the misted windows.

"Goodbye Hannah."

"I'll write, as soon as I get home, don't you worry now."

"You'll make a good midwife, Hannah. But I'll miss your Tendring Pie."

Hannah chuckled. "Oh no you won't. But I'll see what they make of it in Donegal. Well I'll be gone then, Mrs Harkness."

This was the crossroads at which Suhani was supposed to stand, turn and smile, to give a warm embrace without regret, to say that they would see each other soon, and in the moment they would believe it. But the gesture would be too painful so instead she remained transfixed by the crows casting long shadows as they pecked at the bread crumbs Hannah had discarded on the grass the night before. Then, suddenly, the crows lifted and flew away as one connected wave across the treetops. Suhani could detect nothing that had disturbed them, no signs of danger and yet, she thought, they must be in flight from something. Or could it be they just flew for the sheer joy of it? She envied them.

The silence had to be broken, but Suhani was not yet ready to say goodbye, and if she didn't ask the question now, she never would.

"Did you see his face?"

"Ma'am?"

"That night. Did you see his face?"

The crows settled in the trees opposite and Hannah's voice dropped to a whisper.

"It was black as pitch, ma'am. Why are you asking me now? Let sleeping dogs lie why don't you? He confessed to Roper, didn't he? Why would I make it up? Why would *he?* Whatever his reasons, he took them with him to his maker, God help him."

"But did you see his face?" The repetition gave her voice a sharper edge. Suhani heard a click that sounded like Hannah closing the library door behind her to give the two of them privacy, but Suhani continued to resist turning her head to look.

"I saw his limp," said Hannah.

"Which leg was it?"

"How would I know, ma'am? What does it matter? A limp's a limp isn't it? The story is written and the book is closed, that's what matters. The man's in heaven now and make no mistake."

"Stephen, or Christopher?"

"Well now, both I suppose. And half of the world along with them, so it seems."

Suhani watched the crows flap and heard them craw in the branches with agitated plans for new flight.

"It must be very crowded up there."

"Angels don't take up much space ma'am."

There was a soft mewing sound, a gurgle which Suhani remembered was the true reason she rose each morning, and which gave her permission finally to turn and look at Hannah, who to her surprise was holding Phoebe's baby.

"You'll have to take him or I'll miss my train, ma'am."

Suhani stood up to walk over to Hannah and then shaped her arms into a folded crook for Hannah to place the baby in.

"She's a fool and make no mistake," said Hannah. "I could have helped her. But he's a bonny boy and I don't begrudge her that. Ignore the wagging tongues, ma'am."

"Ah, Hannah," she smiled, "I've spent my whole life doing that."

"I suppose you have, ma'am." She put on her gloves and adjusted her hat, exactly as Suhani had imagined she would. "No fancy goodbyes now. I'll be gone."

"Goodbye," said Suhani as she watched Hannah turn and walk towards the library door. But then the erstwhile servant stopped, half-turned her head, and muttered some words reluctantly, a cagey afterthought.

"Left leg. Now that you mention it. I think it was his left leg. But I can't be sure."

And then she was gone, like the flight of crows from the lawn, but Suhani had no more space for sadness or regret. Instead Hannah's leaving had always been inevitable from the day she had arrived, the fruit of an unspoken prophecy, and as Suhani lifted the baby up so that its head rested in the curve of her neck, she felt content about Hannah's uncertain memory of events. The two men, Stephen and Jack, were both innocent and guilty at the same time, like the two sides in a war. This was the truth, it was time to let it be, and to remember instead the years when Stephen walked without a limp, because the past was all she had left.

Except, when the war was over, she thought, she would seek out the only place she could truly call home, even though it was a country she had never visited: not England, not India, but France, with its brown fields bruised with poppies and their blood-red petals bending to the breeze.

41

Two weeks later, after twenty years of having ticked and chimed continuously day and night, the clock in the hallway stopped. Hannah was no longer there to wind it, and neither Suhani nor Phoebe had thought to do it themselves. There was no slowing down, no gradual coming to rest, no fading death-rattle, instead time was moving forward just as it always had until it fell abruptly into silence. With the final swing of the pendulum, Tendring gave up on its waiting.

Though she didn't realise it, it was the stopping of the clock that woke Suhani. Every morning, always sitting in the library, always waiting for the mist to clear. She would often close her eyes pretending to sleep, and sometimes would, a refuge from living. There had been no dream, at least none that she could remember, though she had the feeling she had been visited. Perhaps Phoebe had come down to take the baby away for feeding, but glancing into the crib she could see that little Tristan was still there, awake but content. She picked him up and walked over to the window, thinking that probably she had only napped for ten minutes, no time for dreams. As usual the window glass was misty, if anything more difficult to see through than previous mornings. The sun had gone in, the tendrils of frost had regrown and the hot breath of her sleeping had condensed on the inside. The copper beech gently waved its branches in the breeze, and wintery clouds drifted across the sky.

Then some other movement caught her eye. At first she imagined it was Stephen walking across the lawn. But the cadence was too slow, the limp too subtle and awkward, hard to tell which leg it was. In any case she did not believe in ghosts. Her next thought was that it was Jack, that other limping man from her past. What was he doing here? She briefly entertained the absurd scenario in which he had lost his way to the station six months ago and had only just hobbled his way back. The clouded window made it impossible to make out more than a shape and a rhythm, but of course there was no reason on earth for it to be Jack, he was in Rye with his girl, if he still had one. Or in jail. She tried again, already suspecting she was deceiving herself, playing the game of lies, using it like armour. Freddie? The scandal of his leaving had long since subsided in the village, words of his running away had turned from the present tense to the past, but she knew he would not be gone forever and one day would return. She envied his mother for that. In fact she was surprised Freddie had been gone for so long. For a second this seemed the most likely because she saw now that perhaps it was not a limp but merely a fragility, a reticence in his steps that would fit the return of someone who was not welcome. But it was not Freddie either, this figure was simply too tall. All three possibilities – Stephen, Jack, Freddie – flicked through her mind like pages from a picture book, and were dismissed just as quickly. She wiped the condensation from the window with the palm of her hand, but the frost remained on the outside, impenetrable. All she could make out was the vague impression of a uniform ascending the steps to the portico.

There was no knock, just the sound of the front door being opened. It was not yet time to paint it again, but the click of the latch triggered the urge to retrieve the pot of darkest black from the cellar because uniformed men needed warding off, had come universally to mean bad news, or bad luck, despite the fact she had already run out of both. The baby in her arms fidgeted, attempting to find a more comfortable place to rest its head but lifted it twice and ended up in the same position, tucking back into the warmth of Suhani's neck, a warmth that was its only need, that and the flow of milk from Phoebe's breast. Suhani felt envy that it needed nothing more from this world. She could have held him forever, but the sound of the latch caused her to gently place the baby back in its crib.

He stepped into the library but even then she didn't recognise him. Not out of disbelief but because he had lost so much weight, lamb's fat that he could not afford to lose in the first place and which had fallen from his face, leaving the skin stretched over his cheek bones and around his retreating eyes. He had also removed his pencil moustache, the growing of which had never much been worth the effort but, as she had often said to him in the past, and thought it now, boys are too eager to be men. She gasped at the memory of it, put her hands up to her face and called out his name, a visceral, unrestrained entreaty to Shiva that this moment was real and would not be taken away from her in the way it so often had been in the past. She laughed through her tears, tears that had anticipated the situation before there had been time for her to understand it, tears that immediately turned into an uncontrolled weeping, driving her like a firestorm towards him. The howling sound she made was the same as when he had died, and Edward before him, and Arthur before that, all three deaths standing in front of her in the open library doorway. As she hung from his neck and squeezed the breath out of him, she wondered if this young man was an inch taller than he should be. It was not such a trivial question. Could it be so? Could an eighteen-year-old still be growing? She panicked, thought it might not be him after all. But through the smell of trenches and hospitals and cigarette smoke and the sweat of crowded trains, she detected another odour from the crook of his neck that was the same as baby milk, and she cried into it, knowing it was him.

Her weeping gradually fell into silence, her lungs empty, her heart full. But he was taking too long to return the embrace. Instead he seemed confused, and said, simply, "I'm told I live here."

It was like the pinching out of a candle flame. She immediately released the pressure in her arms and around his body, fully expecting winter to blow out the tinders of spring. Then she squeezed more tightly, remembering where she had seen Tristan's lifeless eyes before, in the haunted gaze of Gabriel, and realised her son's return was far from complete. His journey home was just beginning, and it would take time to fathom its mystery. She would have to give birth to him again. Only then did she notice she was once again holding a fragment of Shiva, and it was cutting into the palm of her hand.

The hands of the clock had stopped moving, but time had begun, and finally it chose to put his arms around her. It was of no consequence to either of them that he did not know why. Just as with a newborn baby, the holding was enough.

Epilogue

42

Exeter, 1940

Billie had turned his back on Ellen so that she might read the letter undistracted. Or perhaps it was just that he didn't want to see her reaction. Blowing another lungful of cigarette smoke against the glass of their bedroom window, he couldn't decide whether he had thought of his mother every day since leaving or had barely thought of her at all. It seemed to be both, a constant presence constantly suppressed, memories locked away, like moths in a wardrobe, never opened for fear they might fly out. By the time he had escaped his mother's gravity there had been no need to resist her pull anymore, and it had not taken as long as he had expected, the weeks turning quickly into months. And then, after the enforced isolation brought about by the Spanish flu, the years had stretched on indefinitely until he realised, finally, that he didn't want to be found. The strongest memory he had left of his fugue was the earliest one, of sleeping overnight on a platform at Paddington station amongst the vagrants and third-class passengers twenty-three years ago. It really did seem like yesterday, and of all the unlikely things that might still cause a recurring, sweat-inducing dream, it was that.

He heard Ellen turn the letter over, the flick of paper sounding impatient, suggesting she had got to the end. “You can’t go all that way to deliver this,” she said. “She might not live there anymore. People move. People die. And even if she is there, it’s madness Billie.”

In the fog of cigarette smoke he thought for a moment she was talking about his mother, but of course the letter was not addressed to her. In any case, Ellen did not yet know of his mother’s existence.

She was crying again, and blurted out, “What’s any of this got to do with you?”

He wondered how he might compress his old life into just a few sentences. But he had to try, so he sucked in a lungful of air to begin explaining everything to her as best he could. About to peel away the layers of deception and duplicity, he was curious about whether there would be anything at the centre, whether his soul would have survived its incarceration. Would there be any truth left on the floor of its prison cell?

He began with the biggest lie of all, by saying that his real name was Freddie Lovegrove. She listened, although it was difficult for her to understand. But then he could barely explain it to himself.

It was unusual for the sun to shine on Billie's – Freddie’s – house. At only certain times of the year, with a rare planetary alignment, was it able to fully escape the shadow of the six-floored factory opposite. This morning, the day after Freddie’s soft, sighing explanation to Ellen, was one such moment, the sun casting a golden glow so agreeable that even the row of dilapidated terraced houses that lay on the edge of the Exeter slums in which his own home was gripped, had a shimmering beauty. The sun somehow made his leaving easier. Inevitable, even.

His family stood on the front doorstep, with Freddie himself a yard away in the street, suitcase by his feet. Removing his trilby and leaning forward to kiss Ellen briefly on the lips, he then hugged his nine-year-old daughter and shook the hand of his ten-year-old son. "Don't forget now, you're the man of the house. Until I come back." The boy nodded, unsure and miserable.

Freddie turned his eyes to Ellen who attempted a smile, but it was nothing more than an unenthusiastic acceptance of his leaving, and even less of his new identity. For Billie to return to being Freddie had been for him a surprisingly effortless slipping back, as quick as removing a hat, but he understood that for his wife of sixteen years it would not be so easy, or even possible.

The baby in her arms wriggled and Ellen swung it round from one hip to the other. Freddie tried to sound cheerful as he kissed the top of the baby's head. "Goodbye Millicent Rose. Look after your mother." But his tone rang a false note and fooled no one, not even the baby, or so it seemed from its nonplussed expression. "Well," he said, straightening his face, "better go."

With that, Ellen let the mask slip. "Bye Billie." Her words had a softer edge, warm and kind, like the brief kiss she had given him the night before, proof for Freddie that whatever damage he had done she would, over time, allow him to repair it, as she always did. This was how they loved each other, for there was no other way to show it in the cramped and blackened ghettos that lay half-asleep under the stifling blanket of the factory's shadow. And certainly there was no way he could say it, not outright. It would have to remain hidden in the undertow of what they both said next.

"I'll miss you, Ellen."

"You'll miss your train, more like."

And so Freddie took that as permission to leave without a further word, adjusted his trilby and walked away down the road to make his final delivery. But just before he turned the corner from Trinity Place into Hibernia Street he looked back at his wife and children to wave, and they waved back. Even the baby raised its arm, though only out of hunger, which made him wonder if, on his return, there would be not just one extra mouth to feed but two, assuming his mother was anywhere to be found.

He made the journey in one day. No sleeping over at Paddington, just an hour to get across London and another to wait at Victoria for the Ramsgate train to Little Risborough. He had sat on platform twelve scanning the posters that asked him to *Dig For Victory* and *Hitler Will Send No Warning – Always Carry Your Gas Mask,* which were such ubiquitous appeals these days he wondered if anyone took any notice anymore. Chewing on a cold pork pie he had bought from one of the station's vendors, he was surprised at how much he enjoyed it, more hungry than he realised. Although his days of being sick after eating had long gone, a vestige of it remained, accompanying every meal like cold gravy. At first he couldn't work out what was different this time. Even though this pork pie was barely edible, two days old he estimated, and should have made him nauseous without any cue from the past, it went down easily and stayed there, like it used to in the days before he first put on his shako hat. As he smiled wistfully at a third poster, *Is Your Journey Really Necessary?,* he considered the trivial bite of a station vendor's dish and sensed a change in himself.

Three hours later as he approached Tendring on the road from Little Risborough station, and with each retraced step from the past, the more profound the feeling of change became. In some curious circular journey, he had finally reached adulthood by becoming young Freddie again.

43

The road had changed hardly at all, escaping the epidemic of Tarmac that had afflicted much of the rest of the country between the wars, and was still a dusty track of worn-down parallel furrows with dandelions and buttercups growing up the middle. The verges looked neater now, trimmed no doubt by some new-fangled machine drawn not by horse but sucked along by diesel, and the trees on either side were taller and thinned out. But these were the only differences between now and the last time he had walked this road, between the old war and the new.

He was approaching Bedden's Farm on his left, and was still unsure about whether this was one of the doors he should knock on. The decision was made for him when he saw the house was silent and deserted, falling in on itself. It was possible that for some families the Depression had reached this far south, or maybe Primrose's fatal illness had spread through the rest of their livestock, but as he got closer he saw evidence of a much simpler explanation – the barn was completely missing, replaced with an area of weeds and tall grass that was covering up black, scorched earth. The flick of a cigarette butt, perhaps, had finished them off, a fire destroying their lives in a matter of minutes, giving them the reason they were looking for to move on. Did they take Lester with them, he wondered? But what did it matter, the little fellow was long dead now.

He put down his suitcase and picked his way through the weeds, across the square of concrete where Primrose had once stood, but there was no detritus, no fragments of burnt wood or iron bolts and brackets that would have held the joists together. The whole area of the old barn had been cleared, or looted. And there was no sign of what he was hoping to stumble across, the drawing, Sinistra, or at least the frame that had held it. He felt curiously despondent and wondered where the Beddens might have moved to. Then his heart thumped with the sudden thought that they could have gone to stay with Olive in Exeter. The notion that Millie could have been in the same city for twenty years or more, perhaps even in the same area, in the next road along, sent a wry smile across his face and a snort of air from his nose at the idea he might have unwittingly passed her in the street. Would he have recognised her if he had? Would she have blossomed or gone to seed? Would her rough lips have turned to sweet plums or turnips? Her thrilling, rustic beauty when she was young could have taken her in either direction. Or perhaps, after all, Millie's family had just moved the few miles to Eagley, baking bread to sell in the market. Wherever she was, Millie had her own life and Freddie had the feeling he should leave her be, hers was no door worth knocking on, no alternative life to live. It was too late for that, though he felt regret for the simple, uncomplicated life it would have been. He picked up his suitcase and turned away from the memory of her to head back to the road and the final mile towards Tendring.

He ought to do the same for Mrs Harkness, he thought, leave her be, but the magnetic lure of Tendring had not diminished since he had left all those years ago. If anything it had increased with time and distance. Wearing the mask of Billie Bedden for so long meant he had eventually come to believe in it himself, but Freddie's face was always behind it, and Tendring had never stopped pulling at his heart. Besides, he had letters to deliver.

The stone eagles were still guarding the gate and the path leading up to the house, but there was a new sign on the right-hand gate post which Freddie read with a sinking heart: *Tendring Hotel.* He put his palm up to his breast to feel the letters inside his jacket pocket: letters to deliver, yes, but no one to deliver them to. Suhani had disappeared in the same way as Millie, though no doubt to a different destination. Back to India, perhaps. That was the most obvious and he should have predicted it. He felt foolish. The air of permanence that Tendring disseminated through the air and through the years turned out to be just an illusion after all. Where the magician and enchantress had once cast her spell, the stage was now empty.

He put down his suitcase and lit a cigarette so he could take the time to look at the house properly, forge a new memory of it, one that was not infected by the past but was simply one of bricks and mortar, tiles and windows, an ordinary house bereft of its former magic. A memory that would be easier to forget, or at least less painful to hold on to.

But he found that standing there was not, in the end, enough. He was still curious, the exorcism not yet complete, and he needed to learn how else it might have changed. What would be gone, what would have been retained? The prospect of walking up to the front door suddenly became easy, and he even had the agreeable fantasy he might stay for one night at the hotel. So he dropped his cigarette on the ground, looked down to examine his shoes, that nervous habit he'd never been able to overcome, picked up his suitcase again and stepped up the driveway towards the house.

The gravel was different somehow, the stones a lighter colour, smaller and more consistent in size and shape, presumably imported by the new owners to facilitate a smoother ride in a motor car for the hotel's comings and goings. There were no flowers along the edge of the path anymore but white-painted stones each the size of a loaf of bread lining both sides of the driveway. They would reflect the light from the headlights of any late arrivals, he guessed. But if so, where were all the cars? There was no viable route for an automobile to get round to the back of the house, and no suitable space to park them even if there was, unless the garden wall had been demolished and the roses uprooted.

The front door was still black, looking like it had recently been repainted, and Freddie touched it with his fingertips to check if the paint was still wet, then chuckled out loud for expecting it to be. But the blackness made him feel unsure again, that perhaps the house had one more secret to give up. The sign by the doorbell said Please Ring And Enter. So he did.

Much had been left unchanged in the hallway. Even the grandfather clock was still there, though it seemed to have stopped, its pendulum unmoving and silent. The main difference was a reception desk that had been built next to the library door where visitor and receptionist would handle bookings. A rack of pigeonholes with room keys tucked inside each one hung from the wall behind. Business was not going well, apparently. There was a bell on the desk, its obvious purpose to call for attention, but Freddie wasn't sure he wanted any. There was a stillness that didn't seem to fit with a working hotel and he suddenly felt like a trespasser, so he didn't ring. Instead he put down his suitcase as quietly as possible at the foot of the desk and leant to one side in order to peek through the open door into the room behind, then took two tentative steps forward to get a closer look. Despite the walls still being covered with shelves of books, the library was once more a re-designated space. There were several tables set for dinner, or breakfast, eight of them with white tablecloths and silver cutlery ready to go. But there were no people, not here in the library, nor, it felt, anywhere else in the house. No flow of life, no sound of footsteps coming down the stairs, no clunking of doors or calling out of children's names, no smell of fried bacon coming up from the kitchen, no winding of the clock, no setting of the chimes.

He walked further into the room, sensing the library had undergone a profound change, his slow footsteps sinking into the burgundy carpet. That was it, every sound was absorbed into the floor, even the soft rhythm of his own breath, all the echoes in the library soaked up by the rich pile under his feet. Perhaps he should have removed his shoes. The nerves began to rise in him as he came to a stop in the middle of the room and held his breath, an intruder on high alert.

And there it was, in a discreet gold-lacquered frame hanging above the fireplace, an object he had not expected to see, or ever really thought about during his prolonged absence: the painting of three soldiers staring directly at him, just as they had stared at the artist all those years ago. More unexpected still was that someone had completed it, Tristan's face matching those of his brothers, the style perfectly replicated. Had Suhani commissioned its completion and sold it on? Too expensive to ship back to India? Too poignant to keep, too heartbreaking to destroy? He looked directly into Tristan's eyes and then his skin went cold. The simplest explanation was the most likely. She was still here.

"I'm afraid we're closed."

Freddie jumped, but it wasn't her. Instead he turned to see a tall young man, black hair and dark eyes, with a naïve enthusiasm for life that seemed out of place in the dead silence of the house.

"As of yesterday," he continued, his smile revealing perfect white teeth. "The War Office requisitioned us for, well, something. Top secret I suppose." He smiled again, a genuine connection, not the false note of a desperate hotel proprietor. This fellow was not in charge, Freddie thought.

"Oh right," said Freddie. "Well I'm not..."

"There's The Oak, would you like me to call them?"

"No. No thanks. Not stopping. Actually I'm a bit lost." Another lie, though there was some truth in it.

"Ah. You're not the first. What can I do to help? Directions perhaps?"

Freddie needed to stall, create time to process his suspicions, for his head to catch up with his heart.

"This painting..." he said.

"Oh, magnificent isn't it." It was the sound and delivery of high education, confidence and strong blood, such that when the young man walked up to stand next to him to admire the painting Freddie half-expected to be embraced. This fearless youth seemed delighted to talk about the painting. Perhaps, in this room where you could no longer even hear your own echo, he was delighted to talk to anyone about anything.

"Rather good don't you think?" he said pointing at each figure as he introduced them, left to right. "My two uncles, Arthur, and Edward. Died at Fromelle and High Wood respectively."

Freddie began quickly to process this startling information, his mind raced, his past unravelling before his eyes. He tried to draw a family tree in his head but the connections between this boy and the figures in the painting were blurred, the faces incomplete in the way the painting used to be. Then the young man alighted on the third figure and dropped his voice. "And this is my father. Everyone says I have his eyes. I have his name, anyway, ha-ha. Tristan Harkness. Pleased to meet you."

He held out his hand, but Freddie couldn't take it. The bizarre revelation was too much, he couldn't move in any direction, the chessboard upturned and the pieces of the story strewn across the floor. He glanced at the young man to check his eyes, then back to the painting, and it seemed to be true. They did look the same. There were other similarities too, the high cheek bones, the thick black eyebrows. If it were not for the years between the wars separating them, this youth standing next to him could have been a fourth brother. Freddie began to work it out, was adding up other things, making more important calculations about who this boy's mother might be. Then it came to him unbidden, like the curtains of the theatre opening again, and the young servant girl, Phoebe, filled the stage where the magician once stood. She had been hiding in plain sight the whole time. How easy it was to deceive a liar. Freddie took the young man's outstretched hand and looked into his eyes. It was time, finally, to speak the truth.

"The thing is, I used to deliver the post here. When I was a boy. I know this painting. Except in my day it wasn't finished."

They had been shaking hands but the movement now stopped abruptly, though they didn't let go.

"Ah yes, I've been told that story."

Freddie wasn't sure if he was referring to the story of the painting, or of the postboy. Then the young man, young Tristan, turned to look at him with a smile that was now less secure, their roles reversed, his turn to try to piece things together.

"Funny the things we forget, isn't it."

"Pardon?"

"If you're the postboy, why would you be lost?"

Freddie finally let go of the young man's hand. "Well I'm not the postboy anymore, I suppose."

"I see. Who are you then? Why are you here?"

Freddie thought about telling him he had a final delivery to make, but it was not for this young man and Freddie himself had his own questions to ask so he changed the subject to buy more time, returning his gaze to the painting.

"I'm very sorry indeed about your father."

"Don't be, Freddie."

This time it was as expected, a woman's voice. Freddie didn't need to turn towards it to know who it was. The accent hadn't changed, the rich glow of it, the glottal throwback to an ancient world. He was convinced he could smell delphiniums.

"I saw you from my bedroom window, you looked down at your shoes. I knew immediately it was you." Suhani stood in the library doorway, holding a single flower.

They walked beyond the boundary of Tendring, all three of them, along the edges of the fields and up towards the ridge before taking a right turn that was new to Freddie. It led into land he'd always assumed was private and, though tempted as a boy, had never explored. The hill fell gently away in front of them. Young Tristan was several yards ahead, his keen youthful legs incapable of walking slowly and he was constantly turning round in silent encouragement for Freddie and Suhani to catch up.

She had been asking politely about Exeter, about his job and his family, and Freddie had obliged, so that they both skirted around the real reasons why he was there. After a while he wondered if the subject would ever come up, and even whether it should; that the whole exercise might be a mistake. Why was she being so civil, why had she welcomed him in? Why was she not still angry? Whilst it was a relief, he was nevertheless suspicious. He had spent the entire train journey thinking about what he would say, preparing to force his story upon her if necessary, to raise his voice in order to clear the air and explain as best he could the madness that had befallen him. If nothing else he would attempt to heal some of her wounds by returning her letters to her. But Suhani offered no resistance, her demeanour the exact opposite of what he had expected, and without a barrier there was nothing to push against, no way to move forward. So the conversation remained courteous, her questions kind, and he was totally disarmed by them. In the intervening years they had changed, but their positions had not. She was still the mistress of the house and he was still the postboy, the one who thought much and spoke little, a characteristic he reverted to now, feeling Suhani was holding something back and was even taking some pleasure in doing so.

She was over sixty years old Freddie thought, she must be, but had retained the beauty and stature of her younger self, as if she had barely aged at all. Over the years Freddie had taught himself to look people in the eye when he was speaking to them, part of the pretence of being an adult, so he watched her when she asked questions and saw that her hair was still almost entirely black. And although it was true there were subtle creases round her eyes and perhaps her face was thinner, he felt these changes made her even more radiant and graceful as a result.

As the path by the edge of the field narrowed she stopped and looked up. A Spitfire was opening its throat overhead and growling across the sky, the sound as thrilling to them on the ground as it would be up there in the clouds. A few yards ahead of them young Tristan was waving his outstretched arms over his head and the Spitfire tipped its wings in reply. Tristan left Freddie and Suhani behind as he carried on walking down the gentle incline that took him towards a copse at the bottom of the valley, where Freddie could just make out a man sitting under the trees, painting.

"You'd think we would have learned," said Suhani, still looking up into what was now an empty sky. Then she stared hard into Freddie's eyes, and for the first time the gentleness was gone. The corners of her mouth were very slightly down-turned, and he wondered if she was going to cry, or perhaps she was angry, it was impossible to say. She narrowed her eyes, and said, "But then the bigger the mistake, the harder it is to admit it I suppose." Her words challenged him in some unspecified way and there was no choice but for him to respond. She had opened the door for him, and it was time to walk through. He put his hand in his inside jacket pocket and pulled out the letters tied up in a rubber band.

"I took these. Intercepted them. Stole them, you might say." He held them out to her. "They belong to you. I'd like you to have them back."

She took them from him but did not remove the rubber band, instead she just read the topmost address. Her lips parted and she breathed in as if she were about to speak, but then appeared to change her mind. Freddie got the sense that she was thinking many things at once. Still refusing eye contact with Freddie, she instead lifted her gaze towards young Tristan who was heading down the inclined field towards the painter under the trees. Finally she spoke.

"He wants to be a pilot. Do you think I should let him?"

"Can you stop him? They'll call him up, won't they, in any case?"

She looked up into the sky, ignoring Freddie's question. "They say that's where the war will be lost and won. Up in the clouds." Mindlessly she glanced back down at the letters and picked at the rubber band, only then seeming to remember they required some kind of reply. Finally she held them out perfunctorily for Freddie to take back. "They are addressed to Tristan."

He stared at her. He had required her to take the letters, to be followed hopefully by an act of forgiveness, the closing of a book, neat and tidy. It was the entire purpose of his visit. But instead she was tearing at an old wound across the decades and if he took the letters back the peace between the wars would count for nothing. All these years later, he would still be running from the library. He couldn't give in, not yet.

"I don't deliver to dead people anymore," he said.

She nodded down the path that cut through the wheatfield. "You don't have to."

At first he thought she had become confused, or was displaying the insanity of grief that had fossilised over time, that she thought the young man heading for the copse was her son, a figure with the same eyes and name that allowed her disturbed spirit some comfort. But when she spoke again it was with such serene tones he knew she was of sound mind, could never be anything else, and he was witnessing the magician's final trick: she was talking about the painter under the trees.

"It turns out you were right. You were smarter than you thought. He was injured, and he did have shell-shock. Lies cloaked in truth, that's how they deceive themselves. Life is very hard for him. I tried to find you, but by then you had done a very good job of running away."

Freddie looked towards the distant, impossible figure of Tristan and said, "But I read the letter." He nodded at the letters she was holding. "You can read it for yourself."

"There were many letters, Freddie, across the country and the years, many grieving mothers reunited with their sons. Other postboys luckier than you. To be sure, in the confusion and the untold death, there were miracles. In good ways as well as bad, war always exceeds the imagination."

By then, a hundred yards away, young Tristan had reached the painter and a third figure appeared from out of the trees, a woman, back from a walk by the river. The family was complete. Phoebe threw out a picnic blanket onto the ground and her son helped her, in fact took over, in the way young men always did. The painter was undistracted, dabbing his brush on the canvas, although it was too far away for Freddie to see any details of the picture being worked on.

"Later we found out he got separated from his company the day before. He was nowhere near Rake's Wood, although he doesn't remember. At first he didn't even remember me, not all of me, anyway. But most of it has come back to him. I think he has all the memories he needs now."

She held out the letters again, more insistent, but still Freddie refused. He was consumed by disbelief, wanted to ask a hundred questions but couldn't find the words to begin any of them. In the end he remained silent.

"You have a good heart Freddie. I understand what you did. There is not enough kindness in this world."

There was the sound of another Spitfire, or perhaps it was the same one returning, and Freddie looked up to watch it fly, higher now, across the sky. He took the letters from Suhani's outstretched hand, and in doing so accepted the forgiveness he had come all this way for, drawn by the pull of Tendring across the country and across the years. And more than that, abandoning Billie Bedden in order to reunite with Freddie the postboy, to hand him down some advice. But what would he say to the young Freddie Lovegrove if he was standing there right now, right next to him? Would he really want to change anything? If he hadn't forged the letter, perhaps Tristan would have died in the trenches after all. Could he have manipulated fate in such a way? No, that was too much, another foolish attempt to forgive himself, and the time had passed for such things.

"Go down to the river and deliver your letters, Freddie."

He was breathing faster, aware of blood pumping in his head again, not like the old headaches but the opposite, a feeling of anticipation. He nervously tapped the bundle of letters on the palm of his hand. "What should I say to him?"

She smiled. "The truth?"

Freddie smiled back, even let out a gentle chuckle. "Yes. Good idea." He was about to turn to head towards the river, but as the sound of the Spitfire faded to nothing he remembered the old biplanes he had watched when he was a boy.

"You should let him fly, your grandson, if that's what he wants to do."

"Of course, it's not up to me," she replied. "But yes, I'm sure you're right."

He gestured with the bundle down towards the river. "Are you coming?"

"I'm returning to the house. There are many things to get ready for the War Office. I'm afraid I won't see you again today. Goodbye, Freddie."

Her words implied one thing but her tone quite another, and he wondered if he would ever see her again. What he did know was that she was releasing him, just as she might release her grandson into the sky.

"Goodbye Mrs Harkness." But he had not gone ten steps when Suhani called after him.

"Freddie?"

He stopped, turned to look at her. She stood there in her sari, an Indian woman in an English field, beautifully incongruous yet perfectly placed, the sun reflecting in her eyes, which even at ten paces looked wet with tears.

"Your mother is waiting for you."

44

She had lied. She was not going back to the house. Instead Suhani had walked fifty paces and then stopped, placed herself behind a tree and peered round to watch Freddie make his way down the path that led through the middle of the field towards the copse, where a fragile river flowed but was sometimes dry in the summer. There was no doubt in her mind that Freddie would make his final delivery, but just the same she felt the need to watch the transaction and ensure he didn't lose his nerve. Though he had never done so in the past.

Phoebe and her son were sitting on the picnic blanket and it appeared to Suhani even from this distance that they hadn't noticed Freddie until he was almost upon them. Then young Tristan stood up to make some kind of introduction, followed by Phoebe also rising to her feet and shaking Freddie's hand. Last time, she had swung at him, knocked him to the ground. How restrained they were now, smiled Suhani, how very English. There had been so much anger and fear the last time they had spoken, no sign of it on this day. Twenty-three times the earth had circled the sun. So little had changed, and yet so much.

Suhani knew what her son was feeling, she knew him better than anyone else on earth, better than her own feelings. A few yards away from the picnic, painting under the tree, he would be oblivious to the figures nearby, or more likely was choosing to be. As a small boy he had never liked crowds of people, even small groups. That was her unforgivable crime, sending him into the crowded trenches, and the unending grief for her other two sons was her punishment.

By now Freddie had approached Tristan, who with his left hand rested his brush on his easel and turned to face him, but as far as Suhani could tell at this distance neither of them spoke. The letters were handed over, presumably deemed to speak for themselves.

In fact Freddie did speak to Tristan, but only after Suhani had turned to walk away from seeing it, and with only four simple words. These are for you. He knew he was not doing it for Tristan's benefit but for his own, for some measure of atonement, an opportunity to be forgiven. But it was all too late for that. Perhaps it was just a sense of completeness, or duty, a legal requirement to fulfil his contract with the Post Office. After all, he still worked for them.

Tristan took the letters without a word, without even a sense of surprise. Of course, Suhani would have told him the story, or Phoebe would have, many times by the glow of the fire or the dappled sunlight under the beech tree. Each season they would have filled out the story to make it more real and yet push it further into the past where it could become a kind of fiction, and therefore easier to understand. Freddie suddenly worried that if Tristan were to read the letters they would open up old wounds. Perhaps Tristan thought so too, because he put the bundle of letters into his trouser pocket and picked up his brush to return to his painting. To Freddie's untrained eye the painting looked a mess, frankly – hard to discern a landscape or portrait amongst the spread of colour. And yet at the same time, and despite his prejudices, he could see the patina was beautiful. He presumed its defining shapes were still to come.

The meeting had been unremarkable, deflating, an ordinary moment that had barely disturbed the artist's brushstrokes. Although Freddie did not feel unwelcome, neither did he feel there was more to come, and even saying goodbye would have seemed out of place and unnecessary.

But just as he moved to go, out of the corner of his eye Freddie caught Tristan turning to smile at him. "Will you stay for a bit?" He used the handle of his brush to point at his canvas. "Until it's finished? Won't be long. Now I know what I'm painting."

And so Freddie stayed for an hour to watch his own face appear on the canvas in the way that clouds, for a passing moment, can take on human form. It could have been anyone, yet it could be no one else. The blue eyes, the butter-coloured hair just visible beneath the dark blue shako hat. And then another figure behind him – but no, just a flash of Post Office blue, like a shadow on a wall. The amanuensis? Was it Suhani's stories? How else could Tristan have known?

Her intention had been to go to the graveyard, as she did most days, to check the flowers and sometimes renew them. Usually she would stand at the family monument and feel content, even happy, not because she believed her sons were there in any mystical way, but the opposite, because she was entirely alone and was able to empty her mind of everything, including grief. Occasionally, however, she was tempted into an alternative world, diverted to a place where Arthur and Edward still lived, Stephen too. She would talk to them without fear of being overheard and they would talk back to the mad Indian woman from the house in the valley. But it quickly palled. She was broken-hearted, not a broken-hearted fool.

She would check on Christopher's grave too, try to visualise the young woman in whose heart he still resided. Not so young now, and perhaps having moved on, remembering and forgetting at the same time, as so many wives and girlfriends would have done. And as they would have to do again now that the whole world was repeating its folly, drinking its second glass of poison because the first had not quite worked well enough. What freedom had the men of war won, except to fight another one? What strange mockery would it be to send her grandson up into the clouds to take his chances there? The monument answered: Thy will, not mine, Lord.

Yes, all of this had been her intention: to go to the graveyard and sit quietly with her memory of Arthur and Edward. But almost without realising it she found herself drawn instead across the fields and onto another path, towards the Boer obelisk. She didn't go there often, perhaps once a year. Not on a specific anniversary but simply when more distant memories occupied her mind and the wind blew her in that direction, as it seemed to be doing now.

As she approached the obelisk she wanted Stephen to be there with her. Not the limping shell of a man who had broken her heart a hundred times, the soldier who had died not by bullet but by pride, foolish, English, meaningless pride; not the man who chose a body, had there been one, to be wrapped in a Union Jack to the muted tones of the Last Post, rather than stand naked in front of his wife. No, she wanted back the confident, handsome, beautiful man for whom she would have died a hundred times more.

The obelisk was catching the light, as it often did, the highest place for several miles. She looked up towards the pinnacle and saw in the sky beyond it several more aircraft, too high now for her to be able to identify their roundels, and thought perhaps some military manoeuvre was coming, a battle planned. There had been talk of it. But they banked and turned as one, a murmuration of Spitfires, too graceful for grim battle, rehearsing instead a ballet in the sky and leaving behind their contrails of angel's wings, no death following there.

Shielding her eyes from the blinding brightness of the sky, she imagined Tristan, young Tristan, the son of her son, in a cockpit landing half-burned on alien soil, words muffled by red-soaked bandages to a foreigner nurse who held her patient's hands tightly but did not understand his English, save perhaps for the one word he might repeat over and over and because the sound of a son's call for his mother was much the same in any language. Or, with a different roll of the dice, return unscathed, the fuel tank unstruck, the bullets missing by an inch, a life returned to a world lost or won. It was not for her to say, or even to wish for.

She took off her shoes so that she might get closer to the earth, then sat cross-legged on the grass to watch the cows grazing on the hillside opposite and began to compose a letter in her head, then another, two letters that would never be delivered.

The reddening sky, the cooler air.

Her breathing lightened and her eyes narrowed. A hawk was hanging in the air poised to swoop down and pounce on its prey. Suhani watched the bird's fluttering wings, and waited. She would never send the letters to her two unforgotten sons, but the writing of them, in the end, would be enough.

45

Blast walls had been built outside the school windows and bolt holes cut next to them for the children to escape. There were no signposts in or out of the village, and where the roads used to be the colour of pale earth they were now dark grey, the pavement less frayed, more a clear path to keep people safe from the recent decade's influx of motor cars, and now army vehicles. But something else was different, Freddie realised, as he walked the road through Eagley village. Cars had driven out horses prematurely to the knacker-man, and so there were no piles of manure on the roads for the roses. That, more than anything, seemed to be the main difference.

Otherwise the air felt much the same, an unnerving familiarity of one-hundred-year-old cottages on either side and then, coming up on his right, the Post Office. It was unexpected, hadn't entered his head, his former place of work, because it was not the purpose of his visit. Defiantly unchanged, it was still selling the same things in the window – or so it seemed, they were certainly faded from several years of sun-light. The only noticeable difference outside was the red telephone box, jammed up against the pillar box because there wasn't really room for it, an unwelcome addition elbowed in by a careless future.

He stopped at the door. Even if George Franklin was still alive, and given his fondness for alcohol it seemed unlikely, he would have long ago retired, so it would be safe to step inside. They would be selling nothing he required but he had a wistful need for the old smells, to run his hand along the polished edge of the counter, to read the wartime posters that had changed but chivvied with the same message, the same call to arms. In order to blow out the flame of old memories, one had first to rekindle them. So he pushed at the door to open it, and the bell rang.

A woman behind the counter looked up and smiled. Freddie had to come up with something quickly – the Post Office was not a place where you browsed. He went up to the counter and placed his suitcase by his feet.

"Some stamps, please." It sounded ludicrous. Worse, it sounded like a lie. He carried on, digging further. "And some writing paper. And envelopes."

"How many, sir?" Without waiting for an answer she stretched across her counter to gather up Freddie's requests. He looked around the shop, as much as anything to avoid eye contact. Inside had changed much more than out, more general provisions and a new shelf filled with forms, dog license applications, licenses for guns and game keepers, instructions about air raids and gas masks. There was a machine by the doorway selling cigarettes. The more he looked, the less it seemed like he had ever worked there.

"Six, thanks." Thanks. Even the way people talked had changed, a more casual air to the words, a freedom in the vowels and syllables shipped over in the movies. It had taken this trip back into the past for him to notice it.

"That'll be two shillings and threepence all together please," she said, handing over the stamps and stationery. Realising he had actually to go through with the transaction he dipped his hand into his trouser pocket, took out a handful of change and picked out the necessary coins to place on the counter. The bell rang. Someone else had come in. Freddie continued to look down into his hand. What if they recognised him?

"Morning Leslie," said the woman behind the counter, looking over Freddie's shoulder. He had known a Leslie, delivered to the old woman now and then, but she'd be a hundred now, rotting in the churchyard.

"Morning Hilda," said the voice from behind. She sounded young. His desire to not be recognised suddenly overwhelmed him, and he regretted coming into the Post Office. Regretted walking into the village. He handed over the money and gathered up his stationery.

"Thanks. Thank you." Then he remembered another Leslie, seven years old, Mrs Gardiner's daughter who never went to school. Would she have inherited the mole on her mother's top lip?

"Bye," Hilda said to Freddie as she scooped up the change.

In Exeter he had learnt to say *goodbye my love* but he was careful to avoid it now and kept it simple, replying in kind, "Bye." He had spent half his life pretending to be someone else, now he didn't know who he was. Would he be recognised? The woman behind him took a step forward, her shoe scraped on the wooden floor, anticipating Freddie's exit. It left him no choice so he turned to go and walked past the woman called Leslie. He stared at her, too long, examining her face, her top lip. She smiled, mole-less, and he smiled back. Did he know her? Did she know him? Already having lingered for a split second too long, he headed for the door.

His hand was by now on the handle, the bell already rung, when she said, "Sir?"

How much had he changed, really? He was a foot taller, but still looked young for his age, his hair still full and blonde. He wished he hadn't taken off his hat. When he turned round, the woman, Leslie, was smiling at him. Yes, he wanted to be recognised – that was why he was here – but not by her.

"Don't forget your suitcase."

He'd left it at the counter. "Oh. Sorry. Thanks." They both looked at him, questioning who this stranger was, and Freddie wondered why. Strangers were commonplace in wartime. He went over to pick up his suitcase. "I'll forget my own name one of these days."

He had left the Post Office too quickly, which must have raised suspicions, but was glad to be back out on the street. There were people going about their business and he felt safer as he walked through the village, more able to hide under his hat. The usual route home would take him past Pig Alley, but because it was a cut-through that would eventually curve round to the back of his row of houses, today he took it. That way he would not be seen knocking on his own front door.

The alleyway was muddy even though there had been no rain that day. Perhaps a pipe had burst. He'd have to take off his shoes before entering the house. But he would do that anyway, wouldn't he, in his own home? The hedges either side had filled out to such an extent he barely recognised the alleyway, darker now, and he momentarily wondered if he was even in the right one.

Further down, someone had left a pile of sandbags along the edge of the path with a row of bricks at their base and they seemed to serve no purpose, until he saw water leaking through the gaps between them. And there was an old bicycle wheel propped up just beyond the bags, tyre-less and rusty. He thought of his own bike, wondered what had become of it, if it was still in use and if so who rode it? Or perhaps, as unlikely as it seemed, this rusty remnant was what was left of it.

He tiptoed round the alley's gentle curve as he tried to place his feet in the areas that were least muddy. He nearly stood on a dead bird, a fledgling, surrounded on the ground by fragments of eggshell dripping with a gooey spittle in which he spotted a fleck of blood. But then he jumped when the bird twitched, alive after all, though barely so, perhaps breathing its last breath. What could he do? If he picked it up it would still die, if he crushed it with a brick it would be his own life diminished. Let nature take its course, he allowed himself, he was not its mother, then immediately he hated his decision for it being no decision at all. He went back to pick up one of the bricks and returned to kill the bird. He would bring the brick down hard, he thought, hard enough for the noise of its impact on the path to cover up the other sounds he did not wish to hear. But in the minute he had been gone, and to his relief, the bird had died. He pushed it to one side with his shoe, supper for the foxes.

A flint wall covered in wild blackberries lined the back of his row of houses. Some of the backyards didn't even have gates and no one had ever had a satisfactory explanation why that might be, but other ways through had been improvised long ago by using a neighbour's gate and then another in the dividing fence. He peered through the gap of the gate at number seven, next door to his own. The washing was on the line, blocking the view from the kitchen window, which meant it would be safe to go through and into the yard at number nine, if he was quick about it.

And so he found himself standing in the garden of his childhood with his back to the flint wall looking towards his old house. It was, like all remembered spaces, smaller than he recalled and it would take no more than ten steps to reach the back door, if he chose to do so. His mother had hung her washing out too, but then all the women had, it was Monday and that was life's routine. Life itself.

He wanted to stay there for a moment, so he put his suitcase down and even thought about lighting up, but found he had run out of matches. They sold them in the Post Office; too late now. He looked up at his own bedroom window and wondered if his collection of pennies was still there but it was impossible to see from this angle. He could think of no reason why his mother would either leave them there on the window sill or take them away, and in the end he hoped that she might have spent them on bread, made by Millie in the village, to keep her going during the Depression.

He noticed that on the washing line there were two bed sheets flapping in the breeze, and unexpectedly, shockingly, he began to cry. Not the wet eyes that one could blink away unnoticed, but a profound howling he immediately had to stifle with his hand across his mouth, then his other hand to keep the first in place, pressed hard, intensely shaking, choking on the years of injustice he had brought down on his mother. She was washing his bed sheet, every week, ready for his return.

The back door clicked and she came out. He wanted to hide, before remembering he didn't need to. She was plumper, cowed, her dark hair turned to white, dressed in the same way, perhaps literally in the same clothes, the seams now straining against the tide of the passing years. He had done this, her son, Freddie Lovegrove, he had draped her in these ill-fitting rags of daily grief. He remembered a game he used to play, when he was little. He would pretend not to be there, see how long he could get away with it, sit as quiet as a mouse whilst watching his mother move around the room, her blind eyes scanning the corners until she heard his breathing or detected his smell, or just sensed his presence in the way a blind person always could. She would always know, in the end. Sometimes he fancied she was just playing along. But he was further away now, and outside. Just as well the breeze covered up the muffled noise of his weeping.

His mother stroked the sheet nearest to her with the palm of her hand to see if it was dry. She seemed undecided. Two steps on she tested the next, squeezed one corner of it, then turned and looked towards Freddie with her milky white eyes, though she was staring beyond him, over his right shoulder, as if there were something of interest on the bare flint wall behind.

"Who's there?"

Freddie's hands were still up to his mouth, holding everything in, the stinging brine that had collected between his eyelids causing the figure of his mother to shimmer like a ghost, and he suddenly realised he had got this all wrong. She stepped nearer, no more than two yards from Freddie now, and she tried again, though it was no longer a question.

"Who's there."

It only needed one word, his own name, and the rest would sort itself out. The guilt, the confusion, the apologies...the forgiveness. But he only truly felt the first of these, and was shocked by his reaction which served merely to add to it, the tears piling up until he became afraid she might actually hear them landing on the dry earth next to his shoes. How could he arrive, only to withdraw again? To leave his bed sheet uncreased and unslept in? He shouldn't have listened to Suhani, she didn't know he had one more letter to deliver. He would have to delay, slip away, take the long way home. Return when the time was right. Then a familiar sound, a Spitfire, and another, a leader with his wingman searing low across the sky, rattling windows and bones. A battle was simmering. It might get harder to travel now thought Freddie, more checks on the trains and at the ports. But he had his tickets, bought in advance by the War Office; passport fast-tracked by the Overseas Evacuation Scheme.

She was so close, surely she knew he was there. He examined her face. It was worn out, creased like an old leather chair. Dark liver spots had formed on her forehead and her cheeks had sunk in from rotten teeth having been extracted, or fallen out. Though she must be about the same age as Suhani, she looked older by untold years, from a different epoch. It was a face he had never properly looked at before, not in this analytical way. He was the one who had been blind, and the neglect was all his.

His mother raised her head to the sound of the planes and seemed immediately to forget his presence. Perhaps she did this every day, hear a creak in a branch of the blackberry bush and hope it might instead be a footstep, be the return of her son, and today like every day she gave up, dismissed it as a lost hope, and turned to go back into the house. Freddie watched her slow steps, each one a broken heart. He could call out, and nearly did, taking his hands away from his mouth and inhaling a breath.

But by then the back door had clicked shut.

46

He took the station Fly back to Little Risborough station. Still horse-drawn, it seemed some things never changed. Two hours and thirty-two minutes later he was in London, and during the short walk from Victoria to Euston he must have passed at least fifty food vendors. He ignored the fried fish, the hot eels, the chestnut stalls, and went for pea soup, the safest option.

As the skies darkened into night he turned left off the Euston Road into Judd Street and selected the cheapest boarding house he could find. The landlady barked that he'd have to share, and his heart sank at the thought of it, but he had no choice. If he went to bed late and got up early he might avoid a conversation with his roommate, which, with a rare turn of good fortune, was what happened. The noises from the street outside reminded him a little of chucking-out time in Exeter, though here in London it seemed to go on all night. He looked at the ceiling listening to his roommate's snoring, breathed through his mouth to avoid the smell of stale sheets, and wondered what Liverpool would be like.

Having managed no sleep in his boarding-house bed, Freddie had his eyes shut for most of the train journey the following day, drifting in and out of dreams that were populated by a mixture of his fellow passengers and the people he used to deliver post to as a boy. At one point he thought he was sitting opposite Stephen Harkness, but the similarity waned when the train shook Freddie's eyes properly open.

Twelve hours later, he was looking out across the Irish Sea. The docks were teeming, busier even than London, with soldiers, policemen, dock workers carrying boxes or ropes, and children, scores of them with haunted eyes lining up for their orders. The sound of train whistles and steam rose from behind the arches to his left, and then he spotted it, the office, though in reality it was nothing more than a requisitioned garden shed perched ridiculously near the edge of one of the piers lining the dock. There was a handwritten poster pinned to its door, *Ministry of Health Evacuation Scheme,* and Freddie stepped inside to find himself in front of a small wispy man who sat at a rickety desk, which wobbled as he wrote.

"Can I help?"

"Billie Bedden. William Bedden."

"Oh. You're late."

"I wasn't given a time. I caught the earliest train there was." He put his hand inside his jacket to pull out his passport. "Do you need to see this?"

"You don't need one of those."

Freddie was disappointed. He'd gone to a lot of trouble to acquire a passport without Ellen discovering it.

The man handed Freddie a piece of paper. "This is your list. You're in charge of the first forty-one of them. They've all got labels, keep them together, some of 'em don't want to go. Well, none of them really."

"Why forty-one?"

"Half of eighty-two. That's how many we've got."

Freddie looked down the list, some duplicated surnames, brothers and sisters, mostly from Liverpool and Manchester, but a few from further afield, London, Dover, Ramsgate, all Luftwaffe targets.

"Where do I go?"

"Mrs Gosling is with them at the moment. Take over from her and stay with them until you're called to board. For fuck's sake don't get on the wrong boat. Yours is the Anselm. You'll be met the other end. Just make sure the kids eat and sleep and don't fall overboard."

The convoy survived the journey to Nova Scotia unscathed, the U-boats either missing or ignoring them. Freddie had speculated that possibly they knew there were children on board, or perhaps they just had bigger targets. It would be too much to hope that the journey home would be as uneventful. Beyond all the other arguments he had fought with Ellen it was that one in particular which had been the main cause of her upset, the prospect that she might never see him again. The night before he left they had spent the evening in silence. The children were quiet too, even the baby, all seeming to know something was up, a cold wind of expectation blowing through the house, like waiting for a hearse to arrive. When the children had gone to bed she had switched on the wireless and listened to the dance music that was supposed to cheer the nation up, but on that evening was for filling their silences. If anything the high spirits beamed from Alexandra Palace seemed to mock them, making it ten times worse. It was only when Ellen said she was going to bed that they made contact. Freddie was sitting in his armchair, as stiff as if he had been tied to it, when Ellen stood up and leant over to kiss him on the top of his head, pressing down through his thick blonde hair. A tear fell on his forehead, reminding him of little Millicent Rose's christening, permission to enter the world. This was more like permission to leave it. He wasn't sure if Ellen was forgiving him or if she would not forgive herself if she didn't in some way say goodbye. Perhaps it was both. Or perhaps she simply loved him.

As Freddie stood on the deck of the *SS Anselm* at midnight, mid-Atlantic, he thought about how he had told her everything, unburdened himself of every single detail, but how the weight had not lifted in the way he had expected, instead simply transferring itself onto her shoulders, which was no unburdening at all. Though she was stronger than him it was still an unequal bargain. He wondered if she would ever be able to call him Freddie, now that she knew his real name. If you live a lie for long enough, it becomes the truth, and the past a fiction, impossible to rectify. Perhaps, after all, none of this was about correcting the lies, but about simply loving someone, and the truth would follow in its wake. He pushed the thought away somewhere into the distant future, as out of reach as he felt from home.

Over the six days at sea there had been no rain, though the wind had picked up towards the end and was removing hats when they finally docked at Halifax. It turned out the overseas evacuation of the children was poorly organised, thrown together in haste, sometimes with too many people doing the same job, other times one person doing several. Freddie found himself in the former category and was often a spare part, unable to avoid getting in the way of those who were more desperate to be in charge, and to be seen to be. The children varied in their reactions to their plight, generally the boys were harder to control, acting out battles, shooting imitation guns at each other and playing dead as they queued up in Pier Twenty-One, the immigration shed. Whereas the girls were quieter and more thoughtful. But there were some exceptions to the rule, and some of the lads, especially the smaller ones, were nervous, tongue-tied creatures, while some of the older girls took charge and looked after them. They were natural carers, rehearsing motherhood.

Over the next two days the children were collected by their new families. Some seemed excited, though Freddie suspected it was a pretence. Others were pulled away crying, would have preferred to have taken their chances with the Luftwaffe. Too late for that. One pair of siblings were to be separated, designated different families, until Freddie negotiated a swap after much wrangling with the jobsworths that ran the circus. After that his task was to visit every family on his list, twenty of them spread across Halifax and beyond, to check that the children had settled in. It took him a week. A few of them, the same ones who had so eagerly disembarked, seemed happy, thrilled even by the adventure that had befallen them. Of the rest, some were better at covering up the tightening in their chests than others. The brother and sister who he had saved from separation clung to each other like frightened kittens. In war, thought Freddie, avoiding bombs could destroy lives too.

On his eighth day in Halifax, Freddie booked a bus ride half-an-hour south to Memory Cove.

47

I still help out in my mother's shop when I can. When the children were smaller there was not much time for that, but now I go most afternoons. My mother is getting forgetful and needs the help. I have a happy life with my two children and husband. We had a photograph taken a few months back when we were last in Halifax, so the four of us now sit framed and smiling on the piano where the silver teapot used to be: Joe stands next to me, Marilyn and David sit in front. The piano is still tuned every six months but is never played. Joe says we can't afford it and he's right; but I'm right too, and in the end mother said she would pay.

They are so different, those two, Marilyn the doer, David the thinker. They've never really seen eye to eye but they rub along well enough, keeping their distance when they need to. Marilyn is getting married in the fall to Peter, a boat-builder from Peggy's Cove. David on the other hand has never looked another girl in the eye as far as I can tell. I always knew Marilyn would leave, but I wonder if David ever will. He's talked about volunteering when he's old enough, which I've tried to discourage, but it's difficult when I can't tell him why and I don't want to undermine Joe who thinks it's what young men should do, would make a man of David.

Right now Joe is up the ladder painting the windows and eaves. He's put on weight these last few years – more of him to love he says! – and I worry about him being up there on the outside of the house by our first-floor bedroom window. I've told him before to move the ladder rather than stretch across, but he says he'll be all right. I say, with a laugh, they'll carve that on his gravestone.

My goodness, how quickly the days have turned into years since I last sat on the porch and simply looked out across the sea. There never seems to be the time, the life of a housewife is never dull, is it? Certainly it's a busy one, the cooking, the sweeping, the washing, the raising of children, it's what I signed up for so mustn't complain. But in the end we still call them chores, don't we. Or, I don't know, perhaps the reason I don't look out to sea is in case I catch sight of a deviating ship, sailing against the wind, the path I might otherwise have taken if things had been different. But regret is a fool's game, you can't re-write the past, can you? Then I catch myself re-writing the future, wondering how my life would change if Joe fell off the ladder… I dismiss my cruel, unforgivable fantasy. Life is what it is now, I love my children, proud of Joe.

So here I am, after all, sitting on the porch looking out to sea, wishing to have arms around me, other than my own, to protect me from the wind. To my left in the distance is Cook's Lighthouse, and down to the right, five hundred yards away, is the fishing village itself, with its rock-walled harbor protecting the boats and our livelihoods, though today they are barely visible through the mist of an incoming sea fret, which this time of year is often blown through by the warm air rolling in from the Atlantic. Sometimes I feel the fog is coming to collect me. But today it lifts as suddenly as it arrives, amounts to nothing, and reveals the arrival of the twice-daily bus from Halifax pulling up by the jetty.

Most of the boats have already left for the day's fishing, though Eddie

Hunter is still readying his. Last out of the pub, they say, last out to sea. The story goes his first words he ever spoke were: "Will you marry me?" It's a nice story, with perhaps a grain of truth in it. I don't suppose he cares, he lost his wife two years back and has slipped back into silence. You could hear his wife screaming above the sound of the relentless wind. Honestly, I wouldn't be surprised if one day he didn't come back. Strange to say, in all my years in Memory Cove, I've never set foot on a trawler deck. If I could think of a pretext for boarding Eddie's boat, I'd take it.

Someone's talking to Eddie, a man who got off the bus and who I don't recognise, though it's not unusual these days to see someone new. The war populates every corner of the world with unknown faces for unknown reasons and we don't even question it anymore. But they're conferring for some time, a one-sided conversation admittedly, and the man seems to be asking for directions. Eddie points towards our house. I feel both a violation and an exhilaration – perhaps one is caused by the other. Retreat back inside, that's what I want to do, but I also want to stay and watch, or be watched. Eddie seems to be shaking his head, then the other man adjusts his trilby and sets off up the steep path that leads to nowhere except our house. My first thought is it might be enlistment papers, but Joe is too old, too large, too kind, and David too young. In any case we have our own postboy to deliver news like that. No, this man, who keeps looking up to check his path ahead even though it is hard to miss your steps, has something addressed for me. You know how it is, when the back of your neck feels cold.

A minute later he's within fifty yards and I stand up, then hold down the front of my dress to prevent it catching in the wind. My palms stick to it. I decide to go and meet the stranger halfway, away from the house, away from Joe, though he is oblivious anyway, concentrating on the windows. I can't explain to myself why my heart beats more quickly, except I think it has worked something out, racing ahead of my thoughts. I don't know this man, but I sense he knows me.

And this is what happens next: we get closer until we find ourselves standing a yard apart, like reunited lovers, he and I both seeming to wish to dispense with any formalities, even though after twenty-four years another few seconds would make no difference.

So there is no introduction, the man speaks as if in the middle of a sentence and simply asks if I am Anne Ellis. I say I used to be. He takes out a letter from his inside jacket pocket and hands it to me, saying he used to be Freddie Lovegrove. He's sorry the delivery is late today.

Some gentle rain begins to fall, its cold hand stroking my face. I examine the envelope, read the postmark, late indeed, and am desperate for an explanation but I have a feeling something else will happen next instead. There will be no goodbyes, he will simply smile and leave, exit as mysteriously as he entered and I'll watch him for a while as he negotiates the path back to the jetty. Then I'll go back into the house, sit on my bed and open the letter. On my way though, I'll pause to call up the ladder to Joe and tell him I love him. He'll look down without even noticing the letter in my hand, and reply in the way he always does, with a wink, and say, "Well why wouldn't yer?" That's what will happen, isn't it? Or, I could follow another path, tear up the letter and throw it into the wind, so that I can continue to pretend.

We will see. Perhaps when the wind picks up into a storm, and Joe has gone to bed, I will do both. I'll sit by the fire to read Christopher's letter before throwing it on the last of the cooling embers to watch it catch, become smoke, and disappear.

48

My dearest Anne,

Forgive my haste, I've just a few minutes to write. I'm sorry it has been such a long time since my last letter, the war makes it hard sometimes. I don't want you to worry but I have injuries that make it difficult to write. Today I have an amanuensis called Freddie.

I'll be here for some while. I hope you are looking after our house, and I hope it is looking after you. If I don't get back in time, remember to paint the windows before the storms come, they won't last the winter. Don't forget Joseph said he will help, if you need him to.

I think about you often. In actuality I think of nothing else. Time drags without you and sometimes I don't see an end to it. I can't say for sure when we will see each other again. My leave has been cancelled and as soon as they have put me back together they will return me to the front.

France is beautiful, and England looks after me like a favourite aunt, but it is not home. My goodness, Anne, I even miss the north-easterly blowing across the water and rattling our windows.

Well, I must finish now, Freddie has work to do. He's the postboy here, my Hermes, excellent in all the tricks. Don't worry if you don't hear from me for a while. Get the piano tuned every six months won't you. God bless you Anne.

Your loving husband,
Christopher.

P.S. My darling Angel, don't forget what I once said to you on the steps of our home. Let my hands be the wind. It was something of a joke then, of course. Less so now.

Joe comes downstairs and wakes me. It's late, he says, two in the morning, come to bed. I say nothing, wanting to go and stand outside in the wind, but instead I just smile and let him take my hand to help me to my feet. I look into the hearth but the flames are long gone now, leaving just one smoking ember to fall into the grate, give up its final breath, and break in two. I'll collect the ash in the morning and throw it on the garden. This year I've decided, for the first time, to grow delphiniums.

49

Miriam would often have visitors, although rarely this time of day. A floorboard had squeaked and she thought about calling out, but the old house had started to make noises of its own in recent years and every creak was a hope dashed, so she ignored it and went back to listening to the wireless, a contraption that had been donated anonymously ten years ago. When Mr Lawes had delivered it, he said he was sworn to secrecy. She hated charity, but it had transformed her life almost to the point of saving it. Keeping contact with the outside world was a way of replacing the stories Freddie used to bring home, as well as filling the hours of his absence.

She stopped and raised her head, flicked her eyes as if exploring the space around her, though of course she saw only the flashing colours of her blindness, which always increased to fill the darkness when she was listening intently. There had been another noise coming from the kitchen, this time the sound of clothes brushing against a table edge. She switched off the wireless. Perhaps it was the Indian woman from the house in the valley, who seemed to visit once a year, but never said why. She did wonder if her yearly visits were some kind of anniversary but Miriam never asked, just grateful for the company. They would always talk about the same things: the sumptuous hills and valleys of a childhood in India, her passion for an older man that shocked her home village but never herself, her sons that she had lost, the son that she had found. And then the conversation would inevitably swing round to Freddie, but neither would be quite able to raise the matter of his leaving. It was as if the whole purpose of the conversation was to avoid the subject. In fact she had the sense that there was a great deal left unspoken. But Miriam knew it could not be the Indian woman prowling her house, she would never enter without knocking first. She drew a picture of the kitchen in her head, simpler than standing up and walking through to it.

"Who's there?"

The sound of her voice reflected back to her ears differently, the adjacent kitchen space did not sound as empty as it should. She waited for a reply, as she had done a thousand times before, but none came.

No one ever says a word; there is no need. Only a mother who watches dark clouds pass across her eyes can see her son in another room, standing alone, looking down at his shoes.

Author's Note

Berrington Hall is a bold red sandstone mansion nestling in the Herefordshire countryside. Built in 1778, it was home to Lord and Lady Cawley from 1901. Later, Lady Cawley used part of Berrington Hall as a convalescent hospital during the Second World War. When their son, the 2nd Lord Cawley, died in 1954, death duties meant the estate had to be handed over to the Treasury, who in turn gave it to the care of the National Trust. Lady Cawley continued to live at the house until her death in 1978, at the age of 100.

When I visited Berrington Hall back in 2009 there was an exhibition dedicated to the role that the house and its occupants played during the First World War, and in one of the rooms were displayed three mannequins dressed in army uniform. Even before reading the text beneath the exhibits, there was a sense of the tragic story hanging in the air around them, and in the wool of the old regimental livery one could almost smell the mustard gas, the cordite, and the sweat of fear.

The uniforms belonged to three of the four sons of Lord and Lady Cawley, three young men all killed in battle in 1914, 1915 and 1918. Of course, I imagined the parents' ongoing bereavement, and the unbearable pain as it multiplied across each subsequent death. But I also began to consider the strain on the postboy who had to deliver such terrible news. There was no counselling in those days, no time off for stress-related health issues. This was the era of stiff upper lips, men being men, and emotions being given short shrift, if expressed at all. What chance did he have? What coping mechanisms might he employ?

This is not a novel about Berrington Hall or the Cawley family, though there are clearly resonances that have inspired me. Rather, the story evolved out of trying to understand how my imaginary postboy might deal with his trauma, and to uncover, as far as it is ever possible, the reasons why good people do bad things.

Whilst the phenomenon of a false negative was unusual, it was by no means unheard of. There are several documented cases of "dead" soldiers returning from the front, and no doubt many more undocumented ones. The postal system during the First World War was an extraordinary feat of organisation and was enormously efficient and reliable, but with thousands of letters crossing the channel every day mistakes were inevitably made. Further, errors occurred on the battlefield itself with misplaced or swapped name tags (sometimes deliberately so as a way of escaping the horrors of the trenches) as well as lost paperwork – and lost memories. There is at least one case of a soldier coming home just in time to witness his own memorial service. With war bringing so much tragedy to its participants and their families, these little miracles brought salvation for the few – and hope for the many.

Acknowledgements

When you start to think about all the people who contribute in some way to your novel, the list grows infinitely long. Such a complex web of connections and influences can never be fully acknowledged, or even entirely understood. As such, I will no doubt be leaving some of you out, and a few of you may actually be the most important, if only I knew it. If you fall into that category, I hope my apologies and undying gratitude here will be of some compensation, along with the knowledge that one way or another this book, such as it is, would not exist without you.

Everyone has *that* teacher, the one who believes in your abilities more than you do yourself, and unlocks an imaginative potential you never knew you had. Mine was Dennis Colman who, at Bungay Primary School in the 1960s, unleashed in me a creative freedom I've tried to hold onto ever since. Mister Colman, I wish I could show this book to you now. I hope you had a good life.

Thanks to Claire Baldwin, my editor, who so deftly advised about the shape and structure of my story, as well as addressing all the smaller details of style and content, of which there were hundreds, enhancing my own voice and bringing it into focus. My apologies for the semi-colons that have stubbornly hung on in there.

To Eleanor Alberga and Tom Bowes, both of whom read early drafts and gave me, amongst other things, wise counsel about how to accurately represent the casual – and not so casual – racism that runs as an undercurrent through parts of my narrative. But more than that, their enthusiasm for my novel helped me overcome those self-doubts that plague all creative endeavours.

To Andrew Keener, who has shown constant support over the years for my various projects, championing me in both practical and psychological ways. I will always be grateful for your kindness.

To Adipat Virdi, for his expert marketing advice and encouragement to overcome my fears.

To Gary Mayes, who put up with my back-and-forth, going-round-the-houses indecisiveness and managed to disentangle what I meant from what I said to come up with such a powerful cover design. I am in awe of what you are able to see.

To Adrian Bain, whose work on the screenplay for The Best Postboy in England was passionate, selfless and generous to a fault. Some narrative ideas, directly or indirectly, consciously or subconsciously, have found their way into my novel. It is still my hope that the screenplay will see the light of day. Our regular early morning discussions of plot and character over a fry-up in the Belgian Bar in Ramsgate were essential to the gestation of this book and remain a treasured memory. Here's to the next!

To Tony Harrison, whose exploration of emotional truth was utterly fearless and some of which, I like to think, rubbed off on me, and into this book. You are still flying Spitfires, Tony, and I am still your wingman.

Finally to Tracy Russell, whose encouragement, advice and wisdom enabled me to write. Even so, I cannot find the words to say how much you mean to me.

About the Author

Stephen Frost was born in the Suffolk market town of Bungay in 1959, before leaving at nineteen to study music. A motley life in the music industry followed, exploring various avenues and culs-de-sac from pop to country to rock, until he finally alighted on classical music editing and production.

From his earliest school days a passion for storytelling was never far, an obsession that culminated in writing and directing the award-winning feature film "Leave Now" in 2018.

The Best Postboy In England is his first novel.

Printed in Great Britain
by Amazon

29142692R00247